RETURN BY SEA

TRACEY JERALD

Sigrid ♡

RETURN BY SEA

Don't be torn by love!

xoxo,
Tracey Drudel

Tracey Jerald
101 Marketside Avenue, Suite 404-205
Ponte Vedra, FL, 32081

Editor: One Love Editing (http://oneloveediting.com)

Proof Edits: Holly Malgieri (https://www.facebook.com/HollysRedHotReviews/)

Cover Design by Tugboat Design (https://www.tugboatdesign.net/)

Photo Credit: Wander Aguiar

Model: Thiago Lusardi

For Tony and Addison.
Your hearts astound me with their utter selflessness. And I know of at least eight
others who feel the same way every single day.
All my love.

PROLOGUE

Maris - Sixteen years earlier from present day

"I'd endure any pain for those I love. If only they'd let me." - From the journals of Jedidiah Smith.

"Maris!" I hear my name being shouted above the cacophony of sound as I'm being escorted by a tall, handsome black man into the VIP area. My brother, Jed, face flushed, swings me around to face him. "What the hell are you doing here?"

The guy, whose grip on my elbow makes the bouncer at my father's bar who caught me trying to sneak in when I was eighteen appear useless, raises a brow in a silent question.

I just flap a hand at him. "It's fine. This is my brother. He's one of Nick's best friends."

The impassive face clears, and he winks down at me. "Then you're in good hands, Ms. Smith. The Champ is just beyond those doors. I'm sure he'll be awfully glad to see a woman who could knock someone out as hard as his last punch."

I blush even as Jed drags me closer toward my final destination—Nick. "Thanks for helping me through the crowd!" I call over my shoulder graciously.

1

He flicks out a two-finger salute before he goes back to guarding the entrance of the hall that I just passed through.

My mind is still down at the arena where Nick pulled out a win no one expected—not the sports reporters, nor the announcers based on the way they were screaming into their microphones. But in my heart of hearts, I knew he had it inside him. He always did.

I dig my nails into Jed's arm. "Can you believe it? I thought I was going to lose my voice I was screaming so hard."

"What are you doing here, Sunshine?"

"I got an invitation from Nick."

Jed's face turns a furious shade of mottled red. "I'm going to kill him," he bellows.

More than a few heads of people passing by the mouth of the hallway hear him and turn toward us at the angry sound. I'm a little confused myself. Reaching into my purse, I pull out the letter that came with the credentials I have slung around my neck, identical to the ones my brother has on. "See? This came in the mail a few days ago."

"So you dropped everything and flew here?" Jed's voice holds a note of frustrated bitterness I don't understand.

"It's Nick," I say as if that explains it all, and maybe it does. Of all my brother's friends, the moody, irreverent Nicholas Cain has always been different. Maybe it's because I know deep inside there's something between us that's always been different. There's something between us that heals the pain in the other. "Anyway, it's not like I didn't have a million hours of vacation. Dad said to take off, that he'd watch the bar. See? No issues."

Jed opens his mouth to speak, but before he can, one of the double doors of the suite behind him flies open. Suddenly Nick's standing there. His shredded body is barely covered by an excuse of a towel that's riding just below the title belt he won a short time earlier. "Ernie! Where the fuck are..." His voice trails off when his eyes collide with mine. For just a moment, unadulterated joy shines before a mask drops down over them. "Hey. You came." Stepping forward, Nick pulls the door partially closed behind him as he approaches.

When he leans down to offer me a one-arm hug, a pungent scent fills my nose. I take an inadvertent step away. "Don't touch me." My body brushes back against Jed's. I take comfort in my brother's presence.

Because it's not the smell of his powerful fight I'm recoiling from. Nor is it the booze he so rarely drinks.

It's the smell of sex wafting off his skin.

"Congratulations," I offer coolly.

"What? That's it? I just won the belt! Doesn't that even rate a hug?" His grin splits his handsome face wide open.

I lean away from Jed. I know from the many years of working at the Brewhouse how to deal with arrogant pricks. "It would if you were even halfway decent."

He laughs in my face. "Sorry, Sunshine. I didn't have time to shower once I got back up here."

"But you sure found time to fuck?" I cock my head around his broad chest, and at that moment, I hear a voice whine, "Nick? Where are you going?"

His face pales.

"Apparently had yourself a hell of a time, Champ," I congratulate him mockingly.

"You don't understand." A dark flush stains his cheeks.

"Actually, I do. I thought you sent me the tickets, the pass, because you wanted to share this moment with people you cared about. I should have done what I originally planned."

"Which was?" he challenges.

"Stay in my corner of the world with a front-row seat to pay-per-view. At least I could have maintained my illusions you didn't do this to rub...whatever you've become...in my face. Why the hell did you bring me here, Nick? You promised to keep in contact with me, and you didn't. I'm the fool who jumped when I finally do hear from you. I thought you actually cared." He steps forward, and I hold my hand up to ward him off. "Don't. I should have just let you go in my heart when you never reached out just like Jed told me I should." I turn away and shove past my brother, my long legs eating up the distance to get away.

I make it to the end of the hall before I hear Nick yell, "Maris, no.

3

Wait!" As I whirl, I see Jed physically using every ounce of his strength to hold him back while I make my escape.

Grateful for the intervention, I slip past the same guard who escorted me to the door. The suite is filled with rising noise that overwhelms me. Using it to my advantage to avoid both Jed and Nick's bellows, I escape.

Thank God my hotel's not far from here. Then again, is anything far in this illusion called Las Vegas?

TWO DAYS LATER, I'm curled up next to Jed in my bed at the hotel. I've tried everything possible to get an earlier flight to get out of Vegas, but short of dumping my entire savings, there's just no way possible to leave any earlier than my return ticket has me booked for. I'm stuck in a nightmare of my own making—the last one I'll allow myself.

I'm exhausted from lack of sleep, but to know Jed has essentially abandoned the festivities to be by my side—just like he always has been—is a testament to the man my brother is. "There's no one in the world like you."

"I broke the mold," Jed declares.

"I agree," I say, even as my heart sighs sadly knowing there's no one I'll ever love the way I love my brother.

I just wish Nick would disappear and leave us alone. Instead, he's taken to randomly dialing Jed at all hours asking how we are. The last call a half hour ago involved him asking if we wanted anything to eat. "Someone's running out for me," he claims. "I can have them swing by where you are."

Jed politely declined. I ignored the whole conversation by rolling to my side and texting my best friend, Kara, in Florida. I want to know how her little boy Kevin is since he's been battling a spring cold.

"Probably a euphemism for something. Running out for 'something' to cover his dick," I grumble against Jed's shoulder.

"What's that?" He turns his head just enough for me to catch the wince on his face. He sticks a pen in the book he was taking notes in before placing it on the nightstand.

"Nick. He's probably just calling to placate himself you're not pissed at him. Trust me, we're not going to starve."

Jed's chest lifts up and down beneath me. "Not hardly with the way you're not eating what you've been ordering from room service. I feel like I'm eating for two."

That earns a reluctant chuckle from me.

"Turn down the TV for me, would you?"

I reach for the remote and lower the volume. "Going to try to nap?"

"No. It's time for us to have a little conversation."

I begin to protest until Jed captures my hand, pulling me back into his arms, and places my head over his heart. "From the moment you were born, I've loved you. I think Mom and Dad were terrified I was going to smother you in your crib after we brought you home because I would just wander into the room where you were sleeping and watch you."

"Did you think about it?" I tease him in an attempt to break the tension gripping me.

"Not until you started taking an interest in boys. And then I couldn't be certain if it was because we'd have crushes on the same guys." We both laugh until Jed's face becomes absurdly serious—ridiculous because my big brother is so rarely serious. He's always the sparkle in the sky, the person everyone wants to be around because they know they'll never be left out. But I can't prevent the tears in my eyes when he whispers, "You're the light of my life, Maris."

"I know." Before I can return the sentiment, Jed shocks me to the core.

"And Nick's the darkness." Jed sifts his fingers through my hair as he solemnly holds my attention. "If he wasn't one of the most loyal men I've ever met, if I hadn't had the chance to know him as well as I have, I'd have done anything to have kept you apart. If I thought I wouldn't die in the process, I'd kick his sorry ass for this stunt. I can't even make up excuses about why he sent you that ticket, but if I knew,

I'd have figured out a way to have kept you up in Juneau. He doesn't deserve you."

As much as I want to believe my brother, it's going to take a long while for me to believe that. Still, I nod to placate him.

"He's just lucky I believe that beneath the land mines, barbed wire, and stay-out signs, he projects a heart of pure gold or I'd cut him from my life completely."

That shocks me. "But he's your brother!"

"And you're my sister, my family, and I vowed to protect you. There may never be a man good enough for you, but one who would hurt you deliberately? Maris, I need you to hold on to your heart carefully; otherwise, you're going to send me into an early grave."

"Trying to tell me falling for Nick is stupid? Trust me, I'm already well aware of that." There's so much insincerity in my voice.

"No, Maris. I'm telling you it might be safer to swim in the Bering Sea in the middle of winter than to feel what you think you do for him."

It's not my brother's words that break me. It's the fact I can feel wetness against my face. My big brother is shedding tears for me and my pathetic heart. "Too late. I'm already underwater," I whisper.

As he tucks me against him, I let the saltiness drip out of my eyes and onto his chest. For a long while, the only sound is the occasional choking sound I make. I scrub my face back and forth, scratching my cheek against our grandfather's gold cross Jed always wears.

"It will all work out the way it's meant to," I vow.

Jed pulls me as close as he can, despite the fact I know it must be hurting him. I begin to drift off when I hear him whisper, "In the end, my sweet sister, all I want is for you to find a love that makes you happy."

NICHOLAS

March - Sixteen Years Later

I step out of the small store and scan the parking lot for my mom's dilapidated station wagon. When I don't spot it right away, I let out a sigh and plop down on the sidewalk with the small sack of groceries I managed to buy with the money I earned on small jobs I picked up after school.

My stomach rumbles. Rebelliously deciding if Mom can't be here to pick me up on time like she said she would, well, I can dip into the supply of jerky without her permission.

Food, money—hell, love—has been stingy since we got word that Dad was killed in a boating accident on the Bering Sea. But if I'm honest, if it wasn't for the money he brought in, he wasn't much for supplying much anyway. Definitely not the kind of man I want to be. I gnaw on the jerky while faded memories of a burly man who gratefully ignored me after I started to get older and bigger flit through my mind.

She's not much better, but I guess we're all the other has now. Swallowing, I scan the parking lot again, trying to find the dilapidated car we sleep in as often as not. At least it's something to protect us from the weather that's edging into brutal at night.

Just then, a family passes by as they head into the market. The boy, I'd guess he's about my age, slows. "Everything cool?"

7

I tip my head back and meet the wildest blue eyes I've ever seen. "Yeah, man. Thanks. Just waiting on my mom."

The smile he gives me makes him look like a slightly deranged serial killer. When I tell him so, he laughs hard before heading into the warm store. I debate following him inside to get warm again, but I can't stand the pitying looks I got from the cashier.

One day, there will be no more pity. Not from anyone.

I wake up in a sweat, despite the air-conditioning pumping cool air into my room. "Not again," I whisper aloud, scrubbing my hands over my face.

Some people have reoccurring nightmares when they're stressed. Me? My mind replays one of two memories to punish me for all my misdeeds: the first time I saw Jed Smith on the day I was abandoned by my mother or the night my ego ruined my future with his sister. Instead of having the strength to stick to my plan of using the night I won the title belt to begin wooing Maris, I let my dick do the thinking when I was asked about how I felt my disturbing past impacted the outcome of the fight during the post-fight interview. I was reduced to that teenage boy in the parking lot immediately after winning what I thought was something that would finally prove I had turned my life around.

That night caused me to do something so stupid, so unforgivable, it often makes me wonder if I could go back in time and hand it all back, including the belt, would I?

My past is no excuse anymore. Back then, I'm not sure I had a full grip of the magnitude of what I was losing; otherwise, I wouldn't have stopped until I made Maris listen to me. If not then, then anytime in the sixteen years since that night. And I, despite having just won a huge sporting championship, should have walked away. Even though that reporter opened the door for all of my inner fear to worm insidiously into my mind, I made the rest of the choices. The question just reminded me blatantly why I shouldn't be with Maris, so I set out to demonstrate to her clearly the worst about me in vivid detail. And I wounded us both permanently in the process.

Now, I barely hold on to my pride to not beg her for a chance to explain it all any and every time we interact. When Jed was still alive, the chance to hear about her, how she was doing, came more frequently. I could live with my mistakes. Now, more often than not, it's by pure coincidence I hear about her, and not knowing about her haunts me.

I wince, remembering her voice snapping, "Jesus, will you shut the hell up, Nick? God, you can be such a jackass," when I last laid eyes on her last summer through a FaceTime call one of my best friends had set up so we could talk face-to-face.

"I am a jackass, Sunshine, but I never intended on being one to you. *Never,*" I say fiercely in my empty bedroom.

I reach over to my nightstand and grab my phone, debating whether or not what I'm about to do is a smart move when I decide to go for it anyway. I pull up an empty text and send her a quick message.

I had a dream about Jed.

It's the anniversary of the day her brother, Jed, died three years ago. Maybe she'll understand why I'm reaching out. Since it's 4:00 a.m., I don't expect her to respond. Then again if I'm on a text string with my brothers—guys Jed and I used to work with at the Great Alaskan Lumberjack Show—and their spouses, she rarely does. I never hear a peep from her unless she's saying "Congratulations" to one of our mutual friends about some accomplishment. She's grown into a strong woman with few insecurities. She was raised confident in love. And I'm positive Maris hates me. I gave her too many reasons to.

When my phone vibrates with an incoming text, I almost fall out of bed. *Good dream or bad?*

I start to type and stop. Start and stop again. She responded. *God, what the hell do I say?* I threw words into the inky sky never expecting her to respond. As I hesitate, a second text follows her first. *Nick, for the love of God. This doesn't require a dissertation.*

And I can't prevent my lips from curving upward. This is one of the things I miss most about her—her snarky humor. Maris and I used to trade good-natured barbs back before hers became laced with bitter wariness. Not that I blame her. If the tables were turned, I'm not sure I could have dug down deep enough to have spoken with me again let alone found the strained civility that she's maintained between us for the sake of our friends who have reconnected and fallen in love over the past years.

"God, Jed. What the hell should I say?" My hands pause as I try to figure it out.

I owe Maris an apology dating back almost twenty years. I owe her respect. Well, I owe those to Jed as well—along with so many things I'll never be able to repay.

After Jed steamrolled into my life, he showed me real things worth fighting for extended beyond food and shelter. Like friendship. As long as I live, I'll never forget when he happened to come back to the same grocery store he spotted me at a few days earlier and found me waiting in the parking lot for a woman who never showed up. He demanded the man he was with—I later found out his uncle—call the police in an attempt to find a mother who abandoned me.

And he taught me love truly does exists. All it cost was his blood, the swipe of a pen, and life without him all these years.

Quickly I type, *Both.*

She sends me back a bunch of laughing emojis before, *It took you that long for a one word answer?*

I don't acknowledge her taunt. *What are you doing up? Couldn't sleep either?*

I'm pushing it, pushing her, but after so long we're having a conversation where she's not telling me to go to hell or storming away. And if this means that for this moment I have Maris back in my life, I'll take it however I can.

Not really, comes her reply. *I can't get the date out of my mind.*

I doubt any of us who loved him will.

Maris sends me a broken-heart emoji, and it sums up what I'm feeling on so many levels. Then her next words send me reeling. *He'd hate this.*

Hate what? I hold my breath, wondering if she's going to address the acrimony between us.

No such luck. *The fact that it's been years and we're still mourning him as if he died yesterday. At least, I am.*

Me too.

Really?

I reel back as if she were in the room and literally slapped me. Does she think her brother meant so little to me that I don't mourn him like our friends Brad, Jennings, and Kody do? I start furiously typing out a string of sentences about how emotionally jailed I feel since Jed's been gone, but I realize none of that matters. Not right now. Backspacing them, I end up replying, *Yeah. Really. Every single day.*

The dots move on her side. Then, *He'd tell you to get your head out of your ass, Nick.*

Even as a lone tear falls, I type, *Long term hazard of knowing all of us? Pretty much.*

Before I lose the opportunity, I type, *Maris, can we talk?*

Isn't that what we're doing right now? is her immediate reply.

Really talk. Like we used to?

There's a long pause before I see the dots flash. *I'm not sure that would be a good idea.*

Why not? I practically shove my fingers through the screen as I punch in the two words.

Because, I made myself a promise a long time ago.

I hesitate before asking, *What promise is that?*

Never to be afraid to walk away since I deserve everything and if I can't, it wasn't worth it anyway.

Maris... I start to type her name, but she beats me in responding first.

Goodbye, Nick.

"No. Don't go. Come back. Please." Even reading them, her words are like a knife sliding between my ribs, puncturing my heart.

"God, Jed. If I could change one moment in my past, it would be that night. Even if it meant losing the damn belt. I'd give it all back if I could make it all right between me and your sister. I swear to you, I would. Give me a damn chance." Then I decide to type what I need to. After all, she's a woman whose heart is generous enough to give me potential solace despite her guard being up constantly.

And today, I think we both need it.

Maris, please. Just a few more minutes.

I've got to get some sleep, Nick. It was a long night at the Brewhouse and it's going to be a longer day. But hey. Stop dreaming. Take it from someone who knows. Dreams don't come true anymore.

My thumbs remain frozen over the keyboard as I absorb her words. The sentiment weighs heavily on my chest, as does the gold cross her brother used to wear that he left me in his will. I never take it off, not for any reason—even training. I put my phone aside without saying anything more, my heart thumping so hard it's causing a ringing in my ears.

Realizing I'm never going to fall back to sleep, not when I prefer the reality of being awake, I swing my naked body out of bed. "Might as well get an early start on today."

I cross the vast expanse of my bedroom and snag shorts and a tee out of a chest of drawers. Pausing in the act of grabbing socks and drawers, I catch sight of the imprint of my head on my pillow where I know I'll be chased tonight by one of the Smith siblings through the depths of hell. And as irrational as it makes me, it still offers me some comfort even as it makes my stomach cramp.

"Not the way to begin a run," I mutter. I carry the clothes into my bathroom and quickly change before slipping on running shoes.

Within minutes, I'm out the door—one foot in front of the other. My mind clears of everything except the hills and valleys I'm conquering. And the demons that never quite seem to go away, no matter how many miles I try to put between us.

Maybe I'm not quite as fast as I used to be, but I'm damn close. It's why I enjoy jumping into the octagon to teach these young kids a trick or two. Now, if the rest of my life offered that same level of satisfaction because what I feel most days is something I thought I'd stop feeling when I left Alaska behind to devote myself to mixed martial art training.

It's envy.

And it's brutal especially when the people you're most envious of are your best friends.

After I left the foster care system at eighteen, I took multiple jobs to afford living in a small apartment over a bar in Ketchikan. One of those jobs was being on a rotation as a part of Team Canada with John Jennings. A very quiet man, John wanted to talk about his life about as little as I did, other than for it to be known he wanted to be called Jennings. I shrugged, knowing eventually I'd be known by something else as well. But what astounded me was when Jennings and I reported in for training, I ran into the boy—now man—who had rescued me years before. Whereas Jennings and I were forced to wear kitschy tourist-wear to show off our muscles, the man—Jed—was wearing overalls and an apron, and frankly looked even more like a wild-ass serial killer when he smiled.

And he still laughed when I told him so.

"Come on. Let me introduce you to your other stage-mates, Brad and Kody. Every time you all perform, you guys will be together."

It was Jennings who said, "Then should we meet them?"

Jed laughed. "I guarantee, by the end of the summer, we'll all be inseparable."

And we were.

Over twenty-plus years they've been in my life, and I hate feeling even the slightest lick of jealousy. But it's hard not to envy men who are kings, not merely champions. As I push myself harder through the lather of sweat, I examine why.

Brad kept hold of Rainey through thick and thin to form a bond so strong, nothing can destroy it.

Jennings found the love he lost—and so much more—when he and Kara reconnected at Jed's funeral.

And recently, Kody and Meadow were given a second chance at the first time.

I slow my pace a little when I realize I'm ahead of pace and recall words Jed spoke to me at our last reunion in Montana.

"What in your life will give you contentment, Nick?"

I don't remember what smart-ass remark I threw back, but I recall his deliberate eye roll. "I'll bet you anything you want, anything, Champ. Because you're too afraid to go after what you really want."

"And what's that?" I challenged him.

I'd just taken a drink of bourbon when Jed bluntly spit out, "My sister."

I choked on the drink. "Excuse me?" I wheezed.

"You're too scarred by your past, afraid of your mistakes, and frankly of her, to make a move now that things have changed so drastically in your life. You won't even tell the guys about what you're doing with Razor, with those kids, for fear it will change how they look at you. And that's why I don't think you'll ever be man enough for her."

Jed's words echo as much as my footfalls do on the empty street.

Because he was right. He was always right.

How can someone who's been wounded, who's deliberately taken jabs at others the way I have, deserve to reach out for the only thing I've ever truly wanted?

As I turn down my street, the sun begins to rise above the mountains, turning the clouds above them the exact shade of Maris's indigo-colored eyes. Soon enough, the clouds will burn away much like this urge to haul my ass to Juneau to claim the one woman I have no right to.

Now or ever.

Because as much as I've changed, I'm still that guy who's just not right for her.

I always will be the man who hurt her.

And she needs to find a man who never will.

MARIS

May

"Maris thinks this is the only life she deserves. She couldn't be more wrong. She's stronger than this place, but she doesn't see it. She's letting the past hold her back." - From the journals of Jedidiah Smith.

"I can't believe it's been three years." I sit cross-legged in front of my brother's grave. The graveyard is quiet at this time of day—the exact moment when we lowered the combined ashes of Jed and his husband, Dean, into the ground.

"How are Mom and Dad? Gram and Gramps? Dean? I bet the lot of you are wreaking havoc up in heaven, aren't you? And, of course, since it's your version of the place, you're wearing those blasted flamingo shorts constantly. Come on, Jed, tell me the truth. After all, you've shared so many secrets with me both before and since you passed. There was an outlet you bought them at, wasn't there?"

My smile might be kissed by my tears, but I can't stop thinking about the roar of laughter the first night Jed made an appearance wearing the atrocious swimwear I'm describing in our backyard. "You were up from Ketchikan with the Jacks. Mom and Dad abandoned us for the peace and quiet of the bar—and that's saying a hell of a lot.

God, Jed. It was so long ago. Did we all feel invincible in that moment, or were we just that damn good at hiding our insecurities?"

Suspecting it was the latter, I reach out and slowly trace my finger over each letter of his tombstone. "Well, we did a damn good job, then, didn't we? We used so much to deflect from the fact we were kids who didn't know shit about the depths of hell we'd be forced to live through. And still"—my voice breaks—"you didn't make it. The one person whose very presence unified us all."

Standing, I lean forward and press my lips to the top of the cool marble marker—such a contrast to the hearts of the men whose remains are buried beneath.

Then again, in my heart, Jedidiah Jonas Smith will never be gone. He can't be because if he is, then I truly am alone in this world. Oh, I know I have friends, but I gave up long ago on finding the other part of my soul. Because in those moments of brutal honesty, I acknowledge I already met him. And like an ugly hunger that can't be assuaged, I interact with Nick enough to remind myself exactly why I end up sabotaging every other relationship I've ever been in.

Other men will never call to my soul the exact same way he did those long-ago summer nights when he opened up to me about why he may not believe in anything, but his faith in my brother was absolute. I might have to crawl into the darkest part of the Tongass Forest in the dead of winter to find eyes the same shade as his when he'd scowl at one of us shoving a camera in front of his face. The few times I made him laugh, the rush to my head was more intoxicating than wine.

I fell head over heels in love with the angry young man who let me into his heart when he let no one else close to his skin.

Those summer nights Nicholas Cain warmed me from the inside by opening up about who he was ended by me making more out of them than what they really were. I'm the one who read more into his casual touches that sent shivers all over my body. I put more stock into his brief hugs he grudgingly bestowed upon me, but no one else. I truly thought he meant it when he promised me in a tormented voice that last night, "We'll keep in touch. We *will*."

As time passed after he first left Alaska, and I never heard from Nick, I slowly locked away a part of my heart that was reserved just for him—that perfect memory of first love that hadn't been tarnished by anything else in my life. When Nick did reach out, when he contacted me about coming to Vegas, I opened the door to that protected space and took a chance.

I faced Nick expecting to be swept away on a tide of emotion. But when my heart flipped on the rocks this time, at least I managed to walk away without any physical scars. I just added to my collection of emotional ones.

My brother willingly bore the brunt of my devastation, keeping me and Nick separated for years—maybe too many—in his effort to protect me from further heartache. Now, as every critical word I uttered to Jed about Nick over the years that he didn't rebuke floats through my head, all I can think is, what a waste. All of it.

Jed.

Nick.

And the years I spent pining for something I knew I'd never have a chance at. Ever.

Because the reality is that while Jed died three years ago, a large part of me died well before that. And because I tried to use one man to forget another, I ended up wounding more than just my heart. I ended up drowning my future not far from where I'm standing.

"I'll be back soon." I tell my brother. "I need to get to work."

I can practically feel the disapproval radiating off the rock. "Listen, if you didn't want me running the Brewhouse, you shouldn't have left the thing to me. It's always belonged to a Smith." My bitter laugh escapes along with a new passel of tears. "Wait, what am I saying? You left Grandpa's cross to Nick. Why didn't you leave him the bar too? That would have capped the whole thing off nicely."

Turning away, I get a few steps away before a gust of wind whips me around to face my brother one last time. Shoving my dark hair off my face, I clearly enunciate. "I love you, Jed. I always will. Even after everything, I'm not entirely certain I'll understand you. I wish I could." The wind stops swirling. "Kiss everyone hello for me. I'll be back soon."

And I turn away from where my brother asked to be returned to his final resting place—a small plot by the sea—and make my way down the street.

It's time to go to work. Since everyone else has moved on, I find it's the safest thing to live for now.

"WHAT DO you mean we're out of the IPA?" I drop my head back and roll my head back and forth. "Didn't the shipment come in today?"

My bartender shakes his head. "Not yet."

"Lovely. Let me go up to the office and check on it. Are we missing anything else?" Just as the words come out of my mouth, my chef comes out from the kitchen holding handfuls of rotted produce.

"I can't work with this, Maris." She shakes it in front of me. Her white knuckles start to unclench.

"If a single piece hits the floor while we have customers in here, you'll be looking for a new job," I warn the temperamental woman.

"I simply cannot work with subpar ingredients."

"And you know Skagway's beer is the popular item on the menu."

"Stop, both of you! Give me a few minutes to fix the problems before you keep kvetching at me," I snap. When they finally quiet, I race up the stairs to where my office is located—a converted apartment where I used to crash when nights were too much at the family home.

"If this is how the night is going to go, I'm moving to Vienna. There's a beautiful glacier there I can stare at—no, walk on! And men with accents. And chocolate, lots of delicious chocolate." Reaching my office, I slam the door for two blessed minutes of privacy while I work out how to fix this issue without bankrupting myself.

Just then, my cell phone rings. If it wasn't for the fact it's Kara Malone Jennings, my best friend and former sister-in-law, I'd ignore it. But I'm certain I know why she's calling. I answer her question without her saying a word. "I'm fine."

"Try that with someone who didn't live through this with you." I hear her sniff into a tissue.

I can't refute her words. I just listen to her tears, her grief, and wish

I could get to the stage where that's all I felt. But— "God, Kara, I'm so angry today."

"Why?"

"Because everything's a mess." I give her a quick rundown of what's happening at the Brewhouse. "And I..." I'm ashamed to admit the last.

"What else, Maris?"

I hesitate before answering. "I yelled at Jed today."

"Good."

"What?"

"It's healthy."

"Yelling at my dead brother is healthy?"

"Sure it is."

"What makes you say that, oh wise one?"

"Well, first of all, it saves you from taking it out on me," she retorts.

"Fair." Even as we both giggle, I reach for a tissue to mop up my tears and mingled snot. "What's second?"

"Do you really think the letters I've written to Dean over the years have been all sunshine and happiness? All good news? I'm so freaking pissed at him right now. Especially now."

"Why now?"

"Crap. I was going to wait to tell you until tomorrow."

"Tell me," I demand.

"No. It's a bad enough day."

"Kara, I swear to God..."

"I'm pregnant," she blurts out.

You could hear a pin drop between us. "You're...what?" I don't recognize my voice. It sounds like someone just shoved a knife in my chest and I'm bleeding out.

Because maybe I am.

"Maris, I'm so happy, and so...heartbroken."

"No. You don't get to be sad. Not unless it's because you won't have a chance to break Dean's hands again in the delivery room. Then you can be sad. It's a fucking miracle you're carrying," I hiss.

Kara begins to sob quietly. "I know. I just... I'd give anything..."

19

I practically choke trying to get out, "I know. But that's not the hand I've been dealt, right? And I can only play the hand I have."

A hard silence stretches out between us. "And here I can't even celebrate by lifting up a glass of our best IPA," I finally manage to tease.

"Why not?"

After outlining the issues, Kara says, "Hold on." Then I hear her yell, "Jennings! Pick up the phone!"

"What? Kara, no." But it's too late. Kara's husband, John Jennings, has already lifted the receiver.

"Everything okay?"

"Maris didn't get a delivery. Is anyone on a run to Alaska?" Kara asks as if it's an everyday occurrence for her to order her husband around the fiftieth state for my supplies like it's her local grocery.

"Jasper is. He's running cargo up. What do you need, Maris?"

"I can't ask a favor this big, Jennings," I protest.

"There is no favor too big or small you couldn't ask us," he reassures me. "Now, just tell me where Jas needs to go."

"You two are a damn miracle," I finally manage.

"No, we're your family. I'm not sure what it's going to take to get that through your gorgeous head," Kara admonishes.

"It's not gorgeous."

Jennings snorts. "Whatever."

"While normally I'd be giving my husband hell for noticing, I agree. You're beautiful, Maris. From the inside out."

Their words make me slightly nauseous. I know there's nothing good inside me. Not really. "No, that was Jed." Before they can protest, I fib slightly. "I have to get down to the floor. I'll send you a text, Jennings. And by the way, congratulations, Daddy. Kara, I'll call you tomorrow. My love to all of you and Kevin."

I rush off the phone and send Jennings a quick text of what I need. But just before I'm about to slip my phone back into my jeans, I get a news alert.

Local Family Fosters Child. New Addition Makes Seven!

"You have got to be kidding me. Who is selfless enough to..." I click on the article before gasping. It's my old school friend Sarah Li and her husband, Hung. I knew they had a few kids after graduation, but to foster kids as well? "How utterly selfless."

Saving the page to read later, I leave my office and go to tell my antsy bartender and crazed cook help is coming.

It only cost me what's left of my sanity to get it.

MARIS

June

"I've seen wishes, hopes, and dreams die in my sister's eyes. It makes me want to hurt the men who have done this to her. What's the worst is I'm probably the worst perpetrator as I know Nick's 'why.' Should I have told her? Would it have stopped everything else after?" - From the journals of Jedidiah Smith.

I hug the redhead exuberantly. "It's so good to see you!" Sarah Michelin Li graduated the year before I did from Juneau-Douglas High School, but it didn't stop us from being friends. Like me, Sarah's a "sourdough." Her family can trace its roots back to the gold rush up near Skagway.

"Do you remember when we were little, we used to dress up our Bunny Boots with stickers?" Sarah's eyes dance as she recalls our days in grammar school.

"Which lasted until we stepped out into the snow again?" I recall drolly.

"I told that story to my youngest foster daughter the other day when she wanted to use a glitter pen."

"What did she say?"

"Obviously, Mom, it's because you did it in winter. You should have waited until spring." We both double over in laughter. "I know I said it when I saw you at his funeral, Maris, but I'm so sorry about Jed." She reaches over and takes my hand.

"I could offer you the usual 'thank you,' but somehow, I think you'd see right through that." I squeeze her hand back before letting it go.

"I would. It's a mom thing."

"Actually, that's what I wanted to talk with you about."

"Want to take one off my hands? I have several available?"

"Offering up the ones you made or the ones you brought into your home?"

"Depends on the day." And our laughter chases one another once again. "Seriously, what's going on?"

Just then our waiter approaches. I order the fondue. Sarah's eyes glaze over slightly. "I knew we were friends for a *very* good reason."

I amend our order. "For two."

"Certainly. I'll be back with that in a few moments." Our waiter disappears.

"I saw you're fostering five kids?"

"Yep. My husband was a foster child. We always swore we'd take in as many as we could."

"But you're overloaded?" My head cocks to the side.

"To say the least. We barely passed the home inspection this time."

"Home inspection?"

Sarah goes to open her mouth to answer, but before she can, our waiter is back with a tray filled with cheesy goodness and croutons. "Thank you."

"Bless you," she counters.

We dive in simultaneously. After a few minutes, Sarah picks up our conversation. "It's a huge process, Maris. You have to go through nine weeks of classes. Then there's months of working with a licensing agent to get your home study and background investigation complete —and heaven help you if you have a fire extinguisher out of place. Because there's always going to be periodic checks you have to pass. And if you don't, that would mean more checks. Finally, you graduate."

"And that's when you're placed with a child?"

Sarah snorts. "Honey, that's when the social workers get involved. You could be placed with a child that night, or you could be placed with one in a few months. It depends on whether or not you agree to respite care."

I place my hand to my forehead. "There's so much to think about."

"Maris, are you considering fostering a child?"

I nod. "It's something I've thought of for years. Jed and I had a close friend who was fostered late in his life. It...affected me."

Sarah falls back into her chair with a jarring thud. "You're really considering this?" At my nod, she continues. "Well, I'll be damned."

"Possibly, but likely for something we did in high school. Definitely not for this."

A lightning-quick grin flashes across her face before she her face sobers. "It's not a decision to make lightly."

"No, it isn't."

After scrutinizing me for long moments, Sarah nods decisively. "Okay. When's your next day off?" She reaches for another crouton and dunks it as deep as she can in the gooey cheese.

"Sunday."

"Then come over for the day. You've met my two, but I'm not sure if you've met my fosters. Come experience what my life is like. It's not easy, my friend. Sundays are paperwork days."

"Like I'm not used to those. Only mine involve kegs and lettuce."

Sarah, chewing on her crouton, chokes. "There's a story there."

I realized how starved I am and reach for a piece of bread. "From a few weeks ago. Luckily, I have a guardian angel."

"Jed?" she asks knowingly.

"No. My best friend's husband owns an air transport business."

"God, up here that's worth its weight in gold!" she exclaims.

"Don't I know it. By the next morning, I had beer, lettuce, and tiny donuts from Pike's Place Market."

"Bitch. Do you know how long it's been since I've had those?"

"Educate me on everything I need to know and I'll make sure you get a supply of them," I promise her.

"Deal. But don't say I didn't warn you. The kids are crazy this time of the year."

"Remember Rainey Jones?"

"Who could forget Rainey? She married Brad Meyers, right?"

"Yep. I tell them their kids thaw at this time of the year; they're so out of control."

Sarah manages to hold back her guffaws for two seconds. "I don't care how many times Hung goes after work with the guys to the Brewhouse. This lunch was so worth it."

For me too. Instead I just take another bite of our appetizer as we catch up on our mutual high school friends and where their lives are. And we make plans for Sunday.

I'm so excited I can barely eat.

SUNDAY SEEMS to take forever to come around. I'm not entirely certain if I should bring anything, so I call Sarah. "My two would eat anything. Bea has a peanut allergy, Richie has a seafood one. Diane, Wendy, and David aren't allergic to anything."

"How about ice cream?" I ask faintly.

Sarah hums her approval. "Stick with chocolate and vanilla," she says before hanging up the phone.

I drive up to the Lis' home and find kids everywhere. Sliding from my SUV, I stand back for a moment and observe the two girls battling with the three boys just as ferociously. One boy is chasing another girl around yelling, "I'll get you! Then you'll be it!"

And then the sun lights upon a brown-haired boy sitting in the middle of a mud puddle, building a pie. Happily, he decorates it with bits of grass and rocks before calling out, "Who wants some pizza?"

His "siblings" begin to laugh. "David, you're playing pizza parlor again?"

"Yeah, come play chase with us."

He shrugs, unconcerned. "I like pizza parlor."

One of the girls comes over and screams, "Oh, my! There's a dead bug on his pizza! I'm going to tell Ms. Sarah," before running toward the house at a dead run.

My heart's pounding not out of fear, but at a memory that's shoving its way to the forefront of my mind that was locked away.

"Maris! Let's pretend we're working at the Brewhouse," Jed urged.

I glanced back at the house. "Will we get in trouble?" I knew only adults were supposed to drink. Mama and Daddy had made that very clear to Jed and me.

"No, Sunshine. See? We'll use the tree to mix drinks. The ground will be our bar," he declared.

I frowned. "Daddy doesn't let people sit on the bar, Jed. And Mama's gonna get mad. You're sitting in the mud."

Jed laughed and laughed. He pulled me down onto his lap, his behind sinking deeper in the dirty earth. "One day, we're going to run that bar, Maris. And who's going to care if we sit on the bar or not?"

I thought for a few minutes about his words because I didn't like the idea that one day we'd run the bar. That would mean Mama and Daddy wouldn't be here. Still, I said with authority, "Cust...cust..."

"Customers? Is that what you're trying to say?" Jed gave me his big smile that turned his face kind of weird.

I nodded.

Jed shrugged. "Then we get new customers. People have to accept us for who we are, or they don't deserve our loyalty and love."

I'm ripped from the memory as Sarah is dragged from the house. "David, sweetheart. Just tell me you didn't eat the bug this time." I can't prevent the giggle at the sound of her aggrieved voice.

Her head snaps up at the sound. "Hey, Maris! Come on over and meet the kids."

"Let me get the ice cream out of the car." You'd think I just announced that Santa was coming for the second time in a year. Children flung their swords in every direction. Ones who were chasing each other began to race in my direction. They all found a new toy, and apparently, I was it.

All of them, except David. He observed me from a distance with wise eyes that burned through my soul.

Sarah took pity on me and yelled, "Everyone, go clean up. That means your rooms as well as your bodies. No ice cream for anyone who doesn't pass inspection in one hour. Miss Maris and I will be in the kitchen." Just like they swarmed me, the children scatter. Maybe they were supporting me, because my knees almost give out once I have some distance.

David ambles to his feet. My breath whooshes out as he swaggers to the house with mud all over the back of his little jeans.

"David," Sarah calls.

"Yes?"

"New clothes, and leave those in the laundry," Sarah adds to his list. She walks back over and inspects his work. "That's a mighty impressive pizza though. Good thing it's a special occasion with Miss Maris visiting and we're having it for dinner."

He turns and beams at me. And that's when I see them. One, two dimples pop out in apples of his cheeks.

Just like Jed's.

Holy shit.

My stomach begins to cramp. I press a hand to it. *Don't get your hopes up, Maris. He's probably Sarah's biological child. That's likely why you feel such a deep pull to him.*

"Well, you wanted to meet all the kids, Maris. First impressions?" Sarah's voice is laced with amusement.

"You're a saint. And I'm glad I brought you and Hung a bottle of wine as well as ice cream." I open the car and pull out the bags from our local grocery

Sarah's grin widens. "Just wait until you see pizza prep. That's when you'll begin nominating us for sainthood."

"Should be fun to watch." I tell her the truth as we make our way up the flagstone steps.

"And participate in," Sarah tacks on.

"Wait, what?"

"Everyone makes their own. And trust me, there's a competition on whose pizza is the best."

"You know I practically flunked art," I growl.

"That's why I thought this would be fun," she chirps as we make our way to the side-by-side fridge and freezer.

"Fun? When did your sadistic side come out?"

"I think after child number four." She purses her lips. "Definitely before number six. You have to be creative as a mom, Maris. Might as well start early."

"Why me?" I ask jokingly.

"Exactly. Why you? Are you ready for the never-ending questions? The help they need? The love they have to give?" Even as I'm pondering that, she wedges the ice cream in an overstocked freezer that looks like it's going to explode any moment. "There. Now, while we have a few minutes, let me give you the lowdown on who's who around here and we can prep dinner."

I catch sight of the clock. "You know it's only four, right?"

She nods. "It takes a while to prep for nine."

"Then it's a good thing I'm used to running a restaurant."

AFTER DINNER, dessert, washing of faces, brushing of teeth, and lots of thank-yous, Sarah, Hung, and I are relaxing in their family room. "So, what do you think, Maris? Now that you've spent some time with our brood, is fostering something you're interested in?" Hung asks.

I shake my head. Both of their faces fall. "But adopting is. I'm ready. I want this, the kind of unequivocal love you all have here."

"There's nothing else like it in the world," Sarah agrees.

"What do I have to do to get started?" I ask.

For a long time, we talk about what to do next. And I gratefully accept the invitation to spend time with the Li family to understand more about the fostering process. "Who knows, Maris? You might be able to give me tips on things like paperwork that will be huge time-savers."

"I'd be happy to." And I would.

Suddenly, the clock strikes ten times. "I can't believe I've been here for so long," I exclaim, standing. "You both must be ready for bed."

Sarah and Hung stand as well. "It's been a huge pleasure."

At the door, I turn and hug them both. "For me as well. Please let me know when we can do it again."

"Any Sunday. Just let me know," Sarah throws out as I shrug into my coat.

"I'll take you up on it." I wave as I step out the door. Heading down the flagstone path, I don't know what makes me glance up. But when I do, I freeze.

David's sitting in the window. And on the frosty pane, he draws a tiny cross. Not a star, not a circle. A cross. Then he blows air onto the pane to fog it up and draws it again.

And again.

I finally move my legs and make my way into the car. Turning it on, I blast the heat, not moving for a few moments.

Then I ask aloud what's been tickling my mind me all day. "Jed, is that you?"

Of course, I don't get an answer. With a large amount of regret, I back out of the driveway and head home.

NICHOLAS

August

*S*lap.

Slap.

Slap.

My feet hit the pavement over and over again, demonstrating to the young kids moaning behind me that I—an "old man"—still have the stamina, the reserve in the tank, that pushed me over the top to win the belt. Right now, it's just running a mile, but for this group, that's a long distance.

The Champ has an image to uphold, after all.

For years, I lauded it publicly—even to my best friends—as the greatest night of my life. What it was is a colossal fuckup I can't fathom how to repair. It's always in the back of my head. That one moment of self-loathing spawned years of contempt and revulsion.

And in the end, there's nothing I can do to get her to talk to me. Even on the worst day when we should have been bonded together. I wince as I'm running as pain floods through my pores.

"You okay, Mr. Cain?" A boy, no older than nine who's missing a few teeth, grins up at me.

"You betcha, Richie." I reach down and ruffle the kid's unruly mop of hair. If the little speed demon dressed a little more flamboyantly and was a lot less polite, I'd think he was Jed zapped into a tiny form. Without a break in stride, I call out, "Let's pick up the pace," to a cacophony of groans.

This is my favorite group to train each week. The one group that no matter what, I try to make it back from my travels to work with. Because these are the kids and teens who come in not believing someone gives a shit. Kind of the way I felt the first time I met Jed Smith at a grocery store and then later at the Great Alaskan Lumberjack Show.

"Crazy bastard," I mutter fondly under my breath, feeling the gold cross he left me when he died bouncing against my sweat-slickened chest.

Even though the anniversary of his actual death has passed, the date the guys and I were notified of the wreck that took Jed and his husband's life just came and went. I recall opening that letter all alone in my office and swearing I was having a heart attack. All the blood stopped pumping to my brain. I couldn't move my arms or legs. And I swore I was moving through a tunnel chanting two names.

Jed.

Maris.

I'd fainted on the floor of my office, clutching the letter to my chest. My assistant found me that way a short time later and was debating with my number two, Oliver, whether or not to call an ambulance. I threatened them with, "If you contact anyone other than Jennings to get me on a flight to Ketchikan, I swear to God, I'm firing you both."

They both hurried out.

Later that night, I received a call from the woman I was...dating. "Nick, baby. I went by your office. So, you want me to go with you, or what?" God knows the reason I was with her was because she was the exact opposite of Maris Smith; hell, all the women I'd had in my life to that point were. Anything to keep the memories of Maris out of my mind. But the idea of bringing someone with me to Jed's funeral—which might or might not hurt the woman I'd loved forever—made me violently ill. I hung up without saying a word before I threw up the better part of the bourbon I'd made a decent dent in before she rang.

After that night, all I wanted to do was give up, but damn Jed. He made it so I couldn't by forcing me to look for the one thing that I swore didn't exist: faith. How could something like that exist when it took from me, from us, the greatest man put on this planet? How could Jed expect me to believe in something so nebulous without guidance?

Turns out he was right. Asshole, I think fondly. I couldn't do it when he was alive. But why did he have to die for my days of gluttonous indulgence to end? My unresolved anger over Jed's loss lengthens my stride, making me pull away from the clustered group slightly. Dominica and Raj encourage the kids from the back. "Go get Mr. Nick, kids. You got this!" And just as quickly, I'm thrown back into the octagon.

"Don't give up! You've got this, buddy."

I can hear all their voices—Jennings, Kody, and Brad— yelling something similar, but it's Jed's voice yelling at me the loudest. I hear him above my coach, above my trainer. There's no one in my corner I hear above Jed. His voice once broke through the open-air fandom in an arena in Ketchikan, and it's berated me for daring to think of touching his precious sister if I was going to fuck everything from there to Juneau along the way. It's his voice that overrode them all in the sea of fans when I land a wild haymaker.

And it's his face I search out when my hand is raised in the air as the blood trickles from my face.

Only it's no longer there.

Neither is hers.

I won and, to the two people who mattered most, I became the biggest loser. Instead of becoming the Champ and showing them the man I could be, I ruined it all. But would anything have been different if I'd lost? No, I admit to myself wearily. I'd have been the guy who lost the belt that fucked in order to get a prize. Talk about a real champ.

As we turn to head the final stretch back to the gym, I conclude nothing's been real for me in three years since Jed died. Despite the hellacious recruiting schedule, working with the kids training, I have a massive hole in my head and my heart. I rub away drops of sweat that drip down the side of my face, ruefully acknowledging Jed would have frowned upon my behavior right after he died.

"Would be worried about me. Too much work. Better than the other shit," I gasp. But it's been a long while since I indulged in any sort of vice, years since I've been involved with a woman in any capacity and large amounts of booze. Both came to a halt the night Jennings texted me to tell me Kody was gone.

I remember blindly reaching for my phone and trying to call him, the same way I did Jed. After I was sent to voicemail, I called Jennings and ripped him a new one for daring to tell me Kody died in a text.

Confused, Jennings replied, "He's not dead, Nick."

I slurred, "Then why are you calling? Had a good buzz going on."

Jennings's disgusted "I'm not sure either, asshole" before he slammed down the phone only made me laugh. Until I sobered up the next morning wondering if any of it was real.

Unfortunately, phone logs don't lie.

Not long after we managed to get Kody back in our lives, I took a long look at myself. It's amazing how that happens when the only woman you've ever loved dismisses you as a joke.

Maris Ione Smith holds my soul, and I dare not tell her. After all, I'm just a waste of people's hopes and dreams.

Isn't that what my mother implied by leaving when she left me in Alaska all those years ago and drove away?

"No," I call out. "If you hold your fist like that, you're going to snap your thumb off in a heartbeat the minute you connect with your opponent's body." Glancing around, I find the perfect person to help the young boy. I let out a piercing whistle, and all activity in the gym ceases. "Tatum, get your ass over here and help Scott for a few. You need a break anyway."

Tatum spits his mouth guard into his taped hand before shooting me a grin that reminds me a little too much of Jennings. "You got it, Nick." He bounds barefoot off the elevated ring after exchanging a quick handshake with the guy he was sparring with. "Thanks for working with me."

"No problem, Tatum." The trainer turns to another member of the elite team.

Tatum makes his way over to where we are, and I do my damnedest to suppress my lips from twitching when I recall Kody's almost desperate call to keep him away from his baby sister, Sandra. Despite the beating he took early on that kept him out of training for a few months, the kid's on a fast track to become one of the best. Stepping back, I observe his training techniques with Scott. The few finer points I acknowledge in myself are evident in the young fighter as well as so many more. I look forward to being a part of his team in the future.

Soon, he's done patiently explaining the reasons for certain hand positions. Clapping both of them on the shoulders, I inform them, "Another ten, then Scott, hit the bag for kicks," before I move over to help another struggling teen.

My heart clenches when I approach Darin. He's sporting a massive black eye I damn well know he didn't earn here. Like any after-school and summer programs, I report every injury. The idea of teaching kids mixed martial arts is to instill discipline they may not receive at home, not to get them hurt. But accidents happen just the same.

God, so many of them are like me after that last summer in Alaska. Lost. Willing to do anything to believe that dreams exist. In all the glory, I never forgot where I came from. And one night, I picked up the phone, reaching out to someone I trusted. I asked him if it was crazy to bring the kids in to seek a healthy outlet while there's so much chaos in their lives. I hadn't spoken to him in almost a year at that point. *It's empty, Jed. The win. But I drive to the center to train, and there's clusters of these kids who I think would die if I invited them in. Most of them will never be champions, but what does that matter? God, life feels so fucking empty lately.*

Maybe because there's more to life than a fight or a fuck? There's the people who would lay down their lives for you if you'd just open your eyes? Jed's voice, silent for so long, came through the text loud and clear.

Yeah. There's that.

Welcome back, brother. And I think it's a shitload of work, but you're the perfect guy to take it on.

I made Jed swear not to say anything. To the casual observer, Razor is just a training academy for the most elite MMA fighters. But inside its walls, it's much more. It's a safe place where the walls come down. Laughter rings out on a frequent basis. Warm meals are served. Hell, I have a swear jar on the level where the kids train. And above all, trust is built and never broken.

It's the most sacred of vows.

"Excuse me, Nick?" my assistant, Charmaine, calls from the gym doors. She waves her arm back and forth.

I jog over. "What's up?"

"You wanted me to let you know when the new recruitment files came in. Everyone's sent everything over."

"Great. Thanks." I offer her a smile complete with dimples and flutter my eyelashes.

She reaches up and pinches my ear. "Don't you dare ask me to watch those videos that Oliver, Evan, Veronika, and Royce sent for *you*. Harold had to take me out for margaritas the last time. Why your recruiters have to cause blood to fly, I'll never know." Charmaine, a spry sixty-two, has been dating her man friend since I hired her ten years earlier.

I disengage her fingers from my ear before wrapping an arm around her shoulder. "To make certain their resumes aren't fluffed up," I remind her.

She huffs but doesn't protest. "Oh, I forgot. Ollie's on the phone."

I stop in my tracks. "Now?" A tingle of awareness shoots down my spine.

"Yes. I'd have just left the videos, but then he called and said this was important."

The tingle turns into a chill. "Can you bring me something when you come back from lunch?" I normally wouldn't make the request as it's nowhere in Charmaine's responsibilities to feed me, but I have a feeling I'm going to miss my chance to get away from my desk

"Sure. Do you think everything's okay?"

"No." Then I press a kiss to the top of her silvery-white head. "I think it's going to knock me on my ass."

"Nicholas. Language!" she snaps. "We're on the children's floor."

I pat my workout clothes for my pockets. "Sorry, Charmaine. Add it to what I owe you for lunch."

"Don't think I won't, you heartbreaking menace," she warns.

Knowing damn good and well she'll hold me to it, I head off in the direction of my office, curious about what Oliver has found.

NICHOLAS

"Did you say Juneau?" I repeat into the phone. Leaning back into my chair, my eyes roam the watermelon-tinted peaks I can make out in the distance. But in my mind it's not the beauty of the Sandia Peaks, nor the excitement of adding a new elite fighter to Razor Academy.

It's her—the idea of possibly seeing her.

Maris Ione Smith.

I listen with half an ear to my scout as he extols the attributes of this guy who decided to try professional fighting. "What does he do?"

"Well, he worked for a while for this touristy thing called the Great Alaskan Lumberjack Show. I think you've heard of it."

No freaking way. Immediately, I pull up the website of the show where day after day for four summers, my best friends and I owned the crowds and demand, "Which one is he again?"

"Reece London."

Oliver keeps talking while I scan the guy's bio. "I'm telling you, Nick. I think the guy could heave both of us over his shoulder before submitting us," Oliver concludes.

"What's his fighting specialty?" I close out of the website to scan the very different profile Oliver compiled of Reece London that arrived in my inbox before answering the call.

Oliver laughs. "What's not? He's a black belt in karate and jiujitsu. His boxing skills are strong, but I see room for improvement. Same with his submissions. Guy did some wrestling back in high school but never really took to it. But..."

I pick up where Oliver left off. "Put it all together and you have one hell of a package to start with. How did Reece get to be so well trained? We've had military pass through Razor before; it doesn't always garner your attention." In order for me to be able to spend time working with both the professional-level athletes and the kids, I cultivated a team of scouts to travel around the world based on query letters and word of mouth to seek out new talent. And Oliver Torrence is the best there is.

"In this case it's personal," he admits. "We knew each other growing up in Hawaii."

"Ah." I press Play as I watch Oliver spar with the larger man on video. It doesn't take but a few minutes for Oliver to wind up on his ass. I grin as Oliver rolls to his feet, only to be thrown back down like an annoying gnat. Reece balances before sweeping out, and the two begin to grapple. They roll over and over. I wince as Oliver takes an elbow to the eye socket. "How's your eye?" My eyes narrow as Oliver mounts him and gets a few hard hits in.

"Bled like a bitch, but his ribs will hurt more."

"Hmm. And you think I should take him on because?"

"Reece is already a champ."

Startled, I hit Pause, just as the champ takes a fist to his face. "What makes you say that?" I demand. My eyes drift over to where my prize belt sits protected.

As many times as people refer to that night, I refuse to let my mind go there willingly. Not when I had the chance to have it all and I ruined it.

Again.

"Because his work ethic rivals ours, he trains in every moment of his spare time, and there's no one from his past holding him back," Oliver concludes.

The laugh I let out is a rough, bitter sound. "There's always someone, Ollie. He just may not realize it. Get me more film and I'll consider it."

"On it, boss." Oliver disconnects the call.

Leaning back in my chair, I stare up at my title belt, which winks smugly down at me. What I said was no less than the truth. I made a promise a long time ago, and I've kept my end of it.

No matter how much it hurts every time I hear her voice.

LETTING myself into my adobe oasis I purchased years ago, I relish the security my home gives to me. I spent too many years being shuttled from house to house by my birth parents before they decided I was too much of a burden. A quiver ripples through my stomach as I slam the heavy door behind me.

No, I left those burdens back in Alaska. I refuse to bring them here.

"What I need is a good workout. Oliver prattling about took up my sparring time," I decide aloud. Not caring my voice echoes off the travertine, I wander into the workout room and drop my clothes into a pile in the small locker room I had built. Pulling on a pair of workout shorts, I grab my cell and a towel before heading out into the fully equipped workout room that's bigger than a three-car garage. Picking up a jump rope, I set a timer on my phone and begin to lose myself to the routine that's as second nature to me as breathing after so many years.

After I finish jumping rope, I do reps of heel-to-butt kicks, walk-outs, and lunges—front and back, side to side. Muscles comfortably warm, I stretch lightly, beginning with my neck, moving down to my shoulders and arms, before I stretch my quads and hips. Then I pad barefoot over to my workout chart. Hmm, arms. And here I was in the mood to kick a little ass.

But like Oliver said earlier, you don't get to be the champion without a work ethic and without training. And for years I've done little but both. Especially since Jed died.

The racks of free weights are neatly organized. I reach over and pick up a forty-pound dumbbell. Bracing my arm, I begin doing curls when my cell rings. Lowering the weight, I press a button on my watch and then hit Speaker. "What do you want?" I growl at John Jennings jokingly. At least, I hope after close to twenty years of friendship he knows I'm joking.

"I didn't interrupt anything, did I?" he worries.

I roll my eyes. Despite the fact in my younger days I was a complete douchebag to women, I can't remember the last time I had one in my bed. "I was working out, asshole."

"You do realize you're getting old. Eventually you're going to have to turn over training the new guys you're picking up to the younger guys who work for you," Jennings comments mildly.

"Fuck you, Jennings. Just remember, I'll always be better-looking than you," I counter, unperturbed. "Now, why did you call?"

"Let me get Brad and Kody on the line so I can tell everyone at once."

Before he can add them, I rush out with, "Is everything okay? What's wrong?"

Kody's face appears in the corner of my screen, his blondish-red hair practically glowing in the Montana sunset. "Hey, Jenn— Hey, Nick! What's the occasion?" Kody's framed by the back of his new house in Montana. He's covered in sawdust, not an unusual occurrence for the acclaimed builder.

Before I can speak—or Jennings can—Brad's face also appears. It's a few hours behind in Juneau, so chaos is reigning as usual at the Meyers household. Rainey—Brad's wife of close to twenty years—is bellowing at their two kids to wash up and get ready for dinner. Finally, an almost eerie silence rains down on us.

"Well, now that everyone's here, I can share the news. Kara and I wanted to wait until..." Jennings's hand is shaking, and he's crying.

"What is it?" Kody demands.

"Is someone sick? Is it Kevin?" Brad demands.

But they're not studying his face. There isn't agony on it; there's joy. "Kara's pregnant?" I take a wild guess.

And Jennings lets out a wobbly laugh. "Damn straight she is. So, you might always be better-looking than me, Nick, but I still have enough power to—"

"Jennings!" We all scold him before we're offering congratulations on top of one another. But my hand reaches up and clenches around the gold cross Jed left me when he died. His grandfather's cross.

"He should be here for this, damnit." I can't prevent the bitterness that laces my voice. But for being in the wrong place at the wrong time, he would be. So would his husband. "Jed and Dean would be fantastic uncles."

"Yeah, they would. So, Kara and I expect the three of you to make up for them and to get your asses to Florida as soon as you can after this baby is born." Jennings's words are nothing more than one friend should expect from another after a half a lifetime of friendship, but for a man who has held himself a step back from emotional entanglements of any kind since he was shoved into the Alaskan foster system at fourteen, it's a huge leap of faith for him to expect this from me.

Then again, it's doing what Jed would want me to do when he gave me this cross, damnit. Squeezing it so tightly, I wonder absently if I'm crushing it. I'm the first to respond, "Okay."

"Just that quick?" Jennings wonders aloud. "Just that simple?"

"It's what Jed would have done." And after the other assurances that Kody and Brad will be in Florida as soon as they can make it after the birth of Kara and Jennings's second child and more congratulations, I disconnect the call.

"Can you believe that, Jed? Another Jennings." I pick up the weight in my other hand and begin reps.

A little voice inside my head taunts me, *You could have had that if you hadn't broken her heart.*

Only if I wanted to ruin her life the way mine was.

Feeling the darkness settle over me, I finish my reps and put away the weights. Slipping on gloves, I move over to the heavyweight bag and begin taking out my frustrations—past and present—on it. Punch after punch, I land with lethal force at my intended target.

Myself.

MARIS

"If there was a price to be paid for love, I'd do anything, sell anything, be anything to set that emotion free in my baby sister again. But day after day, year after year, I know it will take a man with a will of steel to breach the barriers around her heart. I pray for them both." - From the journals of Jedidiah Smith.

Sixteen years. It took sixteen years, but I'm finally fulfilling my brother's wish for me.

I found a love that makes me happy.

Tenderly, I reach out and cup his chin. His long-lashed dark eyes hold mine captive before a wary smile flashes briefly. It's gone quickly but not before his cherubic cheeks flash dimples that likely have broken the hearts of everyone he's ever met in his path.

And he's only nine.

Sarah said to talk with him. "All of them are quick as a whip, Maris. The love you show them means so much."

"David, you are such a special little boy." Even though it's not my decision, my heart is already his. He just has to ask for it. If it were up to me, he'd be coming home today. After all, just like Nick was given, the little boy Sarah's been fostering deserves a chance when life has given him so few at such a young age.

"Are you going to be here for always?" he asks.

My heart melts at the way he phrases it. "Well, I do have my own home. But if Sarah says it's okay, you could come to visit. All of you could," I amend quickly.

"I mean, will you never leave?" In his question, I hear his hopes and fears of being let down rolled into one. The black spot that's been plaguing my life since I got the call about my brother's death three years ago is dimming, and it's because I found his soul again here on earth.

No longer feeling like I'm counting days until I can join Jed, I stand, holding my hand out. David's muddy one clasps it trustingly. "I'll do whatever I can not to," I vow.

"I trust you, Maris." His soulful brown eyes smile up into mine.

And another bond of love snaps into place. First came knowledge, then came trust. Now come the promises.

And this time it's up to me to keep them.

AFTER I LEAVE David at his foster parents' home, I call Kara.

She answers on the first ring. "How did it go?"

I immediately burst into tears.

Her reaction is exactly what I expect from the woman who's been my best friend for twenty years. She lets out a war whoop that might be able to be heard by every person across the four thousand miles that separates us. "We're having a baby!" she shouts.

"David's not a baby," I remind her for the hundredth time.

"You want him to be your first child; that makes him your first baby. Trust me, even when they stand over a foot taller than you, they're still your babies." Since Kara's youngest child is seventeen, and as tall as his father, Jennings, I decide to take her word for it.

Then I voice my biggest fear. "God, I hope nothing goes wrong."

Immediately, Kara's jubilance is tempered. "Why would it?"

"Because I've learned that something always goes wrong, Kara. God, it's like someone has a cosmic shit hammer ready to swing. Remember? Jed lived his life for far too many years wondering if he'd

ever find love. He finds it with Dean, and look what happens to them."
I clear my throat. "I didn't tell you I've been clearing out Jed's old room."

"What kind of things have you found?"

"Other than the fact my brother was a damn pack rat?"

"A trait he shared with Dean." We let out watery giggles. "What else?"

"Bits and pieces of old letters, stuff from the Jacks. Memories I'm cataloging that I'll be giving them on birthdays and shit."

"That's incredibly sweet."

"That's not the only thing I found."

"What else?

"I found old journals."

"Oh, Maris. How incredible. What did you find?" There's a rustle of material as Kara gets settled in for a long talk.

"So much." My throat gets tight as I remember words of a man's frustrated words about the way he devised plans only to have them foiled by the actions or inertia of others. His empathy was both more and less than I ever imagined. And I still don't know what to do about this side of my brother that I can't share because to do so would wreck the image of Jed everyone has. "God, I'd give anything to be able to share what I'm feeling with Jed and Dean." Or to hand them back over. Unread.

"So would I." Kara's voice is husky. Even now, though it's been three years since Jed and Dean died in a car wreck that took them from our lives way too soon, part of me is still floored by the fact our brothers fell in love with one another with one look. Then again, as I admire one of the black-and-white photos Kara's wedding photographer, Holly Freeman, took of the two of us while Kara was preparing to walk down the aisle, I'm really not. It only took that amount of time for Kara's and my hearts to connect when we met in Juneau after she answered my family's ad for a room.

So many years and—for me, at least—so little has changed.

I drag myself back to our conversation. "There are days when I come flying down the stairs and I feel like I'm going to see them."

"I know you would never sell the house." It's a statement, not a question.

"Never," I confirm. "I can't imagine it."

"What other things did you find in the journals? Stuff about Jennings?" I hear both amusement and curiosity in her voice.

My hand presses against my stomach, and I try to control my heartbeat. My mind drifts back to curling up next to my brother for both warmth and safety, both of us ignoring the stench of our skin as the days passed by when all I could do was cry silent tears. As clearly as I remember hearing Kevin's first baby cries, I forgot Jed's being there during the darkest days of my life.

And then I read one of his journals.

Kara believes Jed didn't know about her having Kevin until that fateful day in Florida. Admitting he knew everything from the very beginning, every secret, I don't understand how she could forgive me for lying to her. I truly never meant for my brother to find out about her son—Jennings's son—but I didn't remember. I was so strung out on drugs, recovering from one of the most painful procedures of my life, that getting up to the bathroom by myself hurt. I didn't realize what I was saying awake. The answer is obviously too much after I heard Kevin cry as it triggered my own tears.

Tears my brother wiped and then wrote about.

But if I thought I knew physical pain back then, it was nothing in comparison to the night I got the call from Kara about Jed's death. That was the night my heart began to shatter into a million pieces. Nothing, not any pain from having loved Nick, the agony of my medical scars, will ever leave me with the same kind of despair I felt the night I got that call.

Even if Kara walked out of my life tomorrow.

Throwing off a quick laugh, I reassure Kara, "Stuff that requires a lot of wine. Therefore, you and your inquiring mind will have to wait. It's a long time until my newest niece or nephew is going to make an appearance. Speaking of which, when is Jennings going to tell the guys?"

"He told them earlier tonight. So Rainey can finally stop looking so guilty for not telling Brad," Kara chortles.

"What I think is funnier is that Meadow is better at keeping secrets from Kody," I muse.

"I notice you haven't shared your big news with any of them," she reminds me.

"That's because I'd like to get past the initial hurdles since I finally passed the classes." I run a hand over my head, bringing us back around to my original reason for calling. "I've already filled out the licensing application which should trigger the background check and the need for a home visit."

"I'd like to visit," Kara says wistfully. "I miss you so damn much. And with all of this going on, I suspect there's going to be no way you for you to take a trip to come to us this summer."

"Not likely," I concede, my mood plummeting slightly. Every year since Jed moved permanently to Ponte Vedra, Florida, I flew cross-country and spent time with him, Dean, Kara, and her son, Kevin, for a whole month every summer. The thought depresses me, before I realize what I could have at the end—a family of my own. In my mind's eye, David's soulful brown eyes blink up at me before a shy smile crosses his face.

"Do you think you'll be able to make it for the delivery? I'm not sure if I can do it without you or Dean here." The panic from Kara's voice snaps me back to our conversation.

"What? Are you afraid Jennings will wash out as a labor coach?"

There's a sniff before, "No. I think he'll do great. I just want our baby to be surrounded by as much of his or her family as soon as she comes into the world."

"Unless by some quirk of fate that happens to be the week of the adoption, I'll be there for your delivery. I swear that to you."

"You promise?" Kara's tearful exuberance is clear across the line.

I don't hesitate. "I promise. And you know I don't take those lightly. After all." I flip to a picture of David and me. "I promised Jed I'd find love, and I finally have."

Those words set Kara off on a crying binge that eventually has Kevin coming over and lecturing, "Jeez, Maris. Now I need to get her some Powerade."

Knowing he inherited that smart-ass mouth as much from my

brother as he did from his biological uncle, I retort, "Get used to it, buddy. Soon it will be your little brother or sister demanding much worse."

"Oh, God." The phone clatters to the table as Kevin takes off. I can hear Kara's laughter, though she doesn't pick up the phone again.

That's okay. I couldn't speak if she did. I'm crying myself.

CURLED up in front of a roaring fire, the beauty of the Alaskan summer nights allowing me this comfort, the warm embrace of our generations-old family home plus Jed's own words reassure me I'm doing the right thing when it comes to taking this step forward in my life.

Placing the glass of wine aside, I lift the leather journal off my chest and begin to read aloud, *"I want to dare Maris to open up her heart to love someone. She gives of herself from what appears to be a limitless fountain— over and over again. But something has to feed that spring to keep it flowing clean and pure. I have ideas on what that could be, but it's not an easy road. And in the end, it may not be enough."*

Setting the book on the coffee table, I pick up my glass and offer my brother a toast to the cool air that wraps around me. "Jed, I relied upon you so much in our lives, I'm afraid you made it your life's mission to ensure I reached for what you eventually found—a love so strong that it can still be seen. It's practically tangible. But darling, not all of us are willing to open ourselves to that kind of vulnerability. There's a suffering that accompanies the daring of love." I become entranced in the flickering flames. "But maybe I can go in search of my dreams. Maybe I won't ache as badly at night, and I'll still love with everything I can, everything I am. It will be enough. I'll find that fulfillment you want me to have."

A log rolls in the fireplace, startling me. I'd almost believe it was Jed answering me, except an incoming email pops up on my phone. After noting the sender, I immediately open it. Then I let out a war whoop that must be able to be heard in Fairbanks. "They want to do a home study!" I yell to the empty house.

The dare from Jed to find love may have originally suffocated my earlier relationships, but it forced me to evaluate them with a critical eye.

Now I know why.

David, this adoption, this is the course my life is supposed to be on. I immediately whirl around to tell someone the good news only to deflate a bit when I find myself alone. Then I square my shoulders.

No, this is how it's supposed to be; I just know it.

MARIS

"I pity the fool who believes my sister is merely a pleasant woman. She could take on a Kodiak and come out the winner. When pissed, her eyes can skewer you, and her tongue is pure acid if she's riled. I joke about it, but she should come with a warning sign." - From the journals of Jedidiah Smith.

"What do you mean? Smith's Brewhouse is a respectable business," I argue with Sirona Gustofson, the home study case worker who's come to perform an initial home visit.

"It's a bar, Ms. Smith," she repeats her earlier misconception—something Jed and I worked for years to overcome. "What kind of place is that to raise a child?"

Keep calm. I can practically hear my brother's voice warning me. Picking up a glass of water, I take a drink before responding. "First, I own the Brewhouse, Mrs. Gustofson. I don't live there."

"Though, by your own admission, it is possible you may have to cover shifts," she volleys.

"Of course," I say, exasperated. "But doesn't that demonstrate my willingness to support my employees?"

"Well, yes, but..."

"But what?"

She doesn't say anything but continues to scribble in her interminable notebook that I want to snatch out of her hands and toss into the fire I made up before she arrived. Despite the pleasant weather outside, I felt a chill deep inside. Now, I know why.

"I'd also like to address your point about the Brewhouse being 'just a bar.'" My pride in my job crashes up against her insult, leaving my voice somewhere just short of arctic.

That stops her pen moving. Placing the notebook aside, she reaches for a folder. Without a word, she hands it to me.

I flip it open to find printouts for some of the more interesting media coverage we've received for some of the drunk and disorderliness over the last ten years. Even while I flip through them, my heart stops when I come across a picture of me and Jed I didn't know existed beneath an editorial that reads, "Brother/Sister improving Smith's? To be determined."

My fingers trace over my brother's beloved face. "What would you do, Jedidiah?" I ask aloud.

"Excuse me?" Mrs. Gustofson asks.

Without answering her, I place the folder on the coffee table and stand. I move to the built-ins that are on either side of the fireplace and pull down three thick albums. "Here. Take a few moments to look through these." I hand her three photo albums.

She makes an *umphh* sound under the weight. "What's this?"

"The part of the story you apparently don't want to hear." Moving back over to my chair, I pick up my water as the news articles about how Smith's closed for six months for renovations is told, the interviews Jed and I gave to tout Smith's as a family-friendly restaurant first. I can still remember him booming into the camera, "We want Smith's to grow along with all of the generations of Juneau families. We want to see families, celebrate them, and then watch the next generation come in. That's what Smith's was founded on."

The article Mrs. Gustofson showed me which questioned whether or not Jed and I would make a success of the business was as much to do with Jed's decision to move permanently to Florida. For all we'd worked to sell the idea of being the next generation of Smith's, Jed's decision to move almost derailed the business permanently. But that was something I kept from him. After all, he found something a hell of a lot more precious than the Brewhouse.

He found love.

There were so many things I never got the chance to tell him, I think listlessly. And now, all I can do is write them down as I find scraps of him around this house as I prepare for what I'm certain is his soul trying to come back to me.

"Who would be home with your child while you're dealing with business needs? You'll be out all hours while a young boy entrusted to your care is home." Mrs. Gustofson's words drag me from my thoughts as she once again puts her pen to paper

I frown. "I'll engage someone to be with them, of course." Like I'd leave a stranger with David.

"I need to know who those individuals are, Ms. Smith. It's important I formally inquire about those individuals."

"And what if I was a single woman who was a doctor or a nurse? Would you be quite so interested in their future caregivers?" I can't help the bitterness that seeps into my voice as the blasted woman hasn't said a single word about the part of my soul I bared that's sitting on her lap.

"Excuse me?" Mrs. Gustofson's head snaps up, my question catching her off guard.

Sliding to the edge of my seat, I brace my hands on my knees. "I believe you heard me."

Nothing is said between us, but neither is her pen moving. I continue. "Life will always have emergencies, Mrs. Gustofson. The only thing we can do is prepare for them. And even then, sometimes that just isn't enough. If what you're asking me is would I allow anything at the Brewhouse to supersede my child, the answer is an unequivocal no. It didn't when my parents raised us. But whether I was a doctor, a nurse, a fireman, or a police officer, I have close friends who are the equivalent of my family. I'd lay my life down for their children, and I'm certain they would do the same for mine. Calling them because of an emergency—whether that means sending them to handle it or they stay with my child—is the least of what they would do."

"It's good to know you have friends like that."

"It's good that the child I want to adopt will be raised by a family that includes people who will love him so unselfishly," I counter. "A child needs a permanent, loving home, and this state declares it will permit a single parent, unmarried, to adopt a child. For you to try to block this adoption because you hold some sort of grudge against my profession is—in my opinion—frankly discriminatory. I own a successful business. I delegate responsibilities. And I'm ready to do more of that if necessary. In truth, I'm better off in many ways than a doctor, nurse, or anyone else you're mentally comparing me against because they answer to someone else; I answer to no one but myself and my own conscience."

I sit back, lace my fingers over my stomach, and wait for her response.

Her expression gives nothing away as she makes a few notes in her file. Long minutes pass where the scratching of the pen against the paper drives me out of my mind.

When Mrs. Gustofson finally asks me the next question, I want to slump in my chair in relief. "Your friends? They would be willing to provide affidavits validating their willingness to support you."

Having already anticipated this, I reach down and pull out sealed envelopes from Isler. "Brad and Rainey Meyers. Plus Sarah and Hung Li, the existing foster parents. Brad and Rainey said you are welcome to contact them if you need to visit their home as well."

Nonplussed, it takes Mrs. Gustofson a moment to accept the envelopes. "You've done your research," she comments as the barest hint of a smile crosses her face.

"Yes, I have."

She makes notes in her file before slipping the sealed envelopes inside. She then tears off a receipt and hands it to me. After scanning it, I see it's a formal acknowledgment of the receipt of the letters. Placing it on my box of papers next to me, I sit back and cross my legs.

"A friend who went through the process?" she persists.

I tip my head. "From high school. And another friend of my brothers who was fostered in his teens."

She frowns before flipping back to the front of her file. "I can see where that would make an impact."

Unfolding myself, I lean forward until my eyes hold hers. "I think you have a better understanding of why I appreciate what it's like to be raised by someone who loves you. That no matter what, I will be someone who will love my child exactly for who they are."

I heard similar words from Jed a lot. Especially after the night Nick won the title belt.

Damnit, my brother would have made a great father.

SEVERAL HOURS LATER, Mrs. Gustofson indicates she'd like to come by Smith's one night to get an honest feel for the place. "I deeply apologize that my misconceptions put a tarnish on our initial meeting." Standing in the foyer of my home, she admits, "You have a lovely home, Ms. Smith."

"Thank you. Up until recently, I wished I didn't."

Her head tips to the side. "Why?"

"Because to inherit it, I lost the last member of my family. There is no amount of money worth losing love." I wave a hand dismissively around. "If I could have one more night to speak with my brother, there isn't anything I wouldn't give up, including this home."

"Even the chance at your future with a child?" she probes quietly.

My jaw falls open, but no words come out. Then the realization strikes me in the chest, and I whisper, "No." Tears prick my eyes. "Not even for Jed could I give up this chance at love. He wouldn't want me to."

Shocking me after the hours of interrogation, Mrs. Gustofson's mask of professionalism drops. She reaches out and clasps my hand. "You're a fiery and strong young woman, Maris."

"Young is the one thing I'm really not."

"Try it from my vantage point," she retorts.

My lips curve. "Then thank you."

"I was just going to add, I've experienced loss." And for just a moment, I see the seasoned pain on her face.

"The pain doesn't go away, does it?" I ask tentatively.

She shakes her head. "But life has to go on. Sometimes the days go by and you'll forget. At first, it will be just a moment. Then hours. This—what you're doing—will be good for you. A child, they can bring you such joy." Then her face turns to a blank mask once again. "But anyway, you'll be hearing from me soon." She reaches for the door handle.

"Mrs. Gustofson?" Her head turns back. "Thank you."

"For what?"

"For doing what you do. Otherwise, people like me would never have had a chance all those years ago."

With a brisk nod, she opens the door and sails out. I lean against the jamb until she pulls out of the driveway. Finally, I close the door and head back upstairs to right my living room. Next to my water is the pile of newspaper clippings I was handed about Smith's. "Shit. I'll have to call Mrs. Gustofson to let her know I have them." Rubbing my head wearily, I know I should do it right now, but I just can't.

Besides, I have something important to do first.

Pulling out my phone, I find the article with the image of Jed and me. Quickly using the scan feature, I contact the editor of the local paper and ask him if he can make me a copy of the picture. Then, I call Kara.

She answers on the first ring. "How did it go?"

"Well, I only partially lost my temper when she called Smith's a bar. But I started to cry when I admitted I wanted this more than I wanted to see Jed again. And in between, I answered pretty much every question under the sun that didn't involve a rectal probe."

"So, what you're saying is you need a hug?"

"God, I need one so bad."

She puts her hand over her mouthpiece. "Jennings says I can be there in the morning. Just give him the word and he'll fuel the plane."

"I'm not having you get on a plane."

"Then tell me what you need," she pleads.

"Talk to me. Just talk to me."

"That I'll do anytime, anywhere." With that, Kara begins to tell me

54

all about her day. And for a little while, I'm transported back in time to where we used to do just this. Just talk and be us. Long before each of us met the men we'd fall in love with. Long before Jed and Dean would meet.

And well before they died.

MARIS

"Maris is the most loyal human in the world. She would be utterly devastated if she ever knew I was aware of Kara and her son Kevin before I took that trip to Florida where I fell in love with Dean. But if she ever found out, I knew she would forgive me. She would just never forgive herself." - From the journals of Jedidiah Smith.

"I'm sorry. Would you care to repeat what you said?" I try to get the words out with a straight face.

Rainey growls, "You heard me."

And we all laugh.

I figured a FaceTime with my three best friends would be a great way to relieve my anxiety after my visit with Mrs. Gustafson. Instead, I'm debating pouring more than a respectable amount of whiskey into my cup of tea over the unsurprising yet amusing announcement Rainey just declared about working part-time for Brad. "Anyone else have any updates?" I take a sip of tea.

"Like what?" Kara chides. Her hand rests on her stomach, protectively covering Jennings's and her second child. So many emotions swirl inside me every time her incandescent glow appears on my screen. I want to twirl in a circle with my arms in the air before I lock myself into a room and shed a few tears out of selfish pain. Yet I can't help but think, *Look at what you did, Jed. Even from beyond the grave you managed to get two of the people you loved most in the world back together where they belonged.*

Love. People recognize barriers like air, land, and sea as mere excuses when the reality is the only thing that holds them back from experiencing the purity of the heart is fear. Did I use the so-called heartache over Nick to hide my real fears about love and family after the abrupt loss of my dreams? After all, it was easy to then layer the pain of one loss with another. My own heartache has caused too many vicious words to lie between us now. Hasn't it? But now's not the time to think about Nick. Tonight's a night to celebrate.

I force a wonky smile onto my face. "God, I can't believe you got knocked up again and can't drink with us."

Meadow and Rainey are wearing shit-eating expressions as well. The two sisters tied themselves to two of the men Kara and I affectionately dubbed "the Jacks"—a poker vernacular that means to raise the pot. Kara and I used it as a warning the men we were so enamored by were about to encroach on our conversations.

Meadow declares, "I'm glad Kody is happy with the two we have. I can't imagine pushing out another baby."

"Not to mention your hoo-ha being out of commission for Tinker-toy," I drawl, sending all of us into hysterics with my use of Kody's nickname based on his being the owner of a construction company that makes custom homes.

"I'm not saying a word," Meadow demurs, but there's a glint to her eyes that has Rainey asking, "Been on any picnics lately?" before a bright red heat floods across Meadow's cheeks and we all begin to giggle.

Putting her fingers to her mouth and whistling, Meadow redirects us back to Kara. "Have you thought of names? Will you name the baby after Jennings if it's a boy?"

"Half the time, I forget Jennings isn't his first name," Rainey confesses.

Kara twiddles with the hem of her shirt. "I never do."

"It's just something ordinary," Rainey recalls.

"True. But even the ordinary can be complicated and may be distorted when viewed through the eyes of a child." Kara smiles gently, reminding us all of the decisions she made about Jennings's and her first son, Kevin. "If he wanted, needed, to leave his first name 'John' in the past to become the man I love, the man who will be by my side until the sky falls, who am I to question that?"

Jed's voice whispers in my ear. *Do you forgive me yet, Maris? You read what I wrote. If I thought they were in any danger, you know I would have...*

Suddenly Rainey bursts out with, "Maris, did your parents ever debate naming you and Jed something else? Your names are so unique."

Kara snickers. "After the grandparents on her mother's side."

"Really? What are they?" Rainey asks.

"They're perfectly lovely names." I say solemnly.

"What were they?"

"John and Jane."

One second, two, then Meadow yells, "You mean if your parents didn't choose differently you, your brother and you would have been the real life Mr. and Mrs. Smith?"

By this point, I'm can't control my laughter. Kara's in as bad a condition as I am. I can only manage a nod. "When that movie came out, Jed and I both bought copies for our parents for Christmas without the other knowing. Then, years later, we had a special movie poster made with us reenacting the cover art—"

"Which I have because I begged for it, so Dean stole it for me when he and Jed went back for a visit," Kara butts in.

"—that I can't get back no matter what I do," I conclude.

"Tell you what. If you somehow make it here for this child's birth, I will give it back to you," Kara offers benevolently.

"Done," I agree without hesitation.

Meadow is wiping tears of laughter from her eyes. "Kara, is it put away?"

"Oh, hell no. I have it hanging in my home office. Want to see it?"

"No!" I shriek as Rainey and Meadow's simultaneous "Yeses" overrule.

Kara slides from her chair, and we hear Jennings ask where she's going. "To the office. I need to show the girls where I hung the Smiths."

Jennings cracks up.

I begin to yell, "I'm coming for it, buddy! Don't let her fool you! Make sure you know I'm going to be in that delivery room right there with you!"

"Wait, what? Kara, come back here." Jennings is still protesting as Kara moves through dimly lit hallways.

Meadow smirks. "Nice house."

"Don't you like it? The builder price gauged us on the crown molding. I told Jennings I want it put up as a push present." Even as she flicks on the lights to her study, Kara winks to let Meadow know she's joking. "Anyway, when I need a moment of peace and quiet to study when Jennings and Kevin are blowing things up, this is where I am. Meadow, thank Kody for me. It's perfect."

Even though I've seen the room before, the warm oak bookcases that make up an entire wall are so quintessentially Kara. "He did a fabulous job. Okay. Tour's over."

Maniacal laughter escapes Kara. "Are you seriously kidding me? Let me tell you, the opposite wall used to be blank."

"Oh, God," I moan.

Everyone laughs. I simply brace myself. Then Kara touches her screen to adjust her camera so we can see the display. And my heart? It flips along with the view.

On the wall is a collage of pictures meticulously hung—including the dreaded Mr. and Ms. Smith mockup Jed and I did for our parents. But what else is there is a life history of Kara, Jennings, Kevin, Dean, and—I try to swallow so I can say something—me and Jed.

Photos of all sizes, shapes, and ages. From the time Kara and Dean were young to the wedding ceremony of our brothers in the Caribbean. From Kevin's birth, to vacations. The early years of Jennings and Kara to photos taken when we flew to see Meadow. Pictures of Dean and Jed, of Jed alone, a lifetime of pictures.

No, a lifetime of love.

And there's an entire section of the two of us—God, where did she accumulate so many? My eyes burn as Kara holds up her iPad to show us drunken selfies, photos of us from her wedding, pictures of just me when we were thousands of miles apart and time was passing us by when we were desperate to be together and knowing we couldn't.

How do I admit to her I screwed up? That all these years that wall could have been filled with so much more? Tears fall down my cheeks, and choked laughter bubbles out when my best friend steps back so Rainey and Meadow can get the full effect. "Here it is, ladies. Mr. and Ms. Smith," Kara announces grandly.

But Kara knew her announcement wouldn't be met with more laughter. "It's beautiful," Meadow whispers.

"I've never seen anything more...Brad! I have a project for you." That's when the tension around my heart starts to lift.

Kara flips the camera around, and I say the first thing that comes to mind. "I love you. I always will."

"The same is true for me. Now, if you think you're getting that poster out of my hands, we'll just see about that." Her voice is smug with good reason.

Maybe I won't take the original. Maybe I'll just ask for a copy if I make it to Florida.

And if she's still talking to me after I explain the truth.

LATER, as I prepare for bed, I pick up one of the leather-bound books that's caused me such heartache in the last year. The one thing tarnishing my precious memories of my brother.

His journals. Journals that I found hidden beneath a monstrous number of boxes of mementos and memorabilia in his closet that I chose to start cleaning last summer.

I sit down on the edge of the bed, and a sigh rips out of me. "What compelled you to write down what you knew, Jed?"

Because you're not the only one who's ever felt the way you do right now.

"And for the record I wish you'd get out of my head." I slam the book back down on the nightstand. Flopping backward, I press the heels of my hands to my eyes. There are things in there I should never have known. Things that make me ashamed of who I've become in order to protect the wounds I've sustained as a woman, physically and mentally.

And they were secrets that belonged to other people.

I stare blankly ahead at the ceiling as I talk aloud. "Brad wanted to leave Alaska for a little while, but he got Rainey pregnant which is why they got married so early. Then they lost the baby. Kody was in love with Meadow the entire time, but while Jed wanted him to man up, he suspected his advice drove him not to pursue her. Jennings had a childhood that drove him to make something of himself first to prove his self-worth, which is why my brother didn't tell him. And Nick? God, Nick." The heels of my hands press against my eyes.

"I owe you an apology, Nick. I have no right to hold on to old grudges, do I? You needed a friend more than anything. But like every other insipid female you likely came into contact with, I wanted something else. Yet, I *knew* you, Nick. We talked for hours. You told me the reason you stopped in Ketchikan, you jerk. You stopped at that damn grocery store and at the Lumberjack arena to say thank you to my brother for rescuing you because you believed he saved your life. And despite my being a bitch, you ran after me when they finished reading his will." I swallow hard. "And here I am still being as nasty as I can. Why? Because you wrote me a sweet letter and asked me to come to see you on the most special night of your life? The night you won the belt? You made me no promises, and it's time for me to own that. And it's time for me to get over the absolutely nothing you did. So, no more." Then thinking about his supreme ego, I amend my vow. "At least, I'll try."

I lie there for a while thinking of the other things I read in the journals I found buried in the back of Jed's suite. I began to clean it out thinking it was time, and as I found pieces of the Jacks, I sent it to them. Without thinking, I reach over to the nightstand and pluck the latest journal I'm reading from. I left a bookmark in the spot where I finished last night. Ruthlessly, I pull it open.

"I'm worried about Maris. There's a storm in her eyes that I'm terrified is uncontrollable. It's almost as bad as the ones I saw in Nick's when he and I were still living in Ketchikan.

If there was ever anything that's convinced me the two of them were not meant to be right now, it's this. They'd self-destruct. And instead of worrying about Maris's broken heart, or Nick's recklessness, I'd be worried about losing them both.

I know what it is, of course. It's the anniversary of the accident. You don't go through something that life-altering and not expect it to..."

I slam the book closed as I recall the details of that night.

I was twenty-three, closing a Saturday night at the Brewhouse with my father. I was young, outgoing, and carefree as I raked in money hand over fist waitressing. Men were often the best tippers when they were slightly inebriated because they would flirt under the watchful eyes of my brother and father. I remember Brad and Rainey being there, raising a few shots and laughing. I stopped by and gave them a quick hug as I wove myself in between patrons carrying a tray of drinks.

But there was one man who caught my eye. It was the first time since Nick had left, and I was hurt deep inside since he'd broken his promise to keep in touch. The attention I was getting was flattering as all hell.

Jed grabbed my arm as I passed by, warning me, "Be careful, Sunshine."

"Knock it off, Jed. I don't tell you what to do. Besides, he's not one of your precious friends, is he?" Jed was shocked, but finally, he let me go.

Over and over, no matter where I was in the crowded bar, my eyes kept drifting back to the stranger. Finally, I worked up my courage and made my way over. "Carter Jones," he introduced himself before taking a pull of his longneck.

"Maris. But I guess you knew that from the name tag." I fluttered my eyelashes at him, and his throaty laugh sent shivers down my spine.

"Maris!" my father bellowed over the din. "Drinks up!"

"Right. See you around, Carter." I spun on my heel, but before I could move an inch, Carter's lips were at my ear.

"I hope so."

Since it was a Saturday night and early, I honestly don't remember how many drinks Carter was served that night. And I had to answer that question and many others later on the stand after he stood trial for drunk driving and leaving the scene of an accident. After all, he didn't stick around when he hit my car while showboating on a long stretch of road, causing me to roll over and over, leaving me trapped, and sped off without calling the police.

I found out later it was an hour before someone found me and another to cut me out. I was—fortunately—unconscious most of the time. After being airlifted to Fairbanks, I was triaged and then sent into surgery.

It wasn't until Jed and my parents were by my bedside the next day that I came around enough to find out the accident caused me to hemorrhage blood from an unknown ovarian cyst that had ruptured.

"Did you have cramps during your cycle?"

Embarrassed to be talking about this in front of my dad and Jed, I nodded. "Just on one side."

"Often?" the doctor probed.

Mom squeezed my hand, and I whispered, "Yes."

"When was your next cycle due?"

"What do you mean, was?" Mom asked quietly. Dad slipped an arm around her.

"What happened to Ms. Smith is called an ovarian teratoma tear. There were complications." The surgeon patted my hand as he explained. Patted my hand. After all, it wasn't his life that had changed in that cramped white room.

It was mine.

"What do you mean complications?" My voice shook.

"It's often referred to as 'unicornuate uterus,' where only half of the uterus forms, with one ovary and one fallopian tube," the doctor informed us all.

Mom started to cry. Dad and Jed began yelling simultaneously.

As for me, I couldn't process the news. I began to shake as pain—both physical and mental—swept over me. I began to repeatedly click the button for the pain meds as the rest of the surgeon's words flowed over me. My singular ovary. Apparently I'd only been born with one, something I had no idea about until they had to remove it.

"Why the hell would they name it something like that? Who the fuck was trying to be funny?" I snapped. The room became still at my outburst. "Because I'm sure as hell not a unicorn anymore. I just lost my fucking horn." That's when I began to cry.

My mother and Jed wrapped their arms around me as my father shooed the doctor from the room. All I remember from the following days are two things.

Jed being by my side and asking for more drugs to haze the pain. And I remember talking with Kara when Kevin was born. I just don't recall Jed being in the room as I tried to drown out the pain of surgery and the pain in my heart as I repeatedly clicked the button to inject myself with pain meds.

But he must have been.

And somehow I have to find a way to tell my best friend her life could have been so different if Jed had made different choices because I have no idea why he made the ones he did. None.

NICHOLAS

The docking of the ferry leaves me with a multitude of feelings, most of them tinged with regrets.

I've made my pilgrimage to Jed in Ketchikan by stopping by the grocery store. I can't come back to Alaska and not go back to the place where he saved my life by demanding in a very clear voice to his uncle, *"We have to do something. It's just wrong if we don't."*

As the cool air washes over my face off the harbor, I remember Jed's words to the police officers. *"There's no question. This guy was here two days ago. In the same outfit."* "God, Jed. Did I ever tell you thank you? Foster homes may not have been the best, but they sure as hell were better than the shit I lived with at home. And later when we met up again at the show, you never said a word. It took until that final summer that I didn't feel like a wounded animal, afraid to believe the nonsense you had been spouting at me summer after summer; that you were really my brother even if there wasn't an ounce of blood that ran between us. And now I'll never have the chance because you're gone."

Time. No matter what financial success I've managed to accumulate with my career, the distance I've managed to place between Nick Cain and the boy abandoned years ago, I can't buy back time. And I'd give everything I own to have more of it with the people I love, to make restitutions to the people who deserve them. In the last few years since Jed's death, I've had too much time for retrospection, and my thoughts are as turbulent as the water crashing up against the hull of the boat.

So many memories were made those long-ago summers. Humor makes my lips twitch as I swing my duffle up on my shoulder before it dies just as quickly. It's easy to pull up the flashes of days when we'd all take this exact same ferry from Ketchikan to Juneau to visit the Smiths. The four of us would be in varying degrees of anxiousness—or not—to get off the boat. Every step I take brings a new memory that's seared in my soul.

I hate this place as much as I love the people it brought to me, which leaves me conflicted each step I take down the ramp and onto the dock. Would life have eventually brought Brad, Jennings, Kody, or Jed into my orbit if I hadn't been dealt such a crushing blow as a teenager? On the other hand, that agony fueled me in a way nothing else ever could. Alaska gave me the ability to create my own freedom, which I've enjoyed lavishly.

Moving inside the waiting room, I glance around, trying to spy Brad among the many people lingering around. Still distracted, I think about the difference of what getting off that ferry would have meant twenty years ago. Despite the anger I'm positive I couldn't quite hide, there was a young man terrified of being left behind again. And that fear would only intensify the moment we'd hit Juneau where there was this woman who somehow saw through the bluster. Leaning my shoulder against the wall, I contemplate why finally coming to the conclusion that the secrets I tried to keep—so poorly hidden, they may as well have been spoken aloud—were in danger of coming to light here. Closing my eyes briefly, I can hear the roughness of Jed and Maris's father's voice as his hand clasped the back of my neck when he dragged me away from the others.

"Figure out your shit, Nick. Once you do, come back and look at my daughter with eyes that actually see her. Then maybe I'll let you get near her with that expression on your face." Jed's ghost isn't the only one who haunts me.

Albert Smith was a man who took no crap from anyone. He built Smith's Brewhouse from a simple watering hole for fishermen to a year-round moneymaker which his children carried on. Years later, when the man himself called to congratulate me on winning the belt, I reached out to Jed, who was holed up with Maris—somewhere. "I just took out Troy Martinez for the belt. So, tell me why I'm shaking because your father just called?"

Jed just laughed as he hung up in my ear.

Smiling to myself now, I know Albert Smith wasn't just a good man; he was a great one. Despite my initial wariness around him, he taught me a lot about managing a business that I put into practice today—the importance of always keeping your fingers in the pie, of understanding important decisions, and above all, "The hardest part about owning a business is trusting people. Me and Vi can't tell you how many times we've been burned."

An incandescent fury rose inside my twenty-year-old self. "Then why continue to do it, Mr. Smith? Why not hire a manager?"

He turned eyes—Maris's eyes—on me and frowned, not in anger but thoughtfully. "No matter what happens, there are things that are going to hurt in life, Nick. But cutting yourself off from people, that just leaves your soul empty."

My brows drew together, not really understanding the bad side. He chuckled. "One day you'll understand, Nick. Now, why don't you go over and talk to those kids your age." Then he shook his meaty finger at me. "But..."

I held up both hands. "I know. I know. No flirting with Maris."

"You, I trust to listen. It's my damn daughter who's as wild as the wind and is growing up to be more beautiful than I can handle." His tone was so aggrieved, I actually grinned.

When first Violet, then Albert, passed away, both Jed and Maris were torn apart at their loss. It was one of the few times I willingly came back to Alaska without having to be browbeat by my friends. Then again, how could I not? In a world where I was too used to people of authority who publicly outcried they wanted to help the abandoned child while behind their hands they whispered in undertones about my lack of control. What they didn't understand was I was choking on my own voice. The Smiths did more than that. They became my surrogate parents years too late.

And then there was Maris. During those summers she somehow forced me to talk, she dug out my dreams. Then she did something worse—she listened.

I never told Maris about falling for her while she wore a polka-dot bikini and cutoffs as Jed held her and Kara in a headlock. Instead, I made some asinine comment and hit the closest convenience store for more liquor. Back then, being a brooding jackass around Maris was the only way I could prevent myself from doing something that would have destroyed us both and broken my promise to her father. Because it wasn't her I couldn't see with different eyes; it was myself.

And judging by the disappointment in Jed's eyes every time I ignored his sister, he knew it.

Swearing I'd never return, I packed my bags and caught a ferry to Seattle. From there, it was easy to do the research I needed to get into the Extreme MMA Championship, the world-renowned mixed martial arts organization. Their training and recruiting center—located outside Las Vegas, Nevada—was as different from my life in Alaska as my childhood was from Jed and Maris's slice of perfection.

In other words, it was perfect.

I don't have time to recall the memories of my early days in Vegas because a strong hand clamps down on my shoulder. I whirl around, dropping instinctively into a fighting stance, before my whole body relaxes. Then I surge up and clap Brad in a one-arm hug. "Used to be once a year was enough to see your ugly mug," I joke.

"I was thinking the same thing. Welcome home, brother. It's good to have you back."

My insides twitch at the words. This place will never be my home.

Brad just continues. "How was the ferry? Weather's getting choppy." He nods toward the boat I just left.

"Not too bad. Not like that trip I took from Cozumel to Playa del Carmen." I shudder in remembrance.

"If I recall, you called me drunk off your ass about two hours after you got off the boat,"

"I figured I booted enough in the boat ride I deserved to have the hangover to accompany it." We both laugh as we make our way out of the terminal.

"How's life down in New Mexico? Are you still dating Roxy? I think she's the last woman I remember you talking about."

I cringe. That's the woman I was involved with before Jed died. "No."

"Maybe it was Misty?"

"That was like five, six years ago."

Brad shakes his head. "Then you're just hanging loose?"

Instead of explaining to him I haven't been with anyone since I found out Jed died when the explanation about that belongs to exactly two people, I make a vague sound of acknowledgment.

Brad grins. "Rainey's going to be disappointed. She has an online bingo board with the others on the name of your next hookup. She's one spot away. She was hoping for a 'Trixie.'"

I choke. "Are you serious or just fucking with me?"

"I'm just telling you what I know. I'm not sure if there's bragging rights involved or actual cash."

"For fuck's sake." Scrubbing a hand over my face, I swallow down my laughter over the absurdity of this before pain lances through me when I realize Maris is likely involved with this shit. For the sake of that alone, I don't mention I banged a "dancer" who went by Topless Trixie when I first got to Vegas in an attempt to forget a woman with mahogany hair and deep blue eyes. I'll go to the grave with that before I let Rainey win.

Because then we all lose.

"Have to admit I'm amazed you're here," Brad says after we're on the road to his place.

Sights and memories flash by as he accelerates past downtown Juneau. "Got a line on a new fighter. I'm here to put them through their paces."

"From Juneau?" Brad's shock is understandable. Never before have I personally scouted someone from Alaska, though members of my team have.

"Yep. If you can believe it, he's a former Lumberjack." I mentally count to three because I know my friends and...

Brad throws back his head and roars. "Tell me this is a joke. You're really up here to give a statement for the fostering, right?"

I let out a long-suffering sigh. "Why would I make up something so...wait, what? Are you and Rainey adding to your family?" It wouldn't surprise me. Last spring, they had a full house hosting Rainey's sister's children until the lot of them moved down to Montana. And despite the internal family struggles that it caused for a short time, I know if Rainey wanted to add to their family, Brad would be on board.

Brad flushes. "Crap. You mean there really is a fighter here?"

Even as a small knot begins to form in my stomach, I answer. "Brad, have you ever known me willingly to travel to Alaska?"

"Well, shit. Me and my big mouth."

"No argument from me."

An awkward silence descends between us as we reach Brad's SUV. "Now, what's this about fostering? Did Rainey finally decide you were too much trouble and decide to put you up at a local shelter?" I drawl.

"Cute, Nick. Really. How about I let her explain the whole thing when we reach the house—that is, after the kids climb you like a tree."

As we pass the cemetery where Jed's buried, I reach up and clasp the gold cross I'm never without. I remember contacting Kody last year on Jed's birthday drunk off my ass because a fighter taunted me after the clasp broke. "Loosened a few of the fucker's teeth. Hope you got to see that," I murmur, remembering the retaliatory beat down when he swung the chain in front of me before pocketing it.

"Did you say something?" Brad asks.

"Just catching Jed up."

"We'll go by and see him. Maybe tomorrow."

"Not going out with your crew in the morning?" Brad owns several fishing boats. He'd prefer to be out with one doing day trips bringing the fresh catch to local Juneau residents and restaurants.

He snorts. "I'd love to. I have to spend the day in the office catching up on paperwork. Rainey said she's going to divorce me if I don't. Makes me miss Meadow more than ever." Meadow, Rainey's older sister, used to manage Brad's office for a while before moving to Bigfork, Montana, as a result of her divorce.

"Who do you have doing the work?" I ask as we pull up into the Meyerses' driveway.

He shakes his head before we both exit the vehicle. I grab my duffle from where I stowed it in the back seat. "Rainey handles most of the day-to-day stuff like payroll. It's the stuff like license renewal, taxes, that kind of crap that Meadow used to rock at and I hate doing."

A very irritated voice adds on, "If you would just hire someone, then all your worries would go away." Rainey comes up on my blind side and wraps her arms around me. "Hi, Nick. Welcome to the Fun House."

"Hey, babe." I press a kiss to the top of Rainey's dark hair and wrap an arm around her shoulder as Brad circles the back of the car. "Being abused by the boss?"

She tips her head back and rolls her eyes. "Listen, I'm about twelve seconds away from begging my sister to give up her job to work for Brad remotely."

We all laugh as we move toward the house. After we mount the steps, Rainey asks Brad, "Did you warn him about the inmates?"

"Yep. Nick knows that his tree duties commence the moment you open that door."

"Good. Are you here to provide a statement for Maris to foster that little boy?"

Suddenly, every single muscle in my body freezes. My hand is on the handle of the storm door. Just beyond it, I can see Josh and Sophie —Brad and Rainey's six- and eight-year-old children—beginning their charge for the door. "What do you mean? Maris is fostering children?" I hold the door firmly closed while I turn to face my friends.

Rainey blows her breath out so hard, it musses her hair. "Oh, boy. You didn't know?"

I shake my head, too stunned to speak.

"He's here to see a fighter," Brad offers.

"Must be one hell of a fighter," she offers before scurrying around me and wrenching the storm door out of my hands. She must have some mother superpower, because I'm certain I had all of my weight on it, and there's no way Rainey Meyers can take me down.

Except with the words she just dropped in the air.

"Come on. Let the kids climb on you, and then I'll get you a drink." Brad grabs my bag.

"Yeah. That's a good plan." And then I want—no, need—to see Maris. I'm not certain my mind will rest until I do.

NICHOLAS

I try not to slam the gin and tonic Brad poured me down on the coffee table. "You mean to tell me she's been taunting you all about having a baby for over a year. That turns out to be Maris just getting a rise out of you because the whole time she's been going through classes to be eligible to foster a child? And Kara and Jennings knew? Why is this the first I'm hearing about this?" I'm incredulous that something so impactful to someone so...important to me hasn't been shared before now.

Brad's about to respond, but Rainey beats him to it. "Why would it matter to you, Nick? Where in the grand scheme of your life does Maris fall? Is she somewhere between sister-from-another-mister or a lost opportunity?" Rainey punctuates her words with a sip of wine.

Rainey's words stun me. "How about friend, or am I not allowed to have those?"

"Touché, but you're not going to talk her out of this."

"Who said I want to?" What I want to do is to hug her and tell her exactly what I'm certain her brother would. *I'm so damn proud of you for going after your dreams.* Because it wasn't just my dreams we talked about all those long-ago summers. I've known for close to twenty years about Maris's deep-seated desire to become a mother. After all, I wasn't a total prick. I listened when she spoke about what she wanted from life: a family, a home, a man who loved her. I just wasn't the one who should give it to her. Despite how much a part of me wanted to.

And always will.

Now, I wonder if my words will mean anything to her based on Rainey's hostility. "When is all of this taking place?" I duck my head and cut into the chicken Brad grilled earlier.

"Right now," Rainey announces.

My head snaps back up. "Really?"

"That's why your timing was circumspect, Nick," Brad explains. "Rainey and I have already been contacted by her home inspection caseworker. Kara has as well."

"Well, gee. Have Kody and Meadow received a golden invitation to this little party as well?" My silverware clatters against my plate as I toss it aside, appetite gone.

"No, but Meadow knew Maris met and fell in love with this little boy..." Rainey's voice trails off. She lays her hand over one of my fists. I didn't even realize I'd clenched them. "Nick, I don't think she deliberately cut you out. But, out of curiosity, when was the last time you checked your personal email?"

"Jed used to know if it didn't get forwarded to my business account I never saw it." I dig into the pocket of my jeans for my cell. Once I unlock it and flip the phone around, Rainey winces when she sees the six-digit number on the bottom of the display. "Right. I bet if you search for an email from Maris, you'll find she officially told all of us at the same time. She isn't cruel like that."

"You're right."

Rainey pauses. "Nick, she probably thinks you didn't care when you didn't respond."

Of all the things I would care about in this world, it would be Maris. "I give a damn about all of you." The understatement of a century. I unclench my hand and turn it around, squeezing Rainey's fingers before letting them go. Standing, I push away from the table. "If you don't mind giving me a few moments?" I stride to the back door.

"Where are you going, Nick?" Brad calls out.

"I need to make a call." I just want to know where Maris is going to be tonight. So much has devastated her in the last few years. If there's some way I can smooth the way to make this easier for her, I will.

I'm already pressing Send on her cell phone number as the back door closes behind me. "Well, this is a banner day." Maris's voice comes through as clear as if she were sitting right next to me.

I don't beat around the bush. "I'm in Juneau. Where are you going to be tonight?"

She sputters. "Excuse me? I grew out of needing a chaperone a long time ago, Nick." She takes a deep breath as if she's about to say more. I brace myself for a mass of vitriol to be spewed, but nothing comes.

I jump in while I have the chance. "Maris, I'd like to see you if you're free."

Silence greets my declaration at first before her voice changes to concerned. "Is everything okay? If not, I can arrange for someone to take the shift I just agreed to cover."

"No. I mean, yes. Everything is fine. Like I said, I just wanted to see you."

An awkward tension descends between us. "Well, if that's the case, I'll be at the Brewhouse. I can't say I'll have a lot of time though."

Aside from our text months ago, it's the most patience Maris has shown me in years. Before I can tell Maris I'll wait until her shift is over to speak with her if I have to, the call disconnects in my ear after a quiet, "Goodbye, Nick."

I hang up, both disquieted with this side of Maris and disgusted with myself for not saying more. "Well, at least I know where I'll be going tonight."

That's when a voice causes my heart to jump out of my chest. "Do you know what a pain it is to get my parents to babysit at the last minute?" Rainey grumbles.

"Christ, Rainey. Did you follow me out here?"

"From the moment you got up from the table," she confirms.

I shoot her a filthy look. She merely shrugs. "No offense, Nick, but you constantly leave everyone guessing. I wasn't sure if you were coming out here to congratulate Maris or be a dick."

Affronted, I step back. "Is that so?"

"The one person who could translate you better than anyone is gone," she throws back before her attitude relents. Coming to stand by my side, she hooks an arm around my waist. "Sometimes without Jed, I feel like the rest of us are drowning. Don't you?"

My heart aches at her words. "Yes. But he isn't the only one who knows me."

Rainey's eyes close. "I figured as much. The problem is you let her go. And you've both changed, so maybe she doesn't know she's close enough to matter." While I take the blow from that verbal hit, Rainey slugs me with another. "She must have recognized you were never going to feel the same way about her she always has about you, so she decided to move on with her dreams. Good for her."

I stagger back. "What do you mean?"

"I mean it's finally time for a woman with a heart of gold to offer her heart to someone who can return that love. Who cares if he's a little boy?" Assuming that shot, like so many others she's fired off at me tonight, would bounce off me like I'm made of steel, Rainey heads back into the house.

Maris's heart? No. That's not possible. If I did, that would make me the stupidest man alive. After all, Jed would have told me...wouldn't he? But how many times did he taunt me and I didn't listen.

A cold sweat breaks out along my back. "Oh, God. I think I'm going to be sick." Bending over, I recall the way I flew after her the day of the funeral when Jed left me his cross. *To Nicholas Cain, I leave my gold cross and chain. There was never a day I didn't wear it. Faith was important to me. You need to believe something, my friend. It wasn't me who saved you. It's time for you to accept that as you look in the mirror. Maybe if you're wearing this, you will.*

How many times have I looked in the mirror since Jed left his cross to me have I thought of Maris?

Every. Single. One.

"Is this the truth you were trying to show me, you crazy bastard?" I yell. "How the hell was I supposed to know?" There's no answer, but somehow I know Jed's up there amused as shit at my mental overload. "Asshole's probably thinking that my perfectly ordered life needs to be messed up. It doesn't, you bastard. I had it all fucking arranged. Wake up, work out, eat, sleep. Once I saw her, I didn't even care about finding someone. Was that part of your grand plan?" Furious, I glare up at the clear blue sky.

The door creaks open behind me before Brad steps out. "We try to keep the cursing to a minimum, Nick. The kids are plastered to the bathroom window watching you. They're asking Rainey what certain words mean."

"I'm sure that's jacking her opinion of me even higher than it was." Planting my hands on my hips, I stand my ground. I demand, "Did you know?"

"Know what?"

"About Maris? About her—" I swallow hard before pushing the words out. "—having feelings for me?"

His face takes on a sorrowful cast. "Nick, man. I think the only one who didn't was you."

It feels like the night I took a kidney shot from Martinez right before I pulled a haymaker out of my ass to turn the title fight around that fateful night. I open and close my mouth before I finally turn away.

"Nick..."

"Have you ever noticed the most critical moments of life are made up of seconds?"

"What do you mean?"

"Actions and reactions. They happen in seconds. The repercussions are what take years to resolve." Without changing my posture, I tell Brad in a monotone, "I would like to see Maris tonight. She told me she's working."

"Yeah, I, uh, overheard Rainey bellowing for a babysitter. Come on, Nick—finish your chow. That is, unless you plan on eating at the Brewhouse. Food's great." Brad's voice holds a note of pride.

Frowning, I turn around. "Food? At the Brewhouse? The place just has a liquor license."

Brad holds open the door. "Brother, you are in for some major surprises tonight. Maybe this will teach you to finally check your email. Whodathunkit? Jed's going to force you to finally join us on the group email from the grave." He laughs as I re-enter the house.

Deciding I've had enough, I wait to reply until I'm reseated. Rainey has a concerned look on her face. I offer her a wan smile as I sit back down. "Or maybe I'll hire someone to check my email and just flag any messages I need to read. You know, kind of like you should be doing instead of tormenting your poor wife."

Rainey beams while Brad groans. "You should listen to Nick, honey."

"Words I never thought I would ever hear spoken at this table," Brad chuckles. "Fine. I'll put an ad in the paper after tax season. Happy?"

But no words are needed as Rainey has run around the table and thrown herself at Brad to give him a long kiss. Now, if only the things I've managed to fuck up were so easy to fix.

Later, I'll get a chance when I see Maris again. Hopefully.

I USED to say nothing good happened in my life during my years in Alaska other than my brotherhood, but I have to amend that to include Smith's Brewhouse. Clay Smith started the popular watering hole and passed it down to his son, Albert. Jed—a few years older than me—used to bubble over with excitement when he talked about becoming the third-generation Smith to work the Brewhouse with his sister.

All of that changed when he flew to Florida for a vacation and fell in love with Dean Malone, the irony of all ironies being that Dean was Kara Malone Jennings's older brother. Two brothers of two best friends falling in love with one another before they died together. Their love was both beautiful and tragic. For a long time after Jed and Dean died in a car accident, I figured it was life demonstrating once again that nothing good came for free—like the night I won the belt and lost Maris. Here was her way of simply slapping down a remarkable man who had managed to finally find his soul mate but lost his life.

As Brad navigates the roads back into Juneau, I think back to the things Jed told me about Dean that most appealed to him. "Let's be honest, Nick. Really it was lust at first sight. The man's a hunk."

I about fell out of my lounge chair in the beach house we rented in Malibu that year. "How utterly shallow of you, buddy."

"Takes one to know one." I grinned, taking no offense. But Jed went on. "But every day, he gives so much of himself to so many people. He lives with his sister and his nephew—who you'd love if you had a chance to meet them."

As I had just started building up the training facility and the kids workout center, I took Jed's comment at face value assuming he meant someday. I didn't understand the clues he was dropping. Then, "What else?"

"Dean doesn't hide who he is. He says what's on his mind. He's just out there, and you can take or leave him. He doesn't get offended by it." Jed became thoughtful. "I know it took Maris aback at first."

"What do you mean?" I immediately became protective.

"I mean my sister's too used to men saying one thing but meaning another when it comes to our species. She's too suspicious. She's too young to be this cynical about men. I hate that for her."

"There's no wrong age for her to be cynical about men," I countered.

Jed laughed at my joke, but I felt his disapproval. In the back of Brad's vehicle, I reach up and clutch Jed's cross. "Especially when I likely caused most of it?" I whisper, as we drive through the streets. I doubt I'm overheard sitting behind Rainey with the music on.

The neon sign declaring our arrival at Smith's has her turning the volume down and facing me. "Please don't make a big deal when we get inside," she pleads.

"I wouldn't do that." Except, I was contemplating it. The urge to wrap my arms around Maris and hug her is riding me hard.

"Nick, despite my dogging you all day, you're you."

"And that means?"

Rainey rolls her eyes at me as Brad parks the vehicle. "It means that most of Alaska claim you as their native son since you won the title belt, despite your disdain for our state. I suspect the moment the word goes out that you're in the bar, your reason for seeing Maris will be just a memory once your fans arrive."

"I'm not going to forget why I'm here," I say, affronted.

"It's not you I'm worried about," she retorts.

Brad chuckles.

I flick him off. Thank God Charmaine isn't here. I'd owe her my next paycheck for the amount of swearing I've done since I got here.

"Get it all out now," Rainey warns as she opens her door. "I give you thirty minutes tops to be Nick. Then you'd better be prepared to be *Nick Cain*." Hopping out, she heads inside the Brewhouse without waiting for me or Brad.

"Come on, it's not really going to get that bad. Is it?"

"No. But Rainey's not wrong either. We're going to be swamped with people trying to get to us. Hey! I have an idea." Brad begins frantically texting.

"What are you doing?" I lean forward and try to peer over his shoulder.

"Inviting the guys from the boat down for a drink. This way, they won't fawn over you like you're a rock star, and you'll be well insulated."

"That's genius. Tell them I'm buying." I encourage this idea. I'd rather answer fight questions all night from the guys who work from Brad than be groped by groupies. I've been done with that shit for a long while, despite the trash talk I've tossed at the guys over the years. To be honest, with my work at Razor, it's been way too damn long since I found a woman even remotely attractive. They don't have the same fall of dark hair or spark in their indigo eyes. And I'm damn tired pretending I don't care about what the people I care about think about me. I care too much; I just don't know how to regain the respect I lost with them.

Brad's fingers finish moving. "Done." Pings start coming in. "Looks like you have a half hour to keep your gloves up."

"Or avoid a rear naked choke," I agree.

"Yeah. I'm going to need a drink for you to explain that one." We both slide out and head inside.

The bouncer's eyes widen comically when Brad and I step up in front of him. "Man, huge fan. Major."

I shake his hand even as he stamps the back of my hand without checking my ID. "Appreciate it."

"Amaq, can you keep a sharp eye for my crew? They're going to be joining us by the pool table." Brad's eyes drop to the kid's and my still-joined hands.

"Sure thing, Brad." With another pump of my hand, he lets it go. "Nice to meet you in person, Mr. Cain."

I nod, smile, and turn. But then it's me who's starstruck.

Because there she is.

Long dark hair tumbling over a body any man would die for the right to touch that's wrapped in a tight black bodysuit. Nothing takes away from her magnificent face except the blank look she's aiming in my direction. Giving in to temptation, I step forward and wrap my arms around her. Tugging her against my chest, I inhale her scent— musky, wild, daring. It's simply Maris.

"Stop, Nick. Let me go." Maris squirms in my arms. Heat rushes into her cheeks

I bend my head and whisper in her ear, "Not quite yet."

"You're making a scene."

Not even close. "Would you believe me if I just wanted to tell you I'm proud as hell of what you're doing for that little boy?"

She jerks back, and her lips part. She wets the lower one, her tongue darting out to slick it down. God, this woman could tempt a saint, and no one ever claimed I was one of those. "No, Nick. Not for a second."

My lips curve in the first real smile since the last time I saw her. *Little Mari Sunshine, my ass, Jed.* I recall his nickname for his sister. Woman's as cantankerous and distrusting as ever. "Good." My arms tighten for just a heartbeat more before I let her go to follow Brad.

MARIS

"Rainey and Brad should have had more time to just be. They went through too many trials too early in their marriage. I have never shared their secret with anyone else, but I need to let the pain of their loss out somewhere. That's the kind of love I want—one that withstands that kind of agony and still pushes on." - From the journals of Jedidiah Smith.

"So, you're really doing it?" Rainey asks. Brad's playing pool on the far side of the room with Nick and what appears to be most of the members of his fishing crew. Instead of joining them, she hiked herself up onto a stool and has been nursing a glass of wine at the corner of the bar while I work filling the orders as bar back tonight.

"I am," I confirm, wiping down the counter in front of her before I place a duo of clean pilsner glasses there. Yanking out two more from the crate to my left, I begin drawing the beer from the center tap—a delicious porter from a microbrewery up in Skagway. Carefully, I switch the last glass out without switching off the tap, a trick I learned long ago to speed up the process of fulfilling orders. Moving the glasses two by two next to the ticket to be picked up by one of my harried waitstaff, I finish explaining to Rainey, "I'm more than this."

"Anyone who knows you would never question that," Rainey declares.

Resting my folded arms on the bar, I try to put the thoughts that have plagued me since Jed's death into words. "I'm a strong woman for the way I was raised. I used to imagine a future with someone who would not only be able to appreciate that but bring their own strength to our relationship. I dreamed we'd have a houseful of children who would understand it isn't physical power but an inner sense of self that drives that." Toying with the edge of the Rainey's cocktail napkin, I say flatly, "Life happened. Then Jed died. And I was finally slapped across the face with the fact there's nothing wrong with my life—if I want to live it alone."

"There isn't." But a flash of something crosses Rainey's face.

"Say it," I demand.

"If this is what you really want, Maris. Somehow, I always hoped..." Her eyes dart to the corner where Brad is racking up the balls again. Nick is chalking up his cue, but as if he can sense my eyes on him, his gaze locks with mine. I wrench mine away.

"I've had enough of putting my life on hold for hopes, wishes, and maybe somedays. I deserve to be happy right now," I state, firm in my decision.

"Then no matter what, Brad and I are behind you," Rainey vows.

Something inside me unknots at her words. I'm about to respond when the front door to the Brewhouse opens. Like someone's just rammed an I beam up my spine, I come to full attention. "I'm really glad you said that because I might need that help starting right about now." Untying the apron strings from behind my back, I slide out from behind the bar. Fortunately, we're still technically in the off-season, so the place isn't jammed as I approach the woman who holds a major key to my happiness in the palm of her hands. "Welcome to Smith's Brewhouse. I'll be happy to seat Mrs. Gustofson, Kristina." I pluck the menu away from the startled hostess and extend an arm gracefully without the older woman saying a word.

The already overwhelming burden of having Nick in my bar that had been crushing me dissipates as I maneuver to a booth that has a clear view of the entire Brewhouse. While I have nothing to be ashamed of, my stomach is pitching like the stormiest of seas. "Tonight's specials are an amazing halibut chowder that I tried earlier. It really isn't to be missed. Halibut is also our Catch of the Day. Tonight it's prepared with a soy, honey, lemon butter glaze. Served with Yukon potatoes, you'll find both prices clipped to the inside of your menu."

Mrs. Gustafson blinks up at me for a moment, disconcerted. "I rather expected to suffer through traditional bar fare this evening."

I can't help my lips curving. "While those items are on the menu, Mrs. Gustofson, I try not to serve them until after 11:00 p.m. I don't like families being impeded by people who come to Smith's to celebrate events."

"Such as?"

"Oh, last week we hosted a joint baby shower." It gives me an incredible sense of pride as the woman's jaw unhinges. "Maybe back in my father's day, this was a dockside bar, but it hasn't been that in a number of years. I believe—strongly—that families should have a warm, welcoming place to dine in. This is now a restaurant with a full-service bar. It's taken a long time to build one's reputation as strong as the other," I correct her quietly.

"I'm beginning to see that," Mrs. Gustofson murmurs as a family of four is sat across from her. She offers them a smile before asking, "If I have the soup, will I be too full for the special?"

I wink. "I have it on great authority the fish tastes fantastic on top of salad for lunch or dinner the next day."

"Then if you add a Diet Coke to the order, I think you've sold me on what I'm eating."

I write down Mrs. Gustofson's order and start to turn away before I pause. Making a decision, I offer, "If you'd like to join us, Rainey Meyers is here tonight. She and I are talking at the bar about everything while her husband and some of his friends play pool."

Instead of the revulsion I expect to cross her face, a twinge of something—maybe regret—does. "You have to work the bar all night?"

"Just a few more hours. The child of my regular bartender became ill. I told her to take the night off—that I would fill in."

"Then I would enjoy that after I enjoy my meal. Thank you." She bends over to fiddle in her purse, and I use it as a chance to escape.

I don't know what it is about that woman that causes my insides to clench up. Maybe it's just the idea she's the key roadblock between me and my dreams.

That must be it.

Whistling cheerfully, I snag a new apron and make my way around the bar to fill the small order of drinks that have piled up.

Rainey smiles. "What was all that about? The last time I saw you move that fast to greet a guest, you swore it was a crew member of the *Deadliest Catch*."

I throw back my head and laugh uproariously, unaware I've garnered the attention of more than one person at the Brewhouse by doing so.

"OH LORD, Rainey, stop telling such lies about me!" I screech. My head falls into my hands as Mrs. G.—as I've now taken to calling her—and one of my sisters have bonded. "I did not have half the boys at school chasing after me."

"I'm sorry, Mrs. G," Rainey begins to correct herself. "It wasn't just Juneau-Douglas High. It was also Thunder Mountain High."

I pick up a crouton from the basket Rainey asked to munch on and fling it at her head. She adroitly ducks and it whacks Mrs. G. right in the chest. "Now see what you made me do?" But I'm laughing so hard tears are welling in my eyes as I reach over the bar for a stack of napkins. I hand one to each of the women. "I'm so sorry, Mrs. G."

The older woman is dashing the wetness away from her own cheeks. Gratefully taking the napkin I offer her, she dabs the rest of the moisture away. "What I want to know, Maris, is how you could be so oblivious to your beauty? And it's obvious from speaking with your friend it's not just skin-deep."

Rainey's hands slap the bar before she pushes herself to her feet on the rail. "Thank you!" Reseating herself, she punches me in the arm good-naturedly. "She doesn't see herself like that," Rainey explains.

"How about shoveling in more bread and letting me answer for myself?" Before Rainey can say anything else, I grab a new crouton and slip it between her teeth. "I honestly don't, Mrs. G. I mean, I'm just me."

Mrs. G. lifts her soda in a toast. "And from what I've witnessed tonight, that's a fine woman. Like you tried to tell me, you're a businesswoman with a good head on her shoulders. And lovely friends who obviously support you."

Rainey grins around the toasted bread that looks like a cigar. Removing it, she dunks it into the special crab dip I slipped from the kitchen and moans, "So good."

"I had the specials myself earlier. They were delicious, indeed. Where did you find your chef?" Mrs. G. wonders.

I'm about to answer when I feel a tingle of awareness before a thickly hewn arm bands around my waist. My body goes rigid with tension as Nick slips around the back of the bar. He leans down to nuzzle my temple. Even as I try to calm my accelerated breathing, I'm shooting Rainey a fulminating glance. *What the hell does he think he's doing?*

Her slack-jawed expression gives me no clue. Unfortunately, the woman next to her, who holds the first key to unlock my future, is scrutinizing my every move.

I swear to God, Jed didn't make me take self-defense for nothing. If I have to, I'm going to smash the glass of water I'm drinking on the counter and jab him in the eye with the shards. "Nick, you have about three seconds to remove your hands from me." My voice could help the scientists on top of Mendenhall recrystallize the snow in such a way we'd be back in the Ice Age. Then I feel like a royal bitch because I promised myself I wouldn't be this person to him anymore.

"You promised we'd talk, and we haven't had a chance all night, Maris." His voice sounds like a seductive purr in comparison to his normally conceited tone.

Damnit, why now? Why here? I mouth, "Brad," to Rainey, who immediately reaches for her cell. To Nick, I calmly reply, "I'm working right now. I told you it might not be possible."

For a brief moment, his arm tightens before he lets me go. "Then when?" He spins me around, and I get my first good look at his handsome face. And a quiver races through me when I find his eyes reflect the same brokenness I see in the mirror every day.

The words fall from my lips without hesitation. "Soon, Nick. I promise. I wouldn't let one of Jed's friends down. Not ever."

His arm slackens further. "One of Jed's friends. Right."

I gesture behind me. "It's just, now's not a good time. Can you understand that?"

"When will be?"

I open my mouth, and I'm not sure which of us is more surprised when what comes out is "Tomorrow. Why don't we meet for coffee at Warm Up?"

"That sounds good. Around nine?"

I snort. "Not unless you want me to be mean, Nick. And you know I can do mean very well."

He laughs and it changes his whole face. The dark circles beneath his eyes seem to fade as the smile causes them to crinkle at the corners. "Ten it is. I'll see you then, Sunshine."

"Don't call..." I start to lecture. But Nick's slipped away before I can plead with him not to call me by Jed's nickname for me.

"Okay?" Rainey asks the minute I face her again.

"Okay? Let's see." I lift my hand and tick off my fingers. "One of Jed's best friends who I've always fought my feelings for has decided to blow back into my life at the worst possible minute. Do you think the universe could cut me some slack?" Angry tears start to form, but I refuse to let them form.

"Umm, not to pry," Mrs. Gustofson interjects.

"Feel free, Mrs. G. That little scene just played out in front of enough people it will be all over tomorrow that *the* Nick Cain was making a play for Maris," Rainey puts in.

At her words, my head thunks to the bar before I start rolling it back and forth. Blindly, I reach over and pinch her. Hard.

She squeals before laughing. "It's true."

"Who's Nick Cain?"

Mrs. Gustofson's innocuous question has my head snapping back so fast I almost clock Rainey in the chin as she was leaning over to get her retribution. "Did you just say that? You don't know who Nick Cain is?" I barely hold myself on the stool as laughter overcomes me and Rainey. "Nick Cain is an Alaskan *legend*." I stress the word.

"He really is, Mrs. G." Rainey nods. "Grew up in Ketchikan, worked for the Great Alaskan Lumberjack Show. Left and moved to Vegas where he was spotted by a sports recruiter. He became one of the top MMA fighters of all time."

"One of?" I parrot Nick's deep voice.

"Sorry. He's 'the Champ.' Now, he runs his own facility down in Albuquerque training the next generation of fighters."

"While he sounds...intriguing"—I roll in my lips to bite them over Mrs. Gustofson's word choice—"I was more intrigued by the reference to your brother. You mentioned he was deceased during our first meeting, Maris."

I grab my glass and take a long drink of water before answering. "Yes, I did. I feel like a large part of me is missing without Jed in my life."

"It's a testament to the man he was his friends feel the same way."

I blink rapidly. Words try to form, but I can't seem to make more than an incoherent sound. Brad, Jennings, Kody, and damnit even Nick *are* a testament to my brother. Spinning around in my stool, I spy him just as he leans down for another shot. The cross my brother left him —our grandfather's cross—falls out and grazes the baize.

And it reminds me of the suffering my heart's endured because I wasn't what Nicholas Cain wanted.

It's why I was so careful to send things to the Jacks they'd appreciate when I began sorting through Jed's things. The Jacks were a huge part of him—his brothers. And I needed to know if his brother had given him an inkling about me so I could move on with life. Not finding it, I searched for the answer within myself.

Then, I found the journals.

And here we are.

"Yes, I guess it is."

NICHOLAS

W arm Up's still hopping as the door opens and closes multiple times by the time Brad slows enough to drop me at exactly ten the next morning. "Just give the house a call if Maris can't drop you off," he calls when I slide from his SUV.

"Got it. Thanks." Making my way inside, I pause almost immediately as soon as my feet cross the threshold. There's a significant line ahead of me, which I scan looking for a specific head of mahogany hair. I frown wondering if she's late when I hear a voice just behind me as the line shifts forward.

"Excuse me. If I could get past you to the guy in the blue coat right in front of you? I appreciate it." Maris squeezes around a couple who snuck in behind me while I was searching for her. Her eyes are covered by sunglasses. "Hi."

"Hey." Her long hair falls around her shoulders like bolts of silk. Like every other time I've ever been in her presence, I want to sink my fingers into it and tip her face up to plunder her mouth. I clear my throat. "Sleep well?"

"No."

"That's too bad. I slept like a rock."

The line shifts forward, but Maris doesn't move. "Nick, tell me now. Are we here to have an actual conversation or to exchange banalities? If it's the latter, I'm getting in my car and going back to my warm bed."

Because that's exactly what my dick needs, to think of Maris in bed. "We're having a real discussion. I just don't want to in here."

"Boy, had this better be worth it," she mutters.

"And one of the things we're talking about is this problem you have with me," I declare as the line moves forward again. I grasp her elbow.

"Problem? Me?" she sputters. "I've treated you the exact same way I have for years."

"I'm well aware. And we have issues."

"When did you come to this conclusion?" Maris snaps. Then she rubs her head. "I'm sorry. I need some caffeine and sugar. I'm good with no sleep if I have them."

I'm not really sure I want to know how she figured that out.

The line surges forward again. We're seconds from ordering. Just as a cashier opens up, I look down into her indigo eyes and mutter, "Do the words 'baby' and 'adoption' mean anything to you?" Stepping up to the cashier while Maris gapes behind me, I give a big smile. "Hi. I'd like a large Americano."

Maris bumps my hip as she comes up next to me. The cashier asks, "Anything else? Oh. Hey, Maris. Didn't see you there. You were too quiet."

"I'll pay you any amount of money for a pot of steaming hot liquid to throw, Cayleigh."

The girl giggles. "Rough morning?"

Glaring up at me, she says, "I'm over my head already."

"So, a large double caramel macchiato with extra, extra caramel, extra vanilla?" the cashier offers.

Maris gives it a lot of consideration before nodding. "Plus, a cookie. There's no way I'm going to survive this without a cookie."

I'm agog over the amount of sugar Maris is about to consume, but I don't question it. If it sweetens her disposition at all, I'm willing to go out and buy a bag of turbinado and spoon-feed it to her myself. Damn, now I have images of doing just that floating in my mind. Leaning down and wrapping my tongue around her nipple before dusting it with the sugar crystals. Then I'd lean down and suck the entire thing back into my mouth...

I whip out my card to pay.

The cashier smiles at us both. "Your order will be right up."

We wait for a few moments for our drinks and Maris's cookie before she jerks her head to the rear of the building. Since I'm not certain whether or not Maris is going to throw the sticky substance at me, I warily follow her. But when we reach the back, I'm pleasantly surprised to find a courtyard that only has a few people in it. "How did I never know this was back here?"

Maris snorts before taking her first sip. She sighs in bliss. "That's because you're never in town long enough to actually spend time here, Nick. You're like a captain with a storm off the sea. To protect yourself, you run the very minute you're threatened whereas the rest of us band together to fight whatever it is were being threatened with."

I had just been about to take a drink, but instead I lower my coffee to the table without taking a single sip. "Excuse me?"

Maris opens her mouth but closes it again just as fast. She reaches out to grab the bag with her cookie, but I snag her hand. "What *is* your problem, Sunshine?"

"Don't call me that, please."

I'm taken aback by the hurt in her voice. "Okay. Maris, tell me what I've done. We used to be friends."

For a moment, her blue eyes widen before she bursts out laughing. "Oh, Nick. We've never been friends. Your friendship with the guys and how you conduct it is your own business."

"Gee, thanks," I drawl, my voice dripping with sarcasm.

"But you don't get to come to *my* home and question me about major life decisions. I demand more from the people in my life."

"Like what? Explain things to me. I may not be one of your girls, Maris, but I am your friend." She snorts and I find myself mildly insulted. "Hey, listen, if it's because I'm a man, I'm sorry. I can't change my sex to make this easier on you. Though, frankly, you wouldn't want me to," I goad her.

Maris reaches for her cookie and this time takes a large bite. She swallows and her head lowers. When it lifts, my dick tightens immediately. Her lids are at half-mast as she peers at me. Her lips are glossy, but there's a little icing stuck in the corner of her mouth. I want to spend hours licking it away.

"Holy shit." The words escape me before I can control them.

"And that, right there, is why we've never been friends and we'll never *be* friends." Between one blink and another, Maris morphs back into the woman who greeted me like a curmudgeon at the door. Shoving another bite of cookie in her mouth, she chews before saying, "I'm just surprised you acknowledged it after all these years."

I lean forward. "So, that little performance was what? To prove you could make me want you?"

She shrugs, seemingly indifferent. "That was your own fault for coming up to me like that at the bar last night. What the hell was up with that?"

I have no damn idea. Brad certainly chewed a bite out of my ass when I did it, especially since he told me before I went over to be on my best behavior since Rainey had let him know the person she was sitting with was from the state adoption agency. "Maybe I was just annoyed because everyone else knew about you and this whole adoption thing before me? When you know there's likely something I could do to help you?"

Maris snorts. "Sorry, Nick. Your name's not going to shoot glitter rainbows in this instance. Mrs. G. didn't even know who you were until Rainey and I told her last night. So, I guess there's at least two females who don't melt at the very sight of you." She takes a long drink of her coffee in satisfaction.

"Who's the first?" When she splutters her coffee all over the court-yard, I grin. I can't help it.

"Me, you ass! That's who! Now, when I get back, you'd better be ready to tell me what you're really doing here other than trying to ruin a dream for me." Maris grabs napkins from the holder and begins to dab at her chin before standing and collecting her garbage.

Just as she's about to pass me, I touch her arm briefly. "A dream, Sunshine?"

She doesn't even take umbrage with the nickname. "The biggest one I've dared to have in a long while, Nick."

"Then come back and tell me about it. And yes, I'll tell you why I'm in Juneau."

Her angry expression softens to the one I remember from so many summers. She reaches over and squeezes my shoulder. "I'm still pissed because you annoy me, but I've missed the real you, Nick."

As she stomps off, I say low enough so she won't hear, "I miss you too. Even though you won't let yourself believe me."

When Maris gets back, she reaches for her phone. Unlocking it, her fingers fly until she turns it around to face me. "This is David."

I pick up her phone. "He appears happy." Then again, who wouldn't with Maris Smith's arms wrapped around them, I think wistfully.

"I hope to make him happier."

"COME ON, this fighter is a former Jack?" Maris lifts a jean-clad leg up and wraps her arm around it.

"Maris, I swear to you, there's no way for me to make this up. Look." I pull up Reece's information from my email and turn my phone around.

"Hmm. Not bad stats. His ground game needs some work."

My shock almost topples me off the picnic bench to the stone patio. "You know what you're reading?"

The filthy look I receive when she hands me the phone back is my only answer before Maris ignores my question by picking up her second cup of coffee. "I could live on Warm Up's coffee. Best thing that ever happened to Juneau was when they opened."

I've already been back inside for round two of coffee, dialing back the sugar for Maris at her request. "I will agree with you 110 percent on that." This time, I'm the one eating as I couldn't pass up the freshly baked triple-nut bread. I break off a piece and pop it into my mouth. "Christ, I'm going to have to run this off later."

"Make sure you get a tourist pass if you plan on staying for any length of time," Maris advises me. "Then you can hit the trails in the parks."

"Thanks for the suggestion." I put my phone away. "I don't know how long I'm going to be in town, but I'd like to spend some time with you."

"Why?" Her brows draw together in confusion.

My fingers brush against one another, removing the residue of food, before I reach inside my shirt for the chain I was bequeathed. "I never take it off." My voice is raspy. It's something we haven't talked about yet, but it's the largest issue between us.

Jed.

Her eyes flick back and forth between mine and the gold cross that used to grace the neck of every man in her family. She swallows hard. "And did you find what he wanted you to? Did you realize you saved yourself? It wasn't your friendship with Jed that did that?"

I shake my head. "Because, to say the Jacks, that Jed, had no role in that is a disservice. It's like fight night. There's the guy fighting in the ring, sure, but there are three guys allowed in your corner—and one of them is mandatory and assigned. The cutman assigned to you has a huge job to get the blood stopping, to decrease the swelling on the fighter's face."

"What does this have to do with..."

I continue. "Then there's the other two guys. Those are the guys you pick. The people at your back because you want them there. Typically your trainer and your coach. But if we look at this fight like it's life, maybe Jed was there to be my cutman. Maybe he was assigned by someone to be the person to help get the blood off of me—metaphorically—so I could kick a little ass. And it's up to me to pick the people to be in my corner. That's the part that's faith, Maris."

I sit back and wait for her reaction.

"Who else is in your corner?" she asks, her voice softer than I've heard it in close to twenty years.

"The guys. The thing is, I can't separate them. They're a collective to me. Jed was different because he patched up wounds and didn't give a shit if he hurt me in the process—the sign of an excellent cutman."

Her head tilts to the side. "And the other? Where else do you want to put your faith, Nicholas? Who do you trust enough to have at your back?"

The answer comes to me without hesitation. "You. You're the only other person who knows everything about me and who still would get up on little sleep, despite how infuriated she might be with me. I figure that has to be a sign of faith."

"Oh, Nick." Maris blows out a long breath.

"I promise I'll work harder at this, us. Friends. We'll be friends." That word when it comes to this remarkable beauty feels repugnant in my mouth, but I'll do anything to have her in my life. "Maris, there's a lot to heal between us—most of it because of me."

A hiccuping sob escapes her. Fuck, this isn't going how I wanted it to go. "But give me a chance to make things up to you. Starting with that night in Vegas."

"Christ, Nick. You're really trying to do me in." Maris lets go of her leg and puts both of her hands in front of her face.

"If I never get another chance to apologize, I..."

"Nick, Vegas wasn't your fault." Maris flips her head back. Her eyes are red, but no tears are falling. "It was mine for misunderstanding your letter. So, what I can't understand is why you would want to have me at your back. Especially since Jed died." Her face is tragic, as if it's the early days when we all first lost Jed. God, has she been mourning him alone like this the whole time?

We've known each other half our lives, and I never thought the day would come when Maris Smith sat in front of me a stranger. But right now, that's exactly what she is.

Because I don't know who this broken woman is.

MARIS

"My father used to mutter — out of Maris's earshot — if Nick ever got his head out of his ass about my sister, either they'd end up together or the world was going to end. There was no in-between." - From the journals of Jedidiah Smith.

"What do you mean? Why wouldn't I want you at my back?" Suddenly a burst of laughter from another table draws Nick's ire. "We can't talk about this here. Where can we go?"

Disoriented, I look around as if a portal to somewhere is immediately going to open, when Nick grabs my hand and drags me from the bench. "No. I know the perfect spot. And God knows, he'll love listening in on our conversation."

Whether it's all the sugar I've consumed or the weight of intuition, I immediately know where he means. Once we clear the front door of Warm Up, I tug at the grip Nick has on my wrist. He stops moving immediately. "What is it, Maris?" His voice is as broken as my heart feels.

"I need..."

"What?" When I don't answer right away, he prompts me. "Tell me."

Without a word, I turn away from him and walk to the flower store next door to Warm Up.

I never visit my brother's grave without bringing him a fresh bouquet.

Nick catches up and I push the door open. The door opens with a tinkling of bells that doesn't seem to annoy me as much today as it normally does. Beth steps out from the back, wiping her hands on her apron. "Oh, good morning, Maris. Do you need a bouquet today?"

"Please, Beth. Do you mind if we wait?"

"Not a problem. It will just take a few moments."

Soon, Nick and I are walking through the iron gates of the ceme-tery toward Jed—technically Jed and Dean's—resting spot. With a clear view of the sea, it's the perfect place for Jed to be laid to rest. I lead the way at the end, stopping off to pick up a new flower holder and filling it with water.

Nick doesn't say a word until I've placed the flowers to the side. Then I sit down, drawing my knees up and burying my head against them. What he finally says burns through my soul. "How can you absolve me from that night, Maris? I hurt you and I never meant to." Aching sadness permeates his voice.

I lift my head, and instead of focusing on Jed's tombstone which is what I normally see when I sit right here, the first thing I focus on are Nick's jean-clad legs. Behind him is the swirling sea. "All I found that night was the truth, Nick."

"Which was?" His voice is a low growl.

"I followed where my heart led. Yours wasn't there. I was wrong to have blamed you for that—punished you for it. I'm sorry for being so brutal. I've wanted to say that for a long time." Some part of me feels clean sitting here saying the things I should have long ago in front of my brother.

After all, he thought them about me. His journals said so.

Out of the corner of my eye, I catch his jeans shifting until he's squatting in front of me. Resting his hands on my knees, he draws my attention from the tumultuous sea. I twist my head just as his mouth opens. Expecting him to accept my apology, I'm shocked when his first word is "Bullshit."

I blink. It takes me a moment before I manage, "Excuse me?"

"You didn't read that letter wrong, Maris. I agonized for hours over how to write it so it didn't come off that I was begging you to fly down and see the fight—I wanted you there so damn badly. I wanted you to see that I'd done it. And then I was going to claim you."

Clean anger whips through me. I shove Nick back on his ass hard as I scramble to my feet. "You bastard! Then what the fuck happened, Nicholas? Couldn't wait until I got through security to sink your cock into something?"

"No! What happened was someone decided to grill me during the interviews about my damned past. And it made me realize—again—I wasn't good enough for you," he roars as he surges to his feet.

Whirling around, I yell to my brother's tombstone, "Do you believe this crock of shit?" I begin to pace back and forth. I feel a pang of empathy for the groundskeeper for the work they're going to have to do on repairing the wear and tear on the grass.

"He should as I told him the next morning." Nick's voice is calm.

That halts my stride as I'm pivoting. "Excuse me?"

"Jed knew. I told him the freaking media circus it became once that damn reporter opened the door. He ripped me a new asshole about how I decided to handle my—how did he put it? 'Emotional turmoil' was the phrase, but..."

"Stop." I hold up a hand. I need a second to process his words because Nick's not feeding me a line.

He's telling me the truth. I should know. Jed used those exact words when he wrote about my emotional state after the fight. He said that Nick's breakdown—his "emotional turmoil"—couldn't be tolerated in this case. Not when it hurt the most important person in Jed's life.

Me.

"Let's leave it at we both made mistakes. We start fresh from here, now. I won't let you down as a friend again, Nick." He starts to speak, but I talk over him. "Can you promise me the same?"

"Yes. Unequivocally." He holds open his arms.

Tentatively, I move into them. This is different than the hug from last night at the Brewhouse; it's about two wounded hearts yearning so badly to be healed because of the pain they heaped on each other. No, I correct myself silently, because of the pain I caused.

After a few long moments, I pull back and wipe my eyes. "So, what do you think about the stone?"

"It fucking sucks," Nick tells me bluntly. Of course, he says this as a teary-eyed couple passes us.

I slap my hand across my mouth to contain my laughter. "Nick..."

"He shouldn't be gone, Maris. So who the hell cares what his damn tombstone looks like?"

Kara waxed poetic about the beauty of the stone. Brad and Rainey thought it was gorgeous. Nick, God love him, said exactly the right thing. I decide to tell him something he might not realize. "I missed you more nights than I hated you."

And that's what brings tears to Nick's eyes. He tries to speak but ends up just running a hand over my hair.

For a long time we stand by the sea, over someone we both loved with our whole hearts, and remember without articulating the many words that need to be said between us. Because sometimes it's not words that need to be said.

Sometimes it's time that's more precious between two people.

And we haven't had nearly enough of that.

AFTER A LONG WHILE, we begin to walk back. "Do you need to call Brad?"

"Actually, he's been locked in his office by Rainey. Do you mind dropping me off?"

"Wait, let me guess?" I stop walking and grin up at Nick. "His business is a mess since Meadow left?"

Nick tosses a friendly arm around my shoulders. "Got it in one."

"I'm not sure if Rainey mourned the loss of her sister or her husband's office manager more," I muse.

Nick barks out a laugh. "I know at the dinner table last night, he was swearing he'd put an ad in the paper."

I scoff. "I'll let you know if that actually happens. He swears that every tax season except the one where Meadow worked for him."

Nick stops. "Seriously?"

I nod. "Not kidding."

"What do you do about all this stuff?"

I think back to those dark days after the accident and the classes I enrolled in once I healed. "I run the books for the Brewhouse."

Nick frowns. "Isn't that a lot?"

I roll my eyes. "Not you too."

"Me too?"

I begin ticking all the people who had an opinion about me working so many hours over the years off on my fingers. "Jed, Kara, Dean, Brad, Rainey, Kevin—when he was old enough, Jennings—after he and Kara got married. All of them have harped on me working too many hours." Before Nick can comment, I break away and stand in front of him. "I'll tell you what I told Jennings. I've cut back on my hours working at the actual Brewhouse. Now I only go in when someone needs assistance. It's why I realized I need more to fill my life than just work." I scrunch my nose and turn my head away, a sure sign I have something else to say.

Nick picks up on it immediately. "What? What else is there?"

"I thought if I filled my life with everything that was the Brewhouse, I would forget the most important thing."

"What's that?"

"I was lonely." Despite Nick's obvious shock, I start walking. He quickly catches up. "It was just me. Jed was in Florida, and then he was...he...."

"Maris. I get it." At the conviction of Nick's voice, I get myself together.

I continue. "When I finally snapped back from the agony"—and after I'd read some of Jed's private thoughts, I think silently—"there was a still heartache. But it was different. It was for what I was missing."

"Then you do whatever you have to in order to rid yourself of that feeling."

I smile. And I'm taken aback when Nick stops walking and stares at me. "What? What is it?"

"Nothing." His long legs catch up.

"Nick, what is it?" I ask impatiently.

"It's nothing."

"It was something," I argue.

"It's just, that's the first time you've smiled at me in almost twenty years. I wanted to enjoy it." He tries to move past me, but I snag his arm.

Then beneath the cloudy Juneau sky, I tip my head back and smile up at Nicholas Cain. Not because I'm trying to flirt with him, but because I've owed him smiles for any number of reasons and I've withheld them.

I didn't smile at him at Kara and Jennings's wedding, nor Meadow and Kody's.

I refused to smile at him when he ran after me to make sure I was okay after the will was read.

I couldn't smile when he came to both of my parents' funerals. I was too heartbroken.

But this smile? It's a smile that belongs to him that's been inside of me waiting a long time to be shared.

Finally after a few moments, I turn my head away and say, "Come on. I'm parked in the garage."

I think he might be too stunned, because Nick follows me without a word.

NICHOLAS

I was never one to hide my emotions. If I believed something needed to be said, I came right out with it. But as Maris drove me back to the Meyers residence, I feel like I'd be a heel to do something like that.

There's no sound in the car, not even music. Our conversation has become nonexistent. We're driving the speed limit, if barely a mile over. I'm about to open my mouth to ask if there's something wrong with her SUV because of the focused way she's concentrating when I notice how tightly her hands are clenched on the steering wheel. Her knuckles are so tight, they're practically translucent. I frown and turn my head out the windshield. Does Maris not like to drive? I rack my brain trying to recall if Jed ever mentioned that to me. I want to ask her about it, but not now. Not when she's so focused on what she's doing.

But as quickly as the thought enters my mind, the minute we turn off the main road, the intensity evaporates as if it wasn't there. "Do you need to call Rainey to let her know when you're arriving?" There's not a hint of the strain she's been under the last few miles.

"No, Brad said only to call if I needed a ride."

Her eyes briefly leave the road. "Mind if I pop in? If she's home, I need to speak with Rainey about a fundraiser she wants to do at the Brewhouse for the kids' school."

Disconcerted because one moment Maris looked like she'd rather be doing anything than driving and the next she's completely at ease, I stumble. "Sure. Guess not. Don't see a problem. Not my house."

"You know, Champ, I'm not entirely sure how those smooth words of yours managed to bag so many women." The saccharine sweetness in her voice swirls together with the venomous sarcasm.

Ah, familiar territory with Maris. I relax. "Despite what the rags report, there haven't been that many women."

"Mere thousands instead of trending towards the millions? You know you have your own hashtag, Nick."

I chuckle. "Maris, the paparazzi is so deranged, they think I'm sleeping with my assistant, Charmaine."

"It's been known to happen." She turns her vehicle down Rainey and Brad's street.

"True. Charmaine is a knockout for her age." I relish the hiss of breath that whistles out between Maris's teeth before I finish my explanation. "Except Charmaine's longtime boyfriend, Harold, would likely find some way to take me out despite our age differences. I wonder if he'd run over my foot multiple times with his scooter to even the advantage."

Her lips twitch. I enjoy as she struggles to prevent the giggle from escaping. "He sounds like a ruthless foe. Even not knowing him, I like his style."

"You would just flat out like him. Your problem is Charmaine though."

"Why?"

"First, Charmaine is much more mobile. Second, if she ever caught Harold flirting with you—which is more than likely to happen since he charms everyone he meets—she'd turn into a barracuda."

Maris parks the car and turns her face fully in my direction. My heart thumps hard in my chest over the devilish sparkle on her face. "And now I know I'd like her as well. Give me an example."

"The last woman who hit on 'her Harold' wound up with a bowl of salsa dumped over her head." I pause for a moment. "It was the waitress at bingo night. Harold told me they needed to roll over the jackpot prize to the next week in order to break up the 'humdrum' Charmaine caused."

Maris's body begins to shake. "I have to hear more. I feel like she's my spirit animal."

I decide to press my advantage while I can. Reaching over the center console, I touch her hand. "Will you let me see you again while I'm here?"

Every inch of the laughter slowly drains away, and it causes an ache I don't want to explore. Maris bites her lip. "Is this such a good idea, Nick?"

"Friends eat. Friends share stories about their lives. Besides, I have it on good authority I don't check my email often enough."

"Well, we know that's the truth. Otherwise, the adoption wouldn't have come as a surprise."

"I plan on slugging through it."

"When?"

I open my mouth to reply before I catch the gleam in Maris's. "Shit. Why do I get the feeling you're going to make me clean out my email?"

"I'll make you a deal, Nick. Show me your email box is empty and we'll discuss it." Maris opens her door and slides from the vehicle.

Well, I know what I'll be doing later after I make plans to meet up with Oliver and Reece. Hopping out, I catch up with Maris, who gives a perfunctory knock before entering. And we're both greeted with chaos.

Rainey is running around after Josh and Sophie yelling, "Pick up your toys or I swear you won't have electronic time for a week. And stop making that awful racket. You were supposed to grow out of your savage years."

I lean down to whisper directly into Maris's ear, "Is this normal behavior? Children deciding to start their own marching band using the clean pots their mother scrubbed?"

Her head tips up, so close our lips are practically touching. "Don't you remember doing anything like this as a child?"

"Honestly, no. I remember running around the woods outside

wherever..." Then I catch myself. I've told Jed more than anyone, but I don't know what he shared about my past with his sister. Anxiously, I try to slow my heart rate while I gauge her reaction.

Maris isn't reacting to my words. Instead, she's looking at the Meyers hellions. Frowning thoughtfully, she finally declares, "They're thawing out."

"Like what? A frozen chicken breast?"

Maris barks out a laugh before patting me on the arm. She puts her fingers between her lips and lets out a piercing whistle. All movement in the room stills. "Kids, outside. Burn off some of that energy before your mother ties you to the bed for the foreseeable future."

The spawns of Brad don't have to be told twice. They drop the pans where they stand, setting off a clang that almost has me reaching up to cover my ears. Racing for the back mudroom, they shove on coats and jam their feet into boots. Rainey waits until they're outside before she drops to her knees and begins bowing before Maris. "I'm not worthy."

"I brought a different form of trouble back with homework." Uh-oh. My testicles draw up in fear when Rainey's head snaps up from her prostrate position the floor.

"Oh? What does he have to do?"

"Eliminate his email." Both women laugh like it's the biggest joke in the world.

"Why do you both find this funny?" I demand. I expect this is going to take me thirty minutes max even if there's a limit to the number of messages I can delete at one time.

"Because you're a man. You planned on just deleting all of the email and starting over, didn't you?"

Busted. I thought it was a great idea, until Maris continues. "There's answers to a lot of unasked questions about all of us in those emails. I suggest you settle in and make a half-assed effort to find them all. Now, Rainey, about this fundraiser..."

"Can we raise enough money to turn it into a boarding school?" she beseeches Maris.

"No. You have to keep your kids until at least they can provide for themselves." Rainey groans as if she's in physical agony. "But here's what I was thinking." Maris steps forward and drags Rainey from the floor. The two women link arms and move toward the kitchen.

"Hey," I call out. Both women stop. "How long do I have to do this?" Meaning my Herculean task of cleaning out my email. Internally I shudder. I might get carpal tunnel from this.

Maris shrugs. "That's entirely up to you, isn't it?" Then she disappears out of sight with Rainey.

PROCRASTINATING A LITTLE LONGER, I call Oliver. He makes arrangements to pick me up the following morning. "Me and Reece spent the weekend together. I put him through a few of your workouts."

"How did he do?"

"Kicked my ass."

"That isn't hard to do," I retort.

"Ha ha. Very funny. We rented some gym space to work on his ground game if you want to get in on that."

Making a snap decision, I agree. "Let's put him through his paces. I want to do the full day with him."

Oliver groans. "Have you ever run here, boss?"

"Many, many times. Not enjoying the hills?"

"My calves feel like they're on fire."

"Then do some more stretches before you tear something," I bark out.

"Already doing that."

"I'll take a look tomorrow. If you injured yourself, you're not going to be the one sparring with your friend." Even as the words come out, a thrill pumps through me. "I can always step in."

"Give me permission to video this," Oliver begs. "I might be able to sell it one day as 'Two Champs' or some shit. Maybe be able to buy myself a house as nice as yours."

If I didn't know he was teasing, I'd kick his ass. "Cute."

"You're no fun," he complains good-naturedly before hanging up.

Now, sitting in Brad's home office with my laptop and an unfathomable number of emails staring back at me, I'm at a loss where to begin. And Maris's words keep ricocheting through my head, tantalizing me, like nothing else has lately. Even the idea of working with a new fighter.

There's answers to a lot of your questions about all of us in those emails.

"When this is done, I'm starting a new account so I can leave this one for spam. Then I swear, I'll double Charmaine's salary to scan it for me," I declare resolutely as I begin to delete a thousand emails at a time—the maximum my email provider will allow. Hours later, I'm left with 5,846 messages from the guys and more recently from their women. It's about a percent of what I started with. I know many have slipped off the system, and I feel a huge pang of regret I'll never get those back.

Especially when I spot Jed's email address.

Before doing anything else, I create a folder and dump all of the messages in there so they're at least safe from being eliminated due to time. Then I open up the oldest and start reading.

They're mostly from Jed, keeping us up to date on trivial matters. There are a few replies from Brad and Kody, very few from Jennings. That is, until the message that causes my heart to stop.

Hey.

I'm going to be offline for a while. I'm not sure when I'll be back on.

Maris was involved in a serious car wreck in the early hours of the morning. She was airlifted to Fairbanks. I don't know much more than that. Mom and Dad left at first light.

Guys, it's bad. Really bad.

There's nothing that anyone can do. Everything's being done that can be done. But somehow, it doesn't seem to be enough. This is my baby sister, my heart, my sunshine. But if you have it in you to say a few prayers, it would be appreciated.

-Jed

There was a flurry of emails right after that from all of the guys—except me. Jed never replied to any of them until he got back from Fairbanks to say Maris had been released. And there's nothing from me because I never bothered to check my email because I wanted to leave everything about Alaska behind as I cocooned my pain over my abandonment tightly.

It was at least a year after this before they heard from me again since I chose to willingly cut all of them out of my life while I tried to run away from the anger and hatred. And when I let the guys back in, this never came up. Not then, not later.

"After all, she was home and healed, so why would they bother to bring it up to you, you selfish prick!" I yell at the reflection I see in the glare of the computer screen. "Motherfucking, selfish asshole. Boo-hoo. You were left by your mother. Who the hell cares? She could have *died*."

The door squeaks as it opens. Rainey steps inside. "Nick, are you telling the truth?"

"Yeah, Rainey." I spread my arms wide. "Take a good look. Why did all of you still give a damn about me?"

"No, I meant about being left by your mother."

I turn away. Christ, Brad never told her in all these years? "Yes."

"That's what Brad knew about you all these years and wouldn't share," she guesses accurately.

"What does that matter? Maris almost died, and because I was too selfish I never knew. I couldn't be there, even to offer support via an email."

"But Maris didn't die, Nick. And why are you still giving your—I hesitate to use this word—mother the power to decide your life?" Storming over to me, she gets in my face and pokes her finger right in the place that aches—my heart.

"Is this why you've always held back from all of us? From Maris?" Rainey demands.

"Yes! He died and she left me behind as if I was disposable. You all resurrected what was left of my heart. I ran so that little piece of perfection couldn't be destroyed again." What started as yelling ends up as a mere whisper.

"So, you did the same thing to us your parents did to you. Only your justification was love. Interesting."

Her words are like a firm crack to the cheek. I stagger backward until I feel the wall catch me. Slowly, I sink down until my rear touches my heels. I open my mouth and close it, unable to refute a single thing. I escaped the love my "family" openly offered me because I was afraid of what would happen if I didn't leave first. And if it wasn't for Jed being my touchstone, having faith in me, would any of them still be here at all?

"I'm so sorry," I whisper. The words are wrenched from me.

Rainey ducks her head to wipe her eyes. Drying her hands, she offers me a hand. I take it and tug her down into my arms to me to wrap her in a tight hug. For long moments, I hold the wife of my brother trying to form words. Finally, I realize the simplest ones are the best. "I'm so sorry."

"You have to stop apologizing. It's not your fault what they did to you."

"That's not what I'm apologizing for."

"Then for what?"

"It was just too soon for me to come back here after I'd finally clawed my way out for your wedding." I brush a soft kiss on the top of her head. "You're absolutely perfect for Brad, in case I've never told you that."

"Damn you, Nick." Rainey shoves hard at my chest. "Now I get why…"

"Why what?" But Rainey just shakes her head. Her lips curve, and there's no malice in them.

She nods at my computer. "There's big and little moments in those emails, Nick. Not all of them are as earth-shattering as the one you just read. But come outside if you need a break. The kids and I will be in the backyard."

"I don't suppose anyone would be up for a run later, would they?"

She snorts. "Dream on, Champ. None of us are into torture in this house. I like being able to move."

With a laugh, I help stabilize her as she gets to her feet before pushing up to my own.

As Rainey heads to the door, I taunt her. "You had kids. Aren't yours a form of sadism?"

"My only exception," she calls over her shoulder.

So, it's with a sense of contentment instead of feelings of complete self-loathing I sit down to read some more email.

MARIS

"One day, Maris will make an amazing mother. If she'll ever let herself get to that place emotionally." - From the journals of Jedidiah Smith.

I haven't heard from Nick in days. It's entirely possible he's left Juneau and hasn't called, which would be a disappointment but not surprising. In the meanwhile, I arranged my work schedule to head to Sarah and Hung's to spend time with David as many days as I can. I want to be there for things like homework, snacks, or just to play.

Today, we're outside with a life-size Jenga set I built in the garage at home for barbecues. Since Sarah and Hung's front yard is on a mild slope, we get about four blocks in before the entire tower falls. That sends us both into fits of hilarity, and we both scramble to set everything back up again. "Let's do it again, Maris!" David yells, after the tower topples to the ground after I pull out the piece that sends it crashing down with a huge bang.

"Anything you want, kid." I ruffle the top of his dark hair.

"Then could I have a hug too?" His insecurity does me in.

"Those I give away without asking." I open my arms, and he rushes in. "Is everything okay?"

He shakes his head, and just like that, another bond between us snaps into place—one of trust. "Want to talk about it?" I ask casually.

"Just some stupid kids at school." He scuffs the toe of his shoe against the still-rock-hard earth.

I hold up a hand. "Fair warning, David. If I don't like what I hear, I'm likely to tell Sarah and Hung."

"Aww, why? Why can't we have this between us?"

"Because they're your guardians. And if it's something they need to address with the school, I have a responsibility to keep you safe by letting the people legally responsible for your welfare know."

He bites his lower lip. "But you're my friend, Maris. There has to be some kind of way I can tell you..."

I rest my hand on his shoulder. "No. There's no bending or, heaven forbid, breaking the rules."

"Then maybe I won't tell you," he says belligerently.

And welcome to motherhood, Maris, I think to myself. Thank goodness I had Kara as a role model all these years. "That's your choice. But I'd hate to spend the time between now and the next time I get to visit worrying about you."

David bites down on his lip. "You'd worry?"

"Well, of course I would." *I love you*, I want to scream. *I want to make you my son.* But I hold those words inside.

"They were saying I'm always going to be here," he bursts out with. "The boys from school. They said there was no way anyone was ever going to want to adopt me. Why would you want a kid my age when you could have a baby?" Tears fill his caramel-brown eyes.

Fury burns inside me, but I don't let that show. I shoot up a request to my brother, which I'm sure he'll ignore since I'm still not certain I've forgiven him. *Jed, can you do me a favor and give those little twerps a rash of acne? That's not too outrageous of a request.* I rein in my anger and drop down onto the grass. Patting the spot next to me, I wait for David to sit down. "Did I ever tell you I have a friend who was fostered?"

"Really?"

"Umm-hmm. He was older than you. I don't know much about it, but my brother did. He knew him very well."

"Wow. You have a brother?" David's captivated.

I draw my knees up and cross my arms as I look out over the seawater. How do I set some of these memories free for someone who never knew Jed? "I did. He died about three years ago. It's still difficult to talk about him since I loved him very much."

I feel a little hand slip into mine. "Did he die like my mom did? Is that why you've never mentioned it?"

Startled, my head whips around to face the little boy who's wormed his way into my heart. David's mother's death was an overdose associated with her seasonal affective disorder—a horrid tragedy for the little boy next to me. "No, sweetheart. He and his husband died in a car accident. I think I'll always miss him."

"Kind of like I'll always miss Mom?"

"Exactly like that." I reach over and wrap an arm around his shoulder. "You remind me of Jed in a number of ways."

"I do? How?" He's so eager to know, it alleviates my concerns about letting him know some of their personality traits.

"Making your own fun, finding joy in life. Having a quick mind and a sharper wit. All of those things. But you're more thoughtful than Jed was. He often leaped before he looked. He would do something first and think of the repercussions after. Wait." I sit up, very serious. "You don't have a thing for flamingos, do you?"

David scrunches his nose at the question. "Tigers and bears are my favorite animals."

"Oh, thank goodness. Jed had these obnoxious flamingo swim shorts all of his friends tried to find ways to destroy. I don't think they make them in your size." I bite my lip. At least I pray they don't. Those shorts should have been sacrificed years ago.

"Black's a good color. So's navy. I suppose when you get to college, you have to go with your school colors, I guess."

"Yeah, I guess you do, buddy. And that might mean purple," I warn him.

"Ugh. Okay. So, your brother..."

"You can call him Jed. He would have been okay with that." If he lived to see the day I get to make this little boy my own, he would have loved Uncle Jed more, but all in good time. I swallow the lump in my throat, imagining Jed's exuberance that I finally made it to this point of healing.

"So does Jed's friend remember what it was like to find a permanent home?" David asks.

"He never found one. I found my brother's journals a while back. But I think he was happier where he was. Overall, he's a pretty special guy, regardless of who raised him." I just wish Nick would realize these things about himself and not let the past define him.

The next thing you know, I'm being toppled back onto the grass by a slightly too skinny boy. "Hey, what's this for?" I say as I absorb the hug.

"Because you're the best, Maris. And..." He doesn't say any more, but his arms hold me tight, conveying what I need to know in my heart.

He's a piece of it.

When we look back on our lives together, I hope David will realize this is the moment he became mine. Not when all the inspections get finished and all the legalities become finalized. It's at this moment, while we're overlooking where the sea begins and ends in perpetual motion.

LATER, after staying to enjoy dinner with David, Sarah, Hung, and their extended family, I drive home.

As is my usual, I remain tense until I pass the crash site. Once I do, I exhale and begin my mental to-do list. I need to make certain there's been no changes to the schedules at the Brewhouse that require a miracle. I have chores around the house. Mentally, I groan when I realize that might mean chopping wood if I can't bribe, beg, or borrow someone to do it. And, most important, I need to check in this week with Mrs. G. to make certain things are progressing on schedule with getting my home licensed to take over as David's foster.

And I should check in with Rainey to see if Nick has gone back to Albuquerque instead of rising to the challenge of clearing out decades' worth of email.

"Was it wrong to do it that way?" I ask aloud in my small tank. I navigate down my street and slow as I pull into my driveway and recognize the Subaru waiting there. "Uh-oh. Rainey's here. I don't think I'm getting much done tonight. I wonder if she needs wine." Because if she does, nothing on my to-do list is getting accomplished.

I pull into the garage and turn off my vehicle. After sliding out, I walk outside into the cooling night air. "Hey. What's wrong? Things getting crazy over at your house?"

But to my shock, it's not Rainey who alights from the vehicle; it's Nick. And his face is relieved. "You're back."

"I hope so. I live here." But just as I'm about to brush past him to climb the front stoop, Nick swoops in and wraps his arms around me. "What's wrong? Is it Brad? Rainey? The kids?"

He shakes his head. Instead he buries his head in the crook of my neck and breathes deeply. "Just give me this. Just for a moment, okay?"

Slowly, my arms creep around Nick's waist. Tentatively, I squeeze him back. It's not the first embrace we've shared since he came chasing after me the day of Jed's funeral, but there's something different about it. "Nick, I can't help if I don't know what's wrong."

He mumbles something I don't quite catch.

"Let me go for just a moment so I can close the garage, then we can talk."

His head lifts and my breath catches. Swirling in his beautiful eyes are contempt, bitterness, and revulsion. I try to step back, but the bands of steel holding me to him preclude that. "Why are you looking at me like that?" I whisper. What on earth happened in just a few short hours?

"Like what?"

"Like I somehow caused your world to end."

He tucks a piece of hair behind my ear. "That only would have happened if you'd actually died in that car wreck."

Oh shit. "You've read your email."

"Most of it."

I rush out, "Nick, I'm so sorry. I realized earlier while I was driving you probably didn't know. I had to make you realize there were other things that had happened. Some big, some small, but we're your

114

friends. As for me, I just can't talk about it anymore. You were dissecting me in the car like I was some kind of science project, and I..."

His finger on my lips stops the words flowing.

I stand perfectly still, not even breathing, while his cool lips brush a kiss across my forehead, each brow, each cheek. He removes his finger, before his lips brush lightly across mine. He pulls back, searching my eyes, before admitting, "I'm not done yet. But I couldn't go another minute without seeing your face. I don't care how I felt about this place, if I would have known you were hurt, I would have been here."

"I wouldn't have seen you," I tell him honestly. "I barely let Jed in."

"And we're going to talk about that." A crooked smile crosses his lips. "But I have a training session tomorrow and more email to read."

Slowly, so slowly, his arms loosen. "You'd better head inside."

I'm confused. "That's all you came for? To see me?"

"That's all you'll let me have until I've finished reading. Right?" Nick Cain is many things, but uncertain isn't one of them. Seeing him suffocated with that emotion does me in.

"Wrong." I step back into his arms and thread my fingers into his dark hair.

"Maris." My name comes out as a rasp from his lips. "I don't want you to look back on our first kiss and regret it."

"The only regret will be if I have to wonder what it's going to be like to wait one more night for it." Then there's no room for words between us as Nick lowers his head. His dark lashes lower, highlighting the fact he keeps his eyes on me as our lips connect and linger.

My head angles slightly as a sigh escapes, traversing from my mouth to his. He pulls back slightly. "Well, the world didn't fall into the ocean."

"Did you think it would?" I demand indignantly. I tug at his hair, but all it does is cause him to laugh.

"I was terrified over it."

"Well, if you're too much of a coward, Champ, then you can just—"
But Nick cuts off my words by sealing his lips hungrily against mine.

Mine part of their own accord. My fingers trail into the hair at his neck. I wrap my arms around his shoulders instead. One of Nick's hands tangles behind my head, holding my head in place as his tongue slides in and out of my mouth. The other moves down and cups my ass, his hips undulating to the same movement. In all the years I've had feelings for Nick, there's no way I could have imagined this kiss. I would have had to stop my heart and restart it all while managing to float in the air with my feet on the ground.

In other words, it would have been a virtual impossibility.

Long minutes later, I eventually draw back. Nick's lips are swollen, and the uncertainty has been replaced by an arrogant daze. I did that. A fierce satisfaction fills me at the sight. "Now, go."

"Go? Are you serious?" He reaches for me again.

I smirk as I avoid his touch knowing I'll melt like warm butter in his hands. "I believe you have some more emails to read, Champ."

"There's something you need to know before I do."

"Okay."

His face turns serious. "I want more from this than just your body, Maris. I didn't wait all these years just for that."

Whoa. Pressing a hand against my lower stomach, I whisper, "Then we're going to need to talk, Nick. No more of this for a while."

"We will. I'll let you know when I'm done with the emails." Without another word, he turns away. Sliding into Rainey's car, he starts the engine. I turn and run into the garage.

When I'm inside, I race up to the bedroom and grab Jed's journal. I frantically flip through the pages until I find the passage I read the other night. When I find it, I read it aloud.

"No man is going to be good enough for Maris, but if Nick ever got his head out of his ass, he might have a chance. The question is, will that happen in this lifetime?"

Flopping back on the bed, I whisper, "I don't know Jed, but I'm afraid to wish for too many miracles. You know? I still have to clean up the fallout from your interfering meddling as it is."

Placing the journal on the nightstand, I stand and catch headlights heading down my driveway toward the street.

Damn. He waited until he knew I was safely inside. How am I supposed to handle this kind of sweet from the very devil himself?

NICK

"Damn, he's a machine."

"I know. It's ridiculous to watch." Oliver wipes the sweat from his brow.

We're both standing aside as Reece London tackles everything we've tossed at him like we just asked him to skip around the school playground. He kept up with my grueling pace during a ten-mile run—a pace I set because I thought it would clear my head from the kiss I shared with Maris the night before. Then when we arrived back at the gym, Reece proceeded to demonstrate his range of motion through a series of stretches and jumps that would make a gymnast weep. As he's pounding out rep after rep on the free weights, I make a snap decision. "Stop him."

Oliver frowns. "Why?"

"Because I want to see him in action."

"The tapes weren't enough?"

My eyes don't leave the broad-shouldered young man. "Have you ever wanted back in the cage since you retired, Ollie?"

"For me, the cage was either the gateway to heaven or hell. I love the sport, but I can't say I miss having my ass kicked regularly. Why?"

"Your boy Reece, he'll be so damn used to viewing crowds through little octagons, he'll forget what it's like not to. Now, let's get him comfortable with someone who also understands that feeling." I reach behind my head and tug off my sweat-soaked tank. Toeing off my running shoes and socks, I begin to stretch.

And my soul soars knowing I'm about to fight.

"Ah, fuck. I thought you were kidding when you said you might spar with him."

"Do I ever kid about these things?"

"Hell, Nick. We're in Alaska. I figured you might demand a chainsaw challenge to see if you still had those kind of mad skills." Oliver whistles to get Reece's attention before I can tell him to kiss my ass.

When the younger man sees me stripped down, ready to do battle, he approaches us with some trepidation. "Mr. Cain? Sir? Are you sure this is such a good idea? I don't want to hurt you."

I mock Reece lightly as Oliver begins taping my hands with quick precision. "Son, you're welcome to try."

Reece turns to his friend, demanding, "This is some kind of joke. Right? A test?"

I flex my fingers, nodding my approval at my former protege. "Nice job, Ollie. The only test, Reece, is whether you can get over your hang-ups enough to strike first. Trust me, it won't be as easy as you think."

I stride away and hop up into the ring. My toes curl into the rubbery softness of the mats while frantic whispers go on behind me. Tuning them out, I bend at the waist and place my hands flat down. With a quick kick, I brace my weight on my arms and begin to press up and down, over and over to warm up the muscles in my shoulders.

Carefully, I lower myself back to a standing position, scooping up the gloves Ollie left there, to find Reece gaping at me. "First strike buys the first round."

That shakes him from his stupor. "You're on." He stalks to the opposite corner and hauls himself in.

"Ollie, head guards?" But Oliver, anticipating me, is already grabbing the necessary protective gear. A black helmet comes sailing in my direction. Quickly sliding it on, I slip in a mouth guard from my pocket and find myself in the zone. I'm ready. Anticipation thrums through my veins. I haven't felt anything like this since...fuck. Since Maris kissed me last night.

"Ready. Fight!" Oliver calls.

I leap back just as one of Reece's long legs is about to make contact. "I thought this was going to be a challenge," he trash-talks.

"Oh, boy. Just you wait." I feint to the left before striking with my right. It's a solid hit directly to the kid's midsection.

"Fuck," Reece grunts in disbelief.

"First strike," Oliver calls out.

"You haven't been fucked yet, kid. That's later." Then I stop playing and see if Reece really has what it takes to be a champion because the first step is mental. He has to stop thinking of me like I'm not a threat because I have a decade on him. I can and have taken down guys his age and size. The other thing he needs to start believing is there's only one champ in the ring. That's what my mentor taught me all those years ago. It's what I've taught everyone under me who's fought for the belt.

The thing is, it should no longer be me.

BY THE TIME we're through, I know I'm going to have some impressive bruises. But I also know Oliver wasn't wrong. Reece London was born to wear the belt.

We're both dripping with sweat as we spit out our mouth guards. Then a ridiculous grin splits his face. "Did that just happen? Did I seriously kick Nick Cain's ass?"

I sniff. "You tried, kid. Your ground game needs some major work." But I give in to his exuberance. "Hell, I'm going to feel that kidney shot later. I just know it."

Reece starts to laugh. "It was an honor, Mr. Cain. Truly."

"Make it Nick. No one who works with me calls me 'Mister' anything."

Reece draws in a breath that in turn makes him clutch his ribs from where I landed a series of lightning-fast punches when I had him pinned to the mat earlier. "You're kidding?"

"Not at all. We're going to have to discuss travel arrangements, stipend, of course. I assume you don't have an agent?"

And just like that, all the joy washes out of his features. "You mean I can't train up here?"

I cut my eyes over to Oliver. His own shock is evident. Oliver is the one to reply. "That's not normally how it's done, Reece."

"It's just...it's my gran. I need to make arrangements for her. And winters up here, they're not easy."

"I understand, kid." Boy, do I understand what the first bite of winter feels like sinking through your bones when you're unprepared for it. "How about Oliver and I have a discussion, figure out schedules, and then we contact you with the details?"

Relief floods his face. "That would be amazing. Thank you. Thank you so much." He reaches out and shakes my hand. Then he grabs Oliver and slaps him on the back so hard, it wouldn't surprise me if he cracked a bone.

"Ollie, stick around," I order as Reece bounds out of the ring and heads for the locker room. When he's out of earshot, I cock a brow.

"I'm sorry, Nick. I completely forgot about his gran."

"Is she ill?" I'm not worried about the fighter; I know what I can do with Reece London once I get him at Razor. I am truly concerned about the guy's family. Because once Reece becomes mine, I want all of him.

Much like I want Maris. Shoving that thought from my head, I focus on the matter at hand.

Oliver's thoughtful. "Frail. I think if Reece went to her and said he wanted to move, she'd tell him to go. But intuitively he knows he'd lose her."

"Where are his folks?"

"Enjoying mai tais on the beach in Hawaii with mine." Oliver's voice doesn't hold the same bitterness it did when I first met him. Not anymore.

"Christ, and I liked the kid even before I knew that. So, he put his life on hold to watch out for gran and..."

"And then you walked in the door," Oliver concludes. "The question is, what are you going to do?"

I'm about to answer when my phone rings from one of the folding chairs. "Hold that thought."

I duck under the ropes and jump down. I grab it just in time to see Maris's face. I quickly answer. "Hey. What's going on?"

"Despite the no going out to dinner until you finish your email rule, I've been invited over to eat at Brad and Rainey's tonight. Since I'm stopping by the grocery store for a bottle of wine, do you want me to grab anything to drink for you?"

"I should say no since I'm training," I say automatically.

"Nick, have you ever not been in training?"

I laugh. "No."

"Then would you like something to drink?"

"Beer. Whatever Brad drinks. And would you mind picking up a bottle of tequila for Rainey since I crushed hers the last time I was here?"

"I don't know what I'm more offended by."

Uh-oh. I feel like I'm being led into a trap. I ask carefully, "What?"

"That the Jacks got lit together at Jed's funeral and didn't invite me or that Rainey didn't give me the gossip about it."

"Go with number two," I urge her.

"Of course you'd say that. I'm hanging up now."

"Drive safely," I say automatically.

There's a long silence before a soft "Thanks." Then she disconnects the call.

Damn, I really need to finish reading the rest of those emails. I turn around and find Oliver with an arrested expression on his face. "Let's table this until tomorrow. Tell Reece I had personal plans come up and you and I are going to meet in the morning."

Oliver backs away slowly, trepidation on his face. "What time in the morning?"

Stopping only to pick up my tee and shoes, I call over my shoulder, "Whatever time is most inconvenient for you, of course, Oliver."

"You're an ass, Nick," he yells, just as the door closes behind me.

"So I've been told by many," I murmur as I strip down to nothing. Padding over to the shower stall, I turn on the taps and step under the warm water, letting the soap and spray take away my aches for a little while.

I PULL INTO THE MEYERSES' driveway right behind Maris. Immediately, my mind blanks and my dick hardens as she slides from her vehicle in a pair of torn jeans and a shirt that has cutouts exposing both shoulders. My mouth begins watering, and it has nothing to do with the smells emanating from the backyard. "Thank you, sweet Lord, for the inventor of jockstraps" are the first words I manage to get out. Because I know if I'd taken a nut shot today, I'd be paying for it badly right about now. I'm fully erect as her body moves and sways.

Jumping from my borrowed vehicle, I snag my gym bag from the passenger seat and approach her. "Need any help?"

"Hey. Were you working out?" She nods at the bag in my arms. She reaches into the back of her SUV, stretching out, and my heart beats harder than it did when Reece had me up against the ropes. Holy mother of God. I just want to find a spot where we can be alone and I can spend a night exploring that magnificent ass.

"No, I met the guy today." At her quizzical expression, I explain. "The guy I flew up here to meet. Reece London."

To my shock, the buoyant expression on Maris's face disappears. "Is that what this party's for? A goodbye celebration? You're leaving?" Her voice becomes hostile, but there's something else there. Something I've never noticed before because I wasn't listening.

It's hurt.

"Shit. No." I drop the bag to the side. I reach out and clasp the smooth skin of her arms. "Did you really think I would just pick up and leave?"

"Why not? It's not as if you don't have a record for it," she flings at me. "What's so different this time?"

"This." And I yank her into me.

This kiss holds none of the exploratory tenderness of last night and all of the passion. I boost Maris onto her tailgate and step in between her legs so I can press her against my raging hard-on. She nips my lower lip before trying to climb me like a tree. Fuck, I know there's never been a woman I've wanted the way I want her. And after the tastes of her I've had, I'm not certain I'll ever find another.

Maris tears her mouth away, breathing hard.

I bend down until our eyes are level. "You made me a promise— dinner for those emails. Don't think I'm not holding you to it."

"But I thought..."

"That I was going. You made that clear. And I'm telling you now, I may have other plans in mind."

"Like what?" she challenges me.

I bop the tip of her nose with my finger. "Jed always said you were such a pain around the holidays. Couldn't hack a surprise and had to know everything."

"You two...talked about me?"

"Much more than you can imagine," I confirm.

She shifts off the tailgate. Our bodies are in perfect alignment. "If that's the case, then why did he not want us together? Why did he warn me away from you, Nick?" Tears well in her eyes. "Do you realize how much could have been different?"

"I don't. But maybe the answers are waiting for me."

"I hope so. Because I've been searching for them for years, and what I've found isn't good. For either of us."

MARIS

"I'm not sure I can forgive Nick for Vegas, even if I — barely — understand the reasons why. He's got to get his head on straight if it takes a year, five, ten, before he comes around her again." - From the journals of Jedidiah Smith.

"So, you and Nick are behaving..."

"Yes?"

"Like you both have a secret," Rainey accuses. She holds out the spoon she's stirring the beans with and points it at me. "Start talking. What happened?"

"Nothing."

"You are such a liar," she accuses.

More than you could possibly understand. "Honestly, nothing. We talked the other morning after the bar. And came to a mutual decision to leave the past where it belongs. Water under the bridge and whatnot," I protest. "Nick's not all that bad."

Rainey's eyes are practically popping out of her head. "If I repeat this conversation to the girls, they're immediately going to demand to know if you're ill or what medication you're taking." She reaches over the counter and feels my forehead. "Nope. No fever."

I can't prevent the grin that leaps onto my face. "Swear to you, I'm not ill. No drugs either."

"Christ, what the hell happened?" she demands.

The smile fades from my face as I slide onto a barstool. "Honestly?" At her nod, I continue. "I think I grew up. Is it Nick's fault I still had feelings for so long? No," I answer myself before Rainey can.

It's a large part of the truth in any case, even if it's not everything. But I can't betray my brother, nor Nick, by disclosing what I read in Jed's journals. Maybe Brad's shared Nick's past, but it's not mine to. Instead I tell Rainey, "I did a lot of soul-searching. And how much of my behavior was overly aggressive towards him because I was bitter over something that happened years ago? There were no promises between us—implied or otherwise. In other words, I wasted my life and I have no one to blame but myself, but I'm taking the steps to rectify that. Going through the process to foster and then—fingers crossed—adopt David? I feel renewed."

Rainey opens and closes her mouth. Then she simply puts down the spoon she was stirring the beans with before she comes around the counter and envelops me in a huge hug. "You didn't waste your life, Maris." Her words are muffled.

"You're one of my best friends. Of course you have to say that."

"When have you ever known me to mince words?"

My lips curve. "Oh, I'm sure I can think of a time or two."

"Since we formed the Jacks' sisterhood," she challenges me.

"Well, if you're putting those kinds of parameters on it," I tease, "I guess the answer is never."

Releasing me, she goes back and picks up her beer. "Damn straight. Not with Brad, not with the guys, not with any of you." She gives me a mock salute as she takes a pull of her drink.

"Then tell me, oh wise one, what I should do about the fact Nick kissed me?" I'm so glad I waited to ask until she'd just taken a drink when a spray of beer comes flying out of her mouth. I lean forward and rest my chin on my fist. "Hmm?"

"This is the shit you tell me the *minute* you enter the door! You've been here for almost an hour!" Rainey slams her beer on the counter and immediately dashes for her iPad.

Within seconds, my phone rings with an incoming FaceTime request. "Dialing me by mistake?" I drawl.

"Just answer your phone," she grouches.

"Why?" But I do as she asks, knowing exactly who else will be waiting.

I'm not disappointed.

Meadow picks up first, Kara right after. "Uh-oh. I recognize that look on Rainey's face. Someone's about to get it." Meadow immediately begins to laugh.

I try for an angelic expression, but Rainey hisses, "Don't you even dare, Maris Ione Smith."

Kara smothers a laugh. "All three names? What on earth could you have done?"

"She. Kissed. Nick!" Rainey screeches.

Then there's absolute silence. I know Rainey's as confused as I am because she begins to shake her iPad up and down. "For Christ's sake, Rainey. You're in the same room as me and you're making me nauseous with that. Either we lost connection, or you sent them into shock."

Rainey stops immediately, becoming concerned. "And Kara's pregnant? God, I didn't even think of that."

I roll my eyes. And that's when I hear it.

Applause.

It's slow and steady, but it comes through my phone and Rainey's iPad a little off sync. I immediately glance down to see which one of our friends is being the smart-ass only to get the shock of my life.

Meadow's on her feet applauding. Kara, on mute, has her hand out to Jennings. He's slapping a twenty into it with a rueful smile before he disappears from screen. Then she too begins to cheer. "It's about damn time!"

"Did I enter a time warp where Nick's head hasn't firmly been planted up his ass?" Rainey asks, confused.

Meadow, Kara, and I all answer, "No," simultaneously. But even as we're all giggling, Kara poses a question that has us all sucking in a breath. "Why did Jed leave Nick his cross? Knowing what Nick and Maris had been through? There had to be a reason. The symbolism of

126

that meant too much. After I was able to look at things analytically, then I was able to add one and one together."

"And Jennings gave you the correct answer." I glare at my best friend. Out of the corner of my eye, Rainey glances away on-screen. There's my confirmation; I can only presume she knows as well.

"No. He wouldn't share those kinds of confidences with me. You should know that," Kara chastises me. I blush to the roots of my hair, because I do. These men consider each other brothers for a reason. "All he did was confirm Nick's been searching for a way to pierce the barrier between you both. Seems like he found it."

I open my mouth, and nothing comes out because how much has really been said between me and Nick versus how much do I know? He broke through some of my barriers because he finally read about the past. That shocked him, that bite of mortality. It made him realize the world was still going to spin around whether he was a part of it or not. But, "It's not quite what you're thinking, Kara. He hasn't shared with me. It's been one-sided."

"Shit," Rainey mutters.

"Damn. And here I was hoping..." Kara says softly.

"Everything I know about Nick, from Nick, is exactly the same. So, Rainey's shock is valid and genuine. I don't know why I kissed him the first time. Or why I let him kiss me the second." I slide off the stool and begin to prowl around the room with my phone in hand. "There's something different. I know it. But can I trust it?"

"I think if you don't give it a try, you'll always wonder," Meadow interjects.

"The thing is, he's going to leave." I can't prevent the crack in my voice.

Rainey lays a hand on my shoulder. "Would you rather a day, a night, or more with Nick or longer with someone else if you knew they would stay?" I open my mouth to answer, but she puts her finger against my lips. "We're not the ones you have to answer, babe."

"Maris?" I whip my head around to find Kara staring at me intently. "You asked me a question. Do you remember what it was?"

My mind whips back to those dark days after Jed and Dean died. She'd just told me about kissing Jennings for the first time since leaving

Alaska the first time, and I asked her, *"Did you ever really get over what you felt for Jennings?"* I swallow convulsively. "I remember."

"Back at you. Did you?" Even amid close friends, it's still possible to have a covert conversation with your best friend.

"I tried," I repeat her words back at her. "God knows, I tried." I certainly didn't live like a nun all these years even if I didn't find a man who I trusted with my heart.

"Don't avoid the question the way I did that night. Pretend you don't give this a chance. What will you feel if he leaves and you don't, Maris?" Kara fires off her question.

And the answer is simple. "I'm not the same person I was then. So, I won't be the same person when it happens. I have no doubt I'm going to be hurt when he leaves. But—"

"But what?" Meadow prods.

"But I'm stronger for everything I've been through. I don't back away from fights. They're just an obstacle to get around. But if I'm going to lose him, I refuse to lose myself in the process."

Rainey's wiping tears away from her eyes. "I'm kicking his ass the first chance I have."

And I laugh, truly laugh, for the first time in a while. "You'll break something with the first punch."

"He'll know I'm serious, damnit!" she yells before wrapping her arm around my waist and squeezing.

Soon, the four of us are a mess of sniffles and tears. Rainey and I are in desperate need of mascara repair when the back door slams open. Nick calls out, "Hey, Rainey, Maris? Brad asked me to check on the beans. He said we're just about ready..." His voice trails off when he takes in our appearance. In an ice-cold tone, he demands, "Who do I need to kill?"

Then he practically jumps out of his skin when from multiple directions, "Hi, Nick!" and "Hey, Nick!" are shouted at him. Taking pity on him, I let Rainey go and move toward him. "No one, Champ. We were having a chat with Meadow and Kara."

Nick rubs a thumb over the apple of my cheek. "You've been crying," he accuses.

"Not all crying is a bad thing, Nick. Sometimes it's cathartic." My hand wraps around his wrist.

"Are you sure?"

"Yep. I'm—we're—fine."

"Okay. Well, if that's the case, I think Brad might eat the kids soon. He's debating if he can slather them with ketchup and mustard."

I chuckle at the imagery. "Tell him just a few more minutes. If you were this upset over a few tears, imagine how Brad would feel if he saw Rainey." Like my words release her from some magic spell, Rainey drops her iPad and dashes for the stairs. "See?"

He nods, a frown still marring his perfect face. I place a hand on his chest. "I'm fine. I promise."

"I'm adding it to our list of things to talk about," he warns.

"All right."

"Just that simple?" he asks, wonderment in his voice.

"It is with me." I spread my arms and twirl in a small circle. "I'm a simple girl, Nick. What you see is what you get."

When I face him again, the heat from his eyes blasts me. But he doesn't say more than a simple "We'll finish this later, Maris." And I don't know if that's a reminder or a warning.

I'm about to head upstairs to borrow a makeup wipe from Rainey when I hear explosive laughter from my phone and Rainey's iPad. Oh. Shit. "You didn't hang up?" I yell as I run and snatch up my cell.

"And miss the inferno? No. Jennings, be a love and go get me some water," Kara calls out.

"Kody, I need a drink. Strong. No, I don't care what it is!" Meadow yells.

Mortification suffocates me for about half a second before I admit, "Hell, so do I, Meadow, but I drove."

"Well, that was a tactical error." The three of us are cackling when Rainey comes down the stairs. In her hands—bless her—is a makeup wipe.

"I figured if Nick already saw you like that, you didn't need a full... why are you all laughing so hard?" she demands.

Dinner is delayed again during the retelling of what just happened.

Rainey's knees give out where she stands, unable to speak. She just points at me and gapes like a fish. Thankfully, the next time there's a scout that comes in to check on the delay of the beans, it's Brad who walks in the door. Otherwise, we might still be trying to find our sea legs.

But as someone who knows the difference between the two, I'm so glad I lost them due to laughter instead of pain.

MARIS

September

"Growing up by the sea, fishing has been a part of my everyday life. I just never gave any thought to the fish they caught until I watched the hope drain out of my sister's eyes. Now instead of animated, they're dead like the fish. What can I do?" - From the journals of Jedidiah Smith.

"Smith's Brewhouse. This is Maris. How can I help you?" I answer the phone on the headset. I'm standing on a ladder taking inventory in between the lunch and dinner crowd. Muttering to myself, I wonder, "How many toothpicks can humans go through? I just reordered these," as I place another order.

"Hello, Maris, it's Rona Gustofson."

And I immediately fumble my iPad to the ground. Thank goodness I sprung for the industrial cover. "Hi, Mrs. G. How have you been?"

"Lovely, dear. And yourself?"

I swallow my panic and try to replicate her calm demeanor. "Well, thank you. I got to spend some time with some friends over the weekend—including the Lis."

"That's good. I'm glad you're so close. It helps to have another foster family to guide you through the process. I wanted to let you know I have to come by to do some additional checks for the home study."

"You do? I mean, not that I mind, but can I ask why?"

"Of course. In this case, I'm glad you did. Based on your home's registered floor plan, there should be additional outlets. I need to validate those aren't a fire hazard."

I frown in confusion as I brace myself against the ladder. "Not to question you, Mrs. G., but I'm pretty certain you checked all of the outlets." And the extinguishers. And the distance of the toilets from the sinks. And a whole list of other things that made me wonder if I was going to have to bribe Kody to renovate my home if I don't pass inspection.

"Yes, I did. But I didn't test the ones behind your wall unit. And when I was talking with my supervisor, he asked if the unit can be moved. It can, can't it?"

Oh, holy hell. I rub my hand across my head. "Yes, ma'am, it sure can."

"Wonderful! Would tomorrow afternoon be too soon to come back out?"

"No, it wouldn't." Like I'm going to say no in any case.

"Then I'll shoot you a formal email in just a few moments. Thank you for being so understanding, Maris. In the end, it's making certain children are put into safe and secure homes."

"I look forward to it." After we say our goodbyes, I add, "And I look forward to the herniated disc I'll have as a result of moving that beast." I'm pretty certain it hasn't been moved since it was installed. I think I was seventeen.

Just then, a text message pops up from Nick. *You owe me dinner.*

My thumbs fly over the keyboard. *I'm impressed. I thought I had a few more days, at least.*

Nope. Now put up.

Selfish, selfish man.

I didn't say I was going to make you pay. Come on, Maris. Let's get some food and have a real date.

Physical or emotional pain? I'd rather scar my soul than move that media unit. So, it's with real regret I type, *I can't. I have to move the TV console in my living room before tomorrow.*

Why the hell are you trying to move the brown beast? That thing might be holding up the second floor of your house.

A wide grin splits my face. Jed dubbed the media unit the brown beast the day he and the Jacks wrangled it inside for my father. And then a lightbulb goes off in my head. Furiously, my fingers begin to type.

I'll buy you dinner wherever you want if you move it for me.

That's a hell of an incentive. Have a whole night to do nothing but spend time with you or risk permanent injury. Let me think...deal. When do you need me there?

Two hours?

See you then.

It's going to be worth whatever hell I pay later to get that thing moved.

A FEW HOURS LATER, Nick shows up with Brad in tow. From where I stand propped in the doorway, I watch the two goofballs do warm-up exercises. "You better not pull a hammie," Nick taunts Brad.

Brad throws him the middle finger as he reaches into his back pocket for a red, white, and blue bandanna that he ties around his forehead like he's a ninja warrior. Nick rolls his eyes before he reaches for a red-and-white one to tie around his own head.

Oh. My. God. The Great Alaskan Lumberjacks. They haven't grown up. I begin to laugh so hard, I can't breathe. "There's no way you two are entering my house without my getting a picture of this testosterone-laden debacle to share with the others." I fumble in my jeans pocket for my phone.

Brad strikes a pose that would do any superhero proud, and Nick? He's the grown-up version of himself, glaring at my cell phone camera. "Could you try for a smile, Mr. Grumpy Pants?" I taunt him, much the same way I did when we were all young.

"No, I can't," Nick grouses. His hand moves to swipe the bandanna off his head. Brad reaches over and slaps it down. Nick's face grows more irritated by the second.

"Fine." I take the shot—which is just perfect as it is. For as long as any of us have known him, Nick has been a pain in the ass about having his photo taken. When I press the button to replay the shots, I collapse against the jamb.

In shock.

Because for half of the pictures, Nick's scowling like normal. The rest? He's smirking at Brad like he's trying to hold back huge guffaws of laughter. "How did we miss this? Is this what you've always done?"

"What?" Nick steps up to the door and plucks my phone from my hands.

"Don't you dare delete those photos," I warn him.

With nothing more than a "Hmm," he flips through them. Handing me my phone back, he leans down to whisper in my ear, his lips brushing against the rim so lightly they send tingles down my spine. "Only when you were taking the shot." Then he slips past me inside the house where the dreaded wall unit awaits.

"The things you find out with modern technology," I murmur.

"Did you say something, Maris?" Brad comes bounding up.

"Nothing. You know where the beast is." I wave him up toward the family room.

"Yeah, I remember the three days of bed rest I needed with Rainey waiting on me the last time I moved it. Of course, she was in the bed with me."

I grin as I close the door and follow Brad up the stairs. Some things never change.

In the time since I got home from the Brewhouse, I've emptied the shelves of everything and piled it on top of my guest room bed. I haven't wiped down the unit because I didn't want to make it slippery when we might need to get a better grip. As Brad and Nick are slipping on gloves, I snatch up a pair I found in the garage. "Where do you need me?"

"Safely out of the way," Nick tells me. Brad agrees wholeheartedly.

"Wrong answer, guys. Even though I'm smart enough to ask for help, I can still remove shelves to reduce the weight."

Both men look appropriately chastised, then slightly embarrassed. "Well, shit, Nick. Think we should have done that when we moved the beast in all those years ago?" Brad muses.

"Might have taken a good twenty pounds off," Nick agrees. Hooking an arm around my neck, he plants a kiss on my forehead. "Sorry, Maris."

"For both of you thinking with your male egos again? You're forgiven." My voice is pure honey.

All of us laugh as the guys start to reach for the shelves. I carefully lay them down on towels set on the dining room table after numbering the rough edge so I know what order they have to go back in. I smile when I hear the guys mutter between themselves about how much lighter the unit feels as they ease it from the wall.

Then Nick's voice freezes me in place.

"Hey, Brad. Don't go any further. There's a book or something wedged behind this damn thing on my side. I don't want it to drop down; I can almost reach it."

I whirl around just as Nick pulls out a leather-bound journal triumphantly, familiar like the other volumes I've been reading. Somehow my legs manage to sustain my weight as I make my way across the room. "Give me that!"

I can't even register the shock on Nick's face as I snatch it from his hands. I immediately flip to the first page to see the opening line.

Maris,

I hope like hell you've rid the house of the beast and found this journal first. Because I shudder to imagine what you're thinking otherwise. Give me a chance to explain before you rush off to tell our friends everything. And please let me apologize...

I slam the book closed. God. Jed expected me to find them eventually. The world begins to spin crazily.

"Maris? Are you all right?" Nick bends down until his dark eyes are in line with my own.

"I...I don't know."

"Do you want to tell me what's in that book?" His eyes don't leave mine as they ask.

"No," I tell him honestly. His eyes narrow. "But I'm going to have to."

As Nick and Brad move the TV unit, I make my way out into the sunroom and reread my brother's words from the start.

Maris,

I hope like hell you've rid the house of the beast and found this journal first. Because I shudder to imagine what you're thinking otherwise. Give me a chance to explain before you rush off to tell our friends everything. And please let me apologize because I should have told you a long time ago about so many things, but I was afraid if you knew you'd never trust me the same way again.

You were in such pain, my Sunshine. Not just physical, even though that was intense, but I swear the emotional became worse as the days passed. You elected to remain perpetually stoned after having learned you would never be able to carry a child of your own due to a condition passed along genetically — that damned Unicorn Uterus.

Why the hell did it have to be a unicorn? They're supposed to be magic? In the worst of your nightmares the week we were in Fairbanks, you'd ask me that over and over. And each and every time, I felt powerless for not having an answer.

But then a man named Dean called. I had no idea who he was. I almost hung up on him, thinking he was just another guy who had a crush on my beautiful baby sister, but suddenly there was a spark of life in you I hadn't seen since before the accident. You wouldn't let me hang up on him. Do you remember any of this? You tried to sit up in bed, demanding to take the call. God, despite the IVs attached to you, the catheter, and drainage tubes, you practically crawled out of the bed to rip that phone from my hands.

It never got that far, but I handed it over not knowing what was going to happen, Sunshine. Even now, I'm not sure if it was the best or worst thing. For both of us.

Through your own agony, you selflessly stayed on the phone for hours and gave everything inside your heart to Kara as Kevin was born. Tears were pouring down your face so hard I used an entire box of crappy hospital tissues wiping them up. Though it was faint because that phone was practically glued to your ear, I too got to hear Kevin's first cry.

It was the second most beautiful sound in the world. The first being the words from the surgeon to me, Mom and Dad telling us you were going to live. But I'm certain I'll never be prouder of anyone. Ever. Because when it was over you hung up the phone, pushed the button for your pain meds, and never said a single word to me about it.

You kept Kara's secret, Maris. And until your dying day, I know you would have. But it was my everlasting hell to know it in conjunction to know the way John — Jennings — grew up. Much like how I was trusted by Brad about the circumstances about him and Rainey. His love for her is everlasting even with a rocky start; it has been from the moment they met at Juneau-Douglas. But neither of them was ready.

Kody will always love Meadow from afar. That's not going to ever change. His heart is just content on the rare occasion he gets to see her. I swear, all these years later, the earth still shifts when they're in the same room together. If only they were free to act upon it...I hold so much guilt where they're concerned as well.

As for Kara and Jennings, well, now that I'm married to Dean I'm trying my damnedest to wear her down. And if the battle I just went through at the lawyer's office today is anything to go by, it may be well after I'm gone, but it will happen. Someday. Sooner if we're all lucky. If she would just allow him to meet his son face-to-face, I know what would happen. But Kara's a stubborn thing, though. Jennings isn't the same man he was, but neither is she the same woman. In other words, they're perfect for each other. Still. I can hardly wait until the two of them are breathing the same air. It's going to change the world as we know it.

And then there's Nick. He's not the same fool idiot who hurt your heart, Maris. He's grown up fighting his own self-image which is wholly negative. Do you remember when we were visiting the Chihuly Museum in Seattle? You said one of the pieces reminded you of Nick. I asked why and you said, "It's fierce, fluid, delicate — despite arguments to the contrary, accessible yet untouchable." Then you walked away with disappointment in your eyes because you couldn't afford to buy the piece of art that so reminded you of the man you love.

So, unless you're doing something awful like remodeling my room – and I can't imagine why you would be – you should find this journal first. The rest are hidden under boxes of mementos in my closet that I know you've stayed far away from because there's memories in there you're not ready to confront. I chose to bring them back from Florida because as Kevin is getting older, I didn't want to run the risk of him coming across them and finding out about his father before his parents had the chance to tell him.

These journals were my only way to let out my inner thoughts, my rage, at not being able to do more — be more — for my friends. Too many times, I let out my rage and often my sadness. Far too often, I was helpless instead of insightful. The words in the other journals were my venting and not how I truly felt about the men and women who I do consider my family — especially you.

Those words were written by a brother, a friend, a man who knew things and couldn't share the truths he knew with the people who would benefit from them the most.

Because would the truth have made Meadow divorce her husband?

Would they have given Brad and Rainey their firstborn baby back?

Could they convince Kara to please, for the love of all that's holy, let me tell Jennings he has a son?

Maybe they would make Nick engage more because he would know for certain he's loved by all of us no matter how he grew up.

But if I could choose one, it would be to give you another horn, because you are magical. To me, you always have been. From the first moment I held you.

I love you, Maris. My everlasting sunshine.

Love,

Jed.

PS - All the way against the wall in the back corner under my bed is a box for you. Did you think I would leave it there when it's been yours since the moment you saw it?

I flip the rest of the pages. They're all blank. I close my eyes as the tears begin to run hotly down my cheeks. I have it. My answer. Finally, it's all clear. "God, Jed. I love you too."

Then, still clutching the journal, I race out of the sunroom. I race past Brad and Nick, who've just entered the kitchen. "What the..." I hear Nick say, but I don't acknowledge him.

Making more sound than a herd of elephants, I climb the stairs as quickly as I can. I race down the hall to Jed's room and fling the door open. His bed is pushed in the corner, under two windows. When I cleaned out his room, I never pulled the bed away from the wall since it was too heavy. Tossing the journal on the dresser, I whirl around and smack right into Nick.

"Tell me what it is," he demands.

My hand raises until I cup his cheek. He turns his face and nuzzles the palm. "Completely touchable," I whisper.

"Hmm?"

"Never mind. I'll explain later. Right now, I need to move Jed's bed."

"This was Jed's room? I forgot what it looked like. Maybe because it's clean." His head swivels from side to side, taking it in.

I nod. "You're right, it's clean. But he...I need...there's something..."

Nick lays his hand on the back of my neck and pulls me close enough to put his lips on my forehead. "Just tell me what to do."

"Can you pull it out? There's supposed to be a box in the corner closest near the wall." I can barely get the words out.

He nods. Moving past me, he shifts the end table aside and jerks the frame. The rustic log headboard drags along the carpet a few inches. Nick tugs again and again. "Do you see it?"

I jump on top of the mattress, and there it is, covered with a layer of dust. I carefully pull it out.

Before I can open it, Nick shoves the bed with me on it back into place. Dropping down next to me, he nods. "Do you know what it is?"

I whisper, "Yes." I'm surprised I can get anything out over the pounding in my heart.

"What is it?"

My eyes rise from the dust-covered box to meet his, dark and full of secrets. Right now, before I open the box, I make myself a promise that I'll tell him what I know. I lift the lid, and the smoky bowl of beautiful Chihuly glass is exposed. Nick sharply inhales over the sheer beauty of what's carefully wrapped inside.

I reach for Nick's hand and lace my fingers through them. "He left me something to remind me of you."

Then, still cautious about the beautiful treasure Jed left me, I lean over and whisper my lips over Nick's stunned ones.

NICHOLAS

"What do you mean, he left you something that reminds you of me?" I demand once we're downstairs.

"Patience, Nick. Patience," Maris teases as she moves around the kitchen, spinning around here and there, grabbing spices from one cabinet, then food from the fridge in a dance so graceful it reminds me of the Whirling Dervishes.

In the hour or so since Brad left and the beast is far enough away from the wall so the home inspector can get to the outlets behind it, Maris has transformed. Gone is the woman carrying the weight of the world on her shoulders, and in her place is a combination of the vixen I first fell for all those years ago mixed with the woman whose life has experienced enormous upheaval and survived. There's a flush riding her cheeks, and her eyes are twinkling even as she's concentrating.

"That's not what I said," I mumble. In fact, it's the furthest thing from the truth. I lost my chance. Didn't I?

Maris stops plants her feet in place so fast her hair floats down to her shoulders. "Let me fix dinner, and then I'll start from the beginning."

Intrigued at the idea of Maris cooking, I hike up onto one of the barstools. "What are you making?"

"Meatloaf."

Just her saying the word sets my salivary glands in overdrive. "Your mom's recipe?"

"Is there any other way?" Maris turns to the refrigerator and grabs milk, eggs, ketchup, parsley, and the beef.

"Did you know I used to ask your mother to run away with me when she would make this? Of course, I had the poor taste to do so when your father would be in the room. I think that's when I learned to start fighting." My lips twitch at the memories as I spy the familiar ingredients gathering on the counter.

"Nick, if you ever asked me to be with you, it'd better not be because I'm catering to your stomach. It's going to be because you can't wait another minute to have me." My head snaps up, but she spins so I can't read her face. "Now unless you want me to screw this up, keep quiet for a moment while I measure the ingredients out."

"Yes, ma'am." And because this is one of my favorite meals of all time and the woman who is the epitome of every wish I've ever had is making it, I do as she asks while Maris molds the meat on the pan.

But as soon as she's done wiping her hands, I'm out of my seat. Caging her against the sink, I lean down. "Now, explain."

She lays her head against my heart. "You're going to have questions."

"That's a given."

"Head into the sunroom. I'll meet you in there with the last two pieces of the puzzle I've been missing. After all, it's due to you I now have them."

Because of me? Even though her words don't make sense, I do as she asks.

"This sunroom is probably my favorite room in the house. I imagine it must be like living inside a storm in the winter," I muse aloud.

"Exactly that." I turn when Maris comes in behind me with the dusty box we pulled from under Jed's bed and the leather-bound book we found behind the console. "You asked me what did I mean by Jed leaving me something that reminds you of me. He also gave you back to me."

"How?"

"It turns out the things we don't say to each other has as much impact as the things we do." Silence lies heavy between us as I grapple with the meaning behind her words. Then she continues. "Despite how it may have appeared, I missed you, Nick—the Nick I knew who I spent summers getting to know just a few yards from here." She nods her head out the glass windows.

"I missed you too. Every day." Regret fills my voice.

Maris smiles, but it doesn't reach her eyes. I cross my arms over my chest to hide the fisting of my hands out of sheer nerves. Somehow I know that the secrets she's about to share with me are about to change us both in ways we'll never be able to come back from. And I'd be lying if a part of me doesn't want her to hold them to herself. Her eyes drift downward, so I can only see the fragile lids when she starts talking. "When you left, I resented you didn't keep your promise to keep in touch because even if you didn't feel the same way about me that I felt about you, I thought we were friends." Maris's eyes flick up at me before drifting out the window, but not before I catch a glimpse of the depth of pain. Pain I would take away if I could. And I can't help but feel guilt because her pain was an indirect result of my carelessness with my friends.

"It took a long time for me to realize I deserved better than that." Her chin lifts pugnaciously.

"You did. You do," I assure her.

"Consciously, yes. I know that. Subconsciously, some part of me didn't believe that. Otherwise I would have avoided a man like Carter Jones that night in the bar."

"Is that the man...?"

She nods. "I paid a great price for my pride, Nick."

"There's no price too high to pay for pride," I defend her, stepping closer. But as I do, I notice her eyes are wet.

"Oh, but there can be. Yes, Nick, there truly can be. Anyway." She presses the box and the leather journal in my hand. "You've done a lot of reading lately. But do you remember my saying I've been searching for the answers and I couldn't find them?"

"Yes," I whisper hoarsely.

"Tonight you helped me find the key. For so long, I felt lost, alone. I thought I lost my brother in the most basic of ways. And tonight, you gave him back to me. After reading this, you might understand why. The rest of the journals I found, that he references, are over there." I follow the line of Maris's arm to a bookcase. "If you want to read them, go ahead. They're in chronological order." She starts to leave the room.

Hastily putting the items down on a chair, I follow her. "Where are you going?"

"I have some work to do before dinner. I'll be in my office upstairs." Maris walks back toward me. As the sunroom is down a step, our faces are perfectly aligned. She leans forward and brushes a kiss across my cheek. "Please read what I gave you first. I can't have you lose Jed the way I did." Then she turns and walks away.

I follow her movement until she's out of sight. Then I lift the box onto my lap. Opening the journal, I begin to read. And almost immediately the burn of tears hits the back of my eyes. And as I continue to read Jed's love letter to Maris, they fall silently down my face.

Carefully, I lift the dusty box cover and find the intricately blown glass bowl that reminded Maris of me. Smoky gray, reflective mirror, and obsidian. It's masculine and hard on the outside with a soft center. I have to slide it to the floor before my shaking hands drop the priceless treasure—priceless not because of who made it, but because of the love of a sibling who likely went well into hock to buy it for his beloved sister. "Jed, you're fucking lucky you're not here. I'd probably crush you half to death with the hug I want to give you, you bastard. We miss you so damn much." My voice crumbles on the last few words.

I care nothing for the fact that Maris knows about my past or of diving into the secrets the Jacks may have kept from one another but entrusted to Jed. I have an overwhelming need to find the man who ran Maris off the road and to punch him until he's a bloody mess missing a few critical body parts of his own. I want him to be weeping for something he always dreamed of having and will be permanently denied. I want him to suffer while others are smiling. I want him to feel an ounce of the pain Maris has held inside her all of this time. And then I want to do it again.

But as much as I want to do that, there's something else I need to do more. I reach my hands behind my neck and unfasten the cross Jed left me. Because he did more than give me faith. He led me to something much more precious.

Maris.

And this belongs to her. Now, it's time to give it to her.

I place the journal on the shelf with the rest. "I don't need to read these. She can tell me what she wants me to know. And to be honest, if the guys want me to know their shit, they can let me in. That's their right—and hers." Then I leave the sunroom in search of the woman who has always held my heart even when I didn't think it was worth anything.

Apparently she's always thought differently.

My footfalls make creaks up the stairs. There's clicking from the computer keyboard guiding me to her. My heart rate increases as I get closer. When I get closer, the clicking slows down, but not my heart. If anything, it speeds up more. I clench my fingers around the gold chain, careful not to squeeze the cross too tightly.

As I reach the doorway, Maris surges to her feet. "That was awfully quick."

"I read what I needed to, Sunshine. And I came to a startling conclusion."

Maris thrusts her hip out, and her hands go akimbo. "Oh? Really? I agonized over those journals for the better part of a year, hating myself for judging you, and after just a few minutes you're done? So do share. Your conclusion is?" The bite in her voice, the scrappy fighter who's struggled to her feet despite having fallen, makes what I'm about to do so right.

Maris needs to find the faith in herself so much more than I do.

I lift my hand and let the gold unfurl from my hands. Maris's gasp is loud enough it might be heard in downtown Juneau. "Jed was right. I needed to have more faith in the people who loved me. Now it's your turn to do the same." I step forward and clasp the chain around her neck.

"No, Nick. He meant for you to have this," she protests. Her hands start to move, but I trap them beneath mine.

"And I believe it belongs to a woman with more strength and courage in her heart than any fighter, than any person—including her brother. Including me in the darkest days when I wondered if my mother was coming back for me."

"That's not true." Maris shakes her head adamantly.

"It takes a strong woman to have dreams. It takes a brave one to celebrate her dying ones with the people she loves," I whisper.

Maris lets out a small wounded noise. Her head drops in defeat.

I slip my arms around her and pull her close. For a long time, we stand like that until an annoying *beep-beep* goes off in the room. "What the hell is that?" I demand.

Maris pulls out of my arms to reach for her cell phone. It feels so wrong to let her go but so right for the glint of gold to be at her throat. "Dinner's ready. And you know the rules, Nick. Whoever cooks..." Her luminous face breaks into a wobbly smile.

"Doesn't clean. I remember." Looping an arm around her, I tug her forward for a smacking kiss. "Come on, Sunshine. Let's go eat."

"Okay." But as I turn to make my way toward the door, she hasn't moved. When I turn around, I find her fiddling with her grandfather's cross. "Nick? Are you sure? Jed wanted you to have this." Uncertainty clouds her magnificent eyes.

"I'm certain." My voice is strong. There's only one thing I've ever been more certain about and that's how much I regret hurting her. But somehow I'll make that up to her as well.

Carefully, Maris tucks it inside her shirt. She visibly shudders.

"What is it?" My voice is frantic.

"I've felt like I've been drifting since Jed died. For the first time, I feel like I have an anchor. At least for a little while."

I go to open my mouth to assure her I'll always be here for her, but Maris waves a hand. "It's silly, I know. You're going to be leaving soon. But thank you, Nick. I'm glad the acrimony is gone between us, if nothing else." And like a wraith, she slides past me into the hall. Her feet make a light dance on the stairs as she makes her way into the kitchen.

And I stand in her office and think for long moments about leaving.

And suddenly dinner doesn't sound so appealing.

MARIS

"My father gave me my grandfather's cross for graduation with the understanding I would leave it to Maris should something happen to me. 'Your grandfather believed in two things, Jed. Family and faith,' my father told me. Tonight, I did something. I broke my father's trust because someone else needs those things more. I just hope he forgives me." - From the journals of Jedidiah Smith.

"He gave you Jed's cross?" Kara gasps.

I lift the chain out of my shirt and show it to her. It's a few days after we had dinner at my house, and I haven't heard a word from Nick, but I know he's still in Juneau. He's been training the fighter he came here to work with. I figure it's only a matter of time until he comes by to tell me he's heading back to Albuquerque, but I'm finally at peace with my relationship with him. No, that's a lie, but what am I supposed to do? I'm finally starting to build a life here, and he's made a successful one there. "There are things I need to share with you. I'm terrified of what you're going to say."

Kara's quiet. When she speaks, her words freeze my blood. "After I returned from Juneau, I received a letter from Dean's lawyer. In the

147

package, there was a posthumous message from Jed. He told me every-thing, Maris—including the fact you didn't remember."

"Oh, God. Kara. I'm so sorry. I broke your trust. How can you ever forgive me?"

"What I want to know is how on earth could you think I would hold something like that against you?"

There's silence on both ends of the line until I whisper, "Excuse me?"

"You were strung out on pain meds from just having surgery. You had just been told you couldn't ever have children and somehow, *somehow* managed to stay on the phone with me while I gave birth to your godchild. You didn't bow or break until after you knew I made it through. And still you're worried about me? What did that do to you?" By the end she's yelling and crying.

"Held that in a while, did you?" I joke through my tears.

"Damn you, Maris, this isn't funny. If I thought for a moment it would have hurt you the way it did, I never would have asked Dean to make that call."

"And I would have been devastated even more if you hadn't. Hearing Kevin cry for the first time is one of the most cherished memories I have. It was as if I was in that room with you, helping push that baby out. I may never have the physical experience, but because of you I have the emotional one." And as I say the words, I know it's the truth.

"You're going to be an amazing mother, Maris." Kara sniffles.

Just as I'm feeling the glow of her words trickle over me, she throws a bucket of water over me. "By the way, Jennings wants you to know that he loves you. And he got over being irritated with Jed a long time ago."

My breath catches. "Oh God, Kara. Tell him, I'm..."

"Maris, it's...not...your...fault. None of this was. You were the strongest friend you could be. And in the end, where did we all end up?"

"Together," I whisper.

"Exactly. Do you think your brother isn't looking down at us with a smug-ass smile on his face?"

I giggle. "No. I think he looks like a serial killer because he's smiling so big."

Kara laughs so hard on the other end of the line, the pieces of my soul ease back into place. "I love you, Kara."

"I love you too, Maris. But you're still not getting the poster back." And on that note, she hangs up the phone.

So it's with a huge smile I toss my cell down on my desk. Less than three seconds later, it rings again. This time, it's Rainey.

"Hey. What's up?"

I barely get the question out before she starts ranting. "You have to get him out of my house. I can't keep these hours anymore. The imps of Satan are starting to keep them."

"Whoa. Slow down. What are you talking about?"

"Nick! He's up at five every. Single. Day. What kind of psychopath goes running at that hour? Now the demons I spawned are doing jumping jacks at that hour. Do you know what I'm normally doing at that hour?"

"Your husband?" I guess. Reaching for the bottle of water on my desk, I take a drink.

Big. Mistake.

"Yes!" she yells. I spit my water everywhere. "What I am not doing is running a boot camp. If Nick wants to take that on, he can take them into the backyard and we can stop being quiet while getting in some NC-17 time."

"Rainey, you just rated your sex according to movies," I feel the need to point out as I wipe off the papers on my desk with a stack of tissues.

"Watch enough cartoons and you will too."

"I look forward to that day," I tell her honestly.

"Oh, honey. I know you do, but before you do, save me from Nick. Please. I'll do anything."

I pause. "Anything?"

"An-y-thing." She draws out the word.

"I'm holding you to that."

"Wait, I was just calling to bitch. Are you serious?" There's such hope in her voice I hate to be cruel and remind her of the agreement we just struck.

"Just remember this when tax season rolls around again next year," I say sweetly.

"Now wait, Maris..."

"You did say anything." I emphasize the word exactly like she did.

"Damn, I did. Well, Brad's going to have someone in the office by then."

I don't delude her of her fantasy. "Where's Nick at now?"

Rainey rattles off the name of the gym. "He's working with the guy Reece and another guy from the camp in New Mexico who is staying somewhere other than my house. Why Nick couldn't do that—"

"Because likely your husband invited him," I interrupt.

There's a silence before, "I'm going to kill him."

"Who? Nick or Brad. Because if you're killing Brad, then the point of my going to talk to Nick is kind of fruitless, isn't it?" I point out.

"True. Nick could become a source of income. No, I'll be creative on how I kill Brad."

"Hanging up now," I tell her before I do just that. Reaching in my desk, I grab my purse and keys. I jog down the stairs and out to my vehicle.

A few minutes later, I pull up to the gym next to Rainey's Subaru and a rental. "Surprised the place isn't mobbed with fans." But as I get closer, I glimpse a sign that reads, "Gym under construction until further notice. Contact management for hours of operation."

I pull at the door and find it locked. Smart man, Nick. I pull out my cell and begin to dial his number when a man at least ten years my junior unlocks the door. He's shirtless with taped hands, and his eyes widen before he apologizes. "I'm sorry, but the gym's closed for construction." He gives me a head-to-toe perusal and swallows hard.

I bite my lower lip to contain my laughter. "Well, since Nick showed me the picture of Reece the other morning when we had breakfast, you must be the guy who works for him."

"You know about...wait. Who are you?" The guy tries to look intimidating, but his boyish good looks don't quite pull it off.

"Maris Smith. And you are?" I hold out my hand.

"Oh shit." He immediately pushes open the door.

I make a sympathetic sound. "You poor thing."

"Why's that, Maris? I mean Ms. Smith?" He stumbles over his words.

"Parents naming you 'Oh Shit'? Probably got into MMA to beat the crap out of people growing up," I ask, tongue in cheek.

"No wonder he's loopy over you," the blond Adonis murmurs. Then louder, "Oliver Drake, and it's a pleasure to meet you, Ms. Smith."

I shake his hand. "Make it Maris."

"Did you just pop by to watch?"

"Actually I..." But as soon as I start to speak, my voice drifts off as what my eyes are seeing in front of me connects with the synapses in my brain. My legs start to tremble, and my nipples start to harden.

Nick's in the ring.

After a few high power kicks from each of them, Nick's got Reece up against the ropes with a hard left hook and a kick right down the middle. Reece doesn't take this for long before he spins Nick around and tries to get a knee up to his head, but Nick hooks his other leg around him, trying to take him to the mat.

Intellectually, I'm surprised Nick is going this route. He's always been a take his opponent down and out kind of fighter, but the glimpse of Reece's stats the other day makes me understand why. Nick is trying to get the kid to have a more well-rounded fight strategy, and if it took me all of twelve seconds to recognize his weakness, it will take a professional camp less than that. It takes him a few, and a good elbow, but Nick finally takes him to the mat.

As they grapple, I grip the back of the chair in front of me, unable to stand on my own. My breath is coming out in short pants as Nick taunts the younger man with slaps, not really hurting him even though he could. He's trying to find the fire, the passion within him.

God knows he's found it within me.

I'm trembling as Nick lands shot after shot, before the man next to me lets out a piercing whistle. "Okay. Reece, he'd have crushed you if he was trying. Let's work on your ground game."

Nick immediately sits back and slaps the other man on his shoulder. Then his eyes meet mine, and time freezes. "Ollie, you didn't mention we had an audience."

"And as I was about to say." I can hear the eye roll in Oliver's voice. "Nick, you have company."

Even before Oliver can finish the sentence, Nick is slipping through the ropes. "Sunshine, what are you doing here? Is everything okay?"

I shake my head.

Nick lifts a hand to push a strand of hair back. "What is it?"

I open and close my mouth, but no words come out.

Cursing, Nick grabs my hand. "Come with me." Turning he drags me past the ring, past the free weights, through a set of doors. Pulling me in, Nick slams the door shut before throwing the lock behind us. "This is as much privacy as I can guarantee us right now."

"Okay." But beyond that, I have no idea of what I'm supposed to say or why I came in the first place. The only thing I can focus on are the layers upon layers of sweaty muscles that are within reach. Involuntarily, my fingers twitch. Somehow, I manage to not touch him. I don't know how, but I do.

He steps closer. I step back. We perform this little dance until my head causes metal to rattle. Lockers. Gym. Right. That somehow jars the reason I'm here. "Rainey sent me."

"Did she?" He braces an arm above my head. I inhale the scent of sweat. My eyes track the hair from under his arm across his pecs as it bisects the muscles of his stomach down into the close-fitting workout shorts.

I barely manage a nod. "Yeah. Said you're on duty or something."

"Uh-huh. Did she mention why?" His voice is so deep it's caressing all of my nerve endings.

"Sex" is what comes out of my mouth. I reach between us and slap a hand over my mouth as his lips curve upward. "Not with her."

"Of course not." The hand that isn't braced over my head trails up my side until it reaches my hair. A single finger twirls in my hair over and over. "There's only one woman I want that way."

"Oh yeah? Anyone I know?"

Instead of answering me, Nick leans closer until his lips are brushing against mine. "What did Rainey want?"

"Rainey who?" is what I manage to get out.

"Good answer." Just before his lips capture mine. Releasing my hair, he slides both hands under my ass and boosts me up for me to wrap my legs around his waist.

And in this moment when I want him so badly, I capitulate to the desire and do just that.

NICHOLAS

I have coveted nothing like I do Maris in this moment.

No title, no wealth, no security means more than the thrumming of her pulse beneath my fingers. My lips savor hers when the animalistic part of me wants nothing more than to strip her of every stitch of clothing she's wearing before I press her back against the metal locker pressed at her back and do nothing but take her the way I've yearned for. But even as her low moans devolve my tolerance to next to nothing, I hold myself back. Maris deserves... I lose all train of thought when her lips pull away and begin to trail down the column of my neck. "Christ, your mouth makes me cross-eyed."

Threading her fingers into my hair, she tips my head back to meet my gaze head-on. "Nice to know I have a few moves of my own." Her hand skims over my sweat-slickened chest. "I haven't seen you fight in so long, I forgot what it does to me..." Maris stiffens in my arms to such a degree I almost drop her.

Is there an expression worse than devastation? I didn't think so until Jed died and sitting behind Maris in a church packed with people not far from here to witness her agony over the loss of the person she loved beyond all reason. I brush a finger over her translucent cheekbone, and not a single expression crosses her magnificent face. It's as blank as a doll's. The electricity arcing between us seconds earlier has flicked off like a switch.

"What is it?"

"Nothing. Put me down."

I immediately do so. She slides out from between the locker and my body. I immediately hate whatever went through her mind almost as much as the phony smile she plasters on her face. That's not my Maris, I think fiercely. And when she starts talking, I want to throw something. We've broken through so many things; what put this look on her face?

Maris backs toward the door. "I've got things to do. I just came by to let you know Rainey's losing her mind. You need to speak with her about how long you plan on staying."

"I will. But please, talk to me, Maris. Don't go." But it's too late. Maris's hand is on the lock. I suck in a breath as she whirls around, disbelief on her face.

"About what, Nick?" she lashes out. But in contrast to that devastation, I'll take whatever she has to throw at me. She stomps forward until her nail jabs me in the chest so hard I'm certain I'll feel the press of the half-moons long after she leaves. "We agreed to friends, Nick. Friends. I'm not suddenly about to become one of Nick Cain's temporary toys. I am not disposable."

"I am well aware of that." God, am I ever.

Nonplussed, she jerks back as she realizes she's still touching me. "Good."

"I care about you more than you will ever know, Maris." I bare a part of my soul to her.

Maris scoffs. "Right. And I just became a virgin all over again." My fists clench and release at my side. I have absolutely no room for fury, but something inside of me quivers in rage with her cavalier statement. Narrowing her eyes, Maris continues. "I will have nothing jeopardizing my chances with this adoption. This little boy is my future, Nick. Certainly not a man who changes women as frequently as he changes his boxers."

Leaning in a bit, I just have to antagonize her. "When I choose to wear them at all, Sunshine."

Maris opens her mouth, and a small scream erupts. Quirking my lips, I ask, "I have the perfect solution to dealing with Rainey."

"What do you mean?" she snaps.

"Before you came I was making plans on staying in Juneau for a while. I was hoping my new buddy Maris might allow me to stay with her."

Enunciating clearly, Maris declares, "Fuck you, Nick," before spinning on her boot heel and out of the locker room.

After she leaves, the tension in the air doesn't seem to dissipate. If anything, it coils tighter as I anticipate the welcome I'll receive when I arrive at Maris's later this evening prepared to make my case. Wickedly, I debate whether or not I should use the spare key the Smiths have kept hidden in the same spot forever and cook her dinner on the grill —really bring back her memories to the original scene of the crime as it were.

Whistling, I pad back out to where Reece and Oliver are waiting. Talking softly to each other, they're eyeballing Maris as she climbs into her SUV. For long moments, as neither of them notices I'm directly behind them, I debate how best to punish them. Extra workout? Sparring? I know Oliver—he wouldn't give a shit if a woman as classy and sensuous as Maris gave him the time of day. After all, I was once their age and felt the same way about the same woman. I was just too damn stupid to do something about it—then.

Leaning in between their bent heads, I whisper, "Look all you want, but if either of you try to touch, I'll make sure a body part you both cherish doesn't work properly ever again."

They both jump back as if I've struck them with a cattle prod. "Christ, Nick, way to give us a heart attack." Oliver clasps his chest. "Is she yours?"

"Let's just say I'm working it out," I say.

Oliver bellows with laughter. "You? You're working out something with a potential lady friend? Did she turn you down flat? Damn, makes me appreciate the whole package now more than ever." Oliver casts an admiring glance back at the now empty glass doors.

I clap a hand on Oliver's shoulder. "Ollie, Ollie, Ollie. That's a woman who will kick your ass harder than I ever could without ever laying a finger on you."

"In other words, she hates your ever-loving guts."

"No." There are days when it's the exact opposite. Love and hate, best friends, I think cheerfully.

"And you're in love with her," Oliver surmises.

Since the bastard knows me too well for my piece of mind, I merely squeeze his shoulder. Hard. "Be respectful or I might have to rip out your tongue. Understood?"

"You got it, boss." I let up on his shoulder, and Oliver immediately begins rotating it.

When I glance at Reece to see if there's anything he wants to contribute, he doesn't say anything—smart man. He merely accepts his warning and continues the warm-up we began before sunshine blew into our corner of Juneau when all we expected was drizzling rain.

I STOP by the local gourmet grocery store Jennings gave me the heads-up on before pulling into the Smiths' driveway. Loaded up on gourmet cheese, steaks, and salad fixings, I find the spare key and disable the alarm code which Jennings gave me after I told him my plans. After popping all of that into the refrigerator, I head outside to fire up the grill. I set the steaks to marinate and pop those in the fridge before I get the cheese arranged for her to munch on. When I called Jennings to tell him my plan, his first reaction was shock before he immediately said, "Feed her. God, if you never listen to me about anything else, make sure that woman is fed before she begins to attack you. I learned that when Kara and I started out."

Considering how well that ended up, I thanked him and immediately went grocery shopping.

I'm frowning as I arrange crackers around the plate. Tonight, Maris and I are going to have it out about the past—my past—and why I never believed I was good enough for her. Then again, I think as I uncork the wine to let it breathe, she likely knows this since Jed wrote most of it down. I pause.

And only one thing bothers her still. That she'd be disposable.

"Well, hell. I'm a stupid ass."

"You're also breaking and entering. I really don't think that would look too good in the media." Maris's voice washes over me.

My head snaps over to where she's standing holding a bottle of the same wine I'm carrying. "Hi."

"What are you doing here, Nick?" Her voice is weary but not surprised.

I'm not a stupid man. "Let me guess, Kara called you?"

"Of course she did. Right after she berated her husband for giving you the alarm code to my home." Maris plunks her bottle right next to mine. "At least you had the good sense to listen to him about food. I'm starving."

"You didn't eat?" I frown when she shakes her head. "Why not?"

"I spent the afternoon at Eagle Beach." She pops a cracker laden with cheese in her mouth and lets out a small moan. "Good bribe so I don't kill you. Really good."

I rest my elbows on the counter until our eyes are on the same level. "Thanks. What did you do at the beach?"

"Sunbathed nude?" comes her smart-ass remark.

"Considering the high today was sixty-eight, you'd have frozen that sweet body. Try again."

Her lips twitch. "I just wanted to think. And that's always been my place to do that. It was my place to go with my family. We'd take a picnic there and look for whales, sea lions, and seals."

"And you wanted to be close to them." I reach over the counter and take her hand.

Maris allows the touch for just a moment before jerking away, her frustration palpable. "Why does it have to be you who understands me?"

"Why did it have to be you who understood me all those years ago? Did you think I wanted to feel what I did for my best friend's little sister?" I counter.

That jerks her up short. "Boy, did you have a funny way of showing it. Forget the fact I never heard from you, when I did the humiliation I experienced was beyond anything, Nick." The edge to her voice is so deadly, I'm surprised I'm not bleeding out on the floor.

I bow my head, but I swear I will do whatever it takes to make her understand. I've conquered my past. It may be too late, but she needs to know. "I was disgraced by my past, Maris. If we couldn't afford it, I stole food to survive. I slept in that ratty-ass station wagon most nights. And if it weren't for the showers they have at laundromats, I'm not entirely certain I would have bathed. I was supposedly home-schooled, but..." I turn away, finally ashamed.

"But what?" There's no censure in her voice, not even encouragement to go on. But something in me breaks. I need her to understand.

"But I fell through the cracks. The system isn't perfect. Somehow between what my birth mother knew and I gleaned, I could get by. They kept passing me though I barely knew shit. What I knew was how to avoid being hit when my father came home, and that was by not being there." I glance over my shoulder and find Maris's fists are clenched.

In fury but not at me. For me.

She looks like a warrior goddess, an ancient who'd fight for the life of her young. "You're going to make an incredible mother. Don't let anyone *ever* tell you any different." The words slip out, but when they do, they transform her face like the wash of the ocean crashing on the shore. Gone is the fire and anger. In its place is a softness and pleasure.

She takes a step closer. "Tell me the rest, Nick. Tell me all of it."

I swallow past the lump in my throat. "The foster homes were better than what I had before, but it wasn't until I met Jed the second time around that I began to see there was...more...to a family. And I betrayed that."

"How?" She takes another step to me.

Flawless. Perfect. Not meant for the likes of someone like me.

I wrench myself away and go back to the story. "Jed and your dad made me want to be a better man. I earned my GED. I worked so hard to eliminate my past."

"You mean to run away from it." God, she's right behind me. If I turn around, she'd be right in my arms. So, I just bob my head up and down.

"Yes. I left. I had to. Don't you see? Do you finally understand?" I chance a glance over my shoulder, and my eyes meet her blue ones.

"Tell me why, Nick. Tell me the truth. You're not the same man you were back then. And we both know I'm not the same woman," she demands.

No, she's not. She's stronger. She's more captivating, if that's even possible. She's more beautiful, both inside and out. And she still has a hold of my heart.

I slowly face her. Our bodies brush against one another. Inside, my heart gives a small shudder and sigh. "I left because I had to make something of myself. I stayed away after Vegas because I thought I was giving you what you wanted. What you needed."

"Well, you learned differently, didn't you?" I ache as she backs away. "Nothing stays the same, Nick. People, places, love. It's just like the sea —constantly changing. You should be fucking grateful mine was mired so deep it didn't go very far."

For a second I'm frozen by her words. But in the next, I'm sweeping her into my arms, my lips crashing down on hers when her words penetrate.

MARIS

"I don't want to imagine my baby sister having sex. Ever." - From the journals of Jedidiah Smith.

"**B**e certain," Nick demands against my lips after he lets me up for air.

"I was certain years ago," I taunt. I back away and move toward the stairs. "Maybe you should take a few moments to think. Just don't take twenty years this time."

I walk away and climb the steps to the beginning of us. Or it will be the end. My head bows wearily as I realize I hear footsteps but not the creak on the stairs signifying Nick's following me. Pretending my heart isn't trying to pound its way out of my chest, I make my way to my bedroom. And then I close the door.

At my dresser, I slip off all my jewelry—even the gold cross. I let out a small snort of amusement. If Nick comes through that door, Jed has no place between us in bed. Once that's complete, I move to the window to pull the curtains.

And my heart withers inside my chest.

Nick is striding from the house toward the borrowed Outback purposefully. I pull the blinds, unable to witness him actually pulling away. "Well, that answers that question." I slip off my shirt and walk into my en suite to fling it into my hamper. I pause at the mirror and just brace my hands on the sink. "I found a love that will make me happy, Jed. Now, take your friend and fuck off."

Leaving the bathroom, I realize I forgot to take off my watch. Fiddling with the band, I'm not looking up. I crash into something hard that shouldn't be there. When hands catch me from falling backward on my ass, I let out an ear-piercing scream.

"What the fuck, Maris?" Nick glares at me.

"What are you doing here?" I accuse.

"What do you mean, what am I doing here? Did you change your mind?" Vulnerability crosses Nick's face.

"Me? You're the one who left, you dick." I slam both hands against the solid wall of his chest.

"Well, that explains why you just blew out my hearing. Sunshine, I didn't leave."

"The hell you didn't, Champ. I saw you." I fling an arm out toward the window, my breath coming in shallow pants.

Nick comes closer, trailing his fingers along my extended arm as he does. Reaching my fingertips, he bends it at the elbow and twists it up and behind me. I slam against his body. "I went to the car to get something we need."

Oh. My lips part. I know I can't get pregnant, but yeah. I didn't even think about that.

"Last chance, Maris." Nick's breath fans over my lips before he kisses the corner of one lip. His free hand plays with my bra strap, sliding his fingers up and down. The skin he touches is branded.

Scored.

Desperate for more.

"It's too late, Nick."

"Thank fucking God." His head jerks slightly before his lips cover mine. His one hand threads into my hair. He releases my arm so he can do the same with the other.

Not being a fool, I take advantage to wrap both around his waist, binding him as tightly to me as I can. I yank up his tee in the back, desperate for the feel of his skin however I can get it. Nick rips his mouth away, before quickly tugging his shirt over his head with one arm. He then quickly dispenses with my bra so when our bodies slide against one another, we're flesh against flesh.

Oh. My. God. I can't be saying it as the only air I'm getting is in between kisses, so I know the thought is running on repeat in my mind. His nipples are buried in his dark chest hair. When I find them, I pinch and twist them slightly as I explore the ripples and planes of his magnificent body.

Nick's reaction is to pick me up and wrap my legs around his waist as he makes his way swiftly to the bed. His kisses before were hungry, but now I feel like I'm being devoured. It's wild, raw, and uncontrolled.

And I love it.

As soon as my back hits the spread, I try to roll him over. His head shoots up and the blaze in his dark gaze pins me in place. The devastating curve of his lips leave a trail down my neck before he cups my breasts and lifts his head. "Do they ache for my mouth, Sunshine?" comes his dark whisper.

"Throb. Make it go away, Nick." I lower my lashes until the only thing in my vision is his dark head lowering.

My back arches as his lips cover the straining tip. His tongue rubs it back and forth, rolling it along the roof of his mouth before letting it out with a pop. He shifts over me to take the other one in while his hand skims up my body to pinch and twist the first in much the same way. My legs wrap around his hips. My hips begin to rotate, seeking relief from an agony much worse.

"That's it, Sunshine. Show me how you burn." Nick holds my hands pressed to the bed as I undulate beneath him.

I arch again, my nipples dragging against his chest, and my pussy rubs against the firm column of his cock trapped behind his jeans. "Please, Nick." I don't know what I'm asking for.

"What do you want?" He bends down and presses a kiss to the inside of my breast.

"More, everything."

Nick releases me and sits back.

"Come back." I curl up so I don't lose the warmth of his body.

"I will. Just as soon as I get these damn clothes out of the way." He mutters something about scissors, and I grin before sliding to the end of the bed.

"Strip," I order him.

Nick's hand goes to his waistband while mine go to my boots. I quickly undo the laces before standing up. Nick's frozen in place. Hoarsely he says, "Keep going."

I pop the buttons on my pants, and nabbing my panties, I slide them off. Within moments I'm nude, and Nick's still standing there half-dressed. Nick starts to lunge for me, but I step back. "Your turn."

He mutters under his breath, but I crawl quickly onto the bed. Flopping over to my back, I spread my legs. Nick's got one boot off when he catches me drag my fingers through my wet folds. "Fuck this." Nick crawls onto the bed with one boot still on, one pant leg still trapped. He grabs my ankles and pulls. Cupping my ass, he lifts me to him as his head lowers.

Each lash of his tongue against the swollen bud of my clit is sheer torture. "I'll never survive this," I manage to gasp.

"You will. Now just go over," Nick orders before he suctions his mouth over my lower lips and gives me a particularly devastating kiss that sends shivers coursing through me.

I cry out as I come, unable to keep in the sound. But nothing, I swear nothing, feels better than Nick Cain's smile against the entrance of where he's about to thrust his cock right before he mutters, "That's my girl."

Twisting around, still hampered by the jeans and boot, Nick finds a condom and slips it on. He tries to toss the wrapper over the side of the bed. I giggle as it flutters and lands right next to my head.

He just shakes his head. Lifting one leg up over his shoulder, I feel on display—as if Nick could see inside my body all the way into my heart. When he presses his chest forward and lines up his cock with my opening, dragging the heated flesh against my still-clenching entrance, I close my eyes to give myself some sort of shield.

Nick merely blows past it by notching his cock against the entrance at the same time his lips crash into mine. My eyes fly wide open. At that moment, he pushes inside me.

Physically, emotionally, I'm spread wide open for him. His cock is penetrating me in long slow thrusts much as his tongue is. But it's nothing in comparison to the way his heart claimed me years ago. I'm certain it all shows on my face as I do what I can to mark him in the same way he's done to me—with emotion, with my body.

"Harder, Nick. I want to feel you whenever I move," I gasp into the air after I tear my mouth from his.

It's like setting a caged lion free.

Leaning all his weight down, he shifts his weight to his knees. My eyes grow round as his thrusts become harder, deeper, more intense. "Fuck, Maris, take more," he bites out.

"All of you. Give it to me, love."

Like it was some sort of secret incantation, Nick sets the animal that lives inside him free. His eyes narrow. The arm beneath me pulls me into his thrusts as he tips my hips into receiving them. When I feel myself start to go over, he holds me in position before curling his lip and sliding his hand up my body and pinching my nipple.

My breath catches as the clenching starts again. My head whips back, and my hips lock against his.

And then I feel him go over.

He thrusts once before he buries his pulsating cock inside me. As he leans forward, the depth of his penetration sets off another spasm.

For long moments, I can't form a coherent thought. Nick has shifted his weight to the side, though he's still resting partially on me. But just as I'm about to pass out, I whisper into the air. "That was worth waiting for."

And what does Nick do? He lifts his head and kisses me. "Yeah, it was. Let me know when you're up for round two."

Faintly, I ask, "Round two?"

Nick pulls out and rolls completely off me. The pants whip against the nightstand. He curses before stripping off the boot and his jeans. Nabbing a tissue off the nightstand, he wraps up the spent condom and tosses it in the trash basket. Spinning around, he faces me.

My heart stops beating. I actually feel it stop when I check out his well-muscled shoulders, flat stomach with those damn Vs, narrow hips, and thighs I want to ride just to see if they can make me come.

Fuck, I want to ride him.

"Did you hear that?" Nick asks as he crawls across the bed.

"Hear what?" I start to sit up, but Nick puts a hand to my chest to hold me in place.

"That was the sound of the second round." Then he lowers his head.

I have a feeling I'll never be able to forget feeling him inside me after tonight.

MARIS

"Pain isn't always physical. Anguish is often harder to deal with than the scars. If I were to psychoanalyze him — hell, it's my thoughts, so why can't I? — I'd guess that's why Nick chose to be a fighter. He can't deal with abandonment. It's why he backs away from all of us." - From the journals of Jedidiah Smith.

Nick trails his fingers along my spine. "Will you talk to me about the surgery?"

I stiffen briefly but relax under his ministrations. "Bad circumstances," I try to joke.

"Maris." Just my name. From anyone else, I'd have stormed away. But not after what Nick and I shared in this bed, the physical exchange of emotions that have always lived between us.

Tucking my arm beneath my head, I swallow my pride and declare, "I made a foolish mistake, and it cost me something infinitely more precious."

"I doubt it was that cut-and-dried, Sunshine." His hand tangles in the ends of my long hair.

Instead of answering him right away, I release a pressure valve I didn't know was still ready to blow. "I used to dream about having a little girl with my hair. I'd remember how my Mom would curse every day trying to run a brush through it. She'd say, 'One day when you have a daughter...'" My eyes sting with remembrance. "The last time she ever said it, I was in the hospital room. Dad and Jed had stepped out to get food. I couldn't brush my own hair. I almost borrowed scissors from the nurses' station to hack it all off. Mom knew me too well, or there was a note on my chart to keep sharp implements from me. They refused to give them to me when I asked a nurse for them."

Nick doesn't say a word, just continues to let me speak. But my next words shock him. "Jed told me about the guys' get-well wishes. I was so glad I never heard from you."

His fingers clench against my scalp.

"But Nick, that wasn't because I hated you. I would have hated for you to have seen me like that. I was worthless as a woman."

He releases my hair and rolls me to my back. "Don't you ever say that. Ever."

My shame drips from the corner of my eyes. "I lost everything trying to give up on what my heart knew it couldn't do. It was my punishment for trying."

His thumbs brush back and forth, smoothing away the wetness. "What was that?"

"Saying goodbye to you. I tried to let you go since you'd walked away from me, us, without a glance."

His head bows. His shoulders heave. "Stop talking."

"Then, a year later, I got your letter. I thought it was a sign that maybe everything was going to be okay. That my time in purgatory was over." Now that I've opened the dam, the floodgate of my emotions is pouring out.

"Maris." Nick's voice is shredded.

I turn my head aside. "I felt so small in those days. I was still learning who I was all over again."

"And I fucked up."

I face him. It's time to relieve him of his guilt. "Maybe yes, maybe no. We're not the same people today we were then. I'd have followed you anywhere, been anyone, done anything, but is that the kind of woman you need?"

"Who I've always needed in my life is you. And no one has ever come close to filling the gap in my heart not having you in my life left. Not any woman, not the guys, not your brother. There's only one you, Maris. No one else can invoke these feelings in me."

I cup the ball of his shoulder and drag my fingers down his arm. "Annoyance?"

"Aggravation," he counters before plucking a kiss from my lips.

"Brashness." I push him.

"Bossiness." Nick rolls to his back so I'm sitting astride him.

I smirk. "Confidence."

He thinks for a moment. "Consideration." I bend down and kiss him.

"Devastation?" I lean over and kiss the inside of his elbow.

"Desperation." He leans up and kisses the underside of my jaw.

"Emotional." I'm loving this word game we're playing, but Nick shakes his head, causing me to frown. He sits up and cups my face.

"Everything. You're simply everything." His eyes bore into mine before he leans forward and brushes his lips against mine. "It wouldn't have mattered if it was twenty years ago or twenty minutes ago, I need you to understand that."

I wrap my arms around his shoulders and press against him. I bury my head against his neck, and a harsh sob is pulled from me.

Nick doesn't say anything, just holds on until the storm has passed. After it does, he whispers, "Better?"

"Yes. No."

He laughs before tipping up my chin. "That clears up a lot."

I grin. "Blame hormones. I should have them checked. It's been a while."

Nick's face gets serious quickly. "There's a number of competition-level women athletes at the gym. We get them checked for a number of issues—hormones, among other blood imbalances. Is this something we need to have you checked for regularly. How often should you be checked?"

If I hadn't been on the edge of falling for Nick Cain for most of my life, the immediate concern about my medical welfare—not about the fact I can't have any children—would have brought me to the edge.

Instead, it nudges me clean over. I brush my lips against his before whispering, "It was a joke."

With his lips still against mine, he mutters, "Nothing about keeping you safe in my arms is a joke."

I tip my head so far back, I can feel the ends of my hair brush against the top of my ass. My eyes drift shut before I silently think, *I think he's got it from here, big brother. Love you.*

"Maris?" Nick hesitantly asks.

"I was just thanking Jed," I tell him honestly.

"For what?"

I smile secretively. Instead of telling Nick I push him back on the bed and kiss him.

It's a long while before either of us think about Jed again.

"DO YOU THINK HE'D APPROVE?" Nick asks me hours later.

I'm snuggled up against his chest still damp from our latest love-making. "Jed?" I ask instinctively.

"Yeah." He tries to sound cavalier, but I can hear the anxiety behind it.

"You read what he wrote." I shrug the whole thing off because now I know what Jed truly meant. Despite his worries over the years, he wanted this.

"And I know everything he said to me. It was almost a perpetual stay-away warning." Despite the joking note in his voice, there's a lingering hurt that has fed into Nick's image of himself over the years. Something I unknowingly haven't improved with the callous words between us.

I prop my elbow on his chest and contemplate how to tackle this topic. As I do, he reaches beneath my armpits and hauls me on top of him. I let out an involuntary screech. "Nick!"

"I want you as close as I can possibly have you."

"For as long as you can?" I say softly.

"For as long as you'll let me," he corrects.

"Then that will be an awfully long time." A breathtaking smile breaks out across his face. Holding my hair back, I lean down and press my lips against his. "Now, despite the hours we've wasted talking, there's something we need to do."

"What's that?"

"Talk about Jed so he doesn't get in the way." At his nod, I continue. "He told me that Mom and Dad used to wonder if he was going to murder me in my sleep because he would just watch me when I slept."

"Was that his intent?" Nick's amusement shines through.

"No. It was like he was born a guardian angel." Thoughtfully, I draw my finger through the sprinkling of hair on Nick's chest. "All my friends used to complain about their siblings. Constantly."

"Were they more in line with the Spawns of Brad?"

"Pretty much. But I had Jed. So, when I fell for one of his friends, I'm not surprised he went crazy."

"Maris, I hate to speak ill of Jed, but he was crazy long before any feelings developed between us." Nick murmurs into the top of my hair before he presses a kiss into the crown.

The madness of the world stops suddenly, or maybe that's simply the beat of my heart. "Would you mind repeating that?"

"What? That your brother was a crazy bastard?" Nick's body is shaking with laughter beneath mine.

"Nick."

"Oh, you meant the 'us' part."

"Yeah." My head lifts slowly until our eyes are on the same level. "That part."

"You don't think we'll cause natural disasters if we say it so soon?" Nick's voice is calm, but the thundering of his heart is anything but.

"Frankly, I don't care. The time between when I first started feeling these emotions for you and now has been filled with so much loneliness and despair. Erase it, Nick. Tell me," I plead.

He rolls me to my back and cups my face. "It started with your smile. I never had a smile like yours aimed in my direction. I was blinded by the glorious light of it. I understood why they named Jed's sister Sunshine, even though I still thought that was the most fucked-up name in history."

I bite my lip even as a laugh bubbles up. "He never told me that."

"Swear to God, he constantly called you that. It wasn't until you introduced yourself as Maris I realized your parents weren't insane." He pauses. "Just Jed."

The laugh bursts out. "Just Jed," I agree. My arms loop around his neck. "Did you feel it when we shook hands the first time?"

His eyes narrow on mine, filled with heat. "Yes, I felt it. Why do you think I pulled my hand back so fast after? You were barely eighteen. I was twenty. And Jed was ready to kill me dead. I feel it every time we touch, every time we speak, every time I see you."

"Nick..." I begin, but he lays a finger over my mouth. And there it is.

That zing between us. That something that's been lying dormant for over twenty years because it needed to be protected from his pain, my pain. And then from our shared pain over losing Jed.

Now, now it's time to set it—us—free.

"Tell me." I'm practically begging as I kick my legs free from the covers and wrap my legs around his hips.

"Love, hate, it didn't matter what you felt for me as long as you kept feeling. Then, I almost felt like you cut my heart out when I realized you weren't talking to me anymore." His head bows before it snaps up. "Until I realized it was the other way around. I'm so sorry, my love, for almost giving up on us. I'm a fighter, but you make me weak."

"Say it, damn you." I rake my nails up his back into his hair and press his head until his lips are touching mine

"Didn't I?" His lips curve against mine. The sensation makes my nipples harden like stones against his chest.

"Nick..."

"I love you, Maris. I have from the time I was a terrified boy, and I will until the day they lay me in the ground. There's never been another I've said those words to. There never will be."

And there it is. We might not be able to go back in time and redo our pasts, but the future is ours alone. And no one can take that away from us.

My lips curve beneath his. "I love you, Nick. I—"

I don't get a chance to finish because Nick's done talking. As he captures my mouth with his, and his hand roams freely over my body, I have to agree.

We'll talk more later.

NICHOLAS

"I always said nothing good happened here." After a long doze, I roll to my side and prop my head on my hand to gaze down at Maris. "I lied."

She tsks me. "I'm shocked, I tell you."

"That includes the way I've always admired the way you call me on my shit."

Maris grins up at the sky. "All part of the hospitality here at Smith's B&B. Kill your guests off from breakfast or words—their choice."

Our laughter mingles together sending sparks out like fireflies. "I didn't realize how much I missed being with you on the most basic of levels," I admit.

Maris rolls to face me. Her brows form a V. "What do you mean?"

I reach out and rub it away casually as if I've performed the gesture a million times, not just in my mind. I'm not so lost in my thoughts I miss the way her breath hitches.

My lips curve. "So, now that we're no longer friends, when can I move my shit in?"

She swats at me. "Arrogant ass."

I capture her hand and lift it to my lips. Her irritation flees, and in its place is a look so soft I want to capture it for those times I have to travel and she can't be with me. Instead of reaching for my phone, I roll onto my back and try to put my thoughts into words. "I can't remember the last time I came home from work and just talked about my day, Sunshine. Honest to God, I think the last time might have been with you. Sometimes things happen that are just so over-whelming."

Maris reaches over and rubs her hand up and down my arm. "Why didn't you call any of the guys?"

I can't stop the year's worth of pain from seeping into my voice. "I used to. The problem is he died leaving a gaping hole in the world. I didn't know who to reach out to after. Jed seemed to be the only one who got me." I turn my head just in time to catch her reaction.

Her face pales to match the color of her ivory shirt. "I don't know what to say."

I roll my head back so our heads are touching one another as we peer up at the sky. "I never thought I would be the kind of person worthy of maintaining the friendships we established that summer. I felt I needed to prove I was better than how I grew up. Better than..."

"Than the rags made you out to be?" Maris concludes softly.

I nod, brushing our heads against each other. "Don't get me wrong; I lived up to my rep the first few years."

"Of that, I have little doubt." Her dry response has me roaring.

"Minx," I accuse fondly.

She shrugs. "Takes one to know one. I'm not going to be nomi-nated for sainthood myself, Nick."

Her words shouldn't cause a fire to erupt inside my gut, but I'd be lying to myself if I didn't admit the truth. "I kind of hate any man who's ever touched you."

One heartbeat. Two. Then Maris is laughing so hard her knees curl into her chest and she's rolling onto her side.

"It wasn't that funny," I grumble.

"Oh, yes. It really is," she manages to get out. "Nick, you're a damn man whore."

"Was," I correct her.

I'm not sure if I should be offended or amused at the piglike sounds that escape from her lips. "Not kidding, Sunshine. Completely reformed."

"Let's see if our definitions line up. Excluding kissing, because I feel that's a respectful thing to do at the end of a date, when was the last time you were intimate with a woman?" she challenges me.

I roll over and pin her to the grass. I need to see her face when I give her the answer. "The night before I found out Jed died."

Maris opens her mouth to refute the statement, but I hold her gaze steadily. Her body goes limp beneath mine. "Nick?" She swallows convulsively. "Why?"

"Because I came back and was given something much more precious than a gold cross." I let go of one of her hands and caress the side of her face. "You were still free. And as much as you told me to get the hell away from you when I came after you, it was a sign. Maybe if there was something called faith in this world, I could make the past up to you."

"All you needed to do was tell me the truth. You know, talk to me."

"It took me three years and being forced to come to Juneau to work up the courage. Don't you think I wanted to that weekend?" I brush the wetness away from Maris's cheeks. "The story of David and Goliath is true for a reason, Sunshine. Those of us with strength can be felled with the smallest of stones, particularly if those stones are words."

Maris tugs me down until I wrap her in my arms. Not wanting to give her my full weight and hurt her, I shift to the side, and we lie silently for a while content to just be in each other's arms. An eagle flies overhead, regal and all-knowing. I remember spitting out my beer the first time I saw one swoop past in the Smiths' backyard. Jed cackled until he cried. It's like he's giving us his blessing or some shit, bringing us full circle. *Thanks, you crazy bastard.* I begin to shake with suppressed laughter.

Maris, who had been drifting off, murmurs, "What is it?"

"Nothing. No, wait. Now's the time for the truth. All these years, was half your antagonism due to the fact you thought I was fucking around with half of the women I was photographed with?"

"You're such an ass," Maris pronounces.

"Yeah, but I'm your ass," I announce proudly.

"Yes. You are." Reaching over, Maris pulls down my head and kisses me softly right before she jams her fist into my solar plexus.

I groan as the eagle takes another circle overhead. *Got it, buddy. On the not-to-be-mentioned list.* I'm grinning when I tuck Maris next to me.

MARIS IS AFLUTTER as Mrs. Gustofson squeezes behind the beast and checks the outlet. "Again, I'm sorry I had to put you through such an inconvenience, Maris."

"It's not a problem at all, Mrs. G.," Maris says. Even though I know it was. Forget about the physical strain, the emotional one was a huge issue she had to shoulder as well, but I keep my mouth closed.

The woman stands up and makes notes on her clipboard without saying anything. "That's all I needed."

Maris bites her lip anxiously. "I know you normally don't give any indication about the report—"

"You know I can't, dear."

"But before I move the unit back in place, can you let me know if everything is okay? I had friends who were gracious enough to help me move it. I would hate to have to impose on them if I have to move it again," Maris explains.

My temper slips a notch, and I'm not certain if it's because the most self-sufficient woman I know is kowtowing to this woman or because she classified me back to a friend when we've expressed our love to one another. But I step back into the shadows because this isn't my deal; it's Maris's. I have to trust her to handle this as she sees fit.

It turns out that is the best way. "Let me call my supervisor and ask if I can give you a verbal preliminary about just these two outlets. I understand your concerns. How about that?"

Maris's whole body sags in relief. "That would be great, Mrs. G. Just those two outlets. I can wait on everything else."

"Then give me a few moments. I'll place the call outside." Mrs. Gustofson steps outside to make the call.

When she does, I turn to Maris. As if she's anticipating my words, she holds up a hand. "Not now, Nick. Please? All I'm asking is that you wait until after she leaves."

"Maris, I've never seen you so...supplicant to anyone in your life."

"I've never wanted anything more in my entire life."

I fall back as if I've taken a high kick to the jaw. "Nothing?" I manage.

"No, Nick. Nothing. You could go out tomorrow and..." Her voice breaks, but she continues. "Have a baby of your own seed. A biological child. I can *never* have that. Never. And the bond I felt with this little boy... The closest way I can explain it is to say it's like what I had with Jed. That's how strong and pure it is."

I'm about to open my mouth to reply when the front door opens. Mrs. Gustofson's footsteps clamor up the stairs. "Good news, Maris."

"In more ways than one, I hope," she jokes.

"Actually yes. I can tell you about those two outlets, so whomever you strong-armed into helping you move that unit can help you shift it back into place. And yes, both outlets are fine. We do recommend if they don't have anything plugged into them you purchase some baby plug protectors so no dust can get into them so they don't become a fire hazard."

Maris immediately says, "I'll go pick up some today."

"Wonderful. If you could text me a picture before you move the unit back in place, then we'll consider that matter closed." Mrs. Gustofson makes a few notes, then calls Maris over. The two women speak softly. Maris opens her mouth and then closes it. Mrs. Gustofson frowns before her face smooths out. She rubs a hand up and down Maris's arm. Then she hands Maris a pen and points to several locations on a piece of paper.

Maris signs the first few spots quickly. If I wasn't watching her so intently, I'd have missed her glance at me before she signed the final space. *Don't think I won't be asking about that, Sunshine.*

The two women shake hands. Mrs. Gustofson offers her hand to me as well. I add the slightest bit of pressure. She's startled. "Goodness, I think I know who one of the individuals was who helped you move the wall unit."

Maris rolls her eyes heavenward.

"There's nothing I wouldn't do to help Maris, Mrs. Gustofson."

Her cheerful smile fades. "That's good to know, Mr. Cain. Both of you have a nice day."

I bide my time until the front door closes and her car pulls out of the driveway before I turn and face Maris. "Tell me what she said to you."

"It was nothing, Nick." Maris starts to pass me, but I reach out and hook my arm around her to drag her in front of me. "You do realize I have to drive to town to find stuff to babyproof my house before I can beg you and Brad to move the beast back into place?"

"What did she say, Maris? And don't try to tell me nothing. I caught that little look before you signed that document—whatever it was."

"It was nothing that concerned you, Nick. I promise."

"Maris..."

Her voice filled with exasperation, Maris lets it all out. "All she wanted to know was if I was still applying for adoption as a single parent. She gave the implication it would make a difference on the application. I told her I was. End of story. Okay?" Maris breaks free and storms off to go get her purse.

No. Not okay. None of this feels okay. In fact, it hurts. Everything from her comments before to this make my heart ache in a way I want to talk about, but I don't feel like I have the right to because I'm not the one who lost everything.

But somehow, I still feel like I am.

I'm still standing in the exact same spot when two arms wrap around me from behind. "I'm sorry. None of this is your fault. Not the accident, not people's antiquated minds that believe a two-parent household is better than one. Certainly not a television unit that my parents bought that weighs half a ton." She shifts around until I hold her in my arms. "Do you forgive me?"

"There's nothing to forgive," I tell her honestly.

Except there is.

She's making a life here in Juneau that doesn't include me. So how am I supposed to convince her to leave it?

She seems intent on building a life without me in it. And somehow I have to figure out a way to change that.

MARIS

"In a perfect Utopia, I'd get to arrange everyone to reconnect with their true mate. Remember, since it's my perfect world, there would be no barriers to stand in my way. Brad and Rainey, of course. But I'd have Jennings read his fucking email. Kody would have ignored my stupid advice and asked Meadow out anyway. And Nick? He'd have figured out a way to explain who he really is as a person to Maris. Hell, to all of them.

And all of this would have happened before so many people struggled." - From the journals of Jedidiah Smith.

Nick and I are curled up on the couch after he and Brad managed to shift the wall unit back in place. Watching his muscles ripple beneath his tee earlier, I wanted nothing more than to say screw it, kick Brad out, and back Nick up to the nearest available flat surface. But oddly, this is better. It's normal. And it gives me something I've been missing for a long time.

Hope.

As I lie on top of him, I snuggle closer as the announcers for the pay-per-view MMA Title Fight I purchased months ago compare the fighters. "Sorry it's not one of your guys?"

I'm shocked when Nick shakes his head. "Not tonight."

"Hold on. Do I have the real Nick Cain here? Can you do something to make certain you don't have a forked tongue? Maybe I need to get a couple cans of bug spray to battle you or something?" I reference the original *Men in Black* movie.

Nick swats my tush. "Is that a good enough reminder?"

"I don't know. Why don't you do it again?" I suggest.

He laughs before pressing a quick kiss to my lips. He reaches to the floor and grabs a handful of popcorn, offering me a bite before munching on the rest.

I lay my head back down on his chest. My eyes begin to drift shut as Nick's heartbeat lulls me. In that perfect dreamscape where miracles happen, I can picture David rushing down the stairs yelling, "Mom, is the fight on yet?"

Right before Nick answers, "Not yet, son."

My hand brushes across his chest, and I feel the raised edge of his nipple through his T-shirt. "Hmm." Even as relaxed as I am, I can't get enough of his body. "How is it you still have a body this ripped at your age?"

That earns me another whack. I just smile as Nick asks indignantly, "At my age?"

"I am younger than all of you but Meadow," I remind him.

Nick growls, "I was holding my own with Reece in the ring the other day."

"You were, though he's shredded. Christ, I don't know how you managed that. Despite your kicking his ass, he seemed to have enough gas in his tank to...Nick!" I screech as he flips me over.

Nick unceremoniously dumps me onto my back. Picking up the remote, he hits Record. "We'll watch the fight later."

"When later?" I demand.

"After I teach you a very important lesson."

"About what?"

"About endurance." And then Nick lowers his head and proceeds to show me that he still has the determination to make me forget my own name. The only thing I remember is his as I call it out repeatedly. That and the fact I want his hands all over my body before he thrusts inside, causing me to clench around his cock so hard he moans out my name next to my ear.

Neither of us give a shit who won the fight—either the one on my flat-screen or the one we were having.

THE NEXT NIGHT, Nick and I lie in the backyard talking about his home in Albuquerque. "What made you choose there?" I ask curiously.

"Have you ever been?"

"No. I was supposed to. Even had the ticket booked, but then..."

Nick rolls us until we're facing one another. "What happened?"

"I got the call from Kara." My voice is haunted.

Nick's body stills. "What?"

"Nick. I was flying to Albuquerque. I was going to meet Jed there for a week after he got back from his vacation with Dean. I promised him I'd go somewhere fun with him. He told me I'd suit the southwest —that Albuquerque would be my kind of town." My hand blindly reaches for his.

"God damn, crazy bastard. You were trying to get us together. Fuck. What if she wasn't ready?" Nick surges to his feet, pulling me along with him. Wrapping me in his arms, he rubs his hand up and down my back. Jerking me back, Nick's penetrating stare tries to read me. Since the main thing I'm feeling is shock, he mutters, "Shit," before yanking me back into his arms for long moments before I gather my thoughts.

"He was trying to play matchmaker."

"Yeah, Sunshine. He was." Nick's voice is cautious.

I burst out laughing.

Nick's body locks. I pull back and grab his face down by the cheek before laying a smacking kiss on his lips. "Don't you get it?" I yell.

"Obviously not."

"You were wondering if he'd approve of me and you? Well, despite his vacillating back and forth in his journals, he did. Why on earth would he bring me around you? He had to know what would happen."

"He'd have brought you to Razor."

"Keep going," I encourage.

"What would you have done?" he asks.

"I'd have seen you working with the kids and my heart would have been in a puddle. What about you?"

"I'd have laid claim to you within the blink of an eye before beating the shit out of anyone who looked at you," Nick declares immediately.

I toss my head back and start to laugh. "I love you, Jedidiah! You meddling moron!" I yell, once I catch my breath.

When my head rights, Nick bends me back over his arm, drinking every drop of joy from my lips, pouring every ounce of his into me. I moan under the pressure of his lips. He growls before his tongue duels with mine. Blessing us, the sun shines down on us in its glory instead of the seasonal rain.

It's a heady feeling to know the love you've waited a lifetime for has been blessed by the only person you both love unconditionally. Because I know all too well in the blink of an eye, the crush of a wave, the smash of a car, so much about life can change. But for this moment, I feel invincible. Certainly the feelings I have for Nick are.

When Nick draws back from our kiss, I feel frozen in place by the emotions chasing themselves across his face. But the one that I know I'll never forget is love. "I want to bring you to Albuquerque," Nick proclaims.

"Okay," I agree without hesitation.

"Soon," he presses.

"As soon as I can, Nick."

He yanks me tightly against his chest. His heart is pounding against my ear. Safe, certain in his love for me, I wonder aloud, "Do you believe he's looking down at us?"

"He's sitting at a bar laughing his damn ass off, Maris. And you know it just as I do. First night I was here, I yelled at him."

I jerk back. "You did?"

"Don't sound surprised; I talk with your brother."

"I thought I was the only one."

Nick scoffs. "Please. Since Brad didn't offer to escort me to the nearest mental institution, I suspect he does as well."

Thoughtfully, I tip my head to the side. "I know Kara talks with Dean through email."

"And if Jennings knows that, then he's regularly communicating with the lunatic. And let's not forget Kody."

My eyes go wide. "No way."

Nick nods. "Drunk birthday chat revealed that one. Then again, I told him first." Nick runs his finger along the chain I'm wearing before admitting, "I almost lost this."

I suck in a deep breath. "What happened?"

He drags me over to a chair. Pulling me onto his lap, he recounts how a fighter he was training from a visiting camp broke the clasp and then taunted him with melting it down to put the gold in his mouth. "I hope you bloodied his damn mouth." I fist my hands.

Nick tucks me close. "I did better than that. I took out the two teeth with a kick. Bled like a bitch in the ring. Only time Charmaine didn't bitch me out for cursing or the blood."

"Good. Wait, Charmaine doesn't like cursing? Or blood? How the hell does she work with you?"

Nick blushes.

"Oh, this is going to be good. I might need her number."

"I'll give it to you, but um, yeah."

"Tell me." I start bouncing like a little kid in his lap.

He wraps his arms around my waist and explains how Charmaine won't preview any fight videos anymore. "Okay, fine. Now, fess up Cain. How does your badass assistant keep your potty mouth from tainting the fight floor?" I tease.

"I have a swear jar."

I collapse against his chest. "You are so full of it."

"Actually, because of the kids, we all do."

I sit back up. "You're not kidding."

"Nope. We donate it to local charities including a local organization that helps out with supplying foster families with additional supplies." He runs his hand over my jaw. "And this was before I knew about you. Imagine the donation they're going to get now." His smile tells me they're going to get everything they need including the sun, the moon, and the stars.

Because that's what he wants to give me.

I slide off his lap and reach for his hand. "I need you, Nick."

Nick pushes to his feet before scooping me up into his arms. "Right here. In the grass."

"Where I first lost my heart," I murmur.

"Where I first found mine," he counters.

"Yes." Nick takes a few steps away from the stone and lowers me to the soft grass. Slowly, his hands on my body, we drain the sunlight from the sky and feed it into each other's souls.

Because in the end, whether our hearts were lost or found, they're one and the same.

LATER THAT NIGHT IN BED, I stir when I feel the badass Nick Cain drawing something on my back. At first, as I come out from the sexual slumber I fell into after Nick loved me to sleep, I wonder if he's just drawing doodles.

Then I realize it's the same pattern all over my body.

He's writing his name followed by mine. Then he's surrounding both by a giant heart.

Over and over.

Nick.

Maris.

And a heart.

I twist around to face him, and he blushes like a schoolboy caught passing a note in school. "My turn," I say hoarsely. And directly over his heart, I repeat exactly what he did to me.

Nick.

Maris.

And over his heart, I lay my own. Then again, he's had it for years.

I seal my drawing by placing my hand on top of the faint scratch marks I left. "It's always been you. Even when it wasn't," I admit.

"I will never stop trying to erase the years between us. Every day. Every minute. I'll never believe you're here even though it's always been you in my soul." The low timber of his voice makes me catch my breath.

"Nick..." I need him to stop talking.

"Jed knew. He knew I was too afraid of you shoving me out the door and what would happen if you did. I've never held myself in high regard. Why on earth would a woman who had everything choose me?"

"I think the better question is why wouldn't I?" I smooth my hand up his chest and up to his jaw. Forcing his chin down, I can see from the nightlights sprinkled around the room his eyes are damp. I kiss them closed, tasting the tang of salt on my lips.

Nick crushes me to him. "I may not deserve you, but I'm never letting you go."

My eyes widen comically. "Is that a commitment?"

His face forms a fearsome scowl. "There will never be another after you, Maris."

And his next words steal all my thoughts away.

"Instead of sailing on an ocean of pain, we're finally on the same limitless journey. Together."

My lips part. "Nick..." But I don't get to say more because his lips are seeking mine.

And the mingled salt from our combined tears is sipped away in that kiss and the many others as we bind our bodies, hearts, and souls.

NICHOLAS

"I said let's go to the best place in town for crab and this is where you take me?" I swallow a bite of the best crab chowder anywhere on the planet while sitting across from Maris at a table down near the water.

"Was I wrong?" Maris challenges me.

"Not in the slightest. What do they do? Drive the boats here and let them pick the best ones before they ship off the rest to the rest of us schmucks around the country?" Scraping up the ends of the soup with a piece of roll, I pick up the imposing king crab leg—my third. Using a plastic utensil that resembles something you'd yank out of a dental cleaning package, I quickly shuck the shell surrounding the crab meat. I've done this twice already, but the way it zips through the crustacean's shell like melted butter still floors me. "Astounding. Every single time." I shove the remains of the shell through a hole in the center of the table and offer Maris a piece of the third leg I've annihilated.

She shakes her head. "I'm stuffed. Besides, I'm enjoying watching you eat. Where do you put it?"

"Why do you think I work out as much as I do?"

"To maintain that ridiculous physique. Not to prepare yourself for a crab-eating food challenge, Nick."

My ears perk up. "Is there such a thing?"

Maris's body shakes as she tries to hold in her laughter. "I'm sure there is. That might be taking that 'Champ' title a bit too far, don't you think?"

Suddenly the sweetness of the crab churns in my stomach when how in the blink of an eye I went from having my whole future planned with the woman across the table from me to reducing any kind of chance between us to ashes on the wind. Wiping my hand on the paper towels, I ask, "If you could go back in time and change something, what would it be?"

She waves my question away with a chunk of sweet crab. "That's a question guaranteed to get me in trouble."

"Why?"

"Because everything has repercussions, Nick. If I bring Jed back to life, would he have succeeded in his endeavors to get his friends together despite it being his most fervent wish? Would there be a Jennings and Kara? What about Kody and Meadow? If I were to be selfish enough to wish for more, how does that alter the future? Is it so much that love doesn't happen?"

Even as I try to absorb her selflessness, she knocks me completely on my ass. "What if I were to change the night between us in Vegas? Would you have changed into the man you are, or would you still be Nick the Dick strutting around trying to see how many ways you could use woman to forget your past? Would you see your past might be a part of you but in a way that you've changed lives as a result of it? How many children's lives have you changed as a result of the things that happened to you? Because of Vegas? That you wanted to prove you could be a better man?" She winks at me to take the edge off her words.

"I was a dick, Maris. I deserved to have you walk away."

"Yes, you were. But again, the blame wasn't entirely yours."

"We'll continue to disagree on that."

She shrugs, unconcerned. God, I love her. Jed was right. I needed a little faith in my life, and Maris consistently offers it up. "That night changed both of us. We both spiraled, Nick. You weren't the only one. And look where it led you. Would Razor be helping children or just training MMA fighters? You're doing wonderful things."

I can't stop myself from reaching for her. My hands grip her forearm. "I find something more to love about you every minute I spend with you."

"Good. But just for the record, I hope you plan to make it clear to your past harem you're off-limits. This includes every female that crosses your path who volunteers to slide in between the sheets with you." Maris picks up the shucking utensil. "Otherwise, I might have to use this to—"

I shudder at her violent tendencies but, "I get your point."

"I hope you do. I'm not very good at sharing. And since you're the one who clearly drew where the lines are between us..."

"Oh, they're clear." I shift my eyes to the side and glare at one of the men at a nearby booth who's checking her out. He averts his eyes and shovels in another bite of food, appropriately subdued. Feeling better, I cheerfully chomp down on another bite of crab.

We're both quiet for a few moments before I burst out with, "I still can't believe you wouldn't go back to change things." She wouldn't change the accident? Her ability to have children?

She wouldn't change the lost years between us.

She lets out a sigh. "It's not that easy. It's hard to say I've put certain parts of my past to bed when I really haven't. I just choose not to look back, but forward."

"Are you trying to make me feel better about the years we lost?"

"Maybe I am. But Nick? If we had the power to go back with no repercussions to what's happening now, I'd do anything for more time with the men I've always loved." Her fingers apply pressure to the tight muscles in my forearm in return.

"In spite of everything?" I manage to rasp, still unable to comprehend how I earned this—Maris's love. But I'll never willingly let it go. I'll fight anyone or anything who tries to take it from me.

"Maybe because of it," she muses. "After all, we know the worst things about each other, and here we are."

"You're right." Then quick as lightning, I use my other hand to reach across the table and snag her buttered roll from her tray.

"Damn you, Nick! I was saving that."

"What can I say? I'm hungry. I worked up quite the appetite earlier."

Her lashes lower, partially covering her magnificent blue eyes. "Yes, you did."

Suddenly, the roll so delicious a moment ago feels like it's going to choke me when I try to swallow. "Maybe we should get an order to go. For a snack later."

Maris hums appreciatively. "You know, Nick, living in the now is pretty damn fantastic."

I couldn't agree more.

I DRIVE SLOWLY as we approach the accident site, both hands on the wheel. I refuse to allow anything to hurt Maris ever again—especially me.

"Nick, you know the way you were driving was fine. I only trigger memories when I'm driving." Her voice is soft, comforting me.

I make a noncommittal sound and concentrate even further.

"The speed limit is thirty-five, not thirty," she offers helpfully.

"I'm going a speed I'm comfortable driving at."

Twisting in her seat, she lets out a sigh. "Except there are ten cars behind you, and I suspect one of them is going to pass you soon."

Recalling her describing how the accident occurred, I curse and begin to increase my speed. "I don't want you afraid."

"Nick, he was drunk."

My hands clench on the wheel.

"He was playing stupid games because he was a stupid man."

"Can you please stop talking about it? At least for now?" I ask her pleasantly as we pass the spot where she indicated her car flipped over. And over.

"I just want to say one more thing, and then the subject is closed." Her hand reaches across the center console and rests on my thigh. The heat burns through my pants and seeps into my thigh. "You would have slammed on your brakes, run to me, and torn me out of that car. You would have carried me to a medical center. You would have demonstrated to the world exactly what I knew back then. You're a man worthy of being loved."

By the time Maris stops talking, we're almost at her home. I pull into the driveway and up to the garage but don't open it. Pressing the button to put the car in park, I undo my seat belt and then hers before hauling her across my lap.

"What are you doing?" she exclaims.

"This." I pull her head down to mine to claim her lips in a kiss so incendiary, I immediately have to have her.

Right here. Right now.

Maris tears her mouth away. "Nick, just pull inside and park the car. There's a couch..."

"No. Can't wait." My voice is guttural with need. I slide my hands up her slim thighs until I reach the apex of her thighs. "Who the fuck invented these things?" I groan, referring to her leggings.

Maris, who was busy trying to get to my chest, snaps her head up. "Why do you care?"

"Because I'm not sure if they should be shot or given an award." I stretch the material so tight I can push my fingers in next to the seam. I give myself just enough room before I render the material useless as I tear it in both directions.

Then we're both speechless: Maris because I destroyed her pants and me because she's not wearing any panties, not even a thong.

The flap of material flops down, blocking her from my view. With a snarl, I reach up and tuck the offending material under her shirt so my view is unobstructed. "Push up on your knees a bit," I order her.

Maris shakily braces her arms on my shoulders—one knee on the armrest on the door, the other on the center console. Her ankles are locked behind her. I slowly take each one of her hands and kiss the palm before I place it on the shoulder rest before I skim my way down her body until my lips are even with her pussy. "Fucking beautiful."

"Are you crazy? There's no way I'll be able to come like this!"

"You don't think so," I dare her. "Oh, I know you'll be able to come like this, Maris. In fact, by the time you come, you're going to beg me to fuck you right here." I trace the line of her bare lips with my finger. "Christ, you're dripping already." I slide the finger with the trace of her essence in my mouth.

She shivers and arches, seeking my touch, my mouth. "Please," she moans.

"Please what, Sunshine? Please do this?" I skate the heel of my palm against her mound and slide one finger inside of her.

Maris immediately bucks her hips against it. "Yes. More, Nick."

I hear her breath catch as I slide in a second finger. Her hips begin rocking back and forth, friction easing as her body's natural essence eases the way for my fingers to thrust into her tight heat.

Using my other hand, I part her folds to seek out the treasure hidden beneath them. When the cool air hits her clit, Maris lets out a small whimper. I give her no quarter as I pluck mercilessly at the straining button of her clit even as my fingers continue to thrust upward. Thousands of muscles tighten on my fingers.

Fuck that. "You're not coming unless it's on my cock," I vow.

"Soon," she manages to gasp. "Let me come first."

"After I taste you." Pulling my fingers away, I lift my head. "I really need to taste you, Maris."

My tongue begins to work at her clit even as I maintain the pressure inside her pussy. Even while I drive my fingers strongly inside her, my tongue is circling, flicking, before finally suckling her into madness.

Maris's head flies back. Her back arches so much her curls dance past her ass, almost into my hands. Her hips begin desperately rocking, rising and falling. Finding her purchase, she reaches down and holds my head to her. I groan, the vibration against her sensitive flesh making her pant harder.

Finally, the words I've been waiting for pass her lips. "Fuck me, Nick. Fuck me the way you want to."

What's left unsaid between us is *Fuck me the way you've always wanted to.*

My mouth is drenched with her. I wiggle my way back to a sitting position. Then I slowly pull my fingers from her pussy. I hold them to her lips. Maris takes them in her mouth and sucks them like she devoured my cock. "God, I need inside you." I grit the words out.

Maris untwists her ankles while I go to work on my jeans. Shucking them down my hips, my cock springs free just as her thighs spread wide over mine. I quickly drag the head through her lips to lubricate it.

She slaps both her hands on my cheeks. "Stop teasing me, Nick. Give it to me."

She's on fire, her glow so bright it's brighter than the sun still burning outside despite the late hour of the night. I hold my cock steady. Maris tips her hips. And like a magnet, we're drawn together.

She sinks down on me achingly slow. I'd think it has something to do with my size if it wasn't for the curve of her lips. "Getting some of your own back?" I question mildly.

"Me? Would I ever..." But she can't finish when I thrust up into her reaching as deep as I can trying to make her explode.

Gasping, shuddering, Maris rolls her hips so every time I press upward into her clenching body, I hit her throbbing clit. Uncertain how much longer I'll be able to hold on, I yank up her sweater and pull down her bra. My mouth immediately hones in on one of the tight buds, sucking it gently against the roof of my mouth just as I push upward.

Maris jerks in my grasp, holding my head in place. She moans long and hard as her whole body shudders. Her nails score against my neck, my head. Her lips seek out mine as her pussy ripples along my cock.

But I wasn't done.

My hips continue to thrust and retreat, powered on by her broken inhales. I can't help it, I have to finish. I have to shoot myself inside my woman. And then it's there, twitching in my spine, my balls, until I explode.

As I hold her clasped against my chest, I wonder if I have enough energy to pull the car into the garage. When I say as much to Maris, she lifts her head from my shoulder and whacks me across the chest. "Should have thought of that before you tore my pants, you idiot."

I just grin, albeit weakly. I pull her head back down. "I'll be fine in a minute."

It's more like ten. But holy hell, was it worth it.

It takes me stripping Maris off upstairs before showering to get her to admit the same.

MARIS

"Miracles happen. After all, I found Dean. And for some crazy reason, he fell in love with me." - From the journals of Jedidiah Smith.

I stop off to visit David on the way to work. Like the ripples on water after rain stops pelleting it after a storm, my heart settles in a way it hasn't for far too long. I luxuriate in the feeling even while I fear being caught exposed and unprepared for the next one.

Nonsense, I think to myself. *You're just not used to being this happy with so many good emotions surging through you.* Nick, David, home. I'm not just fantasizing of what could be; I'm living it.

Now, I'm impatient to finalize everything. The time with Nick has lit a fire in my blood for more of...everything. Especially him. A private smile crosses my lips when I recall the way he couldn't wait to get in to the house last night. I never thought it could be this right between us, but it is. His arrogance no longer infuriates me. Instead I find myself more amused than anything. His strength comforts instead of overwhelming me. And the streak of sensitivity in him he claims exists just for me makes my heart quiver.

I thought I was in love with him all these years? I had no idea what love was until he flooded every chamber of my heart. But as much as I love our now, I soon suspect it won't be enough. We've both admitted we wasted too many years on resentment and regrets. I need to know how he factors into not only my future but the one I'll be building with my son.

Sarah comes out to greet me, finding me buried under the arms and legs of random children. Laughing, she demands, "Let Maris up!"

"Hope you don't mind. I just stopped by to get some quality time in before work."

"Not a problem at all. I was going to call you, see if you were free to come by for a chat."

My brows draw together. "Is something wrong?"

Sarah just smiles. "Why don't you come inside? Kids, I'm stealing Maris."

My heart melts when all of the children groan, but David wraps his arms around my legs. "Don't go!" he shrieks, unwilling to free me.

I run my hand over the top of his hair. "I'll be back soon."

"Promise?"

"Always." I follow Sarah inside where she blessedly has coffee waiting. "One day I'll be as good at this as you," I say reverently when she hands me a mug.

"What's that?"

"Organization. Motherhood. Making coffee at a moment's notice." Our shared laughter releases the coil of tension inside me.

"I just wanted to find out how things were progressing. I haven't heard anything, and I didn't want to say anything in front of the children."

"Slowly. Is it always like this?"

Sarah tilts her head. "It's been so long since we fostered our first, but I'd say you're probably right on schedule, Maris, if not a little ahead."

"Really?" Excitement courses through me. "Do you think it will be soon?"

"How long has it been?"

"Months, but it feels like forever." I draw out the last word.

Sarah rubs my arm sympathetically. "Even having had my own, I felt the same way. I wanted what I wanted, and I wanted it then. Couldn't they see I was perfect?"

I bobble my cup. Thank goodness I've sipped down my coffee. "Sarah, are you sure you don't have a listening device in my house? Pretty sure I said that very thing the other night," I tease.

"Oh? Do tell."

I flush remembering the context that I said it.

"You have that look on your face of a woman in love," Sarah comments drolly. Her eyes are dancing.

At first I blank, uncertain if she means David or Nick. But then I get my wits about me and admit, "It's new." But is it really? No, I acknowledge to myself. The feelings I have for Nick have just evolved.

"Maris." There's a note of concern in her voice.

"What?"

"You do realize if this person is going to be around the children— any child—they're going to have to be investigated as well?" Sarah's words jerk me from my reverie.

"I would imagine that would be the case while I was fostering," I reply cautiously.

She shakes her head. "You don't understand. They could find some-thing, anything, in the person's history and deny an adoption. They could pull the child."

A chill washes over me. "What are you trying to insinuate, Sarah? Just come right out and say it."

"I'm trying to give you the best shot you have at getting what you said was your dream." She puts her cup down and reaches for mine. Her hands clasp both of mine. "You do understand once you signed those papers you gave up your right to privacy when it comes to these children? Tomorrow, if something happened to Hung—"

"God forbid," I whisper fervently.

"But if it did, I could lose all of them. Just. Like. This." She lets go of my hand to snap her fingers. "It doesn't matter to the state I'd be grieving or my children would be. What matters to the social worker assigned to those children are *those children*. And you need to remember that every single day. Every decision you make has to be for the child you bring into your home. Full stop. Period."

My breathing is so accelerated, I'm certain the room is spinning around me.

Nick.

David.

Before I came here, I was so certain I was going to have them both. Now, what if I have to choose? "I can't imagine there's a god who would deny me love." I don't realize the words come out of my mouth until Sarah replies.

"I wouldn't if it was me. But it's not my choice. It's none of our choice if we go through this process. You have to be prepared God assigned angels to watch over these children. It's their mission, and they are vigilant about it. I don't know what they may require you to sacrifice. I pray it's not giving up one type of love in order to embrace another."

My lips part, but I have no words to refute her worry. There's nothing I can do but hope that maybe the sacrifices I've made are enough.

That and enjoy every moment where I can have them both.

"You have to go."

"I don't wanna," he whines.

"Oliver is going to make fun of you. Not to mention Reece is going to remind you you're an old man," I remind him.

Uh-oh. Wrong insult. Nick prowls over my body, pinning my hands over my head with one hand. His muscular thighs hold mine down as he fumbles in his pocket for his cell phone. "Ollie? Nick. Take Reece on the trails for a five-mile run, then put him through the paces today. I won't be in." There's a pause. "I know it's a goddamn gift. Why? Because I need to crack the whip somewhere else this morning."

"Oh, goodie. I like whips," I sass.

Nick glares down at me. Tucking his phone between his chin and shoulder, he rolls me to my stomach and yanks down the covers, exposing my ass. Smoothing a hand up and down over it softly, he gives instructions to Oliver about the kind of run Reece should be taken on.

I mumble a trail name that could be made up for all I'm able to speak right now. Nick rewards my ingenuity by placing a kiss on my shoulder though. That feels nice. I'm almost back in la-la land with that sweet stroking. I need to remind Nick this is how he should put me to sleep all the time.

He tells Oliver and then disconnects the call.

Then, *pop*. Nick's hand smacks down on my ass.

Almost instinctively, my foot kicks up and nails him in the nuts. Then I curse him because he's wearing a damn cup. He laughs and rolls off to the side while he begins smoothing his hand over the heat.

"Hmm, okay. That's interesting."

"Wait. I thought you said you liked whips?" Nick's confused.

I lift my head off my very comfortable pillow. "If I turn my head and that clock has a four as the first number, you're going to die. We didn't fall asleep until after midnight."

Nick, smart man that he is, simply reaches over and flips down my alarm clock.

"Second, you can tell when I'm giving you crap most of the time. Why couldn't you tell when I was doing it just then?"

"Jealousy," he says immediately.

"You are so full of shit." I immediately find the spot on my pillow where my face carved a perfect impression and fall back into it.

My comfort lasts for about 0.3 seconds as Nick decides to make amends for his irrational behavior. And it's not discomfort that floods my system, but a heat that is impossible to ignore.

Starting with the arch of my foot, he trails his mouth slowly up each leg. The tip of his tongue leaves a moist heat in its wake that has me writhing, begging. Until he pops me again on the other cheek. "No moving, Sunshine."

"Is this supposed to be punishment?" I dare to ask him.

"Hell no. I want this to last as long as possible. Do you really think I enjoy running?"

"Then what's with the spanking?" I demand as he draws me to my knees.

Running his nose between my folds, he murmurs, "That's just to see how wet I can get you. The guys are going to try to beat the shit out of me for being a lucky bastard anyway. Might as well make it worth it."

My laugh turns into a groan as Nick sinks two fingers in me as he wedges his broad shoulders beneath me and pulls my hips down to tongue at my clit before making my body burn and hum.

I can't imagine a day without him, not anymore. And for today, I don't have to.

Later that night as I head into work, I'm the one kissing him goodbye at the door. He murmurs, "I'll leave the light on."

"Jed used to say that." I can't help being shaken. How did Nick worm his way into my routine? And what am I going to do if he doesn't stay?

Nick tucks a strand of my hair behind my ear. "Did he?"

"Yes."

"Good." Before he can open his mouth, I tug his hair I'm still holding in my hand. "I'll try not to wake you up when I get in. After the way you woke me up this morning, I'm going to crawl into bed and pass out," I lie. Likely I'll do what I did the night before and the night before that—simply watch him sleep until he rolls over and realizes I'm there.

And draws me under him to fulfill my wildest fantasies.

"It's not my fault you work past ten, Sunshine. Some of us need our beauty sleep."

I burst out laughing before playfully shoving away. "Nick, if you were any more handsome, priests would have to accept certain kinds of sins. Now let me go so I can come home and creep up to bed."

Nick makes a rude noise but kisses me soundly. It's a kiss full of affection. "Drive safely," he warns.

"Always do." I wave as I head into the basement and through to the garage. But my smile slips as I slide into my SUV.

Reaching inside my black jumpsuit for the gold cross that rests there, I whisper, "Jed, what's happening? What did I get myself into this time?" Since he doesn't answer me, I open the garage door and back out.

Once I hit the street, I make a call. I know she's expecting it since she answers on the first ring. "Well, well, well. Something to share?" Kara teases.

"Don't make me cry; I'm driving," I warn her.

"So you chose now to call me? That wasn't the wisest of decisions."

"Has any decision I've ever made been wise?"

Kara inhales deeply. "You stop that. You lived after so much pain when so many people would have just curled into themselves. I will never let you disparage yourself because you had a full life."

"No, this is completely asinine."

"What did you do?"

"I..."

"Maris," Kara snaps.

"Kara, I fell in love."

"God, Maris, you did that years ago."

"It's different. So, so different."

Kara's voice sharpens. "What do you mean?"

I begin to babble. "I didn't expect it to happen like this. So strong, so fierce. I knew him, knew what he could do to my heart. I was so sure I could handle it. It shouldn't have happened so quickly."

"It happened years ago, or did you forget the last twenty years of your life?" she teases softly.

"Kara." My breath shudders. "I may have to make a choice. How do I make a choice?"

"A choice about what?"

I fill her in on what Sarah said yesterday. I'm talking so quickly, I'm at the Brewhouse and parking before I know it. "How am I supposed to choose? I love them both."

"There's a part of me that wants to say love will overcome no matter what, but we live in reality."

"Reality can suck my left tit," I proclaim.

Kara chuckles, but there's a vein of sadness beneath it. "There's only one thing I can say, Maris. After everything Jennings and I went through, after finding our way back to one another. There's only one certainty."

"What's that?"

"You shouldn't have to choose between your child and the man you love. But life sometimes just gets it wrong, no matter how many times you throw wishes and pleas into the air." We're both quiet, remembering. When she speaks again, there's a huskiness to her voice. "If that happens, come to me. My arms are waiting for you just like yours were for me."

"Why do you have to live so damn far away?" The first time I said those words to her, I was dropping her off at the airport to fly home to Florida right after she found out she was pregnant with her son, a little over eighteen years ago. I've never meant them more than I do right now.

"I'm just a flight away." Her exact words back to me.

"Or a few," I retort.

"Better now. We don't get charged an arm and a leg by the airline."

I let out a watery laugh knowing Jennings would fly either of us in either direction if we needed each other. "Okay. I have to go."

"One last thing?"

"What?"

"It's your time to find a love as extraordinary as the one you wanted for me." She disconnects the call in my ear.

In the car, with the summer light streaming through, I whisper, "Damn you," because I'm still left with wondering whose love that is.

NICHOLAS

"Great news, Nick." Reece smiles enormously as he lifts the bar back upward while he's doing reps on the bench press. Oliver is spotting him and merely lifts his chin to acknowledge my presence, his eyes on the bar moving up and down from Reece's slow-moving chest.

I drop my bag and shrug off my sweatshirt before heading over to the jump rope. Quickly getting into rhythm, I ask, "Oh? What's that?"

Reece finishes with his last rep and with Oliver's help reracks the bar. He sits up before he announces, "Talked with my gran last night. Turns out, we were doing the same thing for each other. She's been wanting to move to somewhere warmer for years but was afraid of hurtin' me by sayin' so. She has some friends who RV but made Albuquerque their winter home base. She's all in."

I grin. "That's great news."

"So, when do we go?" Reece demands excitedly.

"Go?" I ask blankly.

"Head to Albuquerque?" His voice is eager.

My mind completely blanks so much so that an exercise routine I've performed over and over daily trips me up. Literally. The jump rope winds its way around my ankles, and as I pull back, Oliver yells, "Look out."

But it's too late. I go flying face forward toward the mats like one of the untried kids at Razor.

And as I'm falling, thoughts flash through my mind: Razor, work, and the most important one. Maris.

Even as my body crashes down hard, I know in my heart she won't turn her back on me just because I have to go home to do my job. I roll to avoid the jarring impact, cursing.

"Nick, you trying to show Reece why we bring in a dance instructor to Razor to work with the athletes?" Oliver calls out.

"Asshole." I throw him the finger to enhance my point before untwining the jump rope from my ankles. "But yes, that is something we do."

"I can't wait." And now that the worry is gone, there's nothing but excitement in Reece's voice.

"How long will it take you to get everything settled?" While this guy needs to be at our camp training, my heart is aching in my chest. *Please let him give me some outrageous date so I don't have to have this conversation with Maris soon*, I beg silently.

"How does two weeks sound?"

"Because if you need...that soon?"

"Technically, the house we live in belongs to my parents," Reece explains. "So, after we made our decision yesterday, I called them and told them our plans. All we have to do is pack and find a flight."

"Don't worry about that," I hear Oliver tell him through a fog. "Razor covers all your moving costs."

Two weeks.

On one hand, I'll be out of Alaska, but I'll be leaving Maris for an untold period of time. I don't know how long it will be until she can wrap things up and join me in Albuquerque. *Assuming she wants to*, a little voice inside me prods. But I shove that niggling doubt aside. We love each other. What is there to hold us back?

Right?

From my sitting position on the floor, I begin making plans for who Reece should train with first. Tatum, absolutely. Even though Tatum's climbing the ladder steadily, it will do him some good to have some in-house competition. Besides, despite the fact he's a weight class lower than Reece, his ground game is unparalleled. Briefly, I wonder how Reece will feel having his ass kicked by one of our women fighters?

"Shit, you're fucked," Oliver cackles. I don't even acknowledge him as I imagine how quickly Veronika would be able to take this behemoth down.

"What? What's going on?" Reece worries.

"Nick's face?"

"Yeah?'

"That's his 'he's planning your training' face."

"So? What's wrong with that?"

"I'll ask you that in about a month when your ass has been handed to you by a woman," Oliver predicts.

Reece scoffs. "Right."

I decide then to put Reece in the ring with Veronika first thing. Clapping my hands together, I push myself to my feet. "Okay. If you two have the workout here under control, I'm going to head back to my place to make some plans. The sooner we get things started, the sooner we're back home."

The sooner I can show Maris my home, I think to myself.

Reece walks over and holds out a hand. "Thank you for taking this chance on me, Nick."

"You'll earn it, Reece. So, the thanks are ours for putting your trust in Ollie, in Razor, and in yourself."

He smiles, and immediately my brain remembers, media kit. Shit, I need my computer pronto.

SIX HOURS LATER, I have first-class tickets booked for Reece, his grandmother, and Oliver out of Juneau in ten days. It's a shorter time-line than I originally intended, but after checking with Reece, he said it's one they can make work. "Like I said earlier, Nick, we just have a few things to pack."

"Right. About that. A moving company will be here in six days. Make certain Ollie is aware you'll be supervising them and that's your day off training. They have about an eighteen-hour window to get whatever you need packed and in a shipping container. Make certain you have enough clothes and gear for you and stuff for your grandmother for about two weeks."

The silence on the other end of the line was so absolute, I was certain the call was disconnected. "Hello?" I prompted.

"This is better than winning the lottery because that's a fantasy. This is real." His words strike a chord deep inside of me.

"No, kid. This is better because you worked for it. You'll never take it for granted. Now, you have my number. Get a pen."

There's some scrambling on the other end before, "Got it."

I rattle off Charmaine's office and cell. "That's my assistant, Charmaine. She runs all our lives. Make sure you have those numbers in your phone, and when she calls, you answer them. I don't care what you're doing—unless it's helping your grandmother." I make a mental note to email Charmaine about Reece's grandmother in the event she needs to change the long-term housing to accommodate her needs.

"Got it. Never forget Charmaine."

"Oh, and Reece?"

"Yeah?"

"Learn to not curse around her now."

"Who? Gran? I don't do that." He sounds affronted.

"No, I mean Charmaine. You'll owe her a whack. And right now, you're not making the kind of money she charges for cursing."

I hang up in the middle of his laughter.

After a follow-up email to my assistant, I flip back over to the airline's website. I can stretch out my time here probably an additional week with Maris. Maybe two. I close the page down, just as the garage door opens. At the same time, the front door opens, and I hear Brad, Rainey, and their kids shrieking laughter.

"Nick?" Maris voice precedes her up the stairs. "Did you get my texts? Brad and Rainey are here for dinner. They brought burgers."

"I'll be right down. Just working on some email!" I shout back.

"Okay, honey. We'll be outside by the grill. Take your time." Maris turns and heads down the stairs.

Just then, an email pops into my box from Charmaine.

Got it, Nick! Oliver picked a real winner. Excited about Reece.

10-4 on his grandmother. I'll make sure they're comfortable.
Looking forward to you being back. Things run smoother when you're here.
~C

There's only one part of me that won't run smoother when I'm there, I think as I close down my laptop. Not anymore.

And that's my heart.

"MARIS, YOU KNEW DEAN WELL, RIGHT?" Brad asks after dinner while we're lounging around the Smiths' backyard much like we used to do in the old days.

"Not as well as Kara, but yes. He was fabulous," Maris replies while leaning into the arm I have wrapped around her.

"Will you tell us about him?" Rainey whips her head toward her husband, who shrugs. "I've always wanted to ask, but I was afraid to ask Kara. And I'm sure Jennings now knows, but he's never shared."

"Bradley Meyers, maybe because talking about Dean means talking about Jed. And maybe Maris isn't ready!" Rainey snaps.

"Shit. Crap. I'm sorry, Maris," Brad immediately apologizes.

"Don't ever apologize to me for wanting to talk to me about my brother." Maris's voice is strong. "I'm just surprised you guys are so dense."

"I mean, I didn't mean to bring up... What?" Brad shouts.

Rainey falls into him laughing.

I squeeze Maris's shoulder as my own begin to shake. "Thanks for the compliment, my love."

"Not a problem. Come on, Brad. You didn't put together the fact Jed said Dean was the epitome of all the things he was searching for about love? My brother refused to settle for anything in this life—that included the man he fell for as well as the quality of his friends." Maris tips her beer in his direction and mine before she takes a long pull.

Brad's head bows, and although I lift my drink in return, there's no way I can swallow any of it.

"But if you want to know about Dean specifically, I'll tell you a secret none of you know." Maris leans toward the center of the table.

We all lean in, anxious.

"Did you know the Jacks all actually met him?"

"Bullshit," I exclaim.

"What he said." Brad points at me.

"You all were on your last reunion. And groceries were delivered by a man who wore a ball cap, jeans, and a long-sleeve T-shirt." Maris sits back and waits for our reaction.

"No fucking way. Why didn't Jed say anything?" I demand.

"Because my brother was flying from Montana to Juneau after the reunion. Dean came with him. Dean wanted the chance to check out the men who were closest to his husband."

"Why?" Brad interjects.

Maris's lips curve, but the smile doesn't reach her eyes. "Because the next week they were here, Jed redid his will. And Dean helped advocate on a certain man's behalf for one codicil of it. Dean wanted the chance to see Jennings in person so he could make a decision on whether or not to give his blessing to Jed's machinations."

I suck in an enormous breath. "He did that just by delivering groceries?"

"I do believe he was around long enough to put them away. Do you remember what conversations you all might have had?"

It's been years since that trip, but Brad whispers, "We talked about regrets. We were on the porch with Jed talking about if we had any regrets in our life."

And like a flash, I recall what I said. *I regret running away. Maybe if I hadn't, so many things would have been different. What about you, Jennings?*

I regret not picking up the phone. There was one call I regret not answering. Jed?

"It was maybe a five-minute conversation," I choke out.

"I've never met a more intuitive man than Dean Malone. He loved, and when he did, he did it fiercely. He was a damn hero, saving Kara long before he ever saved anyone as a fireman. His calmness complemented the storm that always surrounded Jed. He was gorgeous in the way that make people blush, but he never saw looks. He saw souls. He never lied. And he was beloved by anyone who met him." Maris takes a moment to wipe her eyes. "I was so wary of him, despite him being Kara's brother. After all, no man could be this perfect. Ever."

Maris's words, while bringing Jed's husband to life, bring me to my knees. I've never been that kind of man for her, to her. And she deserves a love just like her brother had. But I love her selfishly, and I refuse to let her go.

"He wore me down over time. And he became a perfect older brother—protective and loving. But while he was perfect for Jed, I never want a man that perfect." She grins at a captive Brad and Rainey before turning her head to the side and pressing a kiss to my cheek. "Obviously."

And like a prisoner freed from long captivity, I seek the one thing I haven't had freely in eons.

Sunshine.

I yank Maris into my arms and press my lips to hers for a kiss that declares more than just my feelings. It declares my relief. When I let her up, we find Rainey and Brad kissing each other through their hands like they're five-year-olds on the playground.

Deadpan, I say, "That explains so much about your kids."

Rainey reaches for a hamburger roll and tosses it at my head.

"Maris, do you have pictures?" Brad asks even as I duck and the bun flies over my head.

"Oh, do I ever. Let me go get them. Just be forewarned, their joint bachelor party was at a drag cabaret show in Jacksonville. And I got pictures of Jed up on stage."

I choke on the drink of my beer I'd just taken. "In costume? Christ. He already looked like a deranged lunatic. These I have to see."

Laughter rings out around the backyard as Maris races for the stairs. And for the rest of the night, Maris shares story after story about her brother and Dean.

And I forget about the news I need to share with her especially as there's a wealth of joy dancing like stars in her eyes.

NICHOLAS

"Text when you land." I hold out my hand to Oliver.

He shakes it. "Can I just say how odd this is?"

"What?"

"Me getting on a plane and leaving you here? But hey. It's not like you're going to be far behind, right?" His other hand comes up and clasps mine on the shoulder before he brings me close and bumps our shoulders together. "See you back in the land of warmth, boss." Turning to Reece and a delicate woman I never would have pegged for his grandmother, Oliver gestures them to the security line. Soon, they disappear from my sight.

And I'm left standing there saying nothing because there's nothing to say.

At least not to him.

Time's running out.

"WHY DO YOU STAY?" I trace a strand of hair from her nape down the smooth line of her back. The skin is ivory perfection, not marred or touched by the sun. It's a canvas I paint my fingers over night

210

after night. Taking the ends of her hair in hand, I dance it over her spine.

Maris giggles, the sound flooding my heart with joy. "That tickles."

"That doesn't answer my question," I admonish, brushing her hair over her again.

She starts to scoot away, but I haul her back. Her body was carved by a higher power to fit perfectly against mine. Her flesh against mine reminds me of the power and fluidity of an ocean wave just before it crests. Its force is brutally unstoppable, something destined for eternity.

Like our love.

"Why stay, Maris?" I repeat my question. "What hold does Alaska have on you?"

She doesn't move away, but she doesn't answer right away. I begin to wonder if she's fallen asleep in my arms when she shocks me with her answer. "Memories."

"Trust me, those are portable." Bitterness laces my tone.

"It makes it more difficult when the memories you hold are beautiful, Nick."

"After everything that's happened to you here, you can still say that?" There's skepticism in my voice.

"What you heard were the bare-bones stories. It would take a lifetime to fill in the details." Her voice is dreamy.

Therefore my voice is frustrated when I demand, "Give me an example."

"Like Dad closing the bar the week after I came home from the hospital—despite us needing the money. He carried me outside at least once a day and roasted marshmallows with me. Mom, well, she tried to teach me to cook—"

"You can," I interrupt.

"No, honey. I really can't. The only thing I mastered was her meatloaf. When Jed and I still lived here together, he did most of the cooking." She pauses. "Their graves are here—not just Jed, but Mom, Dad, and the grandparents."

My hand stills. "You could come back to visit them."

"That's true, but I don't have to."

But what about when we leave? I open my mouth to speak them, when her next ones freeze them in my throat.

"I want to raise my children in this home—to be able to tell them the stories of their uncles and grandparents. I want the Brewhouse to go on."

"That could possibly not happen." Maris shoots me a dirty look. "Leaving them the Brewhouse," I tack on hastily. "What if they want to be a hairdresser, or a scientist, or...?" *Or what if they want to run Razor? In an entirely different state?*

She shrugs. "Then I'll cross that bridge when I come to it. But the main one is the love in this home. Don't you feel it, Nick? After all these years, can't you feel the sweet memories from having been here?" She cants her head backward so her eyes meet mine.

And I give her the only response I can in that moment. "I do."

But instead of being smug, her face falls. "It holds rough memories too. I deal with those."

My ears perk up. "What do you mean?"

"I mean when you've lived somewhere your entire life, everything has ghosts."

"Did you ever think about selling the house?"

She chuckles. "So many times, I'm surprised I didn't have Realtors perched on my lawn like dogs in heat."

Just the image of all Juneau's real estate agents in a semicircle barking has me roaring. "Nice, Sunshine."

"No, it wasn't. It was bad. Really, really bad. That is, until Kara and Kevin came."

A ball begins to form in my stomach. "Why then?"

"After I came home in between the funeral we held for Dean in Florida and the one we had here in Juneau, I was alone. So alone."

"Why didn't you reach out?" I ask angrily.

"I couldn't." Her voice is sad. "The way Jed's will was written prohibited me from contacting any of you until you were all notified. This way you all were less likely to wonder why we weren't having the ceremony sooner than we were. I had to hold the ceremony for his husband first before I could hold his ceremony for his brothers."

I recall the letter I received from Jed's attorney notifying me

212

months after his actual death that he had passed and when the services would be held. "And you were alone that whole time?"

"I had Kara." Maris swipes under her eyes. "And let me tell you, if our friendship can withstand the things I put her through during that time, it can withstand anything." Before I can ask her what she means, Maris continues. "I essentially blamed her for their deaths, though she wasn't there. I screamed that if it wasn't for Dean, Jed would still be alive where he belonged—not in fucking Florida. And I said, at least she had a relative left."

"God, Maris." Even I'm wincing at the verbal beating Kara endured.

"All while dealing with her own tragedy and knowing her life was about to be flipped upside down. That's my Kara. And she flew here and dealt with it again from all of you."

I flinch, recalling what I said to Jennings about Kara. "No wonder he took a swing at me."

"Who?"

"Jennings."

"About what?"

"Kara."

She nods definitively. "Good."

"Even without knowing what was said?" I'm not even the slightest bit insulted because tempers were high, and I was so wrong.

"It's Kara." As if that says it all.

I kiss the crown of her head. "In any event, you're right."

Maris becomes quiet. I resume stroking her hair, her skin, just absorbing her. But her words freeze my movements. "So many nights after Jed died, I felt lost, alone, drifting. And cold, Nick. So, so, cold."

Instinctively, I pull Maris's body closer to mine to warm it. But her next words come out jaggedly—a whispered confession. It's the kind of confession that makes my own blood freeze, making me want to throw her ass on a plane tonight, consequences be damned.

"For a long time I questioned whether if it would be easier to succumb to the elements thrown at me year after year—the air, land, sea—just to escape the pain."

"What are you trying to tell me, Maris?" The words are torn from me.

"That I'm here because I choose to be, Nick. I may have had to deal with restless nights, lost dreams, and broken hearts, but this is where I'll reap the rewards of my life. Here is where I'll sow the seeds of love, family, and future."

And as she closes her eyes to sleep, I lie awake, realizing in my arrogance I didn't factor something critical into my plans to whisk Maris away.

Her acceptance.

As I drift off to sleep, I begin to dream. And for the first time in years, it's not of a Smith. It's my mother. And she's driving away from me at the store. Over and over again.

"It wasn't that bad."

"No, you only woke up four or five times. It was such a joy."

"I'm sorry about that." My embarrassment makes me irritated. "Would you like me to sleep in a different room?"

Maris stares down at me incredulously before stalking off to her en suite bathroom and slamming the door. I hear the snick of the lock and then curse roundly. "Great job, you fucking idiot."

While Maris is in the bathroom, I grab my cell phone and check it. Just like I asked, there's a text from Oliver. *Got Reece and his gran all settled. Nice digs Charmaine found. Did you up her budget? Ha ha.*

I type back. *Different budget than yours. Now get to the gym and get him working. You should have his training plan in your email.*

Then I glance at the clock and calculate backward. *Shit. Never mind. You're already there. Let me know how it goes with Tatum.*

I toss my phone to the side as Maris steps out. She's damp from having hopped in the shower but is quickly braiding her hair. "Where are you going?"

"I have work to do. You?" Her voice is saccharine sweet.

"I was planning on taking the day off."

"Well, I'll be in my office for a few hours."

"Come on, Maris. It was just a few bad dreams."

"I decided you were right. It's your business."

Sensing a trap, I tread carefully. "Okay."

"In fact, nothing you do makes no never mind to me, Nick."

What. The. Hell? "How can you say that?" I bellow.

"We haven't exchanged avowals of eternal devotion. You don't share, well, I don't have to either."

I sputter. "So what? It's just sex?"

She gets close to pat my arm consolingly. "Great sex. Fabulous sex. I've just had a couple of the best orgasms I've ever had. But more?" She shakes her head, the braid flipping and flopping instead of her hair rippling all the way down her back in loose curls.

"What utter crap. We have more than that. Look at everything you've shared with me."

Her head turns, and fuck me, I want nothing more than to wipe the manipulative curve off her lips by slamming my tongue down her damn throat. But her words pin me in my place faster than any fighter ever managed to. "That's right, Nick. I've been the one who shared."

Damn. "You know it all anyway," I clip out.

Hurt infuses her features, and her face blanks. "I might know Jed's view, but I don't know yours. And much like you read the emails about what happened about my accident and managed to pry out my emotions... You know what? Just forget about it."

Maris starts yanking clothes from her dresser. I leap up on the bed and cross it in two strides before jumping down. "You don't need those." I wrap my arms around her.

"If you think for a hot second I'm crawling in between the sheets with you right now, you've been hit in the head way too many times." Fury and hurt lace her voice.

I place a soft kiss against the exposed skin of her shoulder. "There's no way in fuck you're getting into the ring wearing jeans. Or boots." I take a wild-ass guess based on the socks she yanked out to wear.

"Who said I'm getting into the ring with you, Champ?"

"Because I'll answer one question for every punch you actually manage to land." She squirms around, breasts pressing up against my abdomen, making my cock harden.

"Why can't I kick?" she demands.

My lips twitch. "I'm wearing a cup. You'll take a cheap shot."

Her smile lightens the room and my heart. "Maybe I'll break it?"

I laugh. "You can try, Sunshine."

"Nick." Maris lifts her hand to cup my bristled chin. "Are you sure?"

No. I want to discuss my past about as much as I want to let go of the woman in my arms. But still I reply, "We'll see how many rounds you can handle."

Her breath wafts over mine as her fingers dance beyond my cock to cup my balls. "I can handle more than you think."

MARIS IS GOOD, damn good. She packs a wallop behind her punches I wasn't expecting. When she lands a roundhouse kick to the back of my knee, I drop to the mat, breathing hard more from the excitement of our sparring than anything else. Her hand whirls out, nails sheathed, the heel aiming for my heart. "Do you really think you can take me?" I pant.

"No. But the object isn't to take you down as much as it's to end this once and for all. I'm sick of wasting what's left of my life on something I'll never truly have."

Just as her hand is about to make contact, her body sags into itself. "I'm not going to apologize to you for being strong enough to tell you I love you. That I care about who you are and what happened to you. I'm only sorry that in the end, if you can't open up who you were to me, it will irrevocably change who we are. Somehow, you managed to make me stronger than yesterday. Why won't you let me help you take some of those ugly memories and make them all right? Do you want to carry these burdens forever?" She turns away, but not before the overhead light catches the film of tears coating her dark blue eyes. "If you can't tell me, find someone to talk with, Nick, because bottling all of this up inside? It will eventually hurt more than just us. It will penetrate every aspect of your life. Trust me, I know. Jed tried to get me to speak with a professional for years, but at least I had him and Kara."

"Maris." But before I can choke out more than her name, she's sliding out of the ring. I surge to my feet. "Stop. Please!" But by the time I get the words out, she's scooped up her shoes and keys and burst out the gym doors.

I vault over the ropes and snatch up my hoodie, heedless of any routine. All I can think about is getting to her. But my heart stops when I hear a slight clink hit the floor.

Her grandfather's cross—Jed's cross. She hasn't taken it off since the first night I made love to her, but she took it off to enter the ring with me. "Why now?" My legs begin to shake as I collapse into the folding chair.

"Maybe I can help answer that," a voice comes from the doorway.

"Christ. Not now, Rainey." Not when the woman I loved for so many years just walked away after I so stupidly assumed we'd finally find a way to make it work.

"Yes, now, Nick." She slides her handbag into the same seat Maris removed her stuff from just moments before. "Tell me about what happened with Maris."

"You mean you didn't hear enough?" I drawl as I loop a towel around my neck. I'm fisting the cross chain tightly.

"No, you ass. I didn't hear shit. I was coming in to invite you both to dinner, and she blew past me with tears on her face. Now before I throw your ass into a car so we can go after her, tell me what happened?"

"Nothing. We got into a disagreement."

"Does it involve why you're running away from her?" Disapproval laces Rainey's voice.

Fury causes me to take an involuntary step forward. "What the hell do you know about it. You don't know dick about my life, Rainey. You weren't abandoned when you were a kid in Ketchikan!" I shout.

"No, instead I watched my husband and his friends get abandoned every time they needed a friend," she yells back. "Want me to list them out?"

Maris's voice interrupts our argument. "That won't be necessary, Rainey." Maris stands there, arms crossed.

Rainey storms away, while my heart sags in relief. "I was terrified you'd left."

Maris shoots me a cool look before announcing, "I'm not stupid enough to get behind the wheel of a car when I'm upset. One wreck to change the course of my life is bad enough."

And unlike the kicks and hits I took in the ring, her words do drop me to my knees. I scrub my hands over my face. "Christ, Maris."

"Let's go, Champ. I'm through with this little exercise." Maris turns on her heel and walks out.

Quickly, I scramble into my sweats. Rainey's still standing by the door like a sentry. When I reach her, I push the door open over her shoulder. She doesn't even look in my direction before she announces, "She doesn't deserve to be hurt anymore, Nick." Then she walks out.

Too late. I've already hurt her more than I should have and for no good reason.

And I'm likely to again.

NICHOLAS

"What is it you want to know" I ask her dully.

Maris doesn't say a word. But the look she shoots me before heading up the stairs makes me realize I pushed things way too far.

Shit. I made the bargain, and ever since we left the gym and I slid the cross around her neck, to which I received a clipped "Thanks," Maris hasn't said anything. Then again, have I asked her any questions? I've been trying to guide—hell, manipulate—her into talking about something, anything, but what I promised. I even bartered with the discussing our future. "Maris, we really need to have a conversation about this." And while it's the damn truth, this isn't the time for it, though fuck if I know when that's going to be even though at one point that would almost have been as terrifying to discuss as the past.

But not now, not since Maris has the future looked as bright. And I actually want her to know there is one for us and the past doesn't impact that. And like a crashing realization, I want to bang my head against something. If the past doesn't matter, then why can't I talk about it?

As soon as that bit of enlightenment hits, I follow her. When I reach the main level, I find her head tipped back as she swallows water from a glass. I pause to admire the way her creamy skin works over the long line of her neck. Her dark hair is pulling away from the tight braids she'd done it up in before we went to spar. Her sweatshirt's partially unzipped, exposing the tops of her breasts captured in her tight sports bra. "Damn thing's holding in my favorite part of you," I remark.

Maris rolls her eyes. Putting the glass on the counter, she reaches under her chest and jiggles her boobs. "As soon as I change, they'll be back in their normal shape."

"Wrong part of your anatomy."

She spins around to try to get a look at her delectable ass in her workout pants, but I stop her by coming up behind her and placing my hands on her hips. "Your heart, Sunshine. And I didn't want to taint it with the memories living in my head."

I know her swiftly indrawn breath has nothing to do with the closeness of our bodies' proximity, despite the fact she can no doubt feel the stirrings of my body's response to her nearness. It has to do with the fact I opened the door to letting her inside the dark places inside me to shine her light. My head lowers down until I inhale the scents that calm me: sweat and Maris. The fact they're mingled together are a balm to my soul. "They need to bottle this scent," I mutter against her neck.

Spinning until she's pressed against me, front to front, Maris fits herself tighter. Our bodies fit against one another as if a great artist created her softness to fit my hollows, and my hardness to be shaped exactly to hold Maris. I marvel in the tactile perfection of us before I whisper, "What's your first question?"

Instead of pulling away like I expected her to, she wraps her arms closer around me. "Were you scared?"

"When my mother left me?"

Maris nods against my shoulder. "Though I vehemently disagree with the use of the word 'mother,' but continue."

Why am I smiling? God knows, I never expected to. "So noted." I give myself a few moments to answer so she doesn't think I'm blowing off the answer. "Maybe at first because I feared what would happen. But, honestly, do you want to know the worst part?"

She nods, still not giving me her eyes. I continue. "The worst part was being so fucking ashamed. All the kids at school knew. There was no way of escaping it. One minute, I was this loner, but then there was all this attention. Christ, I hated the fucking attention—especially for that. I swore, every night I slept in that borrowed bed, wearing those borrowed clothes, that if I managed to get away, I wouldn't come back unless I was *somebody*." I let my words hang in the air between us.

"That explains... Well, you accomplished that in spades. With the help of a handful of Jacks along the way."

I jerk my head back in shock. Did she just say that? But when I do, there's no judgment on it. Instead there's a ferocious intensity I've only seen twice before: when Maris was talking about the child she wanted to adopt and when I told Jed the same story years ago right after we reconnected.

"How is it you don't resent me for not being here?" I ask her the question I've been holding back. "My love for you is just as strong as it was back then. How can you not hate me when so much could have been different?"

She fiddles with the string of my sweatshirt before letting it drop. "There were days I thought I did, don't kid yourself, none worse than Vegas."

The words strike me harder than the kick she landed earlier. "Ouch."

"But if you were drowning and I was sinking, would either of us been able to have saved each other?"

"No. We'd have just pulled each other deeper into the abyss."

"Exactly." Her hands flatten on my chest before she tugs at the cross she's wearing. The cross I figured Jed meant for his sister to have when things were right between us. It never felt quite right to wear it, but damn, it makes my heart skip a beat to see it around her neck. "The last time Jed was home, he tried to talk to me about you. Dean was sitting right over there." She nods in the direction of the family room.

"I imagine that went over well." My voice is full of irony, even knowing Jed was trying to get her to Albuquerque at a later date to fix the breach between us.

She pulls the chain between her lips and slides the cross forward back. "Uh-huh."

I bark out a laugh before tugging the chain out from between her lips so I can kiss her all too briefly. "Do you have more questions?"

"Just one. It's a fairly substantial one."

"What's that?" I brace myself.

"We're not like related or anything? You and Jed ruled that out, I hope?" Her impish smile lights the stars that live inside her eyes.

I don't bother to answer, not with words anyway. Instead, I bend down and catch her around the waist with my shoulder. Standing up, I hook the back of her knees with my arm before announcing, "We both smell. Time for a shower."

"Goodie. Does this mean I get to scrub you everywhere?"

I almost drop her at the provocative image her words conjure up in my brain. To retaliate, I give her ass a love tap.

Which, being Maris, she promptly returns. "Tit for tat, buddy."

"I'll take tit anytime, Sunshine." I bound up the stairs with her musical laughter trailing out behind.

And while I'm soaping up her body and hearing her moans echo off the shower walls a short time later, I send my thanks skyward for several things.

For our timing finally being right.

That Maris's main concern was my well-being and not the nitty-gritty details.

And for the Smiths' foresight in investing in indoor plumbing all those years ago when they built this house.

"Aren't you concerned about loving an adopted child differently?" I ask her as we plow our way through a bowl full of pasta after our shower.

"Now? Not in the slightest. Honestly, the only time I gave it any thought was the years immediately after I had surgery. And for a while, I just debated giving up the idea of having a family at all." I hope Maris doesn't notice my small flinch as I reach for my water because I still can't wrap my mind around the idea she can't have children. I just don't want her misunderstanding why.

I still remember one night when we sat outside by the old fire pit and she boldly declared, "I'm going to fill every one of those bedrooms up with babies, Nick. People are going to get so used to seeing this belly round, they won't recognize me without it." Maris proceeded to bend her back so far out it was almost a vertical back bend.

And one of the many times she secretly had me in stitches. "And what about Jed? Where's he going to live?" I asked instead of rising to the bait of asking about her future husband or baby daddy.

She turned around and finally pointed to a patch of land on the far corner of the property. "He can pitch a tent there."

Even I couldn't hold in my laughter at that point. "So generous."

And to think now, those bedrooms will remain unused unless, "Are you planning on adopting more than one child?" I wonder aloud.

"Let me get through the process with one first, please and thank you. I might have an anxiety attack before I get to hold my son in my arms."

"Fair enough." But the image of that long-ago Maris still won't fade. "You'd be a terrific Mom to one or a dozen though."

Just as she was about to take another bite of pasta, she lays the fork down next to the side of her bowl. "Would you mind repeating that?"

After I do, she presses her hand to her lower stomach. "That's what I thought you said." Maris shoves to her feet and moves to the window. She stands there unmoving.

"What did I say?" I put my own bowl to the side and move in behind her.

"You said those exact words to me one night when I used to joke around about having a big family. After...after everything, Jed used to say something similar, but I blew it off." She lets out a breath that stirs the fine hair around her face. I lift my hand and brush it back. Maris reaches up and clasps my hand against her cheek. "It just threw me off hearing those words from your mouth again. That's all."

I want to open my mouth and volunteer to be the man to give her as many children as she wants. I have a home that's larger than this which we can raise them in. Between us there's so much love, I don't know what's holding me back.

Yes, I do. She doesn't want to leave, and I have no choice but to go. Tick tock.

Even as I pass my hand over and over her glossy mane, I don't know exactly when I'm going to give voice to this problem, but I'm not living without Maris in my life. We'll figure something out. *But what if that's not what she wants?* That voice nags me again.

Like she can sense the disquiet in me through my touch, Maris whirls away from the window and asks, "What is it?"

Instead of telling her right then what I know, what's been eating at me, I just yank her into my arms and kiss her. I feel the chain bite into the palm of my hand, a reminder of who and what she is to me. Not just Maris, but a Smith. I've waited for years to hold her so close to me, I can't let her slip away just because I have to go now that my job's done.

It's been done for days.

The only reason I'm still here is her.

And very soon, I have to leave. Is there any good way to tell her?

MARIS

"I'm not certain if Maris understood how much Nick feels for her. If she did, would she punch him in the face? It's entirely a possibility." - From the journals of Jedidiah Smith.

Tonight is hopping at the Brewhouse. I'm glad Kristina made the decision to call me because we're at full capacity. I sashay past my bartender, KJ, and yell loud enough so she can hear, "Is it a full moon or something?"

"Or something," she shouts back.

"Give me a clue."

"Rumor has it the Champ is in town. Since everyone knows you guys are tight, they're figuring he might drop by."

"Remind me to text Nick to tell him to stay the hell home." I roll my eyes.

"You mean you actually do know him?"

Know him, love him, hope we can figure out how to have a future together. I wink at my bartender and simply grab another IPA bottle from the cooler behind her.

"That's seriously cool, Maris."

Just as I'm about to shout a reply over the din, I hear my name being called repeatedly. I whirl around, drop the beer in front of the impatient patron, and signal to KJ I'll be right back.

Amaq has his arms folded across his chest. "Fire chief's here. Police are outside."

"Is 'Praise the Lord' an inappropriate response?" I joke even as I'm untying my apron to follow him through the throng.

Amaq's lips quirk. "We're not over capacity. But apparently there's some issues with parking and with the way people are lined up outside. They'd like you to come out and handle it so they don't need to issue citations."

"Because I have a lot of control of how people park?" My voice is laced with sarcasm.

"No, and the cops have already taken care of that. It's the people who are *trying* to park they have an issue with."

I stop dead. "There's more trying to come in? I seriously want to know who started the rumor of Nick coming here tonight and stab them."

Of course, I say that just as I reach one of Juneau's patrolmen who I've known since high school. He grins. "Now Maris, watch that mouth. You don't need me hauling you in over terroristic threats and acts."

I roll my eyes as we exchange a handshake. "Matt, can I call Nick and direct him to Mendenhall to sign autographs or something?"

His shoulders shake with suppressed laughter. "Nope. I didn't even know you knew the guy, Maris. You've been holding out." He gives me a friendly punch in the arm.

"Not getting into this now. What do you need me out here for? KJ is up to her elbows in barley and hops."

Getting serious, he asks if I have any problem with putting an "At Capacity" sign in the lot. "Just for a while. It's only eight. If people realize you're this slammed, maybe it will discourage the rest of this."

And that's when I get a good look at the line to get in. "What the hell?" The line is around the block.

As I walk down the line, most of the patrons who recognize me immediately scramble to get their backs against the wall. "And there it is, the Smith fury. That's why we called you out," Pete confides.

"Stuff it, buddy."

He's chuckling as we approach some of the businesses whose entrances face the water. The fire chief is arguing with two scantily clad girls who refuse to move away from the doorway where tourists are trying to exit. I let out a piercing whistle. Everyone jumps. "If you're in line for the Brewhouse and you're blocking a business, I'm bouncing you out of line."

"You and what army?" One with a halter, a mini barely covering her crotch, and boots up to her thighs sneers.

I toss my hair over my shoulder and smooth a hand over my hip. "Chief, mind telling these girls who I am?"

"Maris Smith, proprietress of Smith's Brewhouse," he confirms.

Their jaws fall open, but, "I don't see any movement. These tourists likely have a cruise ship to get back to. They're not trying to cut in line. Now move back or move on," I hiss.

They almost topple over getting back. I step over to the door and open it with a flourish for the tourists. "Thank you for visiting Juneau. I hope you found everything you were looking for and didn't forget to have your cruise packet stamped."

"We didn't. Thank you for the reminder." The couple scuttles away on the sidewalk.

I turn to Pete. "We're at capacity. Period."

He grins, before lifting his megaphone. "Attention, please. Smith's Brewhouse is at capacity. I repeat, Smith's Brewhouse is at full capacity."

"How do you know?" comes a whiny voice.

Pete hands over the mouthpiece. "This is Maris Smith. I repeat, we are at full capacity. I have been warned by the police and the fire chief, no more patrons will be accepted without a reduction of twenty percent. That is all. Find another place to hang out or go home." I flip the mic back in Pete's direction, and the chief falls in lockstep with me.

"Thanks, Maris. I know that's lost revenue for you, but..."

"But nothing. Those people could have missed their ship." I'm infuriated. We get back up to the entrance. I spot Amaq. "Brad, Rainey, Nick. Employees. No one else enters the parking lot. I'll make an announcement for people to move their cars, or they have to work with you. Understood?"

"Yes, ma'am." He gives me a quick salute and goes to lock the gates.

I rub my hand across my forehead before wondering aloud, "God, what else could happen tonight?"

Then I duck inside to go rescue KJ.

ABOUT THIRTY MINUTES ago while taking a quick break to shovel in a few bites of pretzel in the kitchen, I sent Nick a text that read, *If you feel like topping off your ego, come visit me at work. We've got wannabes, skanks, actual fans, and people who just plain want to eat.*

His response amused me. *You'll protect me.*

True, but you still need to make your way from the door to the bar. We're six deep. Oh, and I had to lock the gate.

A few minutes later, he replied. *What utter BS. Brad and I are on our way. Rainey is going to stay with the kids.*

While part of me wanted to protect Nick from this kind of nonsense while he's in town, another part of me recognizes it's myself I wanted to save. It's been a long time since I witnessed Nick Cain in action, and frankly the memories aren't great ones even though I know I'm the only woman in Nick's heart.

KJ sways on her feet. I catch sight and slide up next to her. "What's going on?"

"Just a little hot."

"Did you eat?" I demand.

"Yeah. It just feels like there's no air in here."

I yank my phone from my bra to text Amaq to drop the air when I get an incoming text from him that reads, *Reinforcements inbound. I'm escorting them over. Crazy is coming out of the woodwork.*

I release a sigh. Of course they are. I order KJ, "Sit on the coolers. I can handle this until reinforcements arrive."

"When is that, tomorrow?"

With a quick check of the time on my phone, I chuckle. "Possibly. Still, I don't need you passing out."

"You got it." She hikes up on the cooler as I take quick command of the bar.

For the next several moments, I forget about Nick and Brad being there to help as I race from one side of the bar to the other. I've got two pints going simultaneously while I pour a Jack and Coke double when arms slip around me from behind. I'm shocked I didn't hear a roar announcing Nick. "I don't have time, Nick." I bump him back with my hips. "I have to deliver these drinks, and as you can see I have..." Just as I take the twenty from the customer and spin around to hit the register, I freeze.

Because it wasn't Nick who made his way behind the bar.

It's Carter Jones.

And even though the room starts spinning crazily for me, I hear him say, "It's been a long time, Maris."

I hold up my hand and back away. "No." Even as I say that, I'm reaching for my cell phone. I engage it and type *9-1-1* to Amaq.

I don't read his response. I just tuck my phone back in my bra and stare at the man who left me for dead.

"Get out!" I yell. I reach behind me for a glass and hold it above my head, ready to break it if I have to.

"Listen, I just want to talk. Can we go somewhere and talk?" He smiles at me, as if all he has to do to wipe away every tear, every ounce of pain, is fucking smile.

"No. Now, get out before I call the cops. This is your last chance."

"You won't call the cops. You want to hear what I have to say."

"I do? Then why didn't you take the stand and fucking say it fifteen years ago after you left me for dead, Carter? Last chance." I have my phone out, and I dial 9-1-1. I turn the phone around to face him, my thumb hovering over the green Dial button.

But Carter doesn't take it in time. It changes so many things.

Nick has made his way to me. Overhearing my screaming, he shoves behind Carter, puts him in a rear naked choke hold, before dragging his body away from me. "You dare, you son of a bitch? You dare to come here? To approach my woman? After everything you did to her?"

"Nick! God damnit!" I race after the two of them, which isn't easy because everyone in my fucking bar is there to see Nick Cain. They just never thought they'd get to see him in action.

And most of them are yanking out cell phones.

I hit Dial.

"9-1-1, what's your emergency?"

"This is Maris Smith. There's about to be a fight at Smith's Brewhouse," I announce breathlessly.

"You have a number to call, Ms. Smith..." I start to get lectured.

"This is the same man who hit me and left me for dead!" I scream. Just as I do so, some of my patrons hear me and stop moving. They shuffle out of the way so I can run and save the lives of two men, only one I care about.

A new urgency enters her voice. "We'll have a patrol car there shortly, Ms. Smith. Please stay on the line."

"Right." I cross the threshold of my bar just as Nick throws Carter to the ground. "Don't!" I scream.

"You're defending this monster?" he roars.

"No! I'm protecting you! There's about two hundred people with cell phones aimed at you. The cops are on their way to get this piece of shit."

Behind me, Amaq and Brad come racing up, Brad guarding Nick by standing in front of him. Amaq plants one foot in Carter's stomach when he tries to rise. "Just try it."

The sirens roar in the distance. "Let the police handle it. Please?" I beg the man I love.

Brad says something to Nick I can't hear. He throws up his hands. "Fine, whatever. I'll give the statement to the police. Then I'm gone."

And something in the way he looks at me makes me shiver.

IT TAKES me two hours to clear the patrons and the police from the scene. There's still one more battle I need to have before I get to drive home. I stride into the bar to face whatever Nick's ready to throw at me. But when I get in there, the only remaining people there are my staff.

Amaq passes me with a keg on his shoulder. I follow him over to the bar. "Thanks for everything you did tonight."

"Like it isn't something you wouldn't do for us, Maris." His eyes rake me from head to toe. "You doin' okay?"

"I'd be better once I know this isn't going to negatively impact Nick in any way."

"Yeah." We're both quiet for a moment before Amaq unhooks the keg. "Did he get a hold of you before he left?"

"Left?" A churning in my gut worse than anything I faced earlier with Carter Jones comes back. "What do you mean he left?"

"Uh-oh. He and Brad took off. They didn't say anything to you?"

I clench my jaw. "No. If you'll excuse me, Amaq. I'll be in my office." I spin on my heel and stride across the floor which was packed before.

"Maris!" Amaq's voice stops me in place. I turn my head. "When I yelled you had an emergency, he tore through the restaurant. That's a man stupid in love with you."

"Then where is he when I need him, Amaq? When I need to lean on him, why can't he be here?" Knowing the young man I employ can't give me the answers, I fly up the stairs.

Unlocking the door, I slip my phone from bra, which is where I tucked it again after the police arrived to control the situation. It's what my dad taught me, what Jed taught me. Don't take on a crazy man intent on doing me harm. Call the police and get myself to a safe place.

I did what I know is the best thing to do. So why do I feel like I'm being punished?

I dial Nick's number and wait for it to ring.

It rings.

And rings.

I get his voicemail. I take a deep breath and leave a message. "I'm leaving for home shortly. I love you." Then I press End.

I give it two minutes before I try again. Still no answer. I grab my purse and keys. Then I check my phone. Nothing. Not a word.

Well, at least I know what to expect when I get home. It's a good thing I've seen Nick pissed off in the ring otherwise his size might actually intimidate me. But if he thinks for one moment he's going to get a woman who's about to back down, he's got another thing coming.

I thank my weary employees for their hard work before I stalk off to my car. Sliding behind the wheel, I start the ignition. I drive cautiously past the accident site, victorious when once again I pass it without incident. Then I begin to get mad.

As I turn onto my street, I begin yelling. "Does he not give a damn how I'm doing? Was he not worried if I'd be able to make it home after tonight? What the hell is his problem?"

Then I slam on my brakes.

There's no lights lit.

Nick's not here. He hasn't called or texted to see how I am after being pissed at the way I handled things at the Brewhouse.

"Me. I guess I'm the problem."

My heart aching, I pull into the garage of my darkened home, something I haven't had to do in weeks.

It isn't until I turn off the alarm, I get a text. It's from Rainey. *He's here and safe. How are you?*

I start to type back before I decide to hell with it. He doesn't deserve to know. If he wanted to know, he'd be here. Wouldn't he?

MARIS

"I hate fighting with Dean. In the end, we're both too stubborn to say we're sorry, but we love each other too much to go to bed without saying 'I love you.' Of the two, I'll take the second because I know he'll be with me through thick and thin. Until the end." - From the journals of Jedidiah Smith.

I can't believe Nick crashed at Brad and Rainey's last night. If he disagreed with me, fine. We're two people with explosive personalities, and disagreements are bound to happen. I don't understand why he didn't come back so we could work things out.

"Okay, Maris. Look at it from his point of view. The man who crashed into you trapped you at your bar as if he owned it. You called the cops after Nick stepped in to deal with the situation. Nick's supposed to be your love, the man you turn to. On top of which, he's a fighter. He's overprotective of you. So's Brad for that matter. They had no idea you had things under control."

But what about when he's no longer there? The niggling thought presses in. I shove it aside. Nick hasn't said a single word about leaving, giving me more and more hope every single day he plans on making this work between us.

Still, I reach through my shirt and clutch the cross Jed left. I'm searching for that kernel of faith. "It was late when you got home. Maybe he and Brad tied one on." But that was then.

This is now.

Now, we're going to fix this because he needs to understand I've run this bar for years without his intervention. Carter could have shown up at any time. I am a capable woman, completely able to do what I did—which was contacting the police.

But there's no escaping the fact he didn't speak to me before leaving. That was a personal cut.

Pulling into the gym, I notice it's only his car here. I barely spare a thought for where Reece and Oliver are.

I turn off my SUV, drop my keys in my pocket. I fling open the door to find Nick alone working on the heavy bag. His head swivels to the side. His face is blank.

Ding, ding, ding. Let the fight begin.

I stalk toward him. "Not even a phone call."

"Rainey said she would let you know I was okay." Nick begins to punch the bag again.

"It is not Rainey's job to let me know how you are, Nick. It's yours."

His muttered "Sorry" sounds like a kid who got caught eating one too many Oreos.

"You know what? If you don't want to have an honest conversation, then I'll leave. See you around." I turn and start to walk away.

A large *boom* makes me jump. I whirl around to find Nick using his foot to steady the bag. "You want to talk? Then fine. We'll talk. *What in the hell were you thinking?*" The last is said at such a volume, it seems to echo off the rafters.

"What was I thinking? Maybe you've forgotten, but I'd called the cops, Nick."

"And what were they going to do?"

"What they've done any number of times." I shrug.

"Any number of times?" he asks incredulously. "What kind of place are you running, Maris?"

My eyes narrow to fine slits. "A restaurant and bar. Don't even try to tell me in your vows of purity you've never been to one before."

"This isn't about me."

"No, it's about the fact you can't believe I can keep my head in an uncomfortable situation. You think this is the worst?" My laugh is ugly, but so are my feelings. "No way."

"Unbelievable. Why haven't you ever sold it?"

The question shocks me. "My family legacy, and you want to know why I haven't up and sold it? Are you crazy? It may be gone if no child I adopt wants it, but that's the only way ownership shifts out my hands."

"Don't you want something else? Something different?"

The look in his eyes combined with his words cause my stomach to flutter. "Like what?"

"Days where you can just be a mom, nights with your family. Warmer weather." He steps closer and runs a gloved hand down the side of my face. "Just a chance to be."

"What are you asking me?"

"Come to New Mexico with me."

"For a visit?" I tread cautiously.

He shakes his head, but a small smile starts to spread. "Come with me, Maris. Let's get out of this place with the bad memories for both of us."

"What happened to Reece's training?"

"He and Oliver went back last week. Once Reece's grandmother said yes, we made it happen quickly. Reece is already working with other instructors at Razor."

I rear back. "Excuse me?" More so than his overprotective behavior last night, this is worse. Much worse. "This happened last week?"

Nick opens his mouth, and the only word that comes out is "Shit."

I try not to hear the desperation in his voice as I shove ineffectively against his chest. "Yesterday, today, I thought this was just about the bar. What's next? Is it going to be a fight about David? What the hell is this really about? What are we really fighting about?"

"Maris, no. I didn't mean..."

"Mean to what? Make me question again whether you're going to be able to live in Alaska?" His muscles bunch beneath my fingers as I finally piece together what he's been holding back. "You don't plan on staying," I whisper.

"I'm can't. I have a flight booked to leave." Those soft words from such a strong man make me almost choke on the emotions swirling inside me.

"When?"

"Soon."

"I asked when, god damnit!"

"In three days."

I slap my hand to my mouth and push out of his arms. "I can't do this anymore."

"What? Us?" There's panic in his voice.

"After everything you've just said, is there an us?"

"This wasn't how I planned on talking to you about all of this."

"When did you plan on it? When I came home to find your bags packed by the door?"

A muscle twitches in his jaw. A bitter laugh escapes my lips. "Come on, Nick. Not even you can be offended over a comment like that. You leave in three damn days and you haven't mentioned it to me yet?"

"There hasn't been the right time."

"What? In between slipping your cock inside me you couldn't find the right moment to say, 'Hey, baby. It's been a blast, but time's up."

He storms up to me and grips my arms. He yells, "It has never been like that between us. How can you say that?"

"How can I know differently? Is that really the impression you're leaving me with?" His hands slide from my arms.

"Don't my words, my actions, count, Maris? I'm not saying this is going to be forever."

"No, you wouldn't." I'm not sure how I manage to speak when I can barely breathe.

"I can't fucking believe this." Nick takes his frustration out on the folding chair in front of him. He kicks it and it goes sliding across the floor with a screech.

"So, this is it?" I can barely get the words out.

He's standing at least five feet from me, hands opening and closing at his side. "I guess it is. Unless you want to come with me." The ultimatum lies between us, causing a fissure so great I can't cross it and neither will he.

"To do what, Nick? Sit around your house every day while I wonder about all the people I'm breaking promises to?" My words hold every ounce of my heartbreak.

"And what about the promise you made to me? That you loved me?"

I swipe my fingers under my eye to catch the wetness. "That has never changed, will never change."

"But you're willing to walk away? From us?" he roars.

"I'm not the one leaving. And honestly, Nick, you're acting like it was up for debate. In your mind, you're already gone." At my words, his movements still. As does the beat of my heart when I recognize the truth in front of me. Nick is done. With training, with Juneau.

And with me.

"Right. Then I guess there's nothing more to say." He crosses his arms across his chest, protecting himself from what? Me? He's the one who's running away. Again.

I want to make him hurt, but what pain could I inflict on the man who just told me he's packing up and leaving? I berate myself over and over. I don't know why I had any sort of faith this might work out.

Faith.

Slowly, I reach behind my neck and unclasp the chain. "Actually, I do have one more thing to say."

"What's that?"

"Catch." I underhand the gold chain in his direction. Perversely, I'm glad the shock on his face is even a small semblance to the one destroying my heart. "I think you're going to need to search harder to find something to believe in if you can toss it away so easily. That's not what faith is about. Hell, it's not what family is either. You of all people should know that."

I turn on my heel and walk in the direction of the door. I don't register the footsteps behind me. It's as if all of my senses have been shut down to protect me from further harm.

Until he touches me.

Whirling me around, I come face-to-face with the chest I've lain upon, kissed, whispered dreams to. And it's heaving up and down as if he's gone a full three rounds. Before I can say a word, he whispers, "If there's anyone I'd stay for, it would be you."

My head shakes back and forth. "The only person capable of making the Champ, *the* Nicholas Cain, do anything is himself. Somewhere along the way of falling in love with you, I forgot that."

"Come with me. We can be together anywhere but here."

God, if Nick had come to me before I fell in love with the other part of my heart, I wouldn't have hesitated to say yes. "I can't leave without him, and you won't stay. That leaves us—" I point back and forth between us. "—with nothing."

"The hell it doesn't," he snarls, before yanking my head toward his. His lips crash down on mine for the most savagely beautiful kiss in the thousands we've shared in such a short time. I know that until my dying day I'll remember each and every one, but this one will be seared on my soul since I know it will be the last. I pour all of the love I've held for over twenty years into this single kiss. It holds each tear I've shed and every one I will. And buried beneath it are all the lies I'll tell myself for the rest of my days that having had Nick for even this little while was enough.

Pulling back, I clasp his chin. "Like the sea, you crashed into my life and my heart. When you leave, you'll drag my soul with you." And before Nick can say a word, I break free from his arms and slam through the door. I run for my vehicle, running as far and as fast as I can to keep what I can of my soul intact.

I have to survive somehow when he leaves. After all, I won't be alone anymore. Someone will be relying upon me who will feel my agony if I can't control it.

I HEAD out to Eagle Beach for the rest of the day. I've turned my phone to silent. I want no contact with anyone, especially anyone remotely connected with me or Nick.

I can barely keep my head together, and when I should be leaning on the people closest to me, I can't. So, I'll give myself a few hours to fight for some semblance of serenity, and then I'll go home and rid it of everything related to Nick.

Everything.

After I get home later, I walk upstairs and see Nick's already been here.

And he's gone. Everything that was his is gone: his bag, his clothes, his cologne. It's as if we didn't have the last month. And maybe we didn't anywhere except my heart. How ridiculous was I to believe his was moving in the same direction mine was?

Drifting through the rooms, I collect photos, Jed's journals, and the Chihuly bowl before making my way to the fire pit outside. Then I get the fire roaring.

For long moments, I stare into the flames feeling nothing. Then I remember a passage my brother wrote about me, and my lips curve humorlessly. *"I want to dare Maris to open up her heart to love someone. She gives of herself from what appears to be a limitless fountain—over and over again. But something has to feed that spring to keep it flowing clean and pure. I have ideas on what that could be, but it's not an easy road. And in the end, it may not be enough."*

"Always have to have the last word, don't you, Jed?" Then I hurl the bowl into the flames. I quickly turn as the delicate glass shatters against the wood logs. Once the fragmented pieces begin to warm, they begin to bubble. Then by the fistful, I toss in photos. If they weren't important to the Jacks before now, fuck them. I think viciously. Why do I have to be the one with all these memories?

Then I reach for the stack of journals. I begin to tear the pages out and toss them in the fire. Words I never should have read. "I'd still hate him." Tears cause my eyes to burn more than the smoke. "I would still be whole."

Would you?

"Fuck you, Jedidiah!" I scream. "You didn't live. You don't get to ask. You don't have to sit here and *feel* and *hurt*. You can watch down over all of us and make your judgments just like you did in all of these!" I fling in his letter to me and just sob.

When arms wrap around me, I jerk back in fright, afraid Nick might have forgotten something.

It's not Nick; it's Rainey. And she just pulls me close without a word.

I'm not sure how long we sit there, but the only thing I whisper is "Don't let him come back here."

In that moment, I'm not entirely certain if I mean Nick or my brother.

MARIS

October

"I've only known my sister to run away from her emotions twice. And that's because the pain inside her heart was too enormous for her to handle it in the moment. If she does it a third time, I'm afraid she won't come back." - From the journals of Jedidiah Smith.

It's been just over a month where I've had to train my mind that Nicholas Cain doesn't exist. I worried before about not introducing him to David, but now I wonder if it was simply a mother's intuition. Every single day I've heard from either Kara, Rainey, or Meadow—sometimes all three.

"Just want to see your beautiful face. It's good for the baby to get to see her godmother so soon since you'll likely be catching her," Kara tried to joke last night.

Or when I spoke with Meadow: "Maybe once things are settled with the state, you can come visit? Maybe you'd want to look into expansion down here."

Rainey's not quite as subtle. "Get your ass on the phone before I drive over." I can't blame her though. I was a disaster the night I cleaned out my house of all the memorabilia the last day I spoke to Nick.

Out with the old, in with my son, I tell myself firmly. All I'm doing is creating more room in my heart for David. Each time I go to Sarah and Hung's to play with him and the kids is the only time I feel like smiling. I've been buried under old shop blankets, helped each child paint miniature pumpkins, and even set up a new spreadsheet for Sarah to assist her with tracking her expenses in Excel.

So, it's with a sick anticipation I received a call from Leigh Scott, the state's social worker for our area. Her voice was neutral, telling me nothing. "I hope we can meet at your home next week, Ms. Smith. Unfortunately, I can't make it before then."

"Absolutely. I look forward to it." But the minute I hung up, I raced up the stairs to David's room. Should I paint it? Get new bed clothes? Should I ask him what he'd like in his room? Before it was just a possibility, but this? I allow myself a moment to look inside that place I've fortified and sheltered—the part of me that is permanently reserved to love Nick. A shaft of pain lances through me as my heart bleeds again. This moment is what I gave up love for—the chance to be a mother to the little boy that captured my heart.

I quickly slam the fortress door shut again and nod as I survey the room with the basic twin bed and plaid comforter, nightstand, lamp, classic oak bookshelf filled with children's books of all ages in the event David wants to have his former foster siblings over, and an empty dresser.

"It was all for this," I say aloud.

Closing the door, I head back downstairs.

A WEEK LATER, I feel too much.

Too much confusion.

Too much shock.

Too much devastation.

But I try to rein in my emotions. I place my coffee mug to the side. "I'm sorry, Ms. Scott. I went through this program with the intent on fostering and then adopting a specific child. While Kassidy is an adorable little girl, my intent has always been to adopt David from Sarah and Hung Li."

"Yes, well. I evaluated David and found him well adjusted in his current home."

My stomach curdles. "And you don't feel a permanent home would be better for him? With someone who loves him?"

"It's my job to evaluate the overall health and well-being of the child. Right now, the best thing for David is to remain with the Li family with the boys and girls he considers his 'siblings.' I can't rip a child from their family when there are so many others who need our help."

She lays her hands on top of the stack of files in her lap—as if Kassidy isn't to my liking, here's another option? The problem is, none of them will be. They are not the little boy I've been convinced is mine.

No one prepared me this could happen. My hands begin shaking as I close the folder and sit back trying to gather my thoughts. All these months, all the preparation, everyone knew I was doing this for that little boy. But honesty forces me to admit, *Did Mrs. G.? Did the state? Would they have prepared me? Helped me to shelter my heart a little better?*

Kind of like I should have done with Nick?

Suddenly the air has been sucked out from the room. All along I had the chance for it all, but I threw it away because I wore blinders to reality. Nick's gone, and I can't imagine being a good mother to any of these children. Not right now. Not until I get my head on straight.

"I need time to reset my expectations." I think my words are reasonable, but judging from the look on Ms. Scott's face, I apparently have let down someone else.

Nick. A child. The state. Why don't I add Jed to the list as well since I'm sure he's just as disappointed in me.

"Also, my best friend is giving birth soon in Florida. I'm expected to be in the labor room. I fly out soon, but I wanted to meet with you first. I'm surprised this part is moving so fast since the rest took such a long time," I lie convincingly.

Ms. Scott's face clears up. "Oh, dear. I didn't realize that. How generous of you to do that considering your own issues."

I'm unable to hold back the wince. "It's love, not generosity."

"Of course. That makes me all the more excited to have you in our program, Ms. Smith. A child will be lucky to have you for their mother with your big heart. Now I understand what you mean about resetting your expectations."

I hand her back the file, which along with the others, she slips back into her bag. My heart aches for those children. *Not now. Forgive me.*

After Ms. Scott leaves, I lean my head against the door. I know what I need to do.

I need to leave.

NICHOLAS

November

"No!" I yell at Reece and Oliver, who are rolling around the mat like they're about to embrace instead of do some physical damage to one another. "This isn't huggy-kissy time, boys. Unless we're all just wasting our time for fucking nothing?"

Reece shoves Oliver off him, probably the most impressive move he's shown since the two of them entered the octagon. But it's Oliver who opens his mouth. "Why don't you get whatever it is off your chest and stop being a little bitch, Nick."

"What? I'm a little bitch because I've invested time and money in Reece only to get him back here to Albuquerque for subpar sessions?"

"No, you've been a dick since we got back because you won't face the fact you never should have left."

Oliver obviously has a death wish. "London, out of the ring," I snarl. I'm already stripping off my tee over my head.

His grappling may still suck despite the amount of time we've been working on it, but his ears work just fine. Reece slides out just as I slip in. I point a finger at Oliver. "You're going to be useless by the time I'm through with you."

"I'm quivering over here, Nick. After all, how hard can it be to take down a man who leaves the woman—"

My fist connecting with his mouth isn't fair, but at least it shuts him up. He swipes the back of his gloved hand against his cut lip. "You're a serious dick."

"I've been called worse."

"Hopefully by Maris," Oliver taunts, following up his words with a quick jab.

For the next several minutes, I try to stay out of range while Oliver uses his eagle-length arms to knock some sense in to me. Literally. He's the best at quick effective jabs to rattle the guy he's fighting against. But it's worth a few knocks to take him to his knees when I get the chance to put all my power behind a round kick.

Oliver groans, stumbling back, before dropping to a knee. I can't prevent the smug smile. "Those direct shots to the kidney hurt like a—"

I don't get to finish my sentence as Oliver sweeps my legs out from beneath me. Then he's on top of me. I bring my arms up to protect my face as I stupidly got into the cage without any head gear. My ribs take a few nasty shots before I wrap my legs around his and roll him over.

I hammer him with an overhand looping punch before using my elbows to get some of my own back. I don't do as much damage to him as I can. Because maybe, just maybe, I can let out some of this pain rolling around inside me.

Tatum leaps into the Octagon. "I'm calling it."

I snarl at him.

"You two have an audience, Nick. It's done. Work it out some other way."

My head snaps up, and all around me are little faces of the kids I mentor—kids who I've avoided ever since I returned because they remind me of what Maris wanted more than me.

A family.

God, what the hell am I doing?

I roll off Oliver. The two of us are both breathing heavily. Tatum waits a moment to make certain we're not going to attack each other again before he bounds out of the octagon. "Okay, kids. It's time for jump rope."

There's a loud cheer. Lots of sneakers take off after Tatum. "Remind me to give him a bonus," I mutter.

"Why?"

"Because he's right. I never should have stepped into the ring." I roll into a sitting position and groan. I have ten years on Oliver, and right now I feel every single one. The worst of them on my heart.

I'm about to open my mouth to explain what went down between me and Maris when Oliver says, "I always wanted to be you."

"For fuck's sake, why?"

"I thought, here's a guy who has it all: money, fame, women. The belt. But it wasn't until we were in Alaska I realized you'd give it all away if you could have her."

He's right, so why deny it? I nod.

"Then what happened?" Oliver draws his knees up to rock up. He grunts. "You're such an ass. Was the kidney shot necessary?"

"Yes."

"Why?"

"Because you pissed the shit out of me."

Oliver accepts that before turning back to discuss Maris. "Why did you let her go?" he asks again.

My laugh could cut the tape off our hands with a single slice. "Try the other way around. I wanted—want—her here so bad, my soul aches."

"And she wanted..."

"She chose someone else."

"Who?" I've obviously startled Oliver.

Quickly I recount the process Maris has been going through to foster, then adopt a child. God, maybe she has by now and I don't know it. My email has remained eerily quiet, and I've checked it daily hoping to hear any news about her. But it remains stubbornly silent.

Oliver absorbs my words a moment before leaning over and whacking me upside the head. "Do you want to go another round? If we lose Tatum and the kids, I've got more than enough juice in the tank," I warn him.

"It amazes me that a man who retained as many brains as you—despite the head shots over the years—is so dense."

"Wait. What?" I expected Oliver's support, not his condemnation.

He claps a hand on my arm—whether in support or to restrain me, I'm not certain. "It's pretty obvious to me just from what you've said she wanted you to stay. But did you ask to? Did you give her a reason to ask you? Or did you just assume with the same arrogance you've done everything else in your life that she'd give up everything and follow you?"

I don't say anything, which is answer enough. "I have so many bad memories of Alaska, Ollie," I confess.

"Is she woman enough to help you make new ones?"

I snort "If you doubt that, you don't know her. You should have seen the two of us at..." The grin pulling at my bruised face begins to fade as the implications of leaving Maris finally set in. "What did I do?"

"I don't know. What did you do, Nick?"

I don't bother answering. I'm too busy reliving all the moments with Maris while I was in Juneau none of which sparked my fury over my childhood.

Coffee at Warm Up.

Talking at Jed's grave.

The barbecue in the Meyerses' backyard

All the time at her house.

Spending time at Eagle Park.

Eating king crab like it was going to disappear from the planet.

No matter where we were, she never hid from me the very things that would make her soul complete—love and a family. In fact, didn't I resent she wasn't looking to include me in her future? And then I broke both of us by leaving.

"I'm such a jackass."

"At least we're all in agreement. The question is how do you fix this?"

"I don't know if I can." My voice is hollow.

"Bullshit. You're the Champ." He smacks his hand down hard on the mat beneath us.

"I would give up everything I have, everything I am, to be with her.

If you don't think that, you're still recovering from that elbow to the chin."

"Then let's get changed and figure it out." Oliver's eyes are gleaming like he's just spotted the best recruit of his life.

I tilt my head slightly. "What are you thinking?"

Hours later, and after begging Charmaine to get us sandwiches, it's all done but the paperwork.

Now, I just have to get to Maris.

Figuring I'll call the Meyerses to soften things up, I try Brad first. He immediately picks up. "What's going on?"

My fingers are clicking as I check out flights. I sneer at the limited choices because of the winter season setting in. "I'm flying to Juneau early next week. Are you going to be there?"

"No, sorry, buddy. The kids are on a break. We're escaping to Florida to go out on the boat."

"Oh. Damn." There goes my idea of having a buffer.

"Listen, I'm not sure why you're coming..." Brad starts.

I pull the device away from my ear. "What the hell do you mean? I'm flying to see Maris."

"Are you insane?" Brad's voice is so pleasant, I have to process his words a few times. "You need to stay as far away from her as possible. What you did to her, leaving without a word, was brutal."

"How is she?" My voice aches with regret.

"Hello, numnutz. Are you even listening? She—uh, nothing, honey. No, just telling Nick about our trip to Florida and how we expect brutal weather."

While I mentally applaud Brad's save, I know there's not a chance of him giving me any information. "I'll find out when I get there, then."

"Listen." His voice lowers. "Don't come here. Try Jennings." Brad then hangs up the call.

Immediately, I dial Jennings. He picks up on the second ring. "I will not tell you how Maris is. Other than a phone call to tell me she made it safely, I have no clue anyway." He immediately hangs up on me.

"Thanks for noth—" My body locks. Immediately, I turn back to my computer and begin searching for direct flights to Jacksonville, Florida.

I scan the flights and find one that I can make after I sign the papers that make Oliver a partial owner in Razor in two days. I want that done before I go to Maris with my hat in hand. She needs to know how serious I am about being a part of her life—part of her everyday life.

In Alaska.

MARIS

"Jennings?"

"Hey, Maris. What's going on?"

"I just wanted you to know I'm here."

"Here? At the house? The gate guards didn't call anyone in." I hear the disapproval in his voice.

"No, in Florida. My plane just touched down."

"That's great! Come over for dinner. You know Kara is going to love—"

"No, Jennings. I don't want her to know I'm here yet."

There's a silence between us filled with a million and one questions. Of course, being as smart as he is, he asks the only one guaranteed to start up the tears I'd just managed to get under control. "Is Nick with you?"

My voice is flat. "No."

"I see." And I'm sure he does. Until this moment I never acknowledged Nick's been back in Albuquerque picking up the reins of his life. I hid all of my pain over that loss until I was dealt the second blow of the loss of my dream of adopting David.

The idea of being in Juneau is more agonizing now than it was in those wretched months in between Jed's death and the funeral. I couldn't bear to be there another moment more than I had to. It was an unbearable wait because I wanted to put as much distance between me and my home as quickly as possible so I could recover from losing hope again. I'm not sure there are any words that can cut through the pain. I just need time to process everything, and I couldn't do it with the memories suffocating me in Juneau.

"I need time," I manage.

"Where are you going to be?" Jennings demands. Before I can figure out a reasonable argument to not tell him, he hits me with the single indisputable reason why he has to know. "You're here weeks ahead of schedule, Maris, but what happens if something goes wrong? God, what if Kara goes into labor early? If I can't reach you by cell, I need to be able to contact you."

With a sigh, I tell him, "The Bath and Lodge Club," naming the beachside resort I've stayed in for years when I visited Jed, Dean, Kara, and Kevin.

"Thank you. And Maris?"

"Yeah?"

"Just know you're loved for being you." Jennings says something else I don't quite get with the shuffle of bags and general noise of the other passengers. And then I'm left holding an empty line.

"Jerk! God, I should show up and make your wife who is eight million months pregnant cry! I should encourage her to dream of you slipping and falling on a log during labor. How dare you say that?" I hiss at the device I'm clutching in my hands. Because Jennings just struck at the precious core of me I flew four thousand miles to try to protect.

My heart. Or rather, what's left of it.

I gave up a permanent shot at a future with Nick for a chance at the child of my heart only to be told he was better off remaining exactly where he was—in foster care with the Li family. I've been so strong for so long, I just can't handle the addition of this heartache added to the battering of my defenses. I'd been putting my heart back together, and with one fell swoop, the tide rushed in and dragged away every shard of my heart.

I called Mrs. Gustofson and told them I was uncertain when I would be available for placement. Despite her frustrated arguments, I said flatly, "You really need to give me time to grieve." Then I disconnected the call. Even through I'm sure I just screwed myself out of ever having a child, I can't think beyond the immediate pain that isn't fading away.

I quickly made plans to leave my nighttime assistant manager in charge of the Brewhouse. Truthfully, I don't even care if this piece of my family history gets swallowed up by an earthquake; I'm so numb. All I want is to curl in a ball until Jennings tells me Kara's ready to deliver the newest member of their family. My soul would be eased knowing Kara's going to be okay.

But I don't think I will be. All I want right now is for it all to just fade away. Oh, what would I do if I could leave all the troubles festering inside me behind? Sleep, my weary body tells me. Start with sleep. Jennings knows where you are in the event the baby comes early.

As for the rest, none of it matters.

Not anymore.

Almost an hour later, I'm finally granted my wish. I open the door to my well-appointed suite, and the first thing I do is fling open the balcony door. Closing my eyes, with the ocean breezes whispering over me, I hear the roar of the waves. If I was given fanciful thoughts, I think she's angry with me for leaving. "Who isn't?" I whisper. "In the end, I made my choices."

The ocean answers with a tide that comes perilously close to the sea wall directly beneath my room. If I was feeling fanciful, I'd think she was reaching out to comfort me. But I know better. I've had too much reality slapped in my face recently.

Turning, I strip off everything but my T-shirt and panties and crawl into bed. I don't even think of Jed before sleep finally claims me.

After all, why bother? He's gone.

Just like David.

And Nick.

I WAKE up squinting at the sunrise. It's so different than those in Juneau. I pull my knees to my chest, a poor substitute for Nick's arms around me, but the only one I have. I have no desire to eat. No urge to move. No urge to reach out. I don't even know what day it is. Nor do I really care.

The only person who might need me will call the room if they do. And I should have weeks before that happens.

And with more tears falling, my eyes drift shut again.

I just wish I didn't have to open them again.

NICHOLAS

A fter my rental clears the guard shack protecting Jennings and Kara's neighborhood in Ponte Vedra, I call Jennings.

"I don't have any updates, Nick." His voice sounds strained.

"Tell me that to my face in about three minutes."

"The answer won't be any different. Hold on. What do you mean to your face?"

I pull up to the curb in front of the four-thousand-square-foot residence Kody's company custom built for Jennings, Kara, and their son after they were married. I let out a low whistle. "You mean Kody included all your outside detail and he couldn't throw in the interior trim? Cheap bastard."

"I told him the same thing...holy shit." The next thing I know the floodlights are practically blinding me through the moon roof and the front door flies open. "Is that you?" Jennings demands.

"No, it's Santa. Now do I get to come in?"

Jennings just hangs up the phone.

Taking that as a yes, I don't bother to retrieve my bag. First things first, I need to see Maris to apologize and beg for another chance. I begin to cross the lawn when all of the sprinklers pop up their heads.

"Shit." Making a mad dash, I avoid getting soaked, but I'm still well misted. "You did that on purpose," I accuse an amused Jennings.

"There was no way I could have known you'd be here to change the settings. Not that you don't deserve it."

"Is she here?"

Jennings shakes his head. "That's the reason I'm going to let you in. Neither is Kara. But you may have to leave at any moment. Kara's a bit emotional these days. She won't take too kindly to seeing you."

I follow Jennings through to the great room. "This place is gorgeous, Jennings. It's an oasis." He reaches into the fridge and pulls out a few beers, but I shake my head. If Maris isn't here, I want a clear head when I see her. He hands me a bottle of water instead.

"Thanks. We like it. So, why the fuck are you here, Nick?"

Just as I'm about to start spilling my guts on the multitude of my sins about how I hurt Maris, there's a sign someone's watching out for me. The house phone rings. Jennings frowns down at his watch before answering. "Kara, what's wrong?" Then his entire body freezes. The drink in his hand falls to the floor despite my making a grab for it.

"What the hell do you mean your water broke at school?" He hits Speaker so I can hear the call.

"Jennings? It's too soon. Weeks too soon." Panic surges through her voice.

"Kevin!" Jennings bellows.

Within seconds, Jennings's and Kara's eighteen-year-old son scurries into the kitchen. "What's going on, Dad?"

"Your mother's in labor."

I'm in shock when the boy snickers. "Is this another drill?"

Kara starts to cry. Kevin begins to panic. "Mom! What's going on?" From mature-sounding to scared in a heartbeat, Kevin rushes over to listen to his mother.

"The baby. The baby is coming. Oh, God. Maris isn't here. Jennings, I can't have this baby without her or Dean." Kara beings to cry in earnest.

Jennings shoots me a look over the top of Kara's head to warn me I'd better keep my damn mouth shut—including my awareness of Maris's location. Instead, I listen while he urges her to let her coworkers arrange for an ambulance to take her to the hospital and promises to meet her there. As soon as the line clears, I offer, "Do you want me to try Maris? See if I can get her on the line?"

"Let me first, Nick." He turns to Kevin. "Get shoes, a sweatshirt, and your mother's bag. ASAP. And if you mention to her Nick was in this house, I'm grounding you for the rest of your senior year. Got it?"

"Got it, Dad." Then Kevin's running.

Jennings tries, leaves a message. Tries a second, then a third time. "Here." He sends me a text.

I get the incoming ping. "What is this?"

"The hotel Maris has been staying at. Kara doesn't even know she's in town. Go to the front desk and tell them you need to get an urgent message to her. Have them bring her a message that Kara's in labor. I'll call them after I know Kara's settled. Between the two of us, we should get her to answer."

Sounds like a perfect plan especially the part where I get to see Maris again. "I'm on it." I head back the way I came to go out the front door.

"Nick." Jennings voice is like a whip. "Do not try to go to her. Do not approach her."

"Jennings, if it was Kara and you had the chance to talk with her?"

He hesitates, but his shoulders sag. "There's so much you don't know. And I don't have time to tell you."

Then he bolts for the garage to get his wife.

MARIS

"If there's one thing I'm certain of it's the bond between my sister and Kara Malone is stronger than most blood siblings. She would do anything for her. Anything." - From the journals of Jedidiah Smith.

The next time I wake, I leave the bed to use the restroom before crawling back into my fetal position. A quick glance at the clock on the nightstand shows it's 8:00 p.m. I shut my eyes. Really, who cares what time it is. This time, it's the moon that illuminates my room through the window as I close my eyes again. Fatigue drags me under the waves so quickly.

It's really not so hard to drift away.

But just as I'm about to float off again, there's a furious pounding at my door. I frown and turn toward the door, waiting for the noise again. "Probably the wrong room." I roll over and start to stare off at the moon again. It's so clear over the ocean, I think to myself. I watch the sea come in, crash, and drift out. Much like my emotions. It's a balm I didn't expect to have as I rebuild the wall around myself so I can handle life again when I'm forced to.

Thump!

Thump!

Thump!

"Maris! I swear to God, if you don't open this damn door, Management's going to break it down!" Jennings shouts.

You're so autocratic. Someone should really tell you that one of these days. I can't prevent the amusement from seeping into my thoughts. Then I frown. It's something the old me would have thought. And the old me —the me that thought it was safe to fall in love with Nick—needs to return to somewhere she can never be hurt again. I came here to figure out who Maris Smith should be when all this is done.

I'm just not sure how it's working since I've been asleep most of the time since I stepped foot into the room.

"I'm telling you, sir. She's in there. It's been four days since anyone has entered or exited the room according to our logs."

"Then open the door. I'm telling you, this is an emergency."

"Just a moment, Mr. Jennings. I promise you, I'll check on her, but I can't have you come in behind me. That's a violation of guest—"

"For God's sake, open the door and see if she's in there," I hear another voice urge the unknown woman.

Then, there's a noise before a woman calls out, "Ms. Smith. This is Colleen Johnstone from Security. Can you call out to let me know if you're okay?"

I clear my throat as I sit up in bed. Shoving my hair off my head, I try to send the woman a glare.

I guess it doesn't work when her first word is "Shit." She rushes forward over to where I left the balcony door open and slams it shut. "This is Colleen Johnstone. I may need a medical assist in room 325."

"I'm fine," I manage. She whirls around in astonishment. "Go away."

"Ms. Smith," she immediately protests.

"I'm fine. I've just been sleeping. I'll get some water and be fine." I clear my throat again which triggers me into a coughing spasm.

"You need more than that, Ms. Smith. You're likely severely—" Abruptly she stops arguing with me to face a new foe. "Gentlemen, I ordered you both to stay in the hall."

And Jennings and Nick step into the room. *Nick.* Immediately, I curl into a ball and turn away from him, seeking the solace of the sea. "Get out," I croak.

"Sunshine, no. Let me fix this. Please," he begs.

A week ago, two, I would have done anything to have heard those words fall from his mouth. Now, I know they're just from guilt because Jennings probably called him to find out what happened. I refuse to look at him.

"Mr. Cain, I demand you leave this room," Johnstone demands. "Mr. Jennings, you indicated this had to do with your wife's condition."

"It does. Nick, get the hell out of here," he snaps.

"Both of you can demand all you want, but there is no way I'm leaving the woman I love in this condition."

Why not? You did it before without telling me you were leaving.

But then the room gets deathly silent. The bed depresses, and I feel a familiar hand stroke down my hair. I try to twist away, but his words freeze me in place. "You're right, Sunshine. I did it before because I'm a fucking idiot. Because I didn't realize you wanted me as much as you needed your dreams. But I swear to God, Maris, if you give me this chance—this final chance—I will do anything to be by your side."

I let my silence speak for me. I can't let myself believe his words.

"That's what took me so long to get here. I was making plans to sell part of Razor to Ollie so I could move back to Juneau to be with you."

I had been holding myself away from Nick's touch, but at his words I literally turn into a statue. He smooths a hand over my shoulder, and I don't try to pull away. "What?" I croak out.

Jennings moves into my line of sight. "I know you're furious with him right now—God knows you have every right—but I need you to set whatever this jackass did aside. You promised me you would answer." His voice is accusatory.

"You called?" My brain is still muddled between sleep and Nick's touch.

"Oh, only like twenty times in the last hour. And I got scared when you wouldn't answer. Kara's in labor, Maris. I was on my way but took a detour so I could get your ass. He"—he jerks his chin where Nick's still behind me— "arrived at my front door right before Kara's water broke. When he realized where I was going, there was no way to shake him."

"Why bother?" The words come out choked.

Nick makes an anguished sound behind me matches the one Jennings is making in front of me. Nick buries his head against my back. I feel wetness seep through my shirt as Jennings says quietly, "I think I'll let him explain that to you. I have to head to Kara."

I shake my head frantically.

Jennings pushes to his feet from where he was squatting in front of me. "You're our family, Maris. You're our sister, our friend, our glue. You've been there for all of us through everything. What makes you think we wouldn't be there for you when your heart's hurting?"

"Nick's yours," I counter.

"Nick's ours too," Jennings agrees. "And a very smart man once told me a long time ago, 'I'll be watching from much higher.' Now how do you think that man would react to me letting down two of the people he loved the most in this world?"

Nick's words are for me alone. "He'd kick my ass from here to next week, Sunshine, and don't try to tell me he wouldn't. And that's after he declared I *still* wasn't good enough to be yours."

I start to tremble. I try to twist, but Nick has such a hold on me I can't move. So, my whispered words are to both of them. "Let me go."

"No, Maris." Nick's voice holds a note of franticness I can't quite decipher.

"I have to get cleaned up and go help deliver a baby." I turn and give him my dead eyes. "Then..."

He loosens his arms. "Then," he reluctantly concurs.

I slide from the bed and wobble a bit. Getting my bearings, I go to my still-packed suitcase and yank out some clothes. I'm heading into the bathroom when I hear flesh connect against flesh. Briefly, I wonder how Jennings is going to explain that to Kara. Then I still when I hear Nick's voice. "You had every right, Jennings. I won't even stop you if you want to take another shot."

No, it must be hunger causing me to hallucinate. There's no way Nick "the Champ" Cain just allowed someone to take a potshot at him. "First thing on the agenda, a shower. Then, raid the minibar," I mutter as I enter the bathroom.

Then I close out reality for just a little while longer while I clean up in order to be there for the miracle my best friend's about to bring into the world.

HALF AN HOUR LATER, dressed in jeans and a T-shirt, I exit the bathroom feeling much more stable than I went in. I stop by the minibar and grab myself a large bottle of water, M&Ms, and cheese crackers, ignoring the price tag. I need food and I need it now. "The shuttle can get me to the hospital." I step out into the main part of the room and begin rooting around in my suitcase for a pair of socks, sneakers, and a light sweater.

"There's no need for that, Maris. I'll drive you."

I whirl around at the sound of Nick's voice coming in from the balcony. Involuntarily, I take a step back away from the hurt that wells up inside of me the moment he steps toward me. "Why are you still here?"

"God, after everything, it kills me to hear you ask me that." He reaches a hand out to touch me.

"No! You wasted your time coming here. Just...go. Live your life. Be happy. I am sorry though. You sold that part in Razor for nothing." I whirl around and drop to the bed to begin pulling on my socks and shoes. I need to get to Kara before she has this baby.

"That's not true. You're worth it." Nick sits next to me.

I shake my head vigorously. "Do you understand what happened after you gave up on me? On us?"

His breath hisses out between his teeth before he says, "Tell me."

"It all was for nothing, Nick." I laugh humorlessly as I jerk my arms through the sleeves of the sweater. I shove my head inside and pull it over my head before jumping to my feet. "Absolutely nothing. The social worker came to the house and told me here's a stack of children, but you can't have the one you started this process for. It was all for naught." I start to move away so I can grab my purse when the next thing I know I'm flung back on the bed.

"It wasn't for nothing. I won't have you say that." Nick's dark brown eyes bore into mine. "There's a child or children waiting for us to adopt him or her. This was just a setback, Sunshine. Besides, you needed me to get my head out of my ass."

I shove at his chest. "Don't. Don't you dare say that to me. There is no..." But before I can get the word "us" out, Nick presses his mouth to the one place I can't ignore.

My heart.

Up close, I can see Nick looks as awful as I do. He's lost weight and there's hollows beneath his eyes, which are red-rimmed. The punch Jennings took at him is causing a lump at the side of his jaw. But it's the listlessness and pain in his brown eyes that's a reflection of what's been in my heart. Damn him. How am I supposed to hate him when he's taken as many hits as me and still is willing to lay his heart on the line for me?

I can't.

We have more than a few issues to work through, but I can't think of a couple that's in love that doesn't. My heart speeds up as I lie beneath him, each word he says piercing holes in the fog I've been living in.

"I swear, Maris, I will fight harder to heal this than I've ever fought for anything in my life. I don't care if it takes me another twenty years to get you to believe me."

"Damn you, Nicholas." Tears begin to pour out of my eyes. "You made me break the bowl."

He lifts his head. "I know Jed left it for you, but it was just a..."

"I set all the pictures on fire."

"You did what?" His eyes widen incredulously.

"And I burned all of his journals. I didn't want to have his words if they had anything to do with you."

His head falls onto the bed, muffling his self-directed profanity. When he finally lifts his head, they're wet. "There's no way I can ask for forgiveness for fucking this up. Is there?"

I slowly shake my head back and forth.

Nick climbs to his feet. He holds out a hand, his face pale and stoic. "At least let me drive you to the hospital. Then..."

"Then you'll come inside and celebrate with our family while I'm with Kara bringing a new miracle into it," I inform him calmly.

"Wait. What?" Nick's fingers jerk beneath mine. His mask drops and I see the misery and pain reflected in my own heart. I also recognize something else that's branded all over me.

Love.

And it reminds me of something Jed said. I step close and I touch his face. "Jed once said family never has to ask for forgiveness because over the course of a lifetime we're both right and wrong so many times if we kept count we'd do nothing else. I think he was trying to get out of the fact he chopped off my Barbie doll's hair at the time."

"Maris, this is a hell of a lot more than..." Nick begins, but I lay my fingers across his lips. I smile when he brushes his lips against them.

"Do you love me?" I hold my breath as I wait for his answer.

Nick moves my fingers aside to answer. "I've loved you since you were eighteen and you wore a polka-dot bikini with cutoff shorts in your backyard. If what you're asking me is if I'm always going to be in love with you, the forever-after kind, the answer to that is yes."

"Then don't you think it's time we figured out how to love each other without hurting..." I don't get a chance to finish because Nick's lifting me in his powerful arms, not to kiss me but to bury his face in the side of my neck.

"When will you stop paying the price for me? You've lost your family and your faith because of me." He manages to get those words out before I feel the wetness of his tears against my skin. His shoulders shake under my arms. Each drop knits together a wound. A strong man's outpouring of love sending the lingering hurt away. Slowly, combined with my own, we send the pain floating away, leaving us refreshed and renewed.

When he lifts his head, he looks much like I imagine I did when I first arrived, a shipwreck drifting aimlessly. I thread my fingers into his hair before I reach up and kiss his lips gently. "I love you, Nick. I told you that wouldn't change."

His eyes fire. His arms tighten around me. Before he can swoop in and kiss me senseless, I pull away. "But we have to go. Jennings is going to be a mess in that delivery room. Someone has to go in and help Kara deliver her baby."

He yanks me back into his arms before pressing his lips against mine quickly and setting me back. After weeks of being denied the taste of him, I rock into him. "Then let's go. Now. Otherwise you'll meet the baby sometime next week."

"Baby?" I murmur, dazed.

He just lets loose the private smile that won me over decades ago when he told me my brother should never, as in ever, wear flamingos, causing me to laugh. "Baby. Kara. Jennings."

I snap out of my stupor and race around him to snatch up my purse and room key. "Come on, Nick! Let's go!"

He laughs freely. And in that moment, it's the best sound of the night.

Until Kara's daughter is born a few hours later, that is.

NICHOLAS

"What are you doing here?" Rainey's brows lower suspiciously.

Brad slips an arm around her, whether just to touch her or to hold her back from taking a similar shot to the one Jennings did before he left to be with Kara. His words ring more in my head than the clip I took to the jaw. "Make this right with her, Nick. She may never give you another chance. And then where will you be?" And even though by some miracle, the forgiveness I begged for from the woman I love was granted, it's not just her whom I need to seek amends.

I've wounded people all along my journey by being afraid to let them in. That stops now.

"I flew here to tell Maris I'm late in pulling my head out of my ass because I've been making plans to move to Juneau."

"Perfect. I know where to hide the dead bodies there," Rainey snaps before her body locks in Brad's arms. "Wait? What did you say?" I can barely hear her voice over the cacophony of sound in the hospital waiting room—phones ringing and bodies moving all around us while we're in our own bubble.

My eyes dart over her shoulder to Brad. His serious mien relaxes into a broad smile. "Well, this makes up for you missing our wedding, you douche."

A laugh escapes my lips just as Rainey whirls and slaps her husband in the chest. "This isn't about me and you, Brad! Do you remember the state Maris was in when Nick left?"

"And did you see her face when she walked through the door a few moments ago? When was the last time you saw Maris Ione Smith glowing like that? Maybe we were in our twenties," he challenges his wife.

Rainey scrunches her nose while she thinks, but I keep my mouth shut because I know differently. The last time I remember that glow, it was beaming at me along with the Alaskan sun. We were lying in bed before she got ready to go to work the night that fuckwad Carter showed up. We'd spent the morning loving, then simply lying in each other's arms. Making plans for a house of cards that was about to be blown over with nothing more than my disrupting a single card.

Since the women took to calling us "the Jacks," I researched the meaning behind each of the cards in the deck. The Jack of Diamonds wears a crown of good values. That's our Brad. Rock solid, trying to do what's best for everyone—even now as his wife faces off against me to protect the woman I love. Then there's the Jack of Spades, who devotes his life to works for the love of their job. If that doesn't describe the man Kody became, I don't know which one of us it is. The Jack of Clubs is supposedly a young visionary, symbolizing the future. Here we are—waiting for the future of all of us to continue with Jennings. That leaves me. The last Jack in the deck. The Jack of Hearts. Climbing to immeasurable greatness and an emotional tyrant.

Sounds about right. But somehow, some way, Maris still loves me. For the rest of my life, I'll do whatever I have to in order to protect that and her.

I clear my throat. "I know it's going to take time to repair my relationship with Maris, with all of you. But for her sake, for the years we have between us, I'm asking for a chance to show you I've changed."

"No, you haven't," Rainey declares abruptly.

There's a part of me that begins to pull back, automatically recoiling from any disappointment—much like I did for years. "I'm sorry if you feel that way. Perhaps over time..."

"Oh, shut the fuck up, Nick." I'm taken aback by Rainey's declaration until she breaks away from Brad. Wrapping an arm around my waist, she leans up, presses a kiss on my cheek, and whispers, "We've loved you all these years just as you are. Why do we want you to change from being an egotistical—"

"Closed off," Brad contributes. I shoot him a fulminating glare. He shrugs. "Sorry, buddy. It's the truth."

"Any other names you want to add to the list?"

It's the voice that comes from behind shocks us all.

"Uncle." We all whirl around as a beaming Maris makes her way toward us. Rainey steps back, and Maris slides up against me to rest for just a moment before asking, "Where's Kevin?"

"That quick?" The words are out of my mouth before I can stop them.

Maris hurls herself into my arms. "She was like a damn freight train. The last time, it seemed to go on forever. Then again, maybe that was my perception of it." A frown puckers her brow before her lids lower.

I press a kiss against the wrinkles that have formed due to her disquiet because I know where her mind went—that her brother and Dean should be standing by our sides because damnit, they should be. "You can ask Kara later," I remind her.

Her brow smooths out. "I will. And I'll bring each of you back to meet..." She slaps a hand over her mouth.

"What? We can't even know the baby's name? Still?" Rainey is astounded.

Maris shakes her head. "Not until Kevin does. Now where did he go?" Her voice holds impatience, excitement, and love. So much love.

Inside me, any leftover anxiety about the decision I made to move to Juneau smooths out. I know what a life without Maris is like. I've been living it since I was in my early twenties. And before the last few weeks, I've been given the glimpse of what a life with her will be like. My memories will be with me no matter where I go. Now that they include the ones of Maris, why wouldn't I choose to be with her no matter where that is?

The sound of a can opening cause all of us to jump. "Geez, Maris. I needed something to drink. You know Mom's going to be in labor forever." Kevin takes a quick slug of Coke before he recognizes we're all gaping at him. The can begins to slip from his fingers.

I reach out and snag it midair, sticky sweet soda sloshing all over my fingers. I quickly dry my fingers on my jeans before placing it on a nearby table.

Rainey comments, "You'll handle the 'Dad' part of the job just fine when the time's right, Nick," before her attention returns to Maris.

A warm glow races through me as Brad murmurs, "Big praise," just as Maris moves out of my arms.

She holds out her hands to Kevin. "Honey. I have some news."

"Is Mom okay?"

"Yes. She wanted me to come out and tell you—" There's a collective inhale as Maris announces, "You have a baby sister, Kevin. Her name is Deana Smith Jennings."

"After Uncle Dean?" Kevin whispers, the kid being man enough at eighteen to let tears drip from his eyes. I wish I'd been that strong, that self-assured, when I was his age.

Then again, I hadn't met Maris yet.

"Yes. And Uncle Jed. Your mom told your dad just as Deana's head was about to come out." Maris rubs his arm as she tells him the rest.

Rainey lets out a little whimper before turning into Brad's arms.

"Can I go see them all?" Kevin asks.

"That's why I'm here." Maris tips her head back and smiles so brightly, I'm certain there must be energy grids going mad. When she turns that smile on the rest of us, I'd swear if she hadn't already healed everything inside me by telling me she still loved me, I'd be renewed by it. It's that blinding.

Little Mari Sunshine. I hear Jed's voice in my ear as clear as day.

"I'll be back to escort all the rest of you to our newest family member in a bit," Maris assures us before hooking her arm through Kevin's and leaving Brad, Rainey, and me in the waiting room again.

A minute passes before the sunlight passes and my arms are filled with rain. "Whatever you did to fix her, thank you!" Rainey presses kisses to both of my cheeks before she hugs me tight.

"Rainey," I start, even as I hug her back. Helpless, I seek out Brad to do something with his wife.

Bastard just shrugs.

"She's beaming, Nick."

"I know, Rainey, but I don't know if that's..."

"Then who?" she demands.

I set her back a bit and smile sadly. "Do you not think her brother's not looking out for her? I'm just the schmuck who had his head up his ass for way too long."

"No, what her brother sent her—sent both of you—was the only thing she needed. And by the way, not to add to your already inflated ego, that's love, Nick," Rainey fires back. Throwing up her hands, she stomps back over to a grinning Brad. "And he's moving to Juneau? Life is never going to be the same, is it?"

"No, sweetheart. It's going to be awesome," Brad declares. Stepping forward, he gives me a one-arm slap on the back. "Welcome home, brother. It's good to have you back."

My heart clenches at his words, said each time I've visited, but now that I plan on staying, they mean everything. "Thanks, brother," I manage to get out.

Then we all settle in to wait to meet the newest member of our family. A family I hope Maris still wants to add to one day.

"She's so tiny. Where's this strength coming from?" Deana's gripping my finger with such force, I'm enthralled.

Maris leans over my shoulder, her hair cascading over me. "Isn't it a miracle?"

"How many can we have?" I ask her in all honesty.

She turns her head and presses her lips against my cheek. "We'll talk about it when we get home and see the kids Social Services has available. That's after you pass all the classes and we get recertified. Okay?"

"Deal." I turn and capture her lips in a quick kiss before I marvel again at the strength a newborn can have in delicate fingers.

Jennings's booming laugh startles both his wife and daughter conscious. Kara mean mugs him before realizing he doesn't have the baby. When she spies me holding her little darling, she holds out her arms and says, "Gimme."

Even though I've only had the courage to hold her for a very short time, I don't hesitate to comply. But I falter. "Um, is there an easy way to do this without dropping her?"

Kara and Maris both laugh. Fortunately, Maris rescues me by reaching in between my body and Deana's to cuddle the baby to her. "Come to Aunt Maris. That's right, my precious love. Uncle Nick doesn't know how to do this yet, so I'll give you back to Mama."

My fingers go to my lips as Maris places Deana in her mother's arms. "At least three," I say aloud.

Maris's flashes a smile at me before whispering something to Kara. They both laugh uproariously before they begin whispering again.

I don't know what's being said. I couldn't care less. And judging by the look on his face, neither does Jennings. Because like me, his whole world—including his son—is sitting on that bed. And nothing, certainly not past memories or old hurts, would hold either of us from feeling what we are.

"When are Kody, Meadow, and the kids coming in?" I ask lazily.

"Couple of days. The kids are wrapping up some exams. We should be out of here and at home. You guys planning on staying until they get here?" Jennings asks.

I twist my head slightly and wait for Maris's nod. "Yep. I'll call the hotel in a few and extend our booking."

"Good. Then while you're here, you guys can help me finally give Kara the gift she's always wanted."

"Crown molding?" I jest, recalling the long-running joke that Kody's company was going to charge an arm and a leg over the crown molding Kara and Jennings built their home.

"No." Even from across the room, the light catches the wetness gathering in Jennings's eyes. "A family portrait."

I have to swallow hard before I can respond. "Yeah. That would be perfect."

I don't wonder if Maris overheard our conversation. Her face, which was directed at Kara, is glowing at me. Then the little minx twists back to the new mother and declares, "It will look perfect next to my copy of the Mr. and Ms. Smith poster."

Kara gasps. "I can't believe you made it! You're not really going to take it from me, are you?"

Maris shrugs. "Maybe. Maybe I'll just make a copy."

Kara makes a sound of frustration that causes the baby to protest. After soothing her daughter, she glares at her best friend. "You never did explain how you got here on time."

Maris pulls away and saunters over to me before dropping into my lap. "Blame Nick. It's his fault."

I choke as I both absorb Maris's weight and Kara's ire. But what can I say—it is my fault Maris is here. Then I crush her against me. "It's part of my charm."

Kara mutters beneath her breath.

Jennings groans.

Maris rolls her eyes. "Lord deliver me."

"Listen, I'm holding the ultimate prize. And no one's going to have the chance to take this one away from me," I declare arrogantly.

Maris contemplates my words before tossing her head back and laughing. "Damn straight, Champ." Then she kisses me to prove it.

IN THE WEE hours of the morning, with Maris tucked against my side, I'm loath to disturb the moment of happiness we've been granted. But I have to. If it was just us at stake, I'd believe maybe us being on the same path toward our future together was enough to banish the ghosts in her eyes.

But it's not.

I brush her hair away from her neck and press a kiss against the vein carrying her lifeblood. "I'm in awe by you, Maris."

Rolling around until she faces me, I marvel at the confusion washing over her face. "What do you mean?"

"Sunshine." I pause to order my thoughts. "Earlier, when we walked in—"

"You mean when Jennings convinced Security the world was ending and to open my room," she corrects.

"Pretty much," I admit. I smooth my hand up and down her back. "You were drifting away."

Her chin lowers. "I know."

I hesitate. "Maris..."

"I'm going to give Rainey and Meadow's aunt a call." She lifts a determined face back up. "I don't know if it's the pressure of adopting, which in turn brings me back to the why. I thought I accepted that, but how could I, Nick? I was barely a woman."

"And then twice you sacrificed your heart for your best friend."

Maris waves her hand. "That wasn't a sacrifice; that was a gift. That was me emotionally connecting to the children I've sworn to protect until the day I die."

"I didn't think I could love you more until just now."

Maris kisses my jaw. "But I need to do this for the family I'll have. They deserve all of my heart. Our hearts," she amends.

I hug her close before asking, "Now, why Rainey and Meadow's aunt?"

Maris grins wickedly. And witnessing that smile on her face after entering this room filled with despair earlier fills my blood with fire. And hope. Then Maris reminds me, "Do you recall the stories that used to be told about Aunt Alice in Connecticut?"

And I wheeze like I took a direct hit to the solar plexus. "Crazy Aunt Alice—the shrink who's every dentist's dream?" Rumor has it she also maintains items to hurl around her office to relieve stress as well.

And she and Maris are going to speak?

I start chanting the Hail Mary out loud.

Maris chortles until I'm done. Then she leans on my chest, and in the moonlight reflecting off the sea, I see the stars dancing in her eyes.

And in my heart, I know everything's going to be fine.

MARIS

"I've been blessed with so much family, I'll die a rich man. Hopefully, that family will expand many times over before that day will ever come." - From the journals of Jedidiah Smith.

"I still reserve the right to kick him in the ass," Rainey declares.

"Rainey," Kara admonishes her lightly as she rocks her daughter against her.

We're crowded in Kara's office which we declared a no-guy/no-kid zone as soon as Meadow and Kody walked through the front door. Jennings, wanting time with his brand-new baby girl, immediately agreed until Kara ferociously declared, "Who pushed her out?" Wisely, he backed off and corralled everyone toward the kitchen.

Now, as I confront the memory wall, I catch Kara and Meadow up on what happened, about my past and my inability to have children, with the whirlwind romance between me and Nick—the good and the bad, and the crushing disappointment that fortuitously led to my fleeing to Florida early.

And ultimately the conclusions I came to about myself.

"I'm not ready." My eyes lock on the baby Kara's rocking. There's still a hunger burning inside me for a child, but I need to grieve the possibility of never having children before I can be a mother to the ones I'll have. And I will have them. I have no doubt.

"For Nick?" Meadow's voice is shocked.

"No, for a child. I thought I dealt with all of this long ago, but how could I?"

"Why did you never say anything, Maris? We could have supported you" The deep pain resonating in Rainey's voice reminds me of what I read about her loss of a child. Meadow reaches over and squeezes her sister's hand. "There are things we've all been through that, while not the same, might have helped."

Kara hums, but I'm not sure if that's her agreement or her speaking to her daughter. Either way, I answer as honestly as I can. "Because to admit I needed help meant exposing my heart. And look what happened when I did that?"

"Yet, look at what you gained—what we gained—when each of us did that very thing," Kara murmurs.

We're all silent for a few moments before Meadow resolutely declares, "Family."

"The right members of it," Rainey agrees.

Kara's eyes are locked on mine. I'm breathing through my mouth to try to prevent the tears filling my eyes from falling. Then she whispers, "The best kind of family. The kind that loves you for who and what you are. No matter what. The kind you can always come home to." And I lose that battle.

"You all gave me a gift I never thought to have," I croak out.

"What's that?" Kara asks, while she tries to soothe a fussy Deana.

"Sisters. Women who understand me, trust me, believe in me. You are my family, and I will love all of you for the rest of my life." My declaration sends Rainey and Meadow into each other's arms. Kara gracefully gets to her feet, carrying my niece.

"Good. It's about time you understand that your family didn't end when Jed passed away."

"I understand now." I try to communicate twenty years of friendship in the tremulous smile I send her way. But suddenly a noxious smell permeates the room. "What is that stench?" I demand.

Kara puts her daughter in my arms, spins me around, and flings her office doors open. "That, Aunt Maris, is the smell of first baby poo. It's time for you to get some good photos of Daddy's face as I go make him change it."

"Thank God. I thought you were going to make me do it."

Kara's smile turns pure evil. "No, I'm saving a blowout for you. How dare you call Jennings and not talk to me first? Talk about being on my shit list." Then Kara storms through the house calling, "Jennings! I need your help! Fast!"

I begin to giggle. "Shit list. Kara literally has a shit list. God, I love it." Within seconds, Rainey and Meadow join me. And there we stand laughing until Kara literally drags Jennings back. But none of us are howling as loud as the baby, whose soiled diaper is making her irritable.

And then Jennings tops all of us when he gets a look at the tar-like substance stuck to his daughter's tush. "What the hell is this crap?" he roars.

"That, darling, is your daughter." Kara merely slaps another wipe in his hand.

And I lift my camera for another photo. *Jed, I know damn well you're watching. I love you.*

Deana peeing on her father mere seconds later is my answer. Especially when Jennings begins to shake and then leans over to pluck a kiss from Kara. "Seriously? You know it's our brothers who encouraged her to do that."

"Of course they did. I'll thank them later." Kara winks at me.

And before Jennings realizes I got the whole thing on camera, I duck out of the nursery and out the back door. Nick breaks away from the conversation he was having with Kody and Kevin to come over. "What's wrong, Sunshine?"

I hold up my hand. "Excuse me, may I have everyone's attention?" The backyard becomes remarkably quiet except for the younger hellions. "I have on camera Deana baptizing her father when he went to change her diaper."

Nick tries to snatch my phone from my hands. "No way."

I slap his hands. "Just wait for the family."

His face softens. "I can do that."

Kody, without thinking, hands his beer to Kevin before racing over.

Kevin gives it a glance and starts to lift it to his lips before Meadow saunters by and smacks the back of his head. He scowls and hands her the drink.

Brad, who had been standing at the grill with an arm around Rainey, holds the spatula to her. She whacks him on the butt with it before saying, "Go!" He jogs over, already pulling his phone out.

When they get there, I unlock my phone.

And we relive the perfection of Jennings's first moment of torture with a little girl, knowing this is the first of many.

By the time Jennings and Kara reappear in the backyard, the guys have smeared ketchup and mustard on their faces for Jennings to wipe off. "It's good practice." "Come on, buddy. It can't be worse than shit." "My kids are full grown."

Jennings opens his mouth to respond to all of them at once, but Kara just lays her hand over his mouth. "They're your family."

And that appears to be the answer of the day.

Family. We're family.

THE PROFESSIONAL PHOTOGRAPHER has come and gone, taking pictures of couples, families, and the entire group. The kids are in the media room watching a cartoon under Kevin's supervision. And the eight of us are relaxing around the fire pit reminiscing about who we were then and now.

And those who aren't here.

"Does anyone have a desire to go back and see the Lumber- jack Show? We told the kids we'd take them next summer when we went back to Juneau," Kody asks. Meadow's curled up on his lap.

"You're coming back?" Brad demands. Rainey, who had been relaxed back against his shoulder, pops up.

Meadow grins. "Of course. Probably before that, but we can't fit in a trip to Ketchikan as well as seeing you all."

Brad punches Kody in the arm. "What the hell was that for?" Kody demands.

"We're supposed to talk about these things, dick. Especially because we were figuring out how to visit you all in Montana."

Nick leans up and whispers, "Do they forget you live there?"

I shake my head. "No, but I've always lived there. And besides, with Jed gone..." Nick squeezes me to show he understands.

He raises his voice slightly. "Does this mean you guys are going to blow me and Maris off when you come up? Because if you are, don't ever expect to get good fight tickets ever again."

The silence that falls isn't uncomfortable. It's the guys readjusting their expectations. While the women already have, I can practically feel them trying to calmly accept the new status quo between Nick and me. After a few minutes with nothing said, I burst out with, "Are you all going to be this bad with your daughters? I'm almost thirty-nine years old. Plus, it's Nick."

It's Jennings who speaks for them all. "We're trying to think of what Jed would say, Maris."

The trees around us rustle, and I feel the cross slide against my skin. Without understanding how I know for sure what my brother would say since he already did, I whisper, "He'd say, 'All I want is for you to find a love that makes you happy.'"

"And does Nick do that?"

Nick's arms squeeze me tight. He's not perfect; then again, neither am I. So, I answer Jennings honestly. "The day I fell in love with Nick, he brought back things I didn't know I was missing." Like life. And life is complicated, messy, and full of doubt. It's also filled with miracles, inspiring, and filled with dreams. Together we'll learn how to deal with the ups and downs.

"Yes," I murmur. My eyes convey so much more to Nick.

"Well then—" Jennings doesn't get to finish his thought because Kara elbows him in the stomach.

Instead Kara sums it up beautifully. "Be happy, my friend. Just be your version of happy."

Be happy.

Yes. With the man curled behind me, I can certainly do that.

NICHOLAS

June - Seven Months Later

Brad stands before us, wearing a plaid shirt that, damn me, is a freaking replica of the one he wore when we were Lumberjacks down in Ketchikan. Hell, his whole outfit looks like something we used to wear. And I promised my fiancée he'd take this responsibility seriously. I just hope she forgives me sometime before the end of our honeymoon to New Mexico.

It isn't until he starts speaking that I begin to understand how much thought he put into his role being our wedding commissioner. "We all know who should be standing right here today. Likely, he'd be wearing an outfit much more outrageous than this, but my wife refused to let me wear flamingo shorts to a wedding. Even though I had what I knew was a compelling reason."

Tears burn the back of my eyes. I tip my head down just in time to catch Maris dabbing at hers. Turning her fully in my arms, I laugh right into Brad's face. "Jed wouldn't have listened."

A smile spreads across his face. "I know." Reaching up, Brad yanks down his suspenders and begins unbuttoning his shirt. Within moments, he flings away the flannel to reveal a truly noxious picture of Jed in those damn shorts printed on a T-shirt.

Maris screeches with laughter. Thank God I've got her wrapped so tightly in my arms, or I know she'd have landed in the wet earth in her wedding dress.

"Bradley Meyers, you..." Rainey yells where she's standing with Kara, who's holding Deana, and Meadow. All of whom are wearing bridesmaids' dresses in flamingo pink.

"I, what?"

"You're perfect. Absolutely amazing. Carry on." Then I hear her musical giggle mix together with our guests that include Kevin, the employees of the Brewhouse, everyone from Razor that Jennings could fly up—including Tatum, Oliver, Reece, and of course Charmaine and Harold. It also includes a few other people including Mrs. Gustofson and the Lis.

"Listen, did you think it was just me?" Brad nods to my side of the wedding party. And that's when I start to guffaw. The men are all wearing identical T-shirts under their Team USA or Team Canada plaid shirts.

My wife-to-be exclaims, "This is epic."

Jennings steps forward from his job as best man and smooths a strand of flyaway hair away from Maris's face before leaning down and brushing a kiss against her cheek. Pulling back, he whispers, "Be happy, finally, little Mari Sunshine."

Maris's eyes fill with tears. "I've been happy for a long time, Jennings. You know that."

I entwine her fingers with mine as we face Brad.

But neither of us is prepared for what we're about to hear.

"I had a speech prepared—it was even Rainey approved. Then Jennings stops by this morning with a letter. He explained Kara's been guarding this for a *long* time. She was given specific instructions on when it was to be given to the bride. Nick, if you'll please take Maris's hand."

I face my love, my bride, and twine our fingers.

Brad clears his throat.

"*Dear Maris,*

I knew I'd never be able to tell you how much I love you today of all days. So, I entrusted this letter to Kara.

There are not enough words to tell you how beautiful you look. The sun is glinting off your hair, making your eyes more impossibly blue than they were when I first fell in love with you so long ago."

Maris beams up at me. But I'm trying my damned best to stay upright.

Because I didn't write this letter.

"I know you're going to be happy because I know you've waited for the perfect man." Brad pauses for a moment to let the audience laugh. Maris's brow lowers, her head tips to the side. *"He's going to love you and treat you as well as I do, or I swear, I'll haunt him long after I'm gone. I swear that to you, Little Mari Sunshine."*

Maris gasps, yanking one of her hands from mine to cover her mouth. I slip my arm around her waist to hold her stable. "Did you know?"

"I had no idea. All I knew was I didn't write *this* letter."

Maris leans her body against mine. She takes a few deep breaths to get her bearings before nodding at Brad to continue.

Brad swallows before managing, *"I love you, Maris. You've been the best gift in my life. It's been just a few months since we got back from my wedding where you did this honor for me, yet I can't imagine what it will be like walking..."* Brad falters. *"Walking you down the aisle. Okay, I take it all back, the dumb schmuck doesn't deserve you."*

Everyone starts to laugh, including me. I cup her chin and brush her lips with mine. "Very true."

She just rests her head against my heart as we wait for Brad to finish. He inhales and exhales before he continues,

"I'll just be the guy...in the wings...who will always love you. Near and far.

I love you, Maris.

Your brother,

Jed."

If there's a dry eye from any of our friends, I'd be shocked. Somehow, Jed knew he'd have to be able to conquer his love for his sister on this most important of days.

"Nick, there's a letter for you as well," Brad shocks me.

Maris squeezes my hand so hard, I'm terrified she's going to break it.

Brad rolls his lips together before he slips Maris's letter to the back of the stack he's holding. Clearing his throat, he begins.

"Dear Nick,

It's your wedding day. Wow. I know I'm going to be too happy to speak.

Then again, if you're marrying anyone other than Maris, I'm obviously not at your wedding. But I wish you happiness anyway. Dude, what the hell's wrong with you? Turn around, walk out, and get on a damn plane to Juneau. Can I make it more clear than that?

Get your head out of your ass.

Love,

Jed."

Everyone in the audience is howling including me and Maris. "Who...who was in charge of that one?"

Brad points his thumb at himself. "I've had this letter for years, man."

Jennings is bent over in a squat. Kody is bracing his hand on his shoulder. I squeeze Maris before asking, "Give me a second?"

"Yeah."

I step forward and haul Jennings to his feet, then wrap him in a hug. Kody comes in from behind. And Brad fits himself to my back. When we're huddled together, I whisper, "We miss you, you crazy bastard."

"Every single day, Jed," Jennings affirms.

"It isn't the same without you," Kody concurs.

"It should be you conducting this wedding ceremony," Brad admits.

"So, do it Jed-style. You know Maris will love it," I dare him.

Brad's wicked smile spreads slowly before we all step back.

I take Maris back in my arms. "Do I want to know?" she asks.

I'm about to answer, when Brad proclaims, "It only took these two close to twenty years to realize they met their perfect match. I'm surprised Jed didn't take one of the many sharp implements available to him to make them listen."

Maris starts shaking. A quick check and I grin. She's trying not to burst out laughing.

"So, I'm going to make this as brief as possible. Nick, are you not going to be a dick? Do you promise to love Maris the rest of her life, to be faithful, and to support your beautiful wife in all her endeavors?"

"I do." My voice rings out across the Smiths' backyard.

"Maris, do you promise not to throw beer at Nick unless he deserves it? Do you promise to love him despite his faults—which we know are many? To be faithful and to support your husband in all his endeavors?"

Before Maris can answer, I interrupt. "Wait? I'm not beautiful?"

One of the Lis' daughters yells, "I think so!"

After the laughter dies down, Maris beams up at me. "I do." Then she stretches up and lays her lips upon mine to seal the vow with a kiss.

Everything about this ceremony is completely insane, and it fits us perfectly. It's as if her brother is here. "I know you do, Sunshine. I do too. Are you okay?"

"I'm better than okay. Can you believe he managed to—"

"No. I expected us to bring him here—"

"All of us bring a piece of him with us when were together, Nick."

"Ahem." Oops. We both turn toward Brad. "Do you both mind if I finish?"

"Nope. Go for it, buddy."

"By the power vested in me three days ago, by the great state of Alaska, I now pronounce you married—though let's be serious. I'm not doing anything more than officiating a formality. Congratulations, friends! I'd like to be the first to introduce Mrs. Maris Smith-Cain and Mr. Nicholas Cain. Nick, you may officially kiss your wife."

And as my lips touch Maris's for the first time as her husband, I hear murmured oohs and aahs about an eagle soaring overhead. In the back of my mind as I draw Maris into a deeper kiss, I think, *Nice touch, Jed.*

We wish you were here.

EPILOGUE

Maris - Eight Years Later

"I regret only that I haven't managed to bring everyone together one time so they can understand what I know in my heart. Love binds us all. It always will. In life and beyond." - From the journals of Jedidiah Smith.

"One more," Nick cajoles.

"What do you mean you want to adopt another baby, Nick? We already have three children."

"And we have plenty of room. Your parents saw to that." His arms slip around me. Damn him, the silver streaking his temples now that he's close to fifty only makes him look more gorgeous.

"Maybe in a tent outside." But I feel myself weakening as his lips make their way to that place right under my jaw. "Besides, you're not the one who folds all their laundry." I half growl, half moan.

"Neither do you. You just throw all the clothes into a different hamper and tell the kids to pull out whatever they want to wear." His retort is distracted as he presses me against the refrigerator with his hips. But we're stopped from going further as the back door slams open.

"Mommy, Daddy! Joanie just spotted her first eagle all on her own!" Kassidy—the little girl whose picture I couldn't look at that first day the social worker came over and our oldest daughter—screeches in excitement. Her biological sister trails behind her. Born two years later, we didn't care little Miss Joan Violet Smith Cain was born with some medical issues. She was ours as much as her sister was. And we both cried when the first word out of her mouth was "Dada" in contrast to Kassidy calling me "Mama" first.

Then, on a trip to Albuquerque, Nick took the fall before I did. Literally.

We were there to visit the center over winter break. Ollie, Reece, Tatum, and the kids were due any moment when Nick tripped over this tiny body that was huddled near the doorway. He'd been abandoned there sometime during the night. The tiny boy was terrified at the noise of the sirens, the men and women wandering around, the floodlights. But the one thing he wasn't afraid of was Nick.

Nick, who stormed forward and lifted the tow-haired boy into his arms after draping his own sweatshirt over his arms and head. Nick, who hissed instead of bellowed before moving the child inside to his office. Nick, who ordered Charmaine to get the boy clothes, the guys to get him some mats to rest on, and me to figure out if he could have food and water.

By the time Children's Services arrived, the boy was sitting on Nick's lap listening to Kassidy read a book. I'd already woken up our own social worker to ask what it would take to bring this boy home to Alaska when we came home in a few weeks.

Quite a lot. But as Nick told me later that night when we were separated from the little boy who would eventually become our "little Jed" after many failed attempts to reunite him with blood family— none of whom gave a damn about him other than lifting a little money from the state of New Mexico—he sensed the fighter in our little man. "And he'll be with us when the time's right. One way or another."

It took close to a year, but I'm still grateful to hear Jed's irritated "Can you keep it down? I'm trying to play Fortnite?" We might not have him at all.

And now, "You want to see about having another baby?"

He shakes his head. "You're assuming it's another baby."

"Fine. Another child."

"Sunshine..." Nick starts, but the doorbell rings, and he lets me go. "I'll get it."

A tingle begins at the base of my neck as Nick jogs down the steps that lead to the front door. I hear the murmuring of voices. Kassidy asks me something. I tuck my now shoulder-length hair behind my ear as I bend down. "What was that, sweetheart?"

"I asked what David's car was doing here?" She points out the window.

I straighten and turn around until I meet the light brown eyes of the boy I wanted to adopt nine years ago as he follows Nick up the stairs. We'd always remained close, just as I remained close with Sarah and Hung as they helped guide me and Nick through that final day where Kassidy first came home. But there was always something special between me and David.

And now he's standing here, a full-grown adult. And I couldn't be prouder of the young man he's become than if I had raised him. "Hey, stranger." I walk in his direction with my arms outstretched.

"Hi, Maris." He gives me a hug. "Can we talk?"

I dart a glance at Nick, who just smiles but shakes his head. Confused, I tell David, "Sure. Let's head out back."

The two of us head out the door Kassidy and Joanie raced through so we can sit by the fire pit. Neither of us say a word until we're situated. "How are things at home? It must be strange now that everyone is packing up and leaving."

David straightens his broad—God, when did they become so broad?—shoulders. "That's what I wanted to talk with you about. I have a question for you, and I need an honest answer."

"Oh-okay?"

"Did you want to adopt me all those years ago? Right after we first met?" His voice, his eyes, demand my honesty. Not that I wouldn't give it to him, but I might have tried to check with Sarah first to find out why after so long this is suddenly coming up?

And what on earth does this have to do with the question my husband asked me?

"Yes." The confession flows out of me along with a sigh.

"What happened?" There's a tic in his jaw.

"The social worker evaluated your home and said you were better off where you were..." My voice trails off when David stands. Picking up a rock, he hurls it as far as he can.

"David!" My voice holds my shock as I surge to my feet.

"Did you know I used to pray you were there to pick one of us to be your child? That I begged God that it would be me? That you would be my mom?"

Even as I absorb the blows that this young man wanted to be mine as much as I wanted to be his, I whisper, "How did you find out?"

"I overheard Luna and Karen talking with Mom while they were packing for school. None of them knew I was there."

"You eavesdropped," I scold him slightly.

"Damnit, Maris. I was supposed to be yours! They stopped it."

I'm about to snap at him for cursing when his words penetrate. "What do you mean...they stopped it?" A fissure in my heart I'd long closed with Nick's love and the love of my own children begins to open and weep again.

"Sarah confessed to the girls she suspected you and I were becoming too attached. But you see, they couldn't allow me to leave. Hung was ill."

"I remember." My voice is faint. Hung battled and won a small bout with cancer right after I came back from Kara's daughter's birth.

"And since he couldn't work, they needed the money from the state for me. They couldn't let me go." He blinks and big tears roll down his cheeks. "They denied me my mother."

"No, kid. They didn't. She's been waiting for you." Nick. God. I stagger back, but it's his strong arms that catch me. I rest my head back against his chest at the overwhelming love he has for me, that Nick's always had for me. And it all started right here in this backyard.

Isn't it amazing this is where our family's finally going to be complete?

"I'm no good to anyone." David's words jolt me into action.

"Don't you ever let your brother or sisters hear you talk like that David Cain," I snap, wagging my finger at him.

David rears back, eyes wide. "What did you just call me?"

"David. Cain. It will become your name. Get used to it. Now, everyone in this house who can do them has chores." David physically braces against the chair he was sitting in.

Nick snickers. "Here it comes."

"Yours is folding laundry," I inform him loftily.

"Oh, that's fine. I like doing that. I hate when my clothes are messy."

I whirl around to Nick. "And now, our family is complete."

Nick yanks me back against him. "Told you we needed one more kid."

"You're absolutely right."

Nick pulls out his phone and takes a picture of his watch. "What on earth are you doing?" I demand.

"Marking the date and time. I need proof of when you actually said those words so I can tell the guys."

I can feel my face turn red as my temper begins to boil. While love is the foundation of our marriage, Nick and I have creative ways of letting loose our tempers including a good fight in the ring. Just as I'm about to curse at Nick like I haven't in years, he yanks me into his arms and kisses me.

In the background I can hear the back door slam. Kassidy and Joanie come bounding down the stairs. There's hazy murmuring before David laughs. There's a loud scream before, "I unlocked the Golden Skin! But wait? Why don't his pickaxe and glider turn golden too? Ugh!"

I'll figure out what that means once my children's father stops kissing me. I tighten my arms, and Nick murmurs his approval.

While we settle our discussion in the best way possible while the kids are awake, the gold cross I now wear on a delicate gold chain absorbs the Alaskan summer heat—as I'm sure does the heavy gold chain Nick's never without. We never take off that piece of my brother that brought us together in the first place, that piece of him that forced us to get over our own pasts and open our arms to the other. Which is exactly where we need to be.

When our kiss ends, I whisper against his lips, "Why don't we take the kids to Eagle Beach? All of them?"

"Then to the Brewhouse for dinner? David needs to get his eye on one of the family businesses. We can always head to the lower 48 during the munchkins' school break."

My lips curve as I lean into Nick as we make our way to the stairs that lead to the back deck. "I wonder if Brad and Rainey are free for dinner. They haven't had a good shock from us in a while." Not since last month when Jed asked their daughter to the school dance when she was home from college.

Nick deadpans, "I know. We've become normal."

"God forbid." Then, "I don't suppose you know the process on how we go about adopting an eighteen-year-old anyway."

"Not a clue. We'll figure it out together after we return from a day by the sea."

Together. I love that word.

So would my brother.

THE END

ALSO BY TRACEY JERALD

AMARYLLIS SERIES

Free - An amaryllis Prequel

(Newsletter Subscribers only)

Free to Dream

Free to Run

Free to Rejoice

Free to Breathe

Free to Believe

Free to Live

Free to Wish: An Amaryllis Series Short Story - 1,001 Dark Nights Short Story Anthology Winner

Free to Dance (Coming Spring 2021)

GLACIER ADVENTURE SERIES

Return by Air

Return by Land

Return by Sea

SANDALONES

Close Match

Ripple Effect

LADY BOSS PRESS RELEASES

Challenged by You

ACKNOWLEDGMENTS

The Glacier Adventure Series was inspired by the day I had the pleasure of attending the Great Alaskan Lumberjack show in Ketchikan, Alaska. Whether it was the athletes and performers, or the amazing people I was with, it was an afternoon I will never forget.

To my shipmates, not just those who saw the Lumberjack Show, but the authors and readers who sailed with us throughout the Alaskan journey, you have a special place in my heart. Always. Forever.

Of course, by my side on that trip was my husband, Nate. My beloved, I'm still not certain if I'm saying thank you for hauling my luggage to and from Alaska or calmly accepting the giddy pleasure with which I took hundreds of photos of the "Jacks." Never doubt how much I love you.

To my son and my mother for keeping the home fires burning. You are both loved more than I can put into words. As amazing as Alaska was, there's no place as perfect as home.

Jen, you were never far from my mind that trip as you well know. And you know you're always in my heart, my sister.

To my Meows, bring out the map! It's been too long and there's places to go. I love and miss all of you so much.

To Sandra Depukat, from One Love Editing, for popcorn edits and encouragement. For loving the Jacks as much as I do. For being you.

To Holly Malgieri, from Holly's Red Hot Reviews, a.k.a. my twin, you make everything shine. Thank you for adding some of that to me.

To Deborah Bradseth, Tugboat Designs. Thank you for taking my garbled emails and translating them into something beautiful. You are wonderful!

To photographer Wander Aguiar, Andrey Bahia, and model Thiago Lusardi, thank you for your grace and for your brilliance.

To Gel, at Tempting Illustrations, picture magic! Every single time. XOXO

To the fantastic team at Foreword PR, thank you for taking away the rough waters and making the day-to-day so much calmer. I appreciate everything you do.

Linda Russell, frantic texts from 3,442 miles away started this series journey. Looking back, all I have to say is thank God I have a large data plan! You are my anchor in this perpetual storm. Love you.

To Susan Henn, Amy Rhodes, and Dawn Hurst, you are all a dream to me. And to Nathathida Atirekasâra for swooping in with a quick save! XOXO

For the members of Tracey's Tribe, I appreciate you every single day!

Finally, for all of the readers and bloggers who take the time to enjoy my books, thank you. Every day, I find myself humbled by your support.

ABOUT THE AUTHOR

Tracey Jerald knew she was meant to be a writer when she would re-write the ending of books in her head when she was a young girl growing up in southern Connecticut. It wasn't long before she was typing alternate endings and extended epilogues "just for fun".

After college in Florida, where she obtained a degree in Criminal Justice, Tracey traded the world of law and order for IT. Her work for a world-wide internet startup transferred her to Northern Virginia where she met her husband in what many call their own happily ever after. They have one son.

When she's not busy with her family or writing, Tracey can be found in her home in north Florida drinking coffee, reading, training for a runDisney event, or feeding her addiction to HGTV.

CPSIA information can be obtained
at www.ICGtesting.com
Printed in the USA
BVHW041116080721
611406BV00008B/233